# MANIHARA
AND OTHER STORIES

SELECTIONS FROM GALPAGUCHCHHA 2

# MANIHARA
## AND OTHER STORIES

Rabindranath Tagore

*Translated by*

Ratan K. Chattopadhyay

Orient BlackSwan

*In loving memory of my parents*

The Translator

**ORIENT BLACKSWAN PRIVATE LIMITED**

*Registered Office*
3-6-752 Himayatnagar, Hyderabad 500 029 (A.P.), India
e-mail: centraloffice@orientblackswan.com

*Other Offices*
Bangalore, Bhopal, Bhubaneshwar, Chandigarh, Chennai,
Ernakulam, Guwahati, Hyderabad, Jaipur, Kolkata,
Lucknow, Mumbai, New Delhi, Noida, Patna


First published 2010

ISBN: 978-81-250-4097-2

*Typeset in Adobe Garamond 11/14.2 by*
InoSoft Systems, Noida

*Printed in India at*
Aegean Offset Printers, Greater Noida

*Published by*
Orient Blackswan Private Limited
1/24 Asaf Ali Road, New Delhi 110 002
e-mail: delhi@orientblackswan.com

# Contents


*Translator's Preface* vii

1 Cloud and Sunshine 1
(*Megh O Roudra*)

2 The Ghat's Story 30
(*Ghater Katha*)

3 The Matrimonial Deal 42
(*Dena-Paaona*)

4 Ramkanai's Folly 50
(*Ramkanaiyer Nirbuddhita*)

5 Grandfather 56
(*Thakurda*)

6 Nuisance 67
(*Aapad*)

7 The Matronly Boy 80
(*Ginni*)

8 The Skeleton 85
(*Kankal*)

9 Folly 94
(*Durbuddhi*)

10 Wish-fulfilment 99
(*Ichchhapuran*)

11 The Rift 106
(*Byabadhan*)

12 Reciprocation (*Daan-Pratidaan*) 112

13 Retaliation (*Pratihinsa*) 120

14 Resentment Appeased (*Maanbhanjan*) 136

15 The Wedding Garland (*Malyadaan*) 148

16 The Intervening Woman (*Madhyabartini*) 163

17 The Haldar Family (*Haldargoshthi*) 178

18 Rasmani's Son (*Rasmanir Chhele*) 203

19 Fertility Sacrifice (*Putrayajna*) 244

20 Nature's Child (*Balai*) 250

21 Woman Bereft of Jewels (*Manihara*) 256

22 The Ending (*Samapti*) 274

Glossary 296

# Translator's Preface

*Galpaguchchha* (Bengali for 'bunch of stories') is held among the finest of Tagore's literary creations; in fact, next only to his songs and poems. Besides the domain of poetry, over which he reigns, in the entire range of his prose writings, short stories offered him a medium for his genius to flourish. There his two distinct identities—that of a poet and that of a narrator—have met in perfect harmony. Tagore's communion with Nature, his identification with man, his general preference for real-life tales to romanticised history or myth, his emphasis on theme rather than plot, and on the intricacies of character rather than intrigues set the stories apart. To a reader, these are no mere narration of events by a story-teller: rather they are works of art that retain strong contemporary appeal and can be enjoyed at various levels

It is always difficult to translate any great author. It is even more difficult in the case of a multi-faceted writer like Rabindranath, if only because his prose is often infused with his instinctive rhythm and rhetoric with varied overtones of words: words he often improvises by compounding effortlessly, which in fact enhance the beauty and lyricism of his long sentences with their resonance.

A master of his own language, he adapts it as necessary to suit the topic. In his earlier days, when he used to stay in his houseboat on the river Padma, he wrote simple stories based on the joys and sorrows of riparian rural life that he had observed: the language of those idyllic tales is limpid and lilting like a flowing river. Again, in the stories of his later life, when the theme extends from simple narrative to the complex working of human psychology, when he writes a social or political satire, or when inspired by a profound realisation of life, he wants to show us the way in the garb of a story, he adopts a different style of language—sharp, shining, subtle—that appeals more to the intellect of the modern-day individual. Whether it is the lyrical prose steeped in the colours of Nature, as in *Cloud and Sunshine* and *The Visitor,* or the majestic diction of *Hungry Stones*, or humour, wit and stark, unblinking reality as in *House Number One*, the charm of his language is hard to resist.

It is a challenging task to render the stories in a generally acceptable register appropriate to this language. My aim has been to acquaint the reader with the flavour of the original as far as possible within the natural constraints of translation. I have tried to be faithful to the text, for I feel any addition or deletion would lessen its appeal.

Again, the target language, English, may not always be adequate for getting across to the reader the connotations of the idioms and references in the Bengali context that appear abundantly in the stories. These have mostly been retained as such in italics and either annotated at the end of the story or explained in the glossary. This will I hope enable readers to better appreciate the nuances of Tagore's unique style.

This collection of sixty-one stories had to be divided into three volumes to avoid an unwieldy size. That no definite order in chronology or strict thematic unity was maintained—the latter I feel is neither feasible nor desirable—is because each volume was intended to be self-contained in giving the flavour of *Galpaguchchha* as a whole.

If, in spite of my shortcomings as a translator, the reader emerges enriched, the credit is all Tagore's.

I must mention the invaluable role of my sons Rajib and Somnath in the project. Were it not for their suggestions, of considerable literary and critical value, the work would not have been whatever it is worth.

Kolkata, 15 August 2010 RATAN KUMAR CHATTOPADHYAY

# Cloud and Sunshine
# (*Megh O Roudra*)

## 1

It had rained the previous day. That day, in the rain-free morning, pale sunshine and fragmentary clouds were sweeping their respective brushes in turn over the ripening *aus* paddy fields: the extensive verdant canvas was one moment painted a bright yellow in sunlight, and the next, smeared with shadow into profound serenity.

When on the entire stage of the sky, cloud and sunshine, the only two actors, were playing their respective parts, below on the stage of the world so many dramas were being acted out in so many places.

In the scene, where we lift the curtain on a short drama of life, one can see a house beside a path in a village. Only one outer room is brick-built and along its two sides, a dilapidated brick wall encloses several mud houses. From the road through the barred window can be seen a young man sitting bare-chested on a wooden charpoy, every now and then picking up a palmyra leaf fan with his left hand trying to gain respite from the summer and mosquitoes while absorbed in reading a book held in his right hand.

Outside, on the village path, a girl wearing a striped sari was walking up and down in front of that barred window, while eating some blackberries from her sari-fold one after another. The expression on her face clearly indicated that she had intimate acquaintance with the man who was sitting inside on his bed reading the book and that somehow drawing his notice she wanted to give him the message with silent disdain, 'I'm now busy eating blackberries; I don't care a whit for you.'

Unfortunately, the man was short-sighted; the girl's silent neglect was too distant to affect him. She knew it herself. Therefore, after several times of walking to and fro, instead of silent neglect, she had to use the blackberry seeds. It is so difficult to preserve the purity of wounded pride with the blind!

When two or three hard seeds, as if by chance going awry, hit the wooden door with a bang, he lifted his head from the book and looked out. The wily girl, being aware of it, now engaged even more intently to select the most succulent ones from her sari-fold. Screwing up his eyes watching intently, the man could finally recognise her and putting aside the book, drawing close to the window called out with a smiling face, 'Giribala!'

Giribala, quite unperturbed, remaining completely absorbed in examining the berries, started walking one step at a time.

Now the myopic youth could realise that the punishment for some unknowingly committed offence was being meted out. Quickly coming out he said, 'What happened? You didn't give me any berries today?' Taking no heed of it, after prolonged search and examination selecting one, she began to peck at it, quite unconcerned.

These blackberries were from Giribala's family orchard and daily allotment for the youth. I do not know why the thought of it did not at all occur to her today. Rather, her conduct betrayed that these she had collected exclusively for her own consumption. But it was not clear what could be the meaning of plucking fruits from one's own garden and then making a show of eating them in front of another man's door. The man, then approaching her, held her hand. Giribala at first tried to wriggle out of his hands and then all at once overflowing with tears burst out crying and finally dropping the berries from her sari-fold on the ground ran off.

The fidgety sunlight and the flitting cloud of the morning had given way in the afternoon to a calm and tired look. The white cumulous cloud lay in a heap in one corner of the sky and the languishing light of the afternoon was shimmering on the leaves of trees, on the water of the pond and on every limb and pore of the rain-sodden nature. Once again, the same girl could be seen in front of the barred window, while inside the room, the same young man was sitting. The only difference was that this time there was no berry in the girl's sari-fold and no book in the youth's hand. Some more important and subtler differences were there too.

On what purpose she had come again to loiter at the same spot is difficult to surmise. Whatever other purpose she might have had, the girl's conduct in no way showed that she had any need to strike up a conversation with the man inside the room. Rather, it seemed that she had come to inspect whether any of the berries she had scattered in the morning had germinated in the meanwhile.

However, the chief among other reasons for the seeds not germinating was that the fruits now lay in a pile on the charpoy in front of the youth. Moreover, while the girl, stooping from time to time was engaged in looking for some indefinable imaginary thing, the young man, suppressing his laugh was very gravely picking and choosing his berries and blissfully eating them. In the end, when one or two stray seeds as if providentially fell near and even upon the girl's feet, she realised that he was taking revenge against her resentment. Nevertheless, was this fair? When, sacrificing all the pride of her little heart she was looking for an opportunity to surrender herself, was it not cruel to place an impediment on that arduous path? When it was found out that she had come to surrender, gradually blushing as she was seeking ways to escape, the young man came out and caught hold of her hand.

As in the morning, now too by squirming and twisting, the girl tried hard to flee, but did not cry. On the contrary, blushing scarlet, turning her neck and hiding her face behind the back of her tormentor, she kept laughing lustily, and as though merely under external attraction, gravitated into the prison enclosed by iron railings, vanquished like a captive.

As in the sky the play of cloud and sunshine is trivial, so on the earth the play of these two souls was commonplace and short-lived. Again, as the hide and seek of cloud and sunlight in the sky is neither a trifling thing nor a game, only seemingly so, so the short anecdote of an idle rainy day of these two little-known human beings may seem insignificant among hundreds of incidents of the world, but it was by no means insignificant. The old mighty Destiny who, with his unperturbed solemn face, has been stitching together successive eras for eternity was himself inseminating the seeds of lifelong joy and sorrow into the girl's everyday banal laughter and tears. Nevertheless, this unreasonable pique of the girl seemed meaningless, not only to the audience, but also to the main character of this short play, the man referred to above. Here was a girl, who might sulk some day, keep displaying exuberant love some other day, enhance the daily ration or completely stop it yet another day—the reasons for which were not easy to ascertain. On some days summoning all her imagination, ideas and skill she devoted herself to giving him pleasure; again on some other days, mobilising her limited power and her hardness she tried to hurt him. If she failed to agonise him, her strictness was redoubled; if she was successful, the hardness melted in copious tears of remorse and flowed in a thousand streams of affection.

The first trivial history of this insignificant play of cloud and sunshine is narrated briefly in the next section.

## 2

While all other people in the village were occupied with cliques, conspiracy, sugar-cane farming, false suits and the jute business,

Shashibhushan and Giribala were the only two persons who used to discuss emotional topics and cultivate literature.

In this, there was hardly any element of curiosity or eagerness for anyone – simply because Giribala was a mere ten-year-old and Shashibhushan, a freshly bloomed MA, BL. They were mere neighbours.

Giribala's father Harakumar was once the leaseholder of his village. Now in straitened circumstances, after selling his estate he had accepted the post of *nayeb* of another zamindar. His work concerned the very *pargana* where they had been living, and so he had not to move out of his native land.

Shashibhushan had passed MA, and had passed the law examination, but never took up any job. Mixing with people or speaking at a meeting was not his wont. Since he had short sight, he could not make out known faces; that is why he had to pucker his brows to cast a look, which people construed as arrogance.

In Calcutta, it is not quite unseemly to go all by oneself in the sea of humanity, but in a village, it looks like insolence. When Shashibhushan's father, after acknowledging defeat in his efforts finally engaged his worthless son in managing their small estate in the village, Shashibhushan had to suffer endless teasing, taunting and harassment from the villagers. There was yet another reason for his humiliation: a peace-loving Shashibhushan was not willing to get married, which the maiden-encumbered fathers looked down as unbearable and unforgivable vanity.

The more they harassed him, the farther he receded into his shell. He would keep sitting with some bound books in English on his bedstead in a corner room; whichever and whenever he liked he would read. This was all the work he did: how to keep the property, property alone knew.

I have already said by implication that as for socialising, the only person with whom he had any connection was Giribala.

Giribala's brothers used to go to school and on returning, ask their ignorant sister on some day what shape the earth was and on some other day which was the bigger: the sun or the earth. When she expectedly gave the wrong answer, they would correct her showing great contempt. If the statement that the sun is bigger than the earth seemed untenable for lack of proof, and if she made bold to express her doubt, her siblings even more contemptuously said, 'Oh! It is written in our book, and you –'

Hearing that such things were written in printed books, she was left speechless; no second proof was felt necessary to her.

But she cherished the wish that like her elder brothers, she too would read books. On some days sitting in her room, picking up a random book, opening on any page, she would mutter as if reading and keep turning over the pages in rapid succession. The black, small, unfamiliar letters in print forming rows in hordes and brandishing inflectional signs on their shoulders stood guard at the main gate of some unknown archive of mystery, not caring to give any answer to any question of Giribala. *Kathamala* refused to divulge a single word of its tiger, jackal, horse and donkey while *Akhyanmanjari* (A Twig of Tales) with all its stories kept staring silently as if keeping a vow of silence.

Giribala had made the proposal to her brothers that she wanted to learn to read, but they had not paid any heed to it. Only Shashibhushan had come to her aid.

To Giribala, as *Kathamala* and *Akhyanmanjari* were impenetrably mysterious, almost so was Shashibhushan at the beginning. In his small iron-grilled roadside drawing room, the young man would keep sitting on his charpoy, cluttered up with books. Giribala, standing outside the room holding the bars would keep watching this strange fellow bending forward absorbed in reading; comparing their respective numbers of books, she would conclude in her mind that Shashibhushan was far more learned than her brothers were. Nothing else was more astonishing to her than that. She had not the least doubt that he had finished reading from beginning to end all the principal textbooks of the world like *Kathamala*. For this reason, when Shashibhushan turned over the pages, she stood transfixed, unable to ascertain the limit of his knowledge.

In the end, the wonder-struck girl drew the attention of even the short-sighted Shashibhushan. One day, opening a sparkling bound book, he said, 'Giribala, come and see the pictures.' Giribala at once ran away.

But the next day, once again wearing a striped sari, standing outside the window bars with the same grave, silent attention as before, she kept watching Shashibhushan closely in the act of reading. That day too, he invited her and that day again, she ran away breathlessly, swinging her pigtails.

Their acquaintance having begun in this way, exactly when it gradually grew more intimate, when the girl found herself from outside the bars into Shashibhushan's room and finally amidst the pile of bound books on his charpoy are matters requiring historical research for the determination of precise dates.

Giribala started receiving her lessons in reading and writing from Shashibhushan. Everybody will laugh to know that this master used not only to teach his tiny student the alphabet, spelling and grammar, but also to read out from great poems in translation and even ask for her comments. What the girl made out of all that the Almighty alone knows, but she liked it no doubt. She would draw in her child's heart various imaginary pictures made of whatever she understood mixed with whatever she did not. With eyes wide open, she would sit listening intently, at times asking some utterly incongruous question and at some other times all at once arriving at an unrelated context. Shashibhushan never interrupted her: listening to the criticism, praise, annotations and commentaries of this very small critic on the very great poetical works, he derived a great deal of pleasure. In the entire village, this Giribala was his sole connoisseur friend.

When Giribala was first acquainted with Shashibhushan, her age was eight; now she was ten. In the span of two years, having learnt the English and Bengali alphabets, she had finished reading a couple of simple books. For Shashibhushan too, the village had not proved utterly bleak for lack of company all these two years.

## 3

Even so, Shashibhushan did not get along with Giribala's father Harakumar. At the outset, Harakumar would come to take counsel with this MA, BL on legal matters. The MA, BL would not take much interest in it and would not feel shy of acknowledging his ignorance in jurisprudence to the nayeb who interpreted it as a pretext. Two years or so passed by in this way.

Of late, a hostile tenant needed to be disciplined. The nayeb wanted to file complaints against him on different charges and claims in different district courts, and expressing his intention to Shashibhushan insisted pleadingly on his advice. Shashibhushan, far from giving any advice, told Harakumar calmly albeit with firmness one or two words, which sounded anything but sweet to him.

Meanwhile, in none of the cases filed against the tenant did Harakumar get a favourable verdict. He was convinced that Shashibhushan had aided the unfortunate tenant; he resolved that such a wretch as this must be driven out of the village.

Shashibhushan noticed that cattle strayed into his farmland, his barn of pulses caught fire, disputes arose on his boundary, his tenants refused to pay their rents and on the contrary, threatened to file false cases against him. Rumours were even afloat that when out on the road in the evening, he would be physically assaulted and at night, his house set on fire.

In the end, an innocent and peace-loving Shashibhushan decided to escape from the village to Calcutta.

He had begun packing up his things when the Joint Magistrate put up his tent in the village. The entire village was abuzz with footmen, constables, butlers, dogs, horses, grooms and sweepers. Bands of boys, like packs of jackals following a tiger, hung around the camp of the sahib with tremulous curiosity.

The nayeb, by debiting the expenses to the hospitality account, went on providing the sahib with supplies of chicken, eggs, ghee and milk. He had been ungrudgingly supplying the stuff far in excess of what the Joint Magistrate could consume, but one morning when his sweeper came and demanded all of four seers of ghee for the sahib's dog, as ill luck would have it, it did not go down well with him. He advised the sweeper that although the sahib's dog was used to consuming without regret a greater quantity of ghee than a pariah dog, so much fatty substance was not good for its health. He did not supply the ghee.

The sweeper went back to report that he had gone to the nayeb just to enquire about any shop for dog meat, but because he was a sweeper by caste, the nayeb had shooed him away before the public and even had not shrunk from displaying indifference to the sahib.

For one, the Brahmans' pride of lineage is simply intolerable for the sahibs; on top of that, this man had dared to insult his staff: it was impossible for him to keep his patience. 'Summon the nayeb,' he bade his orderly forthwith.

The nayeb, trembling all over, chanting the name of *Durga*, presented himself in front of the sahib's tent. Coming out of the tent in his creaking boots, the sahib asked him loudly in heavily accented Bengali, what translates as, 'Why did you drive away my sweeper?'

Frightened out of his wits, Harakumar, with joined palms, submitted that the arrogance of driving away the sahib's staff was beyond him. But again, since he had asked for as much as four seers of ghee all at a time for a dog, he, at first for the well-being of the quadruped, making a mild protest, sent across men to different places for collecting the ghee.

The sahib wanted to know who had been sent and where.

Harakumar at once reeled off names as they came to his mouth. The sahib immediately sent forth men to verify whether the persons named had gone to the villages mentioned to fetch any ghee and kept the nayeb waiting in the tent.

The messengers, on returning in the afternoon reported that no one had gone anywhere to fetch any ghee. The magistrate had no doubt that all the nayeb's words were lies and the sweeper had spoken the truth. Howling in anger, the 'Joint' sahib summoned the sweeper and said, 'Holding his ears, make this rascal run around the tent till he is out of breath.' The sweeper lost no time to carry out the order in full view of the public.

Soon the word of it reached every nook and corner. Coming back home, Harakumar took to fasting and sprawled out on the ground as if dead.

In connection with estate-related work, the nayeb had made many enemies; this incident gave them great cause for cheering. But when Shashibhushan, who was headed for Calcutta, heard the news, the blood boiled in his veins. He spent a sleepless night.

Next morning, he went to Harakumar's house; holding his hands, Harakumar began to cry despairingly. Shashibhushan said, 'You must file a defamation suit against the sahib; I will stand as your counsel.'

Hearing that the magistrate himself had to be sued, Harakumar was scared initially; Shashibhushan would not relent.

Harakumar sought some time to think over the matter. But when he found that the word had been widely circulated and his enemies were exulting over it, he could not hold himself any more; soliciting Shashibhushan's help, he said, 'Son, I hear you're planning to go to Calcutta without any reason. That can't be; by no means. A man like you in the village is a source of great inspiration for all of us. Anyway, you must rescue me from this mortal humiliation.'

## 4

Shashibhushan, who had always tried to keep himself in secluded loneliness away from the eyes of people, today made his appearance in the court. On hearing his plaint, the magistrate took him into his antechamber and very cordially said, 'Shashi-babu, would it not be better to dispose of the case by compromising secretly?'

Shashi-babu, with his screwed-up myopic eyes intently fixed on the cover of a law book lying on the table, said, 'I cannot give this counsel to my client. He was insulted publicly. How can it be settled secretly?'

After exchanging a few words, the magistrate realised that this reserved, near-sighted man was not easy to cow down. 'All right, Babu,' he conceded, 'let's see how far it can go.'

With this, after deferring the hearing, the honourable magistrate went on to tour the mofussil.

Meanwhile, the joint magistrate wrote to the zamindar, 'Your nayeb has shown disrespect to me by insulting my servants. I trust you will take appropriate remedial steps.'

Nervously, the zamindar at once summoned Harakumar. Harakumar made a clean breast of everything. Extremely annoyed, the zamindar said, 'When the sahib's sweeper wanted four seers of ghee, why did you not give it then and there without a word? Would it have cost you your father's money?'

Harakumar could not deny that this would have caused no loss to his paternal property. Acknowledging the fault, he said, 'My stars are unfavourable; hence such folly.'

The zamindar said, 'And who told you to complain against the sahib, after all that?'

Harakumar said, 'Your Honour, I had no intention to complain. You know Shashi of our village; he never finds a brief. That lad, almost forcibly, even without my consent has managed to create all this trouble.'

Hearing this, the zamindar was enraged no end at Shashibhushan. He realised that the fellow was a worthless novice lawyer, who, on some pretext, whipping up a craze was trying to attract the notice of the public. He ordered the nayeb that immediately withdrawing the case, he should placate both the lower and the higher magistrates.

With some fruits and sweets, the nayeb presented himself at the joint magistrate's house. He submitted that it was contrary to his nature to engage in litigation with the sahib, except that Shashibhushan, a beardless, puerile, immature lawyer of the village without his knowledge had indulged in this audacious act. The sahib was as much annoyed with Shashibhushan as he was pleased with the nayeb: in his moment of anger, having punished the nayeb, he said he was sorry in his quaintly accented Bengali. Of late, having passed with flying colours the examination of the language, the sahib used to speak in chaste Bengali with the public.

The nayeb, in acknowledgement of the courtesy, said that Ma-Baap (mother and father) might even punish when angry; sometimes again, they pampered as well, but that was no cause for sorrow to the children or their Ma-Baap.

Thereafter giving the sahib's servants suitable tips, Harakumar went to the *mofussil* to see the magistrate, who, on hearing of Shashibhushan's impertinence, said, 'I too was surprised to think that I had always known Nayeb-babu for a good gentleman. How was it possible that without first meeting me for a compromise, he should all at once bring up litigation? Now I can see everything.'

Finally, he asked the nayeb if Shashi had joined the Congress. The nayeb unhesitatingly said yes.

The sahib with his Englishman's acumen clearly understood that all this was a trick of the Congress. By creating uproar and writing articles in the Amritabazar Patrika, the small fry of the Congress were secretly looking out for opportunities to engage in skirmishes with the government. Complaining that greater powers to trample these small pests forthwith had not been devolved directly upon the magistrate, he silently cried fie upon the Indian government for being very weak. At any rate, the magistrate bore the Congress loyalist Shashibhushan's name in his mind.

## 5

In the world, when bigger events keep brewing, threatening to erupt any moment, smaller ones too with their hungry roots and veins do not lag behind in clamouring for their rights.

Shashibhushan was particularly busy with this magisterial trouble, hunting up appropriate sections of the penal code, fortifying his arguments and rehearsing to himself, in imagination already cross-examining the witnesses, and contemplating the crowded court scene and the future stages of the legal battle, frequently trembling and perspiring. His little student, then with her almost torn *Charupath* [textbook] and ink-besmeared exercise book, used to appear at his door bringing from their garden sometimes flowers, sometimes fruits, and from her mother's cupboard, on some day, pickles, on some other day sweetmeats of coconut kernel and yet another day homemade scented catechu.

For the first few days, she noticed that Shashibhushan, with a non-illustrated forbidding tome opened before him, was absently turning over its pages; that he was reading it with any degree of attention was not apparent either. At other times, from any book he might be reading, invariably picking one or the other part he would try to explain it to Giribala. But what about that fat black board-bound book? Were there not even one or two words suitable for Giribala's listening? Well, let there be none. Even so, was that book so very big and Giribala so very small?

At first, to capture the guru's notice, Giribala started reading on her own, loudly with intonation, spelling each word and swaying the upper part of her body together with the pigtail. She observed that it did not produce much effect. She got very angry at the black fat book and looked upon it as an ugly, stern, cruel fellow. Each of its abstruse pages, as if assuming the visage of a mischievous person, silently indicated that the book utterly ignored her for a girl. If some thief were to purloin that book, she would steal all the scented catechu from her mother's cupboard and give him as a reward. The gods had not heard the unreasonable and impossible prayers she had made to them silently imprecating the destruction of that book, neither do I find any necessity for the readers to listen to them.

Thereafter for one or two days, the girl with an anguished heart stopped going to her guru's house, *Charupath* in hand. After that period, to test the effect of this estrangement, she came on a different pretext to the path in front of Shashibhushan's house, and casting a furtive glance saw that leaving that black book aside, standing alone he was delivering lectures in some foreign language with gestures of hands to the iron bars of the window. Perhaps, how to melt the judge's mind was what he was testing on these irons. Inexperienced about the ways of the world, bibliophilic Shashibhushan had the notion that the extraordinary work done by orators like Demosthenes, Cicero, Burke and Sheridan in the past—showering unfailing target-seeking verbal arrows, the way they demolished wrongs, humiliated tyranny and brought down pride to the dust—was not impossible even in these days of stark shop-keeping. How he could make the arrogant and drunk-with-overlordship English ashamed and remorseful in public was what Shashibhushan was practising, standing in his small decrepit house in Tilkuchi village. Nobody can tell whether the gods of the sky laughed at this or their divine eyes were moistening with tears.

Naturally, on that day Giribala did not fall in his line of sight. That day, there were no berries in the girl's sari-fold; once having been detected with blackberry-seeds she had since remained inhibited about that fruit. Even if Shashibhushan ever innocently asked, 'Giri, haven't you brought any berries today?' she took it for a subtle joke and saying, 'Stop it,' resentfully made as if to flee. Lacking berry seeds, she had to adopt a stratagem today. Suddenly, looking into the distance, the girl shouted out, 'Swarna, dear, don't go away, please. I'm coming in a minute.'

A male reader might think that the address was directed at some female companion in the distance, but female readers will easily understand that there was none there; the target was very close by. Alas, for the blind male, the aim missed the target. It was not that Shashibhushan had not heard it, but that he failed to get at the meaning. He had thought that the girl was indeed eager for play; moreover, that day he lacked the tenacity to draw her to studies weaning her away from play, because he too had been aiming pointed arrows at some hearts at that time. As the untrained aim of the girl's feeble hand failed to hit the target, so had the exalted aim of his trained hand, of which the readers have already been informed.

One virtue of berry seeds is that one after another quite a number of them can be thrown; if four shots fail, at least the fifth one can be expected to hit the mark. But howsoever imaginary the creature 'Swarna' might be, after assuring her, 'I'm coming in a minute,' one could not keep standing indefinitely. In that case, people might naturally grow suspicious about the existence of Swarna. Obviously, when that trick proved fruitless, Giribala had soon to make herself scarce. Yet, if her desire to find the company of some friend named Swarna had been sincere, the fast energetic gait that would have been natural could not be noticed in Giribala's motion. It seemed as though she was trying to sense with her back whether anybody was coming behind her. When she was definite that nobody was, with the last minuscule fraction of hope, she looked back for once and finding no one, tore to shreds that minute hope and the worn-out *Charupath* strewing the pieces on the road. If she could possibly return the modicum of learning Shashibhushan had given her, then perhaps like the discarded berry seeds she would have flung all that away with a loud report in front of his door. The girl promised to herself that even before encountering Shashibhushan for a second time, she would forget all her lessons so she could answer none of the questions he might ask! Not one—not even one! How then! Then Shashibhushan would be utterly discomfited.

Giribala's eyes filled with tears. Contemplating how her forgetting the lessons would be a cause for intense remorse to Shashibhushan, she derived some slight consolation in her afflicted heart and further, imagining the misfortune of the future Giribala with her lessons forgotten solely owing to Shashibhushan's fault, she felt a surge of pity for herself. Clouds began to gather in the sky, such as gather everyday in the monsoon. Standing behind a tree at the end of the road, Giribala kept weeping with paroxysms of sobs out of sheer pique. Everyday, so many girls wept like this without any apparent reason; there was nothing remarkable about it.

## 6

For what reason Shashibhushan's legal deliberations and practice of cross-examination fell through is not unknown to the reader. The suit against the magistrate was summarily dismissed. Harakumar was appointed honorary magistrate on their district bench. Wearing a chapkan and an oil-stained puggree, Harakumar nowadays very often going to the district town bade salaams to the sahibs.

On that black fat book of Shashibhushan, now so long after, Giribala's curse started to act. Banished into a dark corner, neglected and forgotten, it began to gather layers of dust. But where was that Giribala, the girl who would exult over its neglect?

The day Shashibhushan first shut down his law book was also the day he suddenly realised that Giribala had not come. It was then that the events of several days one by one kept coming to his mind little by little. He remembered that one bright morning Giribala had brought in her sari-end a palmful of wet *bakuls* of the new monsoon. Even after noticing her, when he did not look up from his book, her upsurge of emotion was hindered. She then took out a threaded needle stuck up in her sari-end and with her head hung low picking one flower after another, began to weave a garland. She wove it very slowly; it took long to be completed; the day advanced pretty far; it was time for Giribala to go back home; still Shashibhushan's reading did not end. Leaving the garland on the bedstead, she went away, disheartened. It came to his mind how her resentment deepened day by day; from when the girl, instead of entering his room, used to show up occasionally on the path in front of it and go away; the day she had finally stopped passing that path as well; that too had been several days since. But Giribala's resentment was not used to lasting so many days. Letting out a long sigh, Shashibhushan sat leaning against the wall, as if confused and idle. His young student having not turned up, his own books seemed insipid: picking one book after another, he had to throw them away after browsing through one or two pages. While writing, every moment his expectant and startled look was being diverted towards the door and in the direction of the path and his flow of writing was impeded.

Shashibhushan feared that perhaps Giribala had been taken ill. On secret enquiry, he came to know that the fear was baseless. Giribala did not come out of her home any more these days. Her marriage had been settled.

The following day after Giri had strewn the muddy village path with the torn pieces of *Charupath*, in the morning collecting various gifts in her tiny sari-end she was coming out of her room hurriedly. In the intense summer, having spent a sleepless night, Harakumar, since early in the morning had been sitting outside bare-chested, smoking tobacco. 'Where are you going?' he asked Giri. She said, 'To Shashi-dada's house.' With a rebuke, Harakumar said, 'You mustn't go to Shashi-dada's house. Go inside.' He then scolded her severely for lack of modesty even though she was old enough to go and stay in her father-in-law's house very soon. That was when her stepping out of home had been forbidden. Now she no more had any opportunity to repair her wounded pride. Dried mango pulp, scented catechu and pickled lemon returned to their respective places in the store. Rain continued to patter, bakul flowers to fall; guavas ripened plentifully in the tree and succulent blackberries detached from the branches by pecking birds continued to litter the bottom of the tree. Alas, that tattered *Charupath* existed no longer, either.

## 7

On Giribala's wedding day when shehnai was being played in the village, Shashibhushan, who was not invited, was leaving for Calcutta by boat.

Since the withdrawal of the case, Harakumar had been looking on Shashi with malice. For, he had concluded that Shashi must surely hate him. In Shashi's face and demeanour, he began to discern a thousand imaginary signs of it. Thinking that everyone in the village was gradually forgetting the story of his humiliation, and Shashi alone had kept alive the memory of his plight, he could not stand his sight. Whenever Harakumar encountered him, there grew in his heart a little bashful embarrassment and with it a strong feeling of bitterness. He resolved that Shashi must be driven out of the village.

It was not so difficult to drive out a man like Shashibhushan. The nayeb's intention was fulfilled in no time. One morning, with a load of books and a couple of tin boxes, Shashi boarded a boat. With it, the happy bond he had had with the village was also going to be severed ceremonially. He had not so far known perfectly how firmly the tender tie had entwined his heart. Today when the boat cast off and the festive music gradually grew fainter, all at once his heart, swelling with repressed tears, choked his voice, the veins of his forehead began to throb with surging blood and all the sights of the world appeared extremely hazy like the illusive mirage of shadows.

A reverse wind was blowing very hard, and so, even though the current was favourable, the boat was making slow progress. Then something happened in the river that thwarted his advance.

From the station *ghat* to the sub-divisional headquarters, a new steamer route had been commissioned recently. The steamer was coming against the current noisily fluttering its sail and raising waves. In the ship, there were a small number of passengers, besides the young manager recruited for the new line. Among the passengers, some were from Shashibhushan's village.

A merchant boat was trying from some distance to compete with this steamer, at times nearly overtaking it, again at times lagging behind. The boatman was gradually seized with stubbornness. He hoisted the second sail on top of the first and finally, even the smaller third sail on the second. The high mast bent forward under the wind speed and the cleaved mass of waves began to dance madly with boisterous murmur on both sides of the boat. The boat then sped like a runaway horse without reins. At one point, the steamer had to negotiate a bend; there the boat took a short cut and overtook the steamer. The manager-sahib, leaning against the railing, was eagerly watching this competition. When the boat had attained its highest speed and beaten the steamer by a few yards, the sahib all of a sudden lifting a gun fired a shot at the distended sail. The sail having burst, the boat sank and the steamer disappeared behind the bend of the river.

Why the manager did this is hard to tell. We Bengalis cannot quite make out the mind of an Englishman. Maybe, he could not tolerate the challenge thrown by a native sail. Maybe, there is an element of savage allure in rupturing an inflated and extended object in a trice with a gunshot; maybe, there is an intense devilish humour in finishing its plying career forever by punching several holes in the canvas of this audacious boat; I do not know for sure. But what is certain is that the Englishman had a degree of confidence in his mind that this little joke entailed no punishment for him and he had the notion that those who had lost the boat, and probably had their lives at stake, by no means deserved to be reckoned as human beings at all.

When the sahib lifting his gun pulled the trigger and the boat capsized, Shashibhushan's vessel had approached the spot. Shashibhushan saw the last part with his own eyes. Quickly rowing a boat to it, he rescued the oarsman and other boatmen, except one who had been sitting inside, grinding spices for cooking; he could be seen no more. The monsoon river went on flowing rapidly.

Hot blood kept boiling in Shashibhushan's heart. The law is very tardy: it is like a vast complicated iron machine; it accepts proofs weighing in a balance and dispenses justice with total unconcern; there is no room for the warmth of the human heart in it. But to segregate eating from hunger, enjoyment from desire and punishment from anger seemed equally unnatural to Shashibhushan. There are crimes which deserve to be awarded instant punishment with one's one hand as soon as witnessed, or else, the Almighty dwelling in one's heart keeps mortifying the witness when the heart feels ashamed to find any consolation on the pretext of abiding by the law. But mechanical laws and a machine-driven ship carried the manager far away from Shashibhushan. What other benefits it had brought to the world is not known, but on that occasion, Shashibhushan's Indian spleen was spared.

Taking along the survivors of the tragedy, Shashi came back to his village. The boat had a cargo of jute, to salvage which he engaged men and told the boatman to complain to the police against the manager.

The boatman was vehemently opposed to it. 'The boat has sunk; there's no saving it,' he said. 'Now I can't sink myself.' The police had to be bribed to start with. Then he would have to frequent the court giving up all work, food and sleep. And then, there was no knowing what trouble he would have to face complaining against the sahib. In the end, when he learned that Shashibhushan was himself a lawyer, he would himself bear the court expenses and there was certainty of getting compensation out of the case in future, he agreed. But those of the passengers on board the steamer who were from Shashibhushan's own village strongly refused to stand witness. 'Babu,' they said, 'we did not see anything. We had been in the rear portion of the steamer; from there, amidst the roar of the engine and the rippling sound of the water it was not possible to hear any report of the gun, either.'

Censuring his compatriots most contemptuously, Shashibhushan filed a case before the magistrate.

No witness was necessary. The manager admitted that he had fired a shot: there was a flight of cranes in the sky, to which he had aimed his gun. The steamer was then running at full speed and that very moment it had curved round the bend. Naturally, he did not even know whether a crow or a crane had fallen to the bullet or the boat had sunk. There were so many quarries in land and air that no intelligent person could willingly waste pellets worth even a quarter paisa on a 'dirty rag'.

Honourably acquitted, the manager-sahib went away puffing his way to the club to play whist; the dead body of the fellow who had been grinding spices inside the boat was swept ashore nine miles off the site and Shashibhushan returned to the village with a mortified heart.

The day he returned, Giribala was going to her father-in-law's house by boat. Nobody had invited him, yet he walked slowly to the riverbank and stood at a spot some distance from the ghat, which was crowded. The boat left the ghat and drifted past him when he could see her for once with a quick glance; the newly-wed bride was sitting with her head hung low, her veil pulled down. Giribala had long hoped that before finally leaving her village, somehow for once she would meet Shashibhushan, but today she could not even know that her guru was standing a little distance away. She did not even lift her face to have a look; only, in silent weeping, tears kept rolling down her cheeks.

The boat gradually went farther and farther away until it disappeared completely. The morning sun shimmered on the water. On a nearby mango branch, a cuckoo singing repeatedly in an exuberant strain was pouring out its emotion seemingly without end. A ferryboat loaded with passengers kept shuttling across. Womenfolk, on coming to the ghat on the pretext of drawing water, started chatting excitedly on Giri's departure for her father-in-law's house. And Shashibhushan, after taking off his glasses and wiping his eyes, went back into that small room behind those window bars by the side of that path. Suddenly once, he seemed to hear Giribala's voice, 'Shashi-dada!' Where are you, Giri? Nowhere! Not in that room, not on that path, not in that village—she was in the middle of his tear-soaked heart.

## *8*

Once again packing up his goods and chattels, Shashibhushan set out for Calcutta. He had no work in Calcutta, no particular purpose of going there, and so he decided to go all the way by boat instead of going by rail.

With the monsoon in full swing then, throughout the length and breadth of Bengal a thousand zigzag networks of water had spread. The veins and arteries of the moist green soil of Bengal having filled with water, the abundance of nature in its wild youth phase had grown unruly and reckless with creepers and shrubs, bushes and brambles, jute and sugarcane, everything luxuriating in every direction.

Shashibhushan's boat went on advancing through those narrow curved currents of water. Water had then levelled with land. Bushes of kaash grass, arrow grass, and at places, cornfields had been inundated. The fencing of the village with its bamboo clumps and mango groves stood right on the edge of the trees: it seemed as if nymphs had irrigated the ridges around the roots of the trees of Bengal.

At the beginning of the journey, the forest beauty, as if glistening from a fresh bath, had been brightly smiling in the sunshine; soon clouds gathered and it began to rain. Then whichever direction one cast one's eyes looked sad and untidy. Just as during the flood, the cattle huddled in their dirty, slushy, narrow cowshed keep drenching in pouring rain patiently with piteous eyes, so did Bengal get soaked incessantly, amidst its own muddy, slippery, densely sodden jungle with a mute, gloomy face. The peasants had been out with field-hats on their heads; women were moving between the huts on housework, getting wet and shrivelling from the cold squally wind and drawing water wearing wet clothes from the pond very cautiously stepping on the slippery ghat. Males in the family were sitting on the veranda smoking tobacco, and if urged by sheer necessity, going out with their chuddar tucked in their waists, shoes held in their hands and umbrella over their heads. The weak womankind holding an umbrella over their heads was not included in the traditional sacred custom of the sun-scalded and monsoon-flooded land of Bengal.

When the rain continued without ceasing, growing impatient with remaining inside the boat, Shashibhushan revised his decision, deciding to go by rail instead. Reaching a point, which was like a wide river-mouth, he moored the boat and went about preparing food.

A lame man's foot falls in a ditch: for that, the ditch is not wholly to blame; the foot of the lame man too has a particular tendency to fall. Shashibhushan was to prove this adage that day.

Where the mouths of two rivers met, putting up a bamboo scaffolding, the fishermen had set a wide dragnet, leaving space on one side for movement of boats. They had been doing this for very long and paying taxes as well for that. Unfortunately, this year on this route suddenly the honourable district superintendent of police had been pleased to visit. Noticing his boat, the fishermen in advance pointing to the alternative lane alerted him loudly. But to take a circuitous route honouring any man-made obstacle was not in the habit of the sahib's boatman. He ploughed his boat right through that net, which bowed before the boat, giving right of way, but its oars got entangled. It took some time and effort before the oars could be extricated.

Furious and red with anger, the police-sahib moored the boot. At his very sight, all four fishermen ran away breathlessly. The sahib ordered his boatmen to cut off the net. And they snipped that vast net worth seven to eight hundred rupees into pieces.

After venting his anger on the net, he ordered the fishermen to be hauled up before him. The constable, not finding the absconding four, brought back whichever four he could lay his hands on. They kept imploring with joined palms pleading innocence. When the honourable police officer was ordering the captives to be taken away, Shashibhushan with his glasses on, quickly slipping into a shirt leaving it unbuttoned, flapping his slippers arrived before the police boat, gasping. In a tremulous voice, he said, 'Sir, you have no right to tear the net and torture these four men.'

As soon as the officer reviled him with a particularly insulting word in Hindi, in a moment from a slightly raised land he hurled himself right on the sahib. He started flailing him with his hands like a boy, madly.

What happened thereafter, he did not know. When he recovered in the police station, the treatment he received, one hesitates to say, hardly enhanced his prestige or physical comfort.

## 9

Shashibhushan's father by appointing lawyers first released him on bail, and then began to prepare for the case. The fishermen who had lost their nets belonged to the same region and were under the same zamindar as Shashibhushan. In times of danger, sometimes they came to Shashi to take legal counsel, too. Those, whom the sahib had detained in his boat, were not unknown to him either.

Shashi had them called, intending to cite them as witnesses. They panicked: if they, who had to lead a family life with wife and children, were to quarrel with the police, where would they flee for safety? Whoever had more than one heart in his body? After they had already incurred the damage that was fated, what trouble was this on top of that with the summons for witness? '*Thakur*, you've left us in a great quandary,' they moaned as one.

It took much persuading before they agreed to speak the truth.

Meanwhile, on the day when in connection with his duty on the bench, Harakumar went to pay obesaince to the district sahibs, the SP sahib smiled and said, 'Hallo, Nayeb-babu, I hear your tenants are preparing to bear false witness against the police?'

The nayeb, as if startled, said, 'Oh! Is it ever possible? Is there so much power in the bones of the sons of impure beasts!'

Newspaper-readers will know that Shashibhushan's case never stood a chance to succeed.

The fishermen came one after the other to testify that the police-sahib had not cut off their nets; calling them over to his boat he was taking down their names and addresses.

That was not all; a few known persons from his village deposed that at the time they were present at the spot as members of a bridegroom's party. They had witnessed that Shashibhushan, without any provocation, accosting the sentries had created all the trouble.

Shashibhushan confessed that having been abused, he had rushed into the boat and assaulted the sahib. But the cutting of nets and tormenting the fishermen were the root cause.

In this condition, the judgement that delivered punishment to Shashibhushan cannot be called unfair. But then, the punishment was rather severe. No fewer than three or four charges: physical assault, trespass, creating disturbance in the duties of the police, and so on, all of which were fully substantiated against him.

Shashibhushan went to serve time for five years, leaving behind his favourite books in his small room. When his father proposed to appeal, he forbade him repeatedly, saying, 'The jail is a better place. Iron fetters do not lie, but the freedom outside the jail throws us into danger deceitfully. And talking of good company, liars and ungrateful cowards are fewer within the jail because the space is limited; they are far more numerous outside.'

## 10

Soon after Shashibhushan had gone to jail, his father died. He had few relatives. One of his brothers had been working in the Central Provinces since long; he could rarely manage to come visiting his native home; instead, building a house there, he had settled with his family. Whatever estate he owned in his native land was mostly usurped by Harakumar through various tricks.

By a quirk of fate, Shashibhushan had to suffer much more hardship than most inmates. Nevertheless, the five long years were over one day.

Once again, on a rainy day, broken in body and empty of spirit, Shashibhushan came and stood outside the prison wall. He did get freedom, but except for that, had no one or nothing outside the prison. So vast a world seemed bizarrely loose-fitting for him alone to stay in, with no home, no relative and no society.

He was pondering where to pick up the severed thread of livelihood, when a big phaeton drew up to him. A servant came up to ask, 'You are Shashibhushan-babu?'

He said, 'Yes.'

At once opening the door, the servant stood aside awaiting his getting on.

Taken aback, he asked, 'Where am I to go?'

'My master has called you,' he said.

As the inquisitive glance of pedestrians seemed intolerable, without standing there any longer, he boarded the carriage, wondering if this was not a case of mistaken identity. But at any rate, he had to move in a certain direction: rather let this mistake make up the introduction to this new life.

That day too, cloud and sunshine were chasing each other. The dark-green, flooded cornfield at the end of the path was looking marvellous in the evanescent light and shade. A gigantic chariot was lying abandoned near the market place and not far from it in a grocer's shop, a band of Baishnava mendicants were singing with their one-string lyre, tom-tom and cymbals in accompaniment:

*Come, come, come back – O my Lord! /Starved and parched and smitten is my heart /Come back, my sweetheart!*

The carriage advanced; the words of the song reached his ears, gradually going farther and farther:

*Thou unkind One, come back, my dear! /My sadly tender One/ Refreshingly beauteous as the nimbus cloud, come back, O dear!*

The song grew fainter and more and more indistinct until it was altogether incomprehensible. But its rhythm raised a tempest in Shashibhushan's heart. Humming in his mind, composing line after line, he went on complementing the verse, seemingly interminably:

*Thou art my day's joy / Thou art my day's sorrow, come again, O dear! /My treasure churned out of all joy and sorrow, come back into my heart! / Thou art my ever-desired One /Ever-abiding in my heart, come again my dear! /O restless One, the eternal One /Give thee unto my embrace! /Come once to my breast /Come into my eyes /In my sleep and my dream, in my raiment and jewels, come down to the universe! /Come to the smile of my face /To the tears of my eyes! /To my dalliance, to my wiles /Come back to my sulks! /Abide in my memories /Abide in my faults /Abide in my belief, deeds and affection, shame, life and death!*

When the carriage entered a walled-in garden and stopped in front of a two-storey building, Shashibhushan stopped humming.

Without asking any question, he entered the building, following the servant.

The room where he was seated had big glass-panelled cupboards on all sides, stacked with rows of books of various covers in various colours. At the very sight, his old life emerged free for the second time from captivity. These gold-lettered variously coloured books loomed before him as a well-known gem-studded gateway to the world of joy.

There were some other things too on the table. Bending over them, with his feeble sight, Shashibhushan saw it was a cracked slate, on it were a few exercise books, an almost torn numeration chart, a *Kathamala* and a Mahabharata by Kashiram Das.

On the wooden frame of the slate was written in bold lettering in ink in Shashibhushan's hand: Giribala Devi. On the books and the notebooks also, the same name was written in the same handwriting.

Now Shashibhushan saw where he had arrived. Streams of blood surged into his heart. He looked out of the window: what did he discern? That small room enclosed with bars, that uneven village path, that striped-sari-wearing little girl. And that tranquil, carefree, cloistered life of his own.

That blissful life of those days was nothing extraordinary or extravagant: it passed by unbeknown day after day amidst little pieces of work and little specks of happiness; in the intervals of his own reading, the teaching of a small girl was truly reckoned among insignificant events. Nevertheless, that idyllic village life, that small peace, that small happiness and the small face of that little girl—everything persisted only in the shadow of imagination of the desired land, transcending the barriers of time and space, and inaccessible, as if like heaven. All those images and memories of that day, intermingling with the rain-obscured morning light of today, together with that gently-hummed Baishnava song in his mind, assumed a melodious, resplendent, splendid form. The last memory of the saddened face of that ignored, unloved, anguished girl on that muddy, narrow, jungle-infested village path was reflected on the canvas of his mind as if like a heavenly panorama of God's creation—unnatural, strange, magnificent, profound and full of deep pathos. With it, the plaintive tune of a Baishnava song kept playing and it seemed as if on the face of that rustic girl, an ineffable sorrow of the cosmic heart had cast its own shadow. With his face hidden behind his hands and bent over that slate, book and notebook, Shashibhushan after such a long time began to dream of the days in the distant past.

After a long while, startled by a mild sound, he lifted his face and looked up. Placing some fruits and sweets on a silver tray in front of him, Giribala had been waiting silently standing at a distance. As he raised his face, Giribala in her widow's garb—shorn of ornaments and clad in white— kneeling down touched his feet.

Standing up after making the *pronam*, when the widow looked with her pitiful, soothing eyes at a withered, pale-looking, wizened Shashibhushan, tears began to drop from her eyes and roll down her cheeks.

Shashibhushan tried to ask after her, but did not find the language: confined tears forcibly obstructed his voice; words as well as tears remained confined at the gateway to his heart and the tip of his throat. That band of mendicant singers in course of begging alms from door to door arrived in front of the building and kept singing, repeatedly chanting: *Come, come, O dear*!

*Ashwin-Kartik 1301* (1894)

# The Ghat's[1] Story (*Ghater Katha*)

If events were etched in stone, you could have read so many tales of old inscribed on my steps. If you like to hear old stories, sit down on my step; listen intently to the murmur of water and you can hear many forgotten stories of the long past.

I remember the story of another day. That was also a day just like this. It was a couple of days before the month of *Ashwin*. In the morning, a very light, pleasant, slightly chilly breeze was bringing in new life to the early risers; with it, leaves of trees were twitching a little at times.

The Ganga was nearly overflowing: only four of my steps were above water; land and water seemed to be locked in an embrace. On the bank, under the mango grove where arum plants have grown, even as far as that the Ganga water had extended. There, near that distant bend, three stacks of old bricks stuck out of the surrounding water. The fishing boats, which had been tied to the *babla* tree on the bank, in the morning floating up in the tidewater, were swaying from side to side: the wildly youthful water was naughtily lapping against their sides and tweaking their ears in sweet jest.

On the overflowing Ganga, the sunlight of the autumn morning that was spread was of the colour of pure gold, of the colour of magnolia; such hues of sunlight are not seen at any other time of the year. It was shining on the sandbanks and shimmering on the kaash fields. The kaash was not yet in full bloom; it had just started blossoming.

Uttering Lord Rama's name, the boatmen cast off. Just as birds with their wings spread in the sunlight were flying joyously into the blue sky, the little boats in like manner unfurling their little sails were out to wander in the sunlight. They appeared like birds: they were floating as swans on the water, but out of joy had spread their wings in the sky.

The old Bhattacharya right at his usual time came to bathe bringing his *kosha-koshi*[2] for performing prayers. Women began to trickle in for drawing water.

This was not too long ago. To you it may seem long enough, but to me it seems it was only the other day. My days drift on playfully along the current, as you know; that is what I have been watching for ages without change; for this reason, time never drags for me. My light of the day and shadow of the night every day fall on the Ganga, and are every day wiped out, nowhere leaving behind their impression. That is why, although I look old, my heart is forever young. Under the weight of many years of the moss of memories my sunrays have not died. Occasionally, a stray moss comes floating by and sticks at my side, and again drifts along the current. That does not mean that I do not have anything. Where the currents do not reach, there in each of my crevices the creepers, shrubs and mosses that have grown are the only witness to my past. They are the ones who, binding the olden times with the snare of love, kept them forever green and sweet, forever fresh. The Ganga is receding from me a step each day; I am also growing older in step with her.

You see the old woman of the Chakraborti family, after bath wrapping herself in a *namabali* going back home shivering and counting the rosary beads; her maternal grandmother was a young girl then. I remember the girl had a whim: every day she would set an aloe leaf afloat—there was a vortex on my right flank—the leaf kept circling in it, and putting down her pitcher, she stood watching it. When I saw that some time later, that very girl after growing up, eventually along with a daughter of her own came to draw water, thereafter this girl in turn grew old, and if little girls played naughtily by splashing water, she would scold and teach them manners, then that floating of the aloe leaf boat would come to my mind and I would find a good deal of fun.

What I think I would say does not come to mind. As I begin to say one thing, another comes floating on the current. Stories come and stories go; I cannot keep them back. Only one or two particular stories keep coming back repeatedly like those aloe boats circling in the eddy. One such story with whatever it has to offer is hovering around my steps today, threatening to sink any moment. It is as small as that very aloe leaf and carries very little: two flowers to play with are all it has. If it sinks, the girl with a tender heart only letting out a sigh will go back home.

Beside the temple, where you see the fenced-in cattle-shed of the Gossains', there stood a babla tree. Under it, once a week an open-air market used to come up. The Gossains had not yet settled then. Where they now have their household shrine stood only a shanty of palm-leaf thatch.

This fig tree, which has spread its limbs through my rib cage, its hard protruding roots forming a ghostly mesh of fingers clasping my fissured soul, was just a tiny sapling then. With its newly sprouted leaves, it was rearing its head. When the sun rose, their shadows played all day over me. Its young roots like a child's fingers tickled my breast. If anyone plucked a leaf, I felt the pain.

Though I was old enough then, I still lay straight in one stretch—not the broken-backed, crooked jumble like *Ashtavakra*[3] that I now am, with a thousand cracks like deep three-fold wrinkles, my hollows sheltering myriad frogs for hibernation. Only on the outside of my left arm, a couple of bricks had worn out, leaving a hole, in which a fork-tailed bird had nested. Early in the morning when it fidgeted to wake up and ducked its fishtail-like double-tail a couple of times before flying away into the sky with a whistle, I knew it was time for Kusum to turn up.

The girl whose story I am going to recount, other girls at the ghat called Kusum; perhaps that was her name. When her little shadow fell on the water, I wished I could keep it with me, I could glue it to my stone—such was her grace! When she strode on my stone, her anklets tinkling, I felt my weeds and moss quivering in delight. Not that Kusum was very much fond of play or liked too much of gossip or frivolity. Yet strangely, she had the largest number of companions. The naughtiest girls wanted her the most. Some called her Kusi for short; others, *Khushi* [joy]; yet others, *Rakshusi* [female demon]. Her mother called her Kusmi. She could be seen at any time sitting at the edge of the water. Water and her heart, apparently, shared special common characteristics. She loved water so dearly.

A few days on, and I saw Kusum no more. Bhuban and Swarna came and lamented her absence. I gathered from their talk that their Kusi-Khushi-Rakshusi had gone away to her father-in-law's house. I learnt that where they had taken her away, there was no Ganga. There again, it is a new house, new people, new surroundings: the water lily had been plucked away to be planted on land.

In course of time, I had almost forgotten about Kusum. A year had passed. The women visiting the ghat did not talk too often about Kusum either. One evening, I suddenly felt with a start the touch of two long-familiar feet. It seemed to be Kusum's feet. They indeed were, but no anklets tinkled on them. They lacked the old music. I had always felt her feet and the tinkle together. Today, the sudden absence of that music made the evening murmur of the waters strangely sad for me; the breeze rustling up the mango grove seemed to raise a wail.

Kusum had been widowed. Her husband used to work at a certain far-off place; she had seen him only once or twice. By post coming to know of her widowhood, at the age of eight years, wiping off the vermilion mark from her head, casting away her ornaments, she came back to her native place by the side of the Ganga. But of her companions too, few remained; Bhuban, Swarna and Amala had gone to their fathers-in-law's houses. Only Sharat was left, but I heard she too would be married off in the month of *Agrahayan*. Kusum was virtually alone. However, when she sat quietly on my steps, her head resting upon her knees, the ripples of the river seemed to be waving to her, calling out, 'Kusi-Khushi-Rakshusi!'

Just as with the onset of the monsoon the Ganga fills little by little to the brim, Kusum kept filling up each day with youth and beauty. But her drab clothes, her sad face and her quiet nature had cast such a pall of gloom over her that this burgeoning youth, this blossoming beauty was not evident to others. That Kusum had grown up was something nobody seemed to notice; at least I did not. I never saw her older than the little girl she had been. She indeed had no anklets now, but when she walked, I could hear their tinkling. In this way, ten years passed, apparently nobody in the village knew when.

As you see today, that year too, towards the end of *Bhadra* such a day had come. Your great-grandmothers, that day on waking up in the morning had seen just such mild sunbeams. With pitchers on their waists, their heads covered with long veils, when for the sake of brightening the morning sun on my stones they would come walking through the trees down the uneven village paths, talking among themselves, not even the possibility of your coming into being ever crossed their mind. Just as you cannot quite imagine that once your grandmothers too really went about playing and that day was also as real and living as today, that with youthful hearts like yours, they too throbbed with joys and sorrows like you, in like manner, this autumn day—in their absence, devoid of the memory of their grief and happiness, this joyous picture radiant with the autumn sun—was even more unimaginable to them.

That day, since dawn the first northerly wind beginning to blow gently was carrying one or two blooming babla flowers on to me.

On my stones, a thin film of dew had formed. In the morning, a tall, fair, young *sannyasi* with a bright, dignified appearance came and took shelter in the Shiva temple in front of me. The news of the sannyasi's arrival went across the village. Women, laying down their pitchers, thronged the temple to make *pronams* to the Baba-thakur.

The crowd of visitors swelled each day. Primarily he was a holy man; moreover, he was exceptionally handsome, and on top of that, he neglected no one: he would sit children on his lap and ask women about their household. In the female society, within a very short time, he acquired considerable standing. Men also came in good numbers. On some days, he would read from the *Bhagabat Purana* on others, expound *sloka*s of the *Bhagavad-Gita*, or discuss other religious texts. Some came for advice, some for indoctrination, some others for medicinal herbs. Women at the ghat talked effusively of him among themselves. 'Oh, how majestic he looks! It seems Lord Shiva has appeared in person to reside in the shrine.'

When the sannyasi every day before sunrise facing the morning star, standing waist-deep in the Ganga, sang the hymn to dawn in a slow resonant voice, it drowned the murmur of water. As I heard that voice every day, the sky of the Ganga's eastern coast grew scarlet, the clouds were lined with streaks of crimson, darkness as if bursting forth like the calyx of a blooming bud receded on all sides and the rosy tint of the blossoming dawn diffused little by little in the pool of the sky. It seemed to me that as the holy man standing in the Ganga and gazing in the east chanted the great incantation, each syllable he pronounced broke the spell of the night, the moon and the stars descended to the west, the sun ascended in the east, and the aspect of the universe was transformed. Who was this enchanter? When he came out of the river, water streaming down his matted hair—his tall, fair, virtuous frame resplendent like a sacrificial fire—the first rays of the morning sun seemed to reflect from his limbs.

Several months passed in this way. In the month of *Chaitra*, during the solar eclipse, throngs of people came to take holy dips in the Ganga. A market sprang up around the babla tree. On this occasion, many people had come to pay a visit to the sannyasi as well. Some women from the village of Kusum's matrimonial home had also come.

In the morning, sitting on my steps the sannyasi was reciting mantras. Looking at him suddenly one of the girls nudged her friend and exclaimed, 'Look, isn't he our Kusum's husband!'

Another woman, parting her veil with two fingers, cried out, 'Goodness me, this is indeed him! The youngest son of the Chatterjee family!'

'Ah, just his forehead, his nose, his eyes!' supplemented another who did not bother much about her veil.

Yet another, without looking at the sannyasi, letting out a sigh, pushing the water with her pitcher, moaned, 'Alas, can he still be alive? Will he ever come back? Is Kusum so lucky?'

Then someone said, 'He did not have such a thick beard.' Another said, 'He was not so slim.' Still another said, 'I think he was not so tall.'

In this way, the matter was somehow disposed of, and had no further chance to arise again. All other people of the village had seen the sannyasi; only Kusum had not. Because of the crowd, she had stopped coming to me altogether. One evening, the sight of the full moon perhaps reminded her of our old association.

There was no one else at the ghat then. Crickets were chirping. Temple bells and gongs had just ceased. Their lingering resonance growing fainter and fainter into the shadowy woods across the river had faded away like a shadow. There was silvery moonlight. The tidewater was splashing against my steps. Casting her shadow upon me Kusum was sitting. There was hardly any breeze; trees and creepers stood still. In front of Kusum, all over the Ganga, there was unrestrained extensive moonlight. Behind Kusum, here and there around her, in the bushes and shrubs, in the trees and creepers, in the shadow of the temple, in the foundation of the ruined house, in the palm grove, darkness sat huddled up, shrouded and veiled. Bats were hanging from the *chhatim* tree. Sitting on the temple spire an owl was hooting out at times. Not far from the locality, jackals raised a howl and fell silent again.

The sannyasi slowly emerged from the temple. Coming to the ghat, he descended one or two steps, and noticing a solitary woman, he was thinking of returning when Kusum suddenly lifting her face looked back.

Her veil slipped off her head. Just as moonlight falls on an upturned blooming flower, in the same way, as soon as Kusum lifted her face, the moon lit up her face. That was when their eyes met, as if they came to know each other. It seemed they had known each other in a previous birth.

Overhead, an owl shrieked and flew away. Startled by the sound, collecting herself Kusum pulled up her veil. Then getting up, she lay prostrate at the sannyasi's feet.

The sannyasi blessed her and asked, 'What is your name?'

'My name is Kusum,' said Kusum.

That night no more words were exchanged. Kusum's house was close by; she went away quietly. For a long time that night, the sannyasi remained sitting on my step. At last, when the moon had traversed from the east to the west, when his shadow had reversed sides, he rose and walked into the temple.

From the following day onwards, I saw that Kusum came every day and touched the sannyasi's feet. When he discussed the scriptures, she would listen standing on one side. After his morning prayers, the sannyasi would call Kusum to talk about religion. It is unlikely she understood everything, but with deep attention, she would sit listening silently. Whatever the sannyasi advised her she would obey perfectly. Every day, she would perform the duties of the temple, never neglect the service of the deity; she would pluck flowers, and drawing water from the Ganga wash the temple floor.

On whatever the sannyasi told her, sitting on my steps Kusum used to reflect. Little by little, as it were, her vision extended, her heart opened up. She began to visualise what she had never seen, hear what she had never heard. The pall of gloom that had overshadowed her serene face disappeared. When in the morning, she prostrated in reverence at the feet of the sannyasi, she looked like a dew-soaked flower offered to the deity. A pure bloom of contentment illumined her entire body.

At this time of the end of winter, a cold wind blows; again, on some days in the evening, suddenly from the south, the spring breeze starts blowing, and the chill in the atmosphere goes entirely—after a long time in the village, flutes are played, and songs are sung. Boatmen, resting their oars and coasting in the current, keep singing Lord Krishna's praise. From branch to branch, birds suddenly out of sheer joy begin to call out to each other. Such is the time now.

Taking in the spring breeze, I felt as if within my stone-heart, little by little, the vibrancy of youth was being instilled; as if by drawing that very surge of new youth from within my heart my plants and creepers were rapidly blossoming in bunches. At about this time, I do not see Kusum any more. For some days, she had not been coming either to the ghat or to the temple: in any case, she is no more seen in the company of the sannyasi.

What had happened in the meanwhile I did not know at all. Some time later one evening, right on my step did Kusum and the sannyasi meet each other.

Kusum said lowering her face, 'Master, did you summon me?'

'Yes, but why aren't you coming these days? Why are you so negligent now about serving the deity?'

Kusum kept silent.

'Tell me what is on your mind.'

'Master, I am a sinful woman; that's why this negligence,' said Kusum, slightly turning her face aside.

The sannyasin said in a very affectionate tone, 'Kusum, I can see that your mind is not at peace.'

Kusum was startled; perhaps she thought the sannyasi had come to know a lot. Her eyes gradually filled up with tears; she sat down there; covering her face with her sari-end, sitting on the step near the sannyasi's feet she began weeping.

Stepping aside a little the sannyasi said, 'Tell me frankly what troubles you and I will show you the path of peace.'

Kusum spoke in a voice of unflinching devotion, but at times halted and fumbled for words. 'If you command me, I must tell you,' she said. 'But I cannot present it neatly; I think you know everything in my mind. Master, I used to revere someone like a god; I used to worship him, and that joy had filled my heart. But one night I saw him in a dream, as if he were the lord of my heart; somewhere sitting in a *bakul* grove, taking my right hand in his left he was talking about love with me. To me, this episode seemed not impossible, not strange. The dream ended, but the illusion did not. The next day, when I saw him, I did not see him as before; in my mind, that dream image kept recurring. In fear, I ran away, but the image persisted with me. Since then, the distress in my heart refuses to leave me; my entire world has gone dark.'

While Kusum was saying this, at times wiping her tears, I could feel a strong tension in the sannyasi's right foot as he stood on my stone.

When Kusum stopped, the sannyasi said, 'You must tell me whom you saw in your dream.'

With joined palms Kusum pleaded, 'That I cannot tell you.'

The sannyasi said, 'For your own good I am asking who he was. Tell me frankly.'

'Must I say?' said Kusum, wringing her hands hard and joining her palms.

'Yes, you must.'

Kusum at once spoke out. 'Master, it is you.'

The moment her own words reached her ears, she fell down in a faint upon my hard lap. The sannyasi kept standing like a statue in marble.

When Kusum broke her swoon, the sannyasi said slowly, 'You have obeyed all I said. Now I will tell you one last thing; you must obey it. I am leaving this place today itself so you cannot meet me again. You must forget me. Promise me you will do this penance.'

Kusum got up, and looking at the sannyasi's face, said quietly, 'Master, so shall it be.'

'I am going away,' said the sannyasi.

Kusum, without saying anything more made a pronam to him and put the dust from his feet on her head. The sannyasi went away.

'He has commanded me that I must forget him.' Uttering this, Kusum slowly stepped into the Ganga.

Since when she was a small girl, she had lived close to this stretch of water. Now that she was weary, if this water, stretching out its hands, were not to take her into its lap, who else would? The moon set; darkness deepened. I heard a splash, but could not make out anything else. In the dark, the wind kept swishing, as if to blow out the stars of the sky, in case the least bit of anything could be seen.

The one that used to play in my lap, today after finishing her play moved away from it to somewhere I could not know.

*Kartik 1291* (1884)

NOTES

1 Stairs or a passage, usually paved, leading down to a river or any water body for private or public use (also means: a mountain pass; mud path; fault); a jetty or landing place where boats moor and people gather for taking bath, drawing water or performing religious rites like funerals; a favourite meeting ground of women especially of villages to discuss local politics and scandals.

2 Copper bowl and scoop, both in the shape of a boat, for holy water, an indispensable item of every rite.

3 Son of sage Uddalak's daughter Sujata by sage Kahore; the child was born with curvatures (*vakra*) at eight (*ashta*) places of his body; hence the name. He was later to attain great scholarship and spiritual height and become a sage who authored a scripture known after him.

# The Matrimonial Deal
# (*Dena-Paaona*)

After five sons, when a girl child was born, her parents, after making a great fuss over her name finally settled on *Nirupama (*incomparable). In this family, such a fashionable name was never heard before. Names of gods and goddesses were almost customary—*Ganesh, Kartik, Parvati*, for instance.

For some time now, they had been considering Nirupama's marriage proposals. Her father Ramsundar Mitra had been making extensive enquiries, but no groom was deemed up to the mark. At last, he hunted down the only son of an affluent *Raybahadur*. Although the Raybahadur's ancestral property had dwindled considerably over the years, theirs was no doubt an aristocratic family.

The bridegroom's family demanded ten thousand rupees in cash and plenty of gifts in dowry. Without a thought Ramsundar agreed to that; he must not allow such a groom to slip though his fingers.

Money was not forthcoming by any means. Apart from mortgaging and selling, even after tapping other unusual resources, he lacked six to seven thousand rupees. Meanwhile, the wedding day had approached.

Finally, it was the wedding day. At an extortionate interest, someone had agreed to loan the deficit amount, but at the last moment, he did not turn up. A great fracas ensued at the wedding assembly. Ramsundar, falling in supplication before the Raybahadur, said, 'Please let the rituals go off smoothly; I will certainly pay up the due.' 'Unless and until I get the cash,' declared the Raybahadur, 'I shan't produce the groom.'

This unfortunate development raised a wail of grief in the women's quarters. The root cause of this disaster was sitting quietly in her Benarasi sari, jewellery and sandalwood paste. She was surely not developing too much respect or fondness for her would-be in-laws.

In the meantime, there was a favourable turn in the situation. The bridegroom suddenly grew rebellious against his father. 'I have nothing to do with this haggling,' he said firmly. 'I have come to marry, and I will marry. That's all.'

His father asked whomever he found, 'Have you noticed, sir, how the young men behave these days?' Among them, there were one or two elderly men, who said, 'They've no training in moralities or *shastras*. That's why.' Witnessing the pernicious effect of modern education manifest in his own son, the Raybahadur lost all interest to pursue the matter further. The wedding got through rather perfunctorily in a sombre mood.

At the time of departure for the father-in-law's house, Nirupama's father, while giving her a parting embrace, could not hold back his tears. Niru asked, 'Won't they permit me to come again, Baba?' 'Why won't they, dear?' Ramsundar assured her, 'I will go myself to bring you.'

Ramsundar did go often enough to visit his daughter, but he had no respect in the matrimonial house. Even the servants eyed him disdainfully. Shown into a separate room outside the inner quarters, he could meet his daughter very briefly on some days and not at all on others.

Such shabby treatment at the hands of the in-laws was indeed not acceptable any longer. Ramsundar decided that somehow he must pay up the money.

But the debt he had already incurred was too onerous for him. He was hard up for domestic expenses, and had to have recourse to many devious means to evade his creditors.

Meanwhile, the in-laws kept tormenting his daughter with acerbic comments at every step. Mortified by the vilification of her parents, she was reduced to weeping secretly in her room as part of her daily routine. In particular, her mother-in-law's resentment showed no signs of abating. If someone said, 'Ah, how pretty the girl is! It's a treat to see her,' she shot back, 'Pretty indeed! As pretty as the family!'

Even her food and clothes were not taken care of properly. If some kindly neighbour pointed to any lapse, her mother-in-law would shut her up, 'That was more than enough!' In other words, if her father had paid the full price, she would have received full care. Everyone pretended as if the girl had no right in the family; she had tricked her way into it.

Perhaps these tales of woe and indignity had reached her father's ears. Eventually, Ramsundar decided to sell off his residential estate.

That he was going to render them homeless he kept secret from his sons. In fact, he had decided that after selling the house, he would continue to live there as a tenant and manage so tactfully that his sons would never come to know it before his death.

Nevertheless, the sons did come to know. They fell at his feet weeping,—especially the elder three sons, who were married, one or two having their children as well; they protested most firmly. The sale was postponed.

Ramsundar then began to raise small loans from various sources at exorbitant interest. The condition so worsened that he did not know how to run the household.

Niru, on observing her father's face, surmised everything. His grey hair, his shrunken face and diffident manner betrayed his destitution and worry. When a father was guilty to his daughter, how could the remorse of that guilt be suppressed? Whenever Ramsundar, on permission from his in-laws, very briefly met his daughter, the way he managed a smile would reveal how a father's heart was battered.

For the sake of comforting that anguished heart, Niru had grown impatient to go on a short visit to her father's house; after she had seen his wizened face, she could no longer keep herself aloof. To Ramsundar, one day she said, 'Baba, take me back home for once.' Ramsundar said, 'Well, yes.'

But he had no right: the natural right a father has on his daughter, as it were, had been mortgaged against unpaid dowry. Even an interview with his daughter he had to beg for with abject humility, and if denied at certain times, he was not supposed to insist a second time.

In any case, when the daughter herself had proposed to come, how could a father have ignored it? Therefore, before approaching his in-law with a request to that effect, how he had managed to collect three thousand rupees, and what meanness, humiliation, and personal loss he had had to endure for this had better remain a secret.

The currency notes wrapped in a handkerchief tied to his chuddar, Ramsundar came and sat close to his counterpart. First, with a smiling face, he broached the news from his own neighbourhood: a daring burglary had taken place at Harekrishna's house, of which he gave a detailed account. Comparing the two brothers Nanimadhab and Radhamadhab, in respect of learning and intelligence and moral character, he spoke well of Radhamadhab and ill of Nanimadhab. An unidentified disease was currently visiting their town; he made up all incredible stories about it. Finally, putting away the hookah, in course of conversation he said, 'O yes, Dada, that unpaid sum, of course. Every time I came here, I would have brought in a part, but forgot it at the last moment. Senile lapse, brother.' After this prolonged ceremony, the three notes like three ribs of his chest he took out most easily and indifferently. As soon as he saw a mere three thousand rupees, the Raybahadur burst into a crude boisterous laugh. 'Keep it with you, *bhai*, I don't need it,' he said, and quoting a Bengali proverb, said he did not want to soil his hands over a trifle.

After this, no one could have uttered the proposal of taking his daughter home. Only Ramsundar felt that any hesitation due to the formalities of matrimonial relation was no longer befitting to him. Utterly shocked, he sat silently for a long while and finally broached the matter in a most submissive tone. 'Not now,' was all the Raibahadur said, and without mentioning any reason whatever, excused himself brusquely.

Ramsundar, without showing his face to his daughter, after tying up the notes at the end of his chuddar with trembling hands, went back home. He promised to himself that until after paying off his dues he was in a position to claim his daughter confidently he would never again visit his in-law's house.

Many days went by. Nirupama kept sending messengers one after another, but her father did not come. At last, out of pique, she stopped sending them. Ramsundar was hurt, but still did not go.

The month of *Aswin* arrived. Ramsundar said to himself, 'This time during *Durga-puja* I must bring my little mother home; otherwise I'll –' He finished with a dreadful oath.

One or two days before the pujas, once again at the end of his chuddar tying up a couple of notes Ramsundar prepared to go. A five-year-old grandson came and said, 'Dada, are you going to buy me a cart?' For months he had been longing to go riding a perambulator in the open, but no prospect of fulfilling his wish appeared forthcoming. A six-year-old granddaughter came and submitted ruefully that she had no good dress to wear during the festival invitations.

Ramsundar was aware of it, and while smoking tobacco the old man had deliberated long on it. When there would be the puja invitation from the Raybahadur's house, his daughters-in-law in their meagre jewellery would have to attend like beggars deserving pity: contemplating this he had heaved many a sigh. But that had done nothing except for digging deeper furrows of age on his brow.

With the whining of an impoverished family ringing in his ears, the old man set foot on his in-law's house. Today, his old diffident looks were gone; that quick furtive glance at guards and servants was there no more; he walked straight in, as if into his own house. He was told the Raybahadur was not home, so he would have to wait a while. Unable to suppress the surge of emotion, Ramsundar met his daughter. Tears of joy rolled down his cheeks. Father wept; so did the daughter; neither could speak for a while. Then Ramsundar said, 'This time I'm taking you along, dear. No more problem.'

At this point, Ramsundar's eldest son Haramohan, his two little sons in tow, suddenly entered the room. 'Baba, so you have wrecked us in the end,' he told his father.

Ramsundar all at once flew into a rage, 'Do you want me to go to hell for your sake? Won't you let me do my duty?' He had sold off his residence. Lest his sons should anyhow come to know, he had taken many sound steps. Since they had nevertheless come to know, he suddenly grew very much angry with them.

His grandson, hugging his two knees firmly and looking up to his face, said, 'Dada, so you didn't buy me a pram?' Getting no reply from Ramsundar whose head hung low, the boy, going to Niru said, '*Pishima*, will you buy me a car?'

Guessing the entire matter, Nirupama said, 'Baba, if you ever give a single paisa to my father-in-law, you shall not see me any more. This I swear by touching your body.'

'Shame, dear child,' said Ramsundar, 'you shouldn't say such things. Apart from that, if I do not pay off the due, that will be shameful to your father as well as to you.'

'If you do, that'll be shameful,' Niru countered. 'Do you think your daughter has no dignity? Am I just a bag of money—I have value as long as I have money? No, Baba, please do not insult me by giving them this money. Besides, my husband never wanted it.'

'In that case, they won't permit you to go, my child,' Ramsundar argued.

'If they don't, what can you do, Baba? You won't insist any more, either.'

Picking up the chuddar with the bundle of notes tied to it, once again like a thief averting the notice of everyone, Ramsundar went back home.

But the fact that Ramsundar had brought the money, and forbidden by his daughter, without giving that money, gone away did not remain a secret. Some snoopy, eavesdropping maidservant shared the news with the mistress. Then there was no end to her wrath.

For Nirupama, her father-in-law's house grew into a bed of nails. Meanwhile, her husband, on promotion to deputy magistrate shortly after marriage, had gone to another district and lest she should pick up meanness from corrupt company, recently Niru's meetings with the relatives from her father's house had been completely banned.

About this time, Niru had a serious illness. But her mother-in-law was not entirely to blame for this. The girl had been very careless about her health. During the chilly weather of *Kartik*, all night long the door behind her head used to be kept wide open; during the winter, she had no woollens on. There was no regularity in eating. When sometimes the maidservants forgot to bring her meal, she would not take the trouble of reminding them. The perception that she had been living on the charity of menials and masters of another family was taking firm roots in her mind. But even this behaviour was not tolerable to her mother-in-law. If she noticed any neglect of her daughter-in-law about taking her meals, she would tauntingly say, 'Isn't she from a nawab's family? How can she eat our poor food?' Sometimes again, she would say, 'O, how awful she looks! She's becoming more and more like a burnt stick of wood!'

When her illness turned serious, the mother-in-law remarked, 'It's all pretence.' At last one day, Niru said humbly to her mother-in-law, 'Ma, I wish to see my father and my brothers once this time.' Her mother-in-law said, 'She never lacks pretexts for going to her father's house.'

No one will believe it, but the evening she went into her last gasps was when the doctor examined her for the first time, and that was his last visit as well.

The eldest daughter-in-law of the family died: the funeral rites were fittingly performed with great pomp and splendour. About ostentatious immersion ceremony at the end of Durga-puja, the Raychoudhuris were renowned throughout the district. About the funeral rites of his eldest daughter-in-law, the Raybahadur earned a similar reputation. A sandal wood pyre for cremation no one in this region had ever seen. Such a grandiose obsequies ceremony too was possible only in a Raybahadur's house, and it is rumoured that in this connection they had incurred a little debt.

While paying condolences to Ramsundar, everyone recounted in detail how grandly his daughter had died. Meanwhile, a letter from the deputy magistrate arrived, 'I have made all necessary arrangements here, so please send my wife immediately.' His mother wrote back, 'Baba, we have fixed up another girl for you, so please come urgently on leave.'

This time, the dowry was twenty thousand rupees, cash down.

*? 1298* (1891)

# Ramkanai's Folly
# (*Ramkanaiyer Nirbuddhita*)

Those who say that at the time of Gurucharan's death, his wife by second marriage was playing cards in the inner quarters are rank slander-mongers who make a mountain of a molehill. Actually, she was then busy, sitting on one leg folded under and raising the knee of the other up to the chin, eating with relish soaked rice with a hotly spiced prawn curry of vegetable stalks enhanced with green tamarind and chillies. When she was summoned from outside, leaving the mound of masticated stalks and the cleaned-out platter she moaned with a solemn face, 'Just a morsel of soaked rice; even for that I am not given time.'

Meanwhile, when the doctor had left giving his final pronouncement, Gurucharan's younger brother Ramkanai sat by his side and said gently, 'Dada, if you want to make a will, tell me.' Gurucharan said in a faint voice, 'Take down as I say.' Ramkanai took out his pen and paper. Gurucharan dictated, 'All my movable and immovable property I give unto my legal wife Shrimati Baradasundari.' Ramkanai did write, but he found it difficult to do so: he had high hopes that his only son Nabadwip would inherit the entire property of his uncle who had no son. Although the two brothers had separate establishments, yet sustained by this one hope,

Nabadwip's mother had not consented to Nabadwip taking up any work. She had him married off rather early, and fortunately for them, it was not a barren marriage, either. Nevertheless, Ramkanai wrote as told, and handed the pen to his brother for his signature. Gurucharan signed with an almost lifeless hand, but whether it was several wavy scratches or his name was difficult to tell.

After eating her soaked rice, when Gurucharan's wife came and saw that he could not speak, she started wailing. Those who had nourished their hope and had been deprived of the property dismissed it as crocodile tears. However, this aspersion is not credible.

Hearing about the will, Nabadwip's mother came running and raised a great commotion. 'Insanity before death! When he had such a gem of a nephew –' she grumbled.

Ramkanai had great regards for his wife—so great that it may be termed differently as fear—even so, he could not hold himself back and rushed in. '*Mejobou,*' he rebuked, 'Your time for insanity isn't come, then why are you behaving like this? Dada is gone, but I am still here. Whatever you want to say, tell me at leisure. This is not the right time.'

When Nabadwip came on hearing the news, his uncle had expired. Threatening the deceased man, he raved, 'All right, I'll see who lights the pyre. I won't be the person to perform the last rites.' Gurucharan was no respecter of rites. He was a pupil of Mr. Duff[1]'s. He most relished the food which the scriptures forbade as the worst. If people called him a Christian, he would be abashed, and swear, 'O Rama, if I am a Christian, I would eat beef.' When such had been his views while alive, it was most unlikely that immediately after death he would be perturbed in the least by any shortcomings in the funerary rites. Nevertheless, for the time being, Nabadwip had no other means of avenging himself. He had one consolation that the fellow, after arriving in the other world, would remain perpetually dead. As long as one lived in this world, one could manage a morsel even without inheriting one's uncle's property, but in the world to which his uncle had gone, one could not beg one's way to salvation. Many were the advantages of remaining alive.

Going to Baradasundari, Ramkanai said, '*Bou-thakurani*, Dada has made you sole successor to his property. Here is his will. Put it away carefully in the iron safe.'

The widow was then chanting high-pitched lamentation in long impromptu verses. A ring of maidservants was lending their matching voices, at times throwing in a couple of new phrases, and with the resulting dirge, banishing sleep from the entire neighbourhood. The sudden intrusion of this scrap of paper broke the tempo as well as the sequence of moods. The matter now took the following incoherent form.

'Oh, dear, what ruin has befallen me, what ruin has befallen! Well *Thakurpo*, whose is the writing? Yours, I suppose? Oh, dear, who will look after me with that much care, who will feel for me?—And you! Would you stop a moment? Don't scream like that. Let me hear him—O me! Why did I not go before you, why do I still live?' 'That is our ill luck,' sighed Ramkanai deep within.

Back home, Nabadwip's mother started venting her fury on Ramkanai. As a miserable bullock, stepping in a rut with a loaded cart stands still helplessly for quite some time in spite of all the prodding from the cart-man, so did Ramkanai bear it long enough patiently. At last, he said in a feeble voice, 'Where's my fault? I am not Dada.'

Nabadwip's mother shot back, breathing fire, 'Indeed, indeed. You are so naïve; you do not understand a thing. Dada told you to write and you wrote down. You are all the same. You're going to do the same thing yourself when it's time. As soon as I die, you will go and marry some terrible witch and abandon my darling Nabadwip. Never mind, I am not going to die anytime soon.'

This is how contemplating the future excesses of Ramkanai, his wife grew increasingly impatient. Ramkanai knew for sure that the least attempt to remonstrate with her trying to wipe out those preposterous fears would have the opposite effect. Fearing this, he stood submissively like a culprit as if he had committed what she apprehended: as if he had departed from the world after writing out the will in favour of his prospective second wife depriving the glorious Nabadwip, so that now there was no reprieve without confession.

Meanwhile Nabadwip, after consulting his clever friends, came to his mother and said, 'Don't worry. I am going to get this property, nobody else. All we need to do is remove father somewhere for the time being. His presence will spoil everything.' Nabadwip's mother had scant regard for his father's wisdom, so, she too found the proposal quite reasonable. In the end, harassed by his mother, Nabadwip's redundant, foolish, bungling father found some pretext of sorts to seek refuge in Varanasi temporarily.

Soon after, Nabadwip and Baradasundari moved court accusing each other of forging Gurucharan's will. The signature in the will Nabadwip had taken out in his own name clearly indicated that it was Gurucharan's handwriting; one or two disinterested witnesses had been enlisted as well. On Baradasundari's side, Nabadwip's father was the sole witness, and the signature on the will was beyond anybody to recognise. Baradasundari had a parasitic maternal cousin who said, 'Didi, you need not worry. I'll stand witness and find some others as well.'

When the matter came to a head, Nabadwip's mother recalled his father from Varanasi. The obedient man that he was, he arrived in time, bag and umbrella in hand, and even tried to exchange some banter. 'Here is the humble servant; what's the empress's order?' He smiled joining his palms as he said this.

'Enough, enough,' said his wife reprovingly, 'No more drollery. So many days blissfully away on some pretext, and did not remember me even once.' And so on.

They carried on such fond recriminations for fairly long until finally the butt of jokes veered from the individual to the race. Nabadwip's mother compared man's protestation of love with a Muslim's affection for chickens[2]. 'A woman has honey on her lips, a razor in her heart,' retorted Nabadwip's father, though nobody could remember when he had ever tasted of this verbal sweetness.

In the meantime, Ramkanai received a summons from the court to stand as witness. Surprised, he was trying to get at its meaning when Nabadwip's mother came and inundated herself in tears. Not only did the horrible ogress want to deprive Nabadwip of his affectionate uncle's rightful inheritance, but she was conspiring to send that gem of a boy to jail as well.

At last, when he was gradually able to guess what had happened, Ramkanai was astounded. ' Have you descended to this?' he cried out. Nabadwip's mother, gradually resuming her usual self, said, 'Why, what has been Nabadwip's fault in this? Won't he claim his uncle's property! Simply forgo it without demur?'

If an accursed hag appearing from nowhere staked her claim, how could a blemishless, pedigreed scion tolerate it? Even if at the time of death and under a gorgon's charm an imbecile uncle had made an error of judgement, what grave misdeed would have been perpetrated if his brilliant nephew rectified that error in his own hand?

At his wits' end, when Ramkanai saw that his wife and son together kept hectoring and haranguing him, with occasional shedding of tears, he cursed himself and sat silently; he gave up eating altogether, and even did not touch water.

Two days went by in this way when the day of the hearing arrived. Meanwhile, Nabadwip, by enticement and intimidation, prevailed on Baradasundari's cousin to such an extent that he easily defected to Nabadwip's side standing witness for him. Just when the goddess of victory, deserting Baradasundari, was preparing to switch over to the other party, Ramkanai was summoned.

Famished and moribund, his lips and tongue parched, the old man clutched the bars of the dock with his frail, shaky fingers. The clever barrister began to cross-examine Ramkanai very tactfully to wrest the truth out of him. Starting from a point, apparently very remotely connected, and making very calculated and tortuous moves, he was zeroing in on the issue.

Then Ramkanai, turning to the judge said with joined palms, 'Your Honour, I am old and very weak; I am unable to talk much. Whatever I have to say let me submit in brief. My elder brother, the late Gurucharan Chakraborti, made a dying will of his estate to his wife, Baradasundari. That will I wrote out in my own hand and my brother signed in his own hand. The will filed by my son Nabadwipchandra is false.' Even as he said this, Ramkanai began to tremble and fainted away.

The clever barrister wittily said to his attorney sitting next to him, 'By Jove! Did you see how I cornered the man?'

The maternal cousin ran up to his sister and said, 'The old haggard had nearly spoilt it; my testimony saved the case.'

The sister said, 'Indeed! Whoever can recognise a man? I thought the old man was a simple fellow.'

Nabadwip was thrown into prison. After a good deal of deliberation, his intelligent friends concluded: sure enough, the fellow had done it out of fear. Once in the witness box, the old wretch had been puzzled. You won't find such a consummate fool scouring the whole town.

Returning home, Ramkanai came down with a violent fever. Muttering his son's name in delirium, Nabadwip's stupid, blundering, unwanted father was removed from the world. Some of his relatives regretted, 'Had he gone a few days earlier, it would have been a blessing.' I would rather not name names.

? 1298 (1891)

NOTES

1 Alexander Duff, missionary and educationist.

2 Earlier, chickens used to be eaten by Muslims and would not even be touched by orthodox Hindus, and naturally, had to be reared by Muslims; so, any affection they had for the chickens in rearing them was for their narrow selfish ends and short-lived.

# Grandfather
# (*Thakurda*)

## 1

The zamindars of Nayanjor had once been very famous as Babus[1]. The standard of babudom then was not very easy to achieve. Just as it now takes a whole lot of dinners, carousals, horse-racings, salaams and recommendations to acquire the title of Raja or Roy Bahadur[2], similarly it took many arduous efforts then to earn the appellation of Babu from the common people.

Our Babus of Nayanjor wore the finest dhotis from Dacca only after tearing off the borders because their dandyish skin was too delicate to stand the coarseness of the edges. They would spend a fortune to celebrate the wedding of kittens. Legend has it that once during some festival, determined to reproduce day at night, they had arranged to light countless lamps and simulate sunbeams by showering threads of pure silver from the sky. Obviously, the extravagant lifestyle of the Babus of that time could not last for generations together. Like a multi-wick lamp, they would squander their resources over a brief spell of pomp and splendour.

Kailaschandra Roychoudhuri was a spent successor to the renowned Babu ancestry of Nayanjor. He was born at a time when the oil of resources had reached the bottom of the bowl. When his father died, Nayanjor babudom gave out its last flicker to light up a couple of ostentatious funeral rites before coming to an abrupt end. Almost the entire property had to be sold off to pay up the outstanding dues. The residue was hardly enough to preserve the family name. Kailas Babu therefore left Nayanjor with his son, came to Calcutta and settled permanently. The son, too, in course of time, left the family of lost splendour and went off to the other world, leaving his only daughter behind.

We were his neighbours in Calcutta. The history of our family was quite different from theirs. My father had earned a lot of money by his own enterprise; he never wore his dhotis in the Babu style[3], maintained accounts to the last paisa, and did not hanker after the appellation of Babu. As his only son, I am grateful to him for this. I consider it a proud privilege that I have received education and inherited enough money to preserve my life and dignity. A father's company bonds preserved in an iron chest seem to me more valuable than the inherited flamboyance of babudom languishing in an empty coffer.

That was perhaps why I could not stand the fact of Kailas Babu making tall claims about their former glory. I felt that since my father had earned money by dint of hard labour, Kailash Babu might perhaps have been holding us in contempt. I would be angry and wonder who really deserved contempt. My father had practised rigorous self-denial all his life, overcoming all temptations, and he never aspired after cheap applause. He had removed all impediments with tenacious pursuit of intelligent strategy, converted every favourable turn to his advantage and built up a colossal pyramid of wealth, layer by layer, with his own hands. Such a person was not to be ignored only because he was not dressed like a babu.

I was young then, hence argued like this and grew angry. Now that I am mature, I tell myself: what is the harm? I have immense wealth; what more do I want? If a man who has nothing is still happy to boast I have nothing to lose; rather, the poor fellow has consolation.

I also noticed that no one except me bore him a grudge, for so innocent a man was rare to find. He had good rapport with his neighbours and participated in all their rituals and festivals, joys and sorrows. Anyone he came across, young or old, he would greet with a smile and an address of endearment; his kind of civility ended only after he had asked after the person as well as every member of his extended family. Hence in any such encounter, an unending stream of questions followed: 'How are you? Is Shashi well? Is our Baro Babu[4] keeping good health? I heard Madhu's son had a fever; is he all right now? I haven't seen Haricharan Babu for long; he isn't ill, is he? What about your Rakhal? Are the women in the family well too? And so on in the same vein.

The man was very neat and organised in his ways. His wardrobe was not well stocked: a kurta, a short coat, a shawl, an old wrapper for a bedspread, pillowcases, and a small carpet were all he had, which he personally sunned, dusted, hung out, pleated and put away on the clothes rack. Whenever you saw him, you found him well turned out as if ready to meet people. Even with the limited furniture, his house always looked shipshape; one would have thought he had much more.

As he had only one servant, sometimes after closing the door, he would pleat his dhoti, and crimp his chuddar and shirt with great care. He had lost huge landed estates and property, but managed to save a few things from the clutches of poverty—a costly rosewater spray, an attar pot, a gold salver, a silver hubble-bubble, a very expensive shawl, old-fashioned attire and a turban. These came out of the cupboard only on special occasions to uphold the glory of the renowned Babu family of Nayanjor.

An unassuming person otherwise, Kailas Babu's verbal bragging was done apparently out of a sense of duty to his ancestors. Everyone used to indulge him and derived much fun listening to him.

His neighbours addressed him as 'Thakurdamashai'[5] and there was always a good cluster of them in his drawing room. Not to burden his straitened circumstances with the cost of tobacco, someone or other would often bring a seer[6] or two of tobacco and say, 'Thakurdamashai, try this; I've got some good tobacco from Gaya.' Thakurda would have a few puffs and say, 'Hmm! Good stuff, indeed.' He would then start praising his own stock of tobacco bought at sixty or sixty-five rupees a tola[7], and ask if anyone of them liked to try it.

Everyone knew that if he said yes, either the key to the cupboard would not be found or after a long search, it would be revealed that the old servant Ganesh was the culprit who never put away things in their place; Ganesh, too, would accept the blame without protest. So, all of us would say in one voice, 'No, Thakurdamashai! That superior stuff won't suit us. This is good enough.' Thakurda would only smile without saying another word. When they got up to leave, he would suddenly say, 'Well then, when do you like to have dinner at my place?'

They would say at once, 'Don't worry, we'll let you know after we fix a date.'

'That's best,' he would say. 'Let the rains come; the weather will be cooler then. Rich food in the summer isn't a good idea.'

When the rains came, nobody reminded him of his offer. Rather, if it popped up during conversation, they would protest unitedly, 'We don't think it would be convenient now. Let the rough spell pass.'

His friends often lamented in front of him that a small rented house was not appropriate to his status, yet they had no doubt that it was very difficult to find a suitable house to buy in Calcutta. In fact, even a larger house on rent—his neighbours could not locate one in the six or seven years he had been living here. In the end, Thakurda would say, 'Never mind. After all, I'm living close to you, and that makes me happy. The big house at Nayanjor is lying vacant after all. Would I find my peace there?'

I believe Thakurda knew it just as well that everyone was aware of his condition. When he tried to live out the bygone glory of Nayanjor and the others participated with willing suspension of disbelief, he felt in his heart that this mutual deception was owing to sheer goodwill.

However, I felt utterly disgusted about this. When you are young, you tend to stamp out even one's harmless vanity. You may ignore a thousand faults, but foolishness is most intolerable. Kailas Babu was not exactly foolish; people often sought his advice and assistance. But, when it came to glorifying Nayanjor, he lost all sense of proportion. Because everyone loved him and found him amusing, no one ever objected to his unbelievable talk, and this encouraged him to exceed all limits. Similarly, when someone, for mere fun or flattery, made any exaggerated remark about Nayanjor's glory, he accepted it freely and could not imagine that others might disbelieve it.

At times I was so exasperated with this old man who was happy to live in a false citadel and thought it permanent that I wanted to demolish it with cannon fire before everyone's eyes. The very sight of a bird conveniently perched on a branch impels a hunter to shoot. A rock resting precariously on a mountain slope tempts a boy to kick and set it rolling down. Something which is likely to drop at any moment, yet is attached to a peg, seems to find its fulfilment only if it is brought down, and then the viewer too is satisfied. Kailas Babu's lies were so overt, so ill-founded and they danced so defiantly before the barrel of the truth-gun that I felt an impulse to shoot them down. That I desisted from it was due to sheer lethargy and compulsions of good form.

## 2

As far as I can recollect from a critical analysis of my past feelings, there was perhaps a deeper reason for my antipathy to Kailas Babu. That should be told in some detail.

I was a rich man's son. Even so, I had taken my Master's degree in due time. I had never kept evil company or indulged in crude revelry despite my youth. There had been no aberration in my character even when I became master of myself after my guardian's death. Besides, my appearance was such that if I myself said I was handsome, I might have appeared vain, but would not be lying.

No doubt, therefore, that I carried an exorbitant price tag in the match-making market of Bengal and I was determined to realise my full worth there. Exquisitely beautiful, learned and the only daughter of a rich father loomed in my imagination as the ideal.

Proposals started pouring in from far and near offering ten to twenty thousand rupees in dowry. I scrutinised each proposal coolly in strict accordance with the standard I had set, but none came equal to me. Eventually I came to believe, like Bhababhuti[8]:

Who knows my compeer shall be born
In the world so vast, in the time infinite!

But it is doubtful whether that rarest thing has been born in the present time and within the small area of Bengal.

Fathers burdened with unmarried girls started to chant hymns in my praise and worship me with various offerings. Whether or not I liked the girls, this ritual seemed to please me. I had decided that as a suitable boy I rightfully deserved this adoration from the girls' fathers. Scriptures say that no matter whether the gods grant you any boon or not, they become furious unless they duly get their puja. Having myself become used to receiving worship had similarly created an exalted feeling of godliness in my mind.

As I have said, Kailas Babu had a granddaughter. I had seen her several times, but never mistakenly thought she was beautiful and so, never imagined marrying her. But I firmly believed that Kailas Babu wishing to offer his granddaughter would either come himself or send a representative to initiate my worship for I was suitable. But he did not do that.

I heard he had told a friend of mine that the Babus of Nayanjor had never approached anyone with a prayer. He would rather keep the girl unmarried all her life than break with that family tradition. This exaggerated pride angered me and the anger smouldered in me for a long time. Only because I was a good boy, I remained calm.

As thunder is accompanied by lightning, so my nature had a humorous streak accompanying anger. Otherwise, it would have been impossible to persecute the old man for the mere sake of it. Suddenly one day, I had a plan; it was so funny that I could not resist the temptation of executing it.

I have already said that people fabricated various tales to please the old man. A retired Deputy Magistrate of the locality often told him, 'Thakurda, whenever I meet the Lieutenant Governor, he makes it a point to enquire about the Babus of Nayanjor. He says that there are only two truly aristocratic families in all Bengal: the Maharajas of Burdwan and the Babus of Nayanjor.'

This pleased Thakurda no end. Thereafter, when he came across the retired official, he would ask, among other things, 'Is the Lieutenant Governor well? Is his wife well? Are their children well too?' He would even express his desire to pay him an early visit. But the former Deputy certainly knew that by the time the famous four-horse carriage of Nayanjor vintage arrived at his door, several governors both at the centre and at the state would have been replaced.

One morning, I called on Kailasbabu, took him aside and said in a whisper, 'Thakurda, yesterday I went to the riverfront and met the Lieutenant Governor. When he mentioned the Babus of Nayanjor, I told him that Kailasbabu of Nayanjor is now right in Calcutta. Hearing this, he deeply regretted that he had not come to call all these days. He told me straightaway that he is coming to meet you secretly this afternoon.'

Anybody else would have seen the absurdity of the story, and if it were to concern anybody else, Kailasbabu himself would have laughed at it. Because it pertained to him, he found nothing incredible about it. He was as much delighted as he was excited. He was at a loss to decide where to seat him, what formalities to perform , how to welcome him—how to preserve Nayanjor's prestige. That apart, since he did not know English, how to carry on the conversation was another problem. 'Don't worry,' I assured him. 'The Governor has an interpreter with him; but he particularly desires that no one else should be present.'

In the afternoon when most people of the neighbourhood had gone to office, while the rest were taking a nap behind closed doors, a horse-drawn carriage arrived in front of Kailas Babu's house. A liveried orderly announced in Hindi, 'The Lieutenant Governor's come!' Thakurda, dressed in his outmoded white attire and turban, had already been waiting to receive him. He had his old servant Ganesh too well turned out in his, the master's, own dhoti, shirt and chuddar.

As soon as he heard the announcement, he rushed to the door, panting and trembling. Bending his body and repeatedly salaaming, he led into the room a friend of mine costumed and made up as an Englishman. There he seated the false Lieutenant Governor on the bed topped with his one and the only costly shawl. Kailas Babu then read out a long grovelling speech in Urdu and offered as tribute a chain of gold coins laid out on a gold salver—austerely preserved and handed down through generations. Ganesh was at hand with the rosewater spray and the attar pot.

Kailas Babu regretted time and again that if His Excellency had graced their Nayanjor home, they could have done their utmost to receive him with due ceremony. Living here in Calcutta, he was helpless like a fish out of water. And much more of the same.

My friend, with his top hat on, bobbed his head very gravely. According to the British custom in such cases, the hat should not have been in place; but my friend had not doffed his hat in his effort to keep his face as much covered as possible to evade detection. Anybody except Kailas Babu and his swollen-headed servant would at once have seen through this disguise of a Bengali person.

After bobbing his head for about ten minutes, my friend got up to leave. The orderlies, as tutored, picked up the chain along with the salver, the shawl from the cot, collected the rosewater spray and the attar pot from Ganesh's hands, and stowed them into the impersonator's carriage. Kailas Babu convinced himself that this was the convention with the Lieutenant Governor. I was watching the spoof hiding in the next room with repressed laughter nearly cracking my ribs. When I could control myself no more, I ran into a room further away and broke out into laughter. Suddenly I noticed a girl lying, face down, on the bed and sobbing.

As she saw me suddenly enter the room laughing, she leapt from her bed and stood confronting me. Charging her tear-choked voice with a howl of fury, a blaze of lightning in her large, dark, tearful eyes, she said, 'What's my grandfather done to you ? Why have you come to trick him? Why?' She could not utter another word. Pressing her sari-end to her face, she burst out crying.

My laughter vanished in a moment. Until now, it had not occurred to me that there could be anything more than fun to what I had done. Suddenly I realised that I had dealt a most grievous blow to a most tender spot; the ghastly brutality of my misdeed loomed large before my eyes. I slunk away in shame and remorse, like a dog that had been kicked. What harm had the old man done to me? His innocent conceit had never hurt any creature. Why then did my vanity have to be so monstrous?

The day's incident opened my eyes to another point as well. So far, I had looked upon Kusum as a commodity put away for the condescending glance of an unmarried youth. I had thought: since I have not chosen her, she has been languishing. If someone ever comes to like her, she will be his. Today I discovered that there was a human heart behind that image of a girl lying in a corner over there. A mind with its own joys and sorrows, likes and dislikes stretched out towards two endless domains of mystery: the unknowable past and the unimaginable future. Does an individual with a heart deserve to be judged merely in terms of dowry and physical features?

I could not sleep all night. Early next morning, I picked up all the purloined goods, priceless treasure of the old man, and sneaked into his house, like a thief. I would have liked to leave them with the servant surreptitiously, without saying anything to anyone.

As the servant was not around, I stood hesitating, when I caught snatches of a conversation between the old man and the girl in a nearby room. The girl was asking tenderly, 'Dadamashai, what did the Governor tell you yesterday?' Thakurda was gleefully putting profuse imaginary encomiums about the Nayanjor family on the lips of the Governor, and the girl was listening encouragingly.

My eyes swam with tears to see this compassionate deception by a small motherly girl of her old guardian. I waited quietly until Thakurda finished his story and left the room. I then went to the girl, silently placed the purloined goods before her and came back.

Following the modern practice, I had never greeted the old man with any form of courtesy; today I touched his feet. The old man must have inferred that the Lieutenant Governor's visit to his house had aroused my respect for him. With great delight, he eagerly started telling embroidered tales about the Governor, and I too joined in without protest. The others who heard it took it as complete fiction and graciously agreed with every word of the old man.

When the others had left, I made a proposal to him with utter shyness and humility. I said that although in lineage we were not to be compared at all with the Babus of Nayanjor, yet if he would etc.

Once I completed, he held me in an embrace and ecstatically said, 'I am poor. I never knew, bhai, that I would be so fortunate. Kusum must have done many good deeds to deserve you.' Tears rolled down his eyes as he said this.

The old man, for the first time today, forgot that he was honour-bound to uphold the dignity of his ancestors, and admitted that he was poor; he admitted that by accepting me the Nayanjor family had suffered no loss of pride. While I had been contriving to ridicule the old man, he had deeply cherished me as a most suitable groom.

*Jyaishtha* 1302 (1895)

## NOTES

1 A dubious distinction for their extravagant and ostentatious lifestyle (distinct from its other senses; see Glossary).

2 Raja: a ruler or landlord, sometimes used as a form of address (as in Roy Bahadur) or as a title preceding a name (as in Raja Rammohan Roy); both the titles were given by the British to respectable, wealthy Indians for loyalty to the Raj.

3 Traditionaly, Bengali gentlemen wear their dhoties ankle-length. The story-teller's father, to economise on the cost, would wear a variety which did not reach below his knees.

4 Address for head of a joint family.

5 Combination of Thakurda (one's grandfather) and mashai (a suffix to the surname or address of any respectable person); Thakurdamashai or Dadamashai is an affectionate and respectful form of address.

6 Seer (or ser): an old unit of weight, usually taken as one-fortieth of a maund which equals thirty-seven kilograms; bulk quantities, such as of rice and milk, were measured by the seer.

7 Tola: a very small unit of weight such that 86.5 units make a kilogram; very costly materials, such as gold, were measured by the tola (or bhori); hence, the high cost of the brand of tobacco Thakurda used compared with that of the neighbours is suggested.

8 Court pundit of king Bhoja, famous Sanskrit dramatist of the eighth century, second only to Kalidas, and author of Uttararamacharita [The Later Deeds of Rama] and Veercharita [The Deeds of the Hero].

# Nuisance
# (*Aapad*)

Towards the evening, the wind grew increasingly stronger. With the lashing of rain, booming of thunder and flashes of lightning, the sky looked like a battleground of gods and demons. Billows of black clouds kept flying in every direction like the victory flag of the apocalypse; rebellious waves started dancing with a gurgling sound across the Ganga; huge trees fluttering their branches kept swaying to the right and left with whistling and hissing.

At that time, in a bungalow in Chandannagar[1], in a lamp-lit closed room, sitting on a mat on the ground in front of the bed, husband and wife were talking to each other.

'If you stay a few more days,' Sharat-babu was saying, 'you'll recover fully. We can then go back home.'

'I've recovered fully,' said Kiranmayi. 'There will be no harm going back home now.'

Any married person will know that the conversation did not end as briefly as I have reported. It was no complex issue, yet the arguments were by no means heading towards a resolution; like a boat without a rudder, they were twirling endlessly until in the end it seemed likely to capsize in the waves of tears.

'The doctor says it is better to stay back a bit longer,' insisted Sharat-babu.

'Your doctor seems to know everything,' countered Kiran.

'Try to understand, Kiran,' Sharat argued, 'This is the season back home when various diseases strike. We should rather stay here for another two months or so.'

'You mean here at this time no one in the vicinity has any disease, is it?' quipped Kiran.

The background was this: Kiran was the beloved of everyone in the family and neighbourhood, even of her mother-in-law. Naturally, when Kiran fell seriously ill, they had become very much worried, and so when the doctor advised a change of air, her husband and her mother-in-law had not hesitated to get away leaving their home and work. Every prudent man of the village had adjudged the optimism about the healing power of a change of air and such inordinate fuss over the wife as a brazen display of uxorious capitulation. They had raised several questions: had no one else's wife ever fallen seriously ill? were people immortal at the place Sharat was taking his wife to? was there any place on earth where the decree of providence was ineffectual? But Sharat and his mother had paid no heed to those questions; rather than the collective wisdom of the village, the precious life of their heart's treasure, Kiran, had seemed more important to them. Such delusions do occur in times of our dear one's danger.

So they had been living at a garden house of Chandannagore; Kiran had recovered as well, only she had not fully regained her strength. A pathetic feebleness lingered in her face, the sight of which makes one's heart tremble: 'Oh, she had a narrow escape,' one muses.

By nature, Kiran was fond of company and fun. She no longer liked to remain here alone: she had no work in the house, no friends in the neighbourhood; she hated tending her own sick body all day. Watch out for the hour to take your medicine, then measure it out and gulp it, keep your temperature chart, follow your diet—it was so tedious. Today in the stormy evening, in their closed room, this was the matter husband and wife were quarrelling over.

As long as Kiran kept giving rejoinders, they had been fighting an equal battle, but at last, when withholding her replies without remonstrance she sat stiff-necked with her face slightly turned away from Sharat's direction, the feeble, helpless fellow had no other weapon. He was just about to concede defeat, when from outside, the servant announced something loudly.

Sharat came out and heard that a Brahman boy whose boat had capsized had swum ashore to their garden.

When Kiran heard this, all her resentment and wounded vanity disappeared. At once, she took out a set of clothes from the wardrobe and sent it to the boy, and then warming a bowl of milk, sent for him.

The boy had long hair and large eyes; no hint of moustache yet. Kiran, after feeding him with personal care, asked him his story.

She heard he was a lad in a *jatra* troupe; his name was Nilkanta. They had been invited to perform at Singha-babus' house in this locality; meanwhile there was this mishap on the way; nobody knew what had happened to the others. He could swim well and had saved himself.

They kept the boy with them. Thinking how close to death he had been, Kiran felt a surge of pity for the boy.

'That's fine after all,' thought Sharat to himself. 'Kiran's got something to do. It'll keep her in good humour for some time.' In the expectation of earning virtue, thanks to the Brahman boy, his mother too derived some pleasure. And having been transferred from the hands of the impresario, as well as *Yama,* unexpectedly into a rich family, Nilkanta felt greatly relieved.

Soon, however, Sharat and his mother started veering from their opinions. They thought they had made enough fuss; now if they could get rid of the boy, a nuisance would be removed.

Nilkanta, in secret, started puffing away at Sharat's hookah serenely. On rainy days, remorselessly flaunting Sharat's favourite silk umbrella over his head, he kept roaming the streets in quest of new friends. A mangy village dog from somewhere was so much spoiled by his petting that foraying into Sharat's furnished room, it kept registering its gracious visit on the clean bed sheet with its footprints in dust. A large circle of admirers soon formed round Nilkanta, and that year the green mangoes in the village orchards had no chance to turn yellow.

Kiran used to pamper this boy excessively, no doubt. Sharat as well as Sharat's mother forbade her often enough against this, but she paid no heed. Clothing him in Sharat's old shirts and socks, new dhoti and chuddar, she just made him a *Babu*[2]. Frequently, at any hour calling him in, she would shower her affection and indulge her love of fun. Kiran would sit on the bed, *paan*-tray beside her, while her maidservant would dry her hair by repeated parting and rubbing, and Nilkanta, standing on the floor would enact the Nala-Damayanti[3] episode with appropriate gestures and flourish of hands. The long afternoon thus ended soon enough for her. She would try to enlist Sharat as a spectator in the same row as her, but Sharat would be very much annoyed, and in front of him, Nilkanta's talents could not be fully displayed, either. On some days, her mother-in-law came in the hope of hearing the praise of gods, but her usual afternoon sleepiness soon overpowered her piety, and sent her to bed.

From Sharat, Nilkanta almost routinely received a tweak in the ear or a smack or a slap, but having been used to harsher modes of disciplining from childhood, he never felt hurt or humiliated. He firmly believed that like the division of earth into land and water, human life was divided between eating and beating, with beating corresponding to water by volume.

Exactly how old Nilkanta was it had been difficult to ascertain. If he was fourteen or fifteen, his face must have outgrown his age in maturity, and if he was seventeen or eighteen, it must not have grown in proportion to his age. He was either prematurely mature or unsuitably immature for his right age.

The fact is that at a very early age after joining the *jatra* troupe, he used to play *Radhika, Damayanti, Sita* and a female confidante to *Vidya*. To fulfil the needs of the impresario, by God's grace, after growing to a certain stage, he had stopped growing further in stature. Everyone used to look upon him as small and he himself thought of himself as small indeed; from no one did he get the dignity due to his age. Because of these natural and unnatural factors, at the age of seventeen, he had looked more like an overdeveloped fourteen-year-old than an underdeveloped seventeen. His lack of moustache had made this impression even more convincing. Whether from tanning by tobacco smoke, or from using language ill-befitting his age, his upper lip gave an impression of adulthood, but his eyes with their large pupils had a childish innocence in them. I presume his inside had an embryonic quality, but his association with the jatra troupe had incubated it fast enough to exhibit maturity.

While he was living in Sharat-babu's shelter at his bungalow in Chandannagore, the rule of nature kept working on Nilkanta without hindrance in its own way. The critical age, at which until now he had abnormally halted for long, he crossed silently after coming here, at some time unknown to him. He looked every inch his seventeen or eighteen years of age.

This change in him did not catch anyone's notice from outside; but its first sign was that when Kiran behaved with Nilkanta in the way suitable to a boy, he used to feel embarrassed and hurt. One day, the fun-loving Kiran had asked him to dress like a *sakhi*[4] in woman's clothes; suddenly it felt very painful to him, yet he could not find out any good reason for it either. These days, whenever he was called upon to act out a jatra part, he would make himself scarce. That he was nothing more than a stripling from a wretched jatra party was something he could not at all accept in his mind.

He even decided to take some lessons in reading and writing from the bungalow manager. But because Nilkanta was the mistress's favourite, the manager could not bear the sight of him, and because he had never learned to concentrate, the letters just swam before his eyes. He would sit for long hours on the riverbank, leaning against a *champa* tree, with a book kept open on his lap. The water splashed, boats plied, birds chattered, and Nilkanta's eyes glided over the page—what he was thinking he alone knew or even he did not know himself. From one word, he could hardly reach another, yet the thought 'I am reading' lent him a great sense of self-glory. When a boat came up close, he would make a great show of reading, holding the book to his face and muttering with even greater enthusiasm; once it was gone, his enthusiasm was gone, too.

Earlier, the songs he used to sing mechanically, as a matter of course, now stirred his heart strangely with their melodies. Their words were most trivial, full of cheap alliteration; neither was their meaning exactly comprehensible to Nilkanta. But when he sang:

> O swan, you twice-born[5] swan,
> How could you be such a heartless one?
> For what purpose best, in this forest,
> Did you imperil a princess?

he seemed to be transported to a different life, a different world. Then the habitual world around him and his insignificant life, being translated into song, took on a new meaning. The swan and the princess of his song brought strangely beautiful pictures to his mind; what he thought of himself cannot be spelt out clearly, but he forgot his identity as a stray waif from a jatra troupe. When the wretched grimy child of a destitute family lying in bed listens to the story of 'The Prince, Princess, and Sapphire', in the dark corner of that dimly lit decrepit house, his mind being delivered from the ties of poverty and meanness, assumes in a fairy-tale Eldorado a new beauty, new lustre, and unchallenged power. So too from the tunes of his songs this jatra boy would remodel himself and his world in a novel shape. The lilt of water, the rustle of leaves, the cooing of birds and the smiling face of the blessed lady that had sheltered this accursed one, her benign bejewelled arms, her pinkish feet of flowery softness and rare beauty—all transformed into a musical strain by some mysterious magic. Again at some time, this mirage of music disappeared into thin air: Nilkanta, the jatra boy with unkempt hair would be revealed; following the complaint from the manager of a local orchard, Sharat would punish him with a couple of thwacks on his cheeks, and as the leader of his admiring followers, Nilkanta would go out to create newer and newer troubles on land, water and tree.

Meanwhile, Sharat's brother Satish came to spend some days with them during his Calcutta college holidays. Kiran was very happy; she had another subject to keep her occupied: in any matter from eating to dressing, she kept teasing and joking with her brother-in-law of the same age. At some time, smearing vermilion on her palms, she would press his eyes from behind; at another time, write 'monkey' on the back of his shirt or bolting the door with a bang from outside run off with a sweet loud laughter. Satish was not one to be outdone, either: by hiding her keys or lacing her *paan* with chilli powder or hitching her sari-end to the bedpost he used to take revenge on her. In this way, together they used to spend the day screaming, chasing, and laughing, sometimes even quarrelling, weeping and coaxing, and finally making up.

Who knew what evil spirit possessed Nilkanta? He could not think out on what pretext and with whom he wanted to quarrel, but his mind filled with a feeling of intense bitterness. He started being unfairly harsh with his loyal boys bringing them to the verge of tears; without any reason kicking that pet country dog, he caused a great din to be raised with its yelps; even, when walking down the street, he lashed away at the weeds with a stick lopping off their branches.

Kiran took great delight in feeding with personal care those who could eat well sitting in front of them. Nilkanta was capable of eating well; he never refused requests for repeated helpings of a good dish. For this reason, Kiran, often inviting him to her room, fed him with solicitous attendance; it was a special pleasure for her to watch the Brahman boy eating to his heart's content. After

Satish's arrival, because of lack of opportunity, Kiran had usually to be absent from where Nilkanta ate. Earlier, such occasional absence no way disturbed his eating; he used to leave his seat only after finally rinsing the milk bowl and drinking water from it. Now, unless Kiran called and fed him personally, his heart became anguished and his mouth unable to get the taste of food; without eating, he would leave his seat, telling the maid in a choked voice, 'I've no appetite.' He hoped that soon after getting the news, Kiran with a repentant heart would send for him and request him repeatedly to sit down to eat, yet, he would not keep that request, and say, 'I've no appetite.' But neither did anybody inform Kiran nor did Kiran send for him, and the maidservant would finish up the food. Putting out the lamp of his bedroom, lying on his bed with a pillow pressed against his face, he burst out weeping with a paroxysm of sobs. But what was his complaint, whom did he want to take notice and who would come to comfort him? When no one came, the kind, universal nurse, sleep, crept in, and with the touch of her tender hands, assuaged the pique of this wounded motherless boy.

Nilkanta's firm conviction was that Satish was always poisoning Kiran's mind against him. On any day when Kiran for some reason kept up a sullen silence, Nilkanta thought that because of Satish's conspiracy it was he whom Kiran was angry with.

From then on, Nilkanta, wholeheartedly and with intense desire, always prayed to his god, 'In our next birth, may I be Satish, and may Satish be me!' He believed that a Brahman's curse imprecated with full force never failed. Therefore, in his mind, trying to burn up Satish with Brahmanical spiritual force, he continued to suffer within, while Satish and his sister- in-law's enthusiastic bursts of laughter and banter coming from upstairs kept greeting his ears.

Nilkanta did not dare to be openly hostile to Satish, but at opportune moments, causing him minor inconveniences, he derived great pleasure. When Satish, leaving his soapbox on the step of the bathing *ghat*, got down in the Ganga and began to take dips,

Nilkanta would swoop down and run away with the soap; duly coming back for the soap, Satish found there was none. One day, while bathing, he suddenly noticed that his much-fancied embroidered shirt was drifting by in the Ganga water; he put it down to the breeze, but from which direction it had blown nobody could tell.

One day, to entertain Satish, Kiran, after calling in Nilkanta, asked him to sing some jatra songs. Nilkanta remained silent. Surprised, Kiran asked, 'Whatever happened to you?' Nilkanta made no reply. 'Why don't you sing that one?' she pressed again. 'That I've forgotten.' Saying this, Nilkanta went away.

Finally, it was time for Kiran to return home. Everyone started getting ready; Satish too was to go back with them. But to Nilkanta, no one said anything whatsoever. Whether he would go with them or stay back did not cross their minds.

Kiran proposed to take Nilkanta with them. To this, her mother-in-law, her husband, her brother-in-law—everyone objected in one voice; Kiran gave up her plan. At last, two days before the departure, calling the Brahman boy she advised him with affectionate words to return to his native village.

After neglect of several days in succession, having heard the tender words he could contain himself no more; he burst out crying. Kiran's eyes also brimmed with tears. She realised with great remorse that it was unwise to have allowed attachment to grow by doting on someone who could not be kept forever with her.

Satish was present there at the time; he was very much irritated to see a grown-up boy weeping. 'My goodness!' he blurted out, 'Nothing is the matter, and he's weeping like a child!'

Kiran rebuked Satish for these harsh words. 'You don't understand, *Boudi,*' said Satish. 'You trust everyone too much. No one knows a thing about him, and he's living here like a king. Afraid to go back to square one[6], he's shedding false tears. He knows very well that if he sheds two drops of tears, your heart will melt.'

Nilkanta hurriedly left the room. But his mind kept assailing the imaginary effigy of Satish, turning into a knife to stab, a needle to pierce, a fire to burn. The real Satish remained unscathed, only Nilkanta's heart kept bleeding.

Satish had brought a fancy inkstand purchased from Calcutta. It had two oyster-shell boats on either side to hold the ink, and in the middle, a German silver swan holding a pen between its parted beaks sat spreading its wings. Satish cared very much for it; often he dusted it very tenderly with his silk handkerchief. Kiran could not resist a dig at him: tweaking the swan's beak half in jest, she would recite, 'O swan, you twice-born swan / How could you be such a heartless one?' and on that pretext there would ensue a duel of jokes between the jesting in-laws.

The morning preceding the day of departure, the inkstand could not be found. Kiran laughed and said, '*Thakurpo,* your swan has gone to look for your Damayanti!'

But Satish became furious. That it was Nilkanta who had stolen it there was not a shadow of doubt in his mind; even a witness was found who had seen him loitering near Satish's room the previous evening.

The accused was brought before Satish. There Kiran was present too. Satish came up straight with, 'Where have you kept the inkstand you've stolen? Go bring it.'

Nilkanta, for various offences, and even for none, had often received a good deal of beating from Satish and always borne it cheerfully. But when in front of Kiran the theft of the inkpot was blamed on him, his two large eyes kept blazing like fire; his heart swelled and thrust upward to his throat. If Satish had said one more word, with all ten nails of his two hands he would have pounced upon him like a cornered kitten.

Then Kiran taking him into the next room said in a coaxing tone, 'Nilu dear, if you have taken the inkstand, bring it back to me quietly; no one will say another word to you.' Big drops of tears trickled from his eyes; at last covering his face he began to weep.

Coming out of the room Kiran said, 'Nilkanta never stole it.'

Both Sharat and Satish kept saying, 'Of course, it was Nilkanta, no one else.'

'No, never,' Kiran firmly protested.

Sharat wanted to interrogate Nilkanta separately, but Kiran said, 'No, you mustn't ask him anything about the theft.'

Satish said, 'His room and his box should be searched.'

'In that case,' said Kiran, 'I'll never have anything to do with you all my life. I won't allow you to cast any aspersion on an innocent.'

As she said this, the lids of her eyes wetted with two drops of tears. The supplication of those sad tearful eyes dissuaded the accusers from taking any further action against Nilkanta.

Such outrageous treatment of an innocent orphan boy raised a well of sympathy in Kiran's heart. That evening, taking two pairs of fine dhoti and chuddar, two shirts, a pair of shoes, and a ten-rupee note, she entered Nilkanta's room. She had thought that without telling Nilkanta, she would just slip those gifts of love into his box. That tin box too was her gift.

With the key at her sari-end, she opened the box quietly, but could not accommodate her gifts into it. It was stuffed with various articles like kite-reel, bamboo-twigs, ground oyster-shell for peeling green mangoes, the bottom of a broken glass, and so on.

Kiran thought that if the box was repacked properly, her gifts could go in. For that purpose, she began to empty the box. First, the kite-reel, a spinning top, a kitchen knife and such other things came out; then some dirty clothes and some washed ones, and then, right from the bottom, out came Satish's precious swan inkstand.

Kiran was surprised; red in the face, she sat pondering for a long time, holding it in her hand.

Meanwhile, Nilkanta had entered the room from behind but she did not know. Nilkanta saw everything and thought that Kiran herself like a thief had come to catch his thieving, and his theft had been found out as well. That he had stolen it not out of greed like a common thief, that he had done this to satisfy his urge for retaliation, that he had decided to throw it into the Ganga, but in a moment of weakness instead of doing that shoved it into his box, how could he explain all these things to her? He was not a thief! Not a thief! What was he then? How could he say what he was? He had stolen someone's thing, yet he was not a thief. Kiran had suspected him to be a thief: the cruel injustice of this he could neither explain, nor bear.

With a long sigh, Kiran put the inkstand back into the box, and like a thief, over it placed the dirty clothes, over them the boy's reel, twig, top, shell and broken glass, everything, and on top of all, her presents and the ten-rupee note.

But the next morning, no trace of the Brahman boy could be found. People of the village said they had not seen him. The police reported him missing. 'Let's now look into his box,' said Sharat.

'By no means,' said Kiran stubbornly. Then having the box brought into her room, she took out the inkstand and secretly cast it into the Ganga.

Sharat and his family went back home. The garden house became empty all at once. Only that pet country dog of Nilkanta kept wandering along the riverside, searching and wailing ceaselessly.

*Falgun 1301* (1894)

NOTES

1 Chandannagar: a town across the Ganga some distance from Calcutta. In *My Reminiscences* (p 125), Rabindranath recalls how he came to stay with his elder brother Jyotirindranath who was living there at the time with his wife Kadambari in a villa known as 'Mr Moran's Garden'.

2 This was the traditional attire of a Bengali middle-class gentleman.

3 Nala-Damayanti: a love-lorn royal couple from the Mahabharata (see Notes to *Aparichita*).

4 *Sakhi* means 'a most beloved female friend, a confidante'; here, a *gopi* or confidante of Krishna.

5 In Bengali, *dwija* literally means 'twice-born'; it usually refers to a Brahman who is believed to be regenerated or reformed by wearing the sacred thread; it can also mean 'a bird' because it hatches from an egg.

6 The text says *punarmushik* from the Sanskrit proverb '*punarmushiko bhaba'* which literally means 'May you be mouse again.' In a parable, a sage, taking pity on a mouse scared of dogs, converts it into a dog that in turn, scared of tigers, is mercifully converted into a tiger; the latter, one day tried to pounce on the sage himself, and was instantly turned into a mouse again by the sage uttering the words, now proverbial.

# The Matronly Boy
# (*Ginni*)

Two or three classes below the Junior Scholarship class[1], our pandit[2] was Shibnath; he was clean-shaven, with his hair close-cropped, and topknot short. The very sight of him scared the boys out of their wits.

In the animal world, species having sting have no teeth. Our teacher had both. On the one hand, punches and slaps rained bountifully like hailstones upon the garden of saplings; on the other, intense tongue-lashing made their lives miserable.

This man used to grumble that the teacher-student relationship of olden days no longer existed; students no more revered their teacher like a god. With this grouse, he would hurl his neglected halo viciously on the boys' heads and often roar loudly. But that explosion was so freely contaminated with vulgar words that there could be no mistaking it for a god's thunder in another form. If aspersions on another's father are cast in booming tones, does it not betray his mean stature?

However, nobody made the mistake of identifying this Class III-Section B god of our school with *Indra, Chandra, Varun* or *Kartik*; only with one god could any similarity be discerned: his name is *Yama*. After all these years, there can be no fault or fear in admitting that in our minds we wished he would not delay much longer in going to that god's abode.

After all, we had realised that there was no nuisance like a mortal god. Heavenly gods do not give any troubles. Pluck them a flower from the tree, and they are content; if you do not, they do not come to remind you. Our mortal gods want very much more, and if there is the slightest lapse, they come charging with blood-shot eyes; then they do not at all look like gods.

Our Shibnath-pandit had devised a novel method for tormenting boys. It may sound trivial, but in fact was terribly cruel: he gave them sobriquets. Though a name is nothing but a word, generally a man loves his name more than he does his own self; to promote his name, what trouble can he not undergo? He will not hesitate even to die if only to save his name. To distort the name of such a name-loving being is to hit him somewhere dearer than his heart. Even if you call Bhootnath[3] Nalinikanta[4], Bhootnath will bristle with anger. From this, it follows that people tend to value the abstract more than the concrete: the cost of making an ornament rather than the gold, self-esteem rather than self, and one's name rather than oneself.

Because of these deep underlying principles of human psychology, when Pandit-*mashai* named Shashishekhar *bhetki*[5], Shashi was terribly upset. Moreover, when he discovered that the nomenclature had taken particular note of his physical features, his heartache doubled; yet very patiently bearing it all, he had to keep sitting silently.

Ashu got the name *Ginni*[6], but there is an anecdote to it.

Ashu was a most innocent simple-minded fellow in his class. He would never say a harsh word to anyone. Very shy, and perhaps the youngest, he had a gentle smile for everyone and everything. He would prepare his lessons regularly. Boys were generally eager to make friends with him, but he would not play with anyone; as soon as the school broke up, without waiting a moment he would make straight for home.

Their maidservant used to turn up at one in the afternoon every day, bringing him his tiffin[6]: a few sweets wrapped in a *sal* leaf, and water in a small bell-metal bowl. Her visit was a great embarrassment for Ashu: if only the maid returned home! That over and above a school student he was something else he seemed mortally ashamed to reveal to other boys. That he was someone of a family, that he was a son of parents and brother of siblings was, as it were, a very secret thing; his only effort was to ensure that in no case was this disclosed to his classmates.

About his studies, there was no fault except that occasionally he was late coming to his class. Asked to explain, he could give no good reason. For that, often there would be no end of humiliation. The pandit would keep him standing near the stairway, doubled up with hands resting on knees: the boys of all four classes could watch the wretched boy in this disgraceful position mortified with shame.

One day, the school had a holiday for solar eclipse. Next day, pandit-mashai came to school, sat on his chair, and looking at the door, saw Ashu entering the class with his slate and books in an ink-smudged cotton bag, more diffidently than usual.

With a wry smile, he said, 'Look, look, Ginni's coming.'

Thereafter, when the lessons were over and the school was to dissolve, he said, 'Boys, listen.' All the force of gravitation kept pulling the boy forcibly downwards. But the tiny Ashu, with the plaited fall of his dhoti and his two legs dangling from the bench stayed put as the target of all the boys of the class. By now, Ashu must have grown old enough; many memorable days of happiness, sorrow and shame must have come to his life; but, no other day can compare with the history of that day in childhood.

Nevertheless, it was a trivial matter; just a couple of words can finish it.

Ashu had a younger sister; she had no sisters or companions of her age, so whatever play she had was with Ashu alone.

An iron railing with a gate enclosed the portico of their house. Thick clouds had gathered that day, and it was raining heavily. The few pedestrians on the road, umbrella over their heads and shoes in their hands, were walking too hurriedly to notice anything. In that darkness of clouds, amid that clattering of rain and with the holiday stretching before them, Ashu was playing with his sister sitting on the portico steps.

It was their doll's wedding day. On that ritual, Ashu was advising his sister very gravely and in a great flurry. Everything arranged, they were discussing who could be the priest. The girl at once ran off to someone and asked him, 'Hello! Will you be the priest at our doll's wedding?'

Turning back, Ashu saw Shibnath-pandit, his clothes half-wet, his wet umbrella folded, standing in their portico; on his way, he had taken shelter from rain, and the girl was proposing to appoint him her doll's priest.

As soon as he saw pandit-mashai, Ashu, abandoning his play, sister and everything else vanished into the house. His holiday plan was a complete washout.

Next day, when Shibnath-pandit, after narrating this episode with wry humour as a prelude, gave Ashu his sobriquet of Ginni, Ashu at first smiling gently as he did to every word, tried to join slightly in the fun. Just then, the one o'clock bell rang; other classes dispersed, and there stood their maidservant at the door, two sweetmeats in a sal leaf and water in a freshly scrubbed bell-metal bowl in her hand. It was then that Ashu burst out laughing; his face and his ears blushed deep red, his forehead began to ache, veins swelled, and tears gushed out in spite of himself.

Shibnath, in his restroom, had his refreshments and sat smoking tobacco peacefully while the boys with great hilarity running around Ashu began to yell 'Ginni, Ginni'. That misadventure of playing with his sister on a holiday seemed to him to be a most disgraceful blunder of his life that he did not believe the world would ever forget.

*? 1298* (1891)

## NOTES

1 Class VI of a secondary school; a scholarship examination was held at the end of this class all over Bengal to select a certain number of talented and indigent students for grant of stipends to defray their expenses.

2 The word in the text was not used in the context of primary schools to mean 'pundit' in its accepted sense. Whether or not they taught Sanskrit, they were called Pundit or rather, Pandit as a surname: such as Shivnath Pandit in this story.

3 The lord of ghosts, Shiva; please see Glossary.

4 The lotus-bodied god, Narayana or Vishnu; see Glossary.

5 A freshwater fish with a rather flat body and a wide mouth and a tapering head.

6 A married woman, homemaker of a family.

# The Skeleton (Kankal)

The room next to ours where we three childhood companions used to sleep had a full-sized skeleton hanging on the wall. At night, the wind stirred it rattling the bones; by day, we had to handle those bones. At that time, we used to read about *Meghnadbadh* with our *pandit-mashai* and osteology with a student of the Campbell Medical School. Our guardian's desire was to make us experts in every branch of learning. How far his desire has been fulfilled need not be told to those who know us, and is best kept secret from those who do not.

Many years have passed since then. Meanwhile the skeleton from that room and osteology from our head had been removed somewhere beyond investigation.

A few days ago, one night, for some reason there being lack of accommodation elsewhere, I had to go to sleep in that room. At an unaccustomed place, sleep proved elusive. I kept tossing and turning until the clock at the church tower struck midnight. Around that time, the oil-lamp that had been burning in a corner, after guttering for about five minutes, finally went out. Very recently, there had been one or two mishaps in our family. So from this dying out of the lamp, naturally the thought of death came to my mind. I thought that the way a flame of lamp melted away into darkness at dead of night was no different from Nature in the way thin flames of lives were suddenly blown out and forgotten sometimes at night, sometimes by day.

This gradually brought back the memory of the skeleton. While contemplating its living state, I suddenly felt some live form groping along the wall around my mosquito net; its heavy breathing could be heard. It seemed to be looking for something, and not finding it, shuffling across the room even faster. I definitely knew that it was entirely a figment of my imagination in my sleepless overheated brain, and the blood that was spinning in my own head itself sounded like footsteps. Yet I had a creepy feeling. Trying to shake off this unfounded fear, I called out, 'Who's there?' The footsteps stopped next to my mosquito net, and I could hear an answer, 'It's me. I've come to find out where my skeleton could have gone.'

I reasoned that there was no point in betraying fear to a creature of one's imagination; so, clutching the bolster with both hands, I said familiarly like an old acquaintance, 'Just the thing to do in the middle of the night! Why must you have that skeleton back, anyway?'

In the darkness, from very close to my mosquito net, the reply came, 'What a thing to say! Wasn't my breastbone in that skeleton? Hadn't my twenty-six-year-old youth bloomed around it? Would I not wish to see it once again?'

I at once said, 'Yes, it's a valid point, indeed. Well, you keep searching. I'll try to get some sleep.'

'You're alone, I suppose,' it said. 'Then let me sit for a while and have a chat. Thirty-five years ago, I too, sitting next to man used to talk to man. All I have done these thirty-five years is wander round the burning *ghat,* moaning with its wind. Today, sitting beside you, let me talk once again like a human being.'

I sensed someone sit near my mosquito net. Feeling rather helpless, I said with some amount of interest, 'That's fine! Tell me something that cheers up the mind.'

'If you want a most interesting story,' said the voice, 'let me tell you about my life.'

The church clock struck two.

'When I was a human being and young, one person I used to fear like *Yama*: he was my husband. I felt exactly like a fish caught with a hook. That means as if a completely unknown creature hitching me to a hook was snatching me away from the deep soothing waters of my birth; there was no chance to escape from its clutches. Just two months after my marriage, my husband died, and my near and dear ones lamented my fate. My father-in-law, after studying several symptoms, told my mother-in-law, "This girl is what the scriptures describe as a poison-girl". I remember that word distinctly. Hey! Are you listening? How do you like it?'

'Very much,' I said. 'The beginning is quite amusing.'

'Listen then,' she continued. 'I returned gladly to my father's house. Gradually I grew up. People would not tell me openly, but I knew very well that my kind of beauty was not found anywhere and everywhere. What do you think?'

'Quite possible. But I've never seen you.'

'Never seen me? How? You've seen my skeleton! Ha-ha ha! I was joking, but how can I prove that in those two empty sockets, there were two large, wide, black eyes, and the gentle smile that lingered on my ruddy lips cannot be compared to the present bare, toothy horrible grin? Such grace, such charm, such consummate fullness of youth was blossoming on those long dry fragments of bones, it seems ridiculous and makes me angry as well to recount to you. That osteology could be learnt from that body of mine was something even big doctors of that time did not believe. In fact, a doctor had once remarked to one of his friends that I was a *kanakchampa,* a golden lotus. This implied that all other humans of the world could be subjects for demonstration of anatomy and physiology, only I was like that flower, beauty itself. Could a golden lotus have a skeleton inside it?

'When I walked along, I could sense that just as on turning a diamond it sparkles from every side, so at every turn of my body the aspects of my beauty broke forth into wavelets in all directions. Sometimes for a long while, I would keep gazing at my own arms—two arms that could muzzle and hold in a passionate grip the imperious manhood of the world. Subhadra, carrying Arjuna by her side, proudly drove away her victory chariot to the amazement of the three worlds[1]. Perhaps she had two such slender shapely hands, rosy palms, and fingers like flames of gold.

'But that shameless, bare, bland, perpetually old skeleton bore false evidence to you about me. I was helpless, so I did not protest. For this, I am most angry with you rather than with anyone else in the world. I wish I could present before you my sixteen-year-old vibrant beauty flushed with the warmth of youth; let it banish sleep from your eyes and your osteology from the country.'

I said, 'If you had your body, I would swear by touching it that not a trace of that learning remains in my head. As for your enchanting full-bloomed youth, it is brilliantly shining in the dark background of night. You don't need to tell any more of it.'

'I had no friends. My elder brother had vowed he would not get married. I was the only woman in the house. Sitting all by myself under a tree in the garden, I used to contemplate that the entire world loved no one but me, all the stars were watching me alone, the wind was brushing past me with deep sighs repeatedly on some pretext, and if the grass where I sat stretching out my legs had consciousness, it would faint away. I loved to imagine that all the young men of the world in the shape of those blades of grass were standing in a cluster quietly at my feet; I felt an unreasoning twinge in my heart.

'When my brother's friend Shashishekhar passed out of the Medical College, he became our family physician. I had previously often sneaked a look at him. My elder brother was a very peculiar type: it seemed as if he did not look at the world with his eyes wide open, as if the world was not spacious enough for him, and so he had edged closer and closer to the extreme end.

'As for friends, he had only Shashishekhar. For this reason, among the young men outside, this Shashishekhar was the only one I always saw, and when in the evening I sat like an empress under the flowering tree, all the young men of the world taking on the image of Shashishekhar stood in supplication at my feet. Hey, are you listening? What do you think?'

I said anxiously, 'I wish I had been born Shashishekhar!'

'Listen to the rest then.'

'One rainy day, I had fever. The doctor came to see me. That was our first meeting. I was lying with my face turned towards the window so that the reddish tinge of the evening might hide the pallor of my sickness. When the doctor on entering the room first looked at my face, I imagined myself in his place looking at my own face. In that evening light, on the soft pillow it was a face tender like a flower, albeit slightly distressed; unruly locks of hair fell on my forehead, and wide eyelashes lowered by bashfulness cast their shadows on my face.

'The doctor politely told my brother that he needed to feel the pulse. I stuck my limp, rounded arm out from beneath the covering. Looking at it for once, I thought if I had worn blue glass bangles, they would have set off its beauty even more. A doctor hesitating like this while picking up a patient's hand to feel the pulse was something I had never seen before. Very clumsily, with unsteady fingers, he examined my pulse; while he felt my temperature, to some extent I too sensed how the pulse in his heart was going. Don't you believe it?'

I said, 'There is apparently no reason not to. Pulse varies under circumstances.'

'After a couple of turns of falling ill and coming round, I found that the vast multitude of young men that hovered at my imaginary evening court gradually petered out to just one; my world became almost deserted; only a single doctor and a single patient remained.

'Secretly in the evening I used to put on an orange-coloured sari, weaving my hair in a firm coiffure with a wreath of *bel* flowers round it, and then with a mirror in my hand sit in the garden.

'Why a mirror? Had I not seen enough of me? Indeed, I had not. For, I would be looking at me not entirely by myself. Sitting alone, I would then become two. Becoming the doctor, I would see myself, would be enamoured of myself, would love and caress myself, yet a deep sigh rose within me moaning like the evening wind.

'From then on I was no longer alone. When I walked, I looked down watching the way my toes trod the earth, and wondered how our newly qualified doctor would like this gait. At noon, it blazed outside the window, there were no sounds anywhere; at times, a solitary kite flew away into the distant sky noisily, and a pedlar outside the compound wall of our garden passed by hawking toys and bangles with intonation. Spreading a sparkling white bed sheet for making my own bed, I would lie down. Stretching out a bare arm, as if negligently, on the soft bed, I would imagine that someone had seen my arm laid out in this fashion, someone had picked it up with both hands, and then planting a kiss on its ruddy palm was going back slowly. How's this for the ending of the story?'

I said, 'Not bad. Of course, it is a bit incomplete, but I can happily spend the rest of the night finishing it in my mind.'

'But in that case, the story would end on a serious note. What happens to the irony of it? How does the skeleton within it emerge baring all its teeth?

'Listen then. When his practice had looked up a bit, the doctor opened his chamber on the ground floor of our house. Then sometimes humorously I would ask him about medicines, about poisons, about how people could die easily, and so on. The talk of medicine unplugged the mouth of the doctor. As I kept listening, death became familiar like a member of the family. Love and Death were the only two things I saw pervading the world.

'My story is almost finished; not much is left.'

I said in a low voice, 'And the night is almost over as well.'

'For some days thereafter, I noticed that the doctor was rather preoccupied and rather too much flustered in my presence. One day, I noticed that having dressed up with special care, he borrowed my brother's carriage—he was going somewhere at night.

'I could contain myself no more. Going to my brother, after talking desultorily for some time, I asked, 'Well, Dada, where's the doctor going tonight by carriage?'

'My brother cryptically said, "To die."

'I insisted, "No, tell me truly, please".

'He said a bit more clearly, "To get married".

'I said, "Really so?"' and laughed a lot.

'Little by little I came to know that the doctor was getting twelve thousand rupees from the marriage.

'But what was the point of slighting me by keeping the news from me? Had I fallen at his feet snivelling that my heart would break if he married? You can never trust a male. In the world, I had seen only one male, and in a moment acquired all the wisdom.

'After seeing his patients, when before the evening, the doctor came into the room, I told him laughing heartily, "Hallo Mr Doctor, today you're getting married, aren't you?" Not only was he embarrassed at my hilarity, but he became very much depressed as well. "How's it that there are no music bands or something?" I asked.

'At this, with a short sigh, he said, "Is marriage a matter for so much rejoicing?"

'I laughed hysterically to hear this. Really, such an idea I had never heard. "You can't get away from that," I said. "There must be a band; there must be lights".

'I pestered my brother so hard that he at once went out to arrange a regular festivity.

'I kept talking incessantly: when the bride comes home, what the things are going to be like, what I will do, and so on. "Well,

Mr Doctor," I asked, "will you still be going around feeling the pulses of patients?"

'Ha-ha-ha! Although the human mind, especially a male's, is beyond conjecture, I can nevertheless say on oath that my words were piercing the doctor's heart like a knife.

'The wedding proper was fixed for the late hours. In the evening, sitting on the terrace the doctor, along with my brother, was taking a pint or two of drinks; it was their habit. Gradually the moon was up in the sky. I came to them laughing and said, "Has the Doctor-babu forgotten about it? It's already time to go!"

'A minor thing needs to be told at this point. In the meantime sneaking into the doctor's chamber, I had collected some powder, and conveniently unnoticed, sprinkled a part of it into the doctor's glass; I had learnt from him which powders were lethal. The doctor drank it in one gulp, and casting a miserable look at my face, in a slightly emotionally charged voice, said, "Then I'm off."

'The flute played on. I wore a *Benarasi* sari, and taking out all the ornaments that had been kept away in the chest, put them on complete with a thick smear of vermilion in the parting of my hair. I then made my bed under the *bakul* tree.

'It was a beautiful night. There was silvery moonlight. The whole garden was thick with the fragrance of jasmine and bel flowers.

"When the flute tunes tapered off into the distance, when the moonlight had begun to wane, and together with these trees and the sky and my household of a lifetime when the world began to fade away like illusion from around me, I closed my eyes and smiled.

'I had wished that when people would come to see me, this hint of a smile would linger on my lips like a hangover. I had wished that when I would enter gently into my bridal chamber of eternal night, I would carry this smile on my lips right from here. Where was the bridal chamber? Where was my bridal attire? Waking up to a clattering sound from within me, I found three boys were learning anatomy from my body! The breast that once used to throb with joy and sorrow, and where a petal of youth unfolded everyday, now suffered a teacher pointing out with a cane which bone was which! Moreover, of the dying smile that I had bloomed around my lips did you find any trace?

'How did you like the story?'

I said, 'It is quite exhilarating.'

At that time, the crow cawed. I asked, 'Are you still there?' There was no reply.

Daylight was entering the room.

*Phalgun 1298* (1891)

NOTES

1 See Glossary.

# Folly
# (*Durbuddhi*)

I had to leave my ancestral home, finally. I shall not be explicit about how it all happened, but just drop a hint or two.

I was a native doctor[1] in a village. My house stood opposite the police station. The depth of my allegiance to the Police Inspector was no less than that to *Yama*. Naturally, I was well aware what conceivable ills could befall man through the agency of man and gods. As gemstones and bangles enhance each other's beauty, so also through our mutual collaboration the Inspector and I had been furthering each other's economic well-being.

Thanks to such clandestine considerations, I had developed a special intimacy with Inspector Lalit Chakraborti, a most successful professional of his time. Pestering me often enough to marry a kin of his who had grown too old to remain unmarried, he had almost persuaded me no longer to remain a widower myself. But Shashi being my only daughter, and motherless at that, I could not bring myself to entrust her to a stepmother. So many auspicious dates prescribed by the new almanac year after year proved useless to me. So many grooms, not all of them entirely eligible, rode palanquins before my eyes; I only joined the bridal party, ate feasts in the outhouse, and returned home despondently.

Shashi had nearly completed her twelfth year of age. If only I could collect a decent sum, I could marry her into a respectable family, which had assured me as much. Once I discharged that duty, I would be able to devote myself to another happy event.

I was meditating on that crucial matter of money, when Harinath Majumdar from Tulsipara showed up and fell weeping at my feet. What he reported was this: his widowed daughter had died suddenly at night; thereupon his enemies had sent an anonymous letter to the police bringing up a false charge of abortion, and now the latter were harassing him no end over the cremation.

With the shock of his daughter's death still raw in his mind, this slander was a blow too hard for him to bear. Since I was a doctor as well as a friend of the Inspector's, he wanted me to use my good offices to see him through.

When the goddess of fortune wishes to favour you, this is how she visits you fortuitously, whether through the front door or the back. I shook my head in apparent desperation and said, 'I'm afraid the matter is a very serious one.' I cited one or two fictitious precedents, and a trembling old Harinath started wailing like a child. Details are unnecessary, but Harinath ended up a pauper getting the matter sorted out for smooth cremation of his daughter.

Shashi came and asked pitifully, 'Baba, why was the old man crying like that at your feet?' I gave her a sharp rebuke. 'Go to your room. What business is it of yours?'

Now at last the avenue had opened up for getting my daughter married to an eligible groom. The wedding date was fixed. As she was my only daughter, I hosted a lavish feast. My household lacked a mistress; the neighbours were kind enough to help. A penniless yet grateful Harinath worked all day.

At about three in the morning on the eve of the turmeric ritual[2], Shashi was suddenly stricken by cholera. Her condition worsened rapidly. After trying my utmost, I flung the phials of useless medicine to the ground, rushed to Harinath and threw myself at his feet.

'Forgive me, Dada,' I pleaded, 'Forgive this sinful wretch. She is my only child; I have no one else.'

Harinath was shocked. 'What are you doing, Doctor-babu? I am indebted to you for life. Please do not touch my feet.'

'I've ruined you, though you had done no wrong,' I said. 'My daughter is dying because of that sin.' Then in front of the crowd, I announced loudly, 'Listen, all of you. I've ruined this old man, and here I take the punishment for that. May God spare my Shashi.' With these words, I seized Harinath's slippers and started beating my head with them. Hurriedly, he snatched those away from my hand.

At about ten next morning, Shashi departed from the world, the ritual turmeric marks still fresh on her body.

The very day after, the Inspector said, 'Well Doctor, what prevents you now? Go on, get married. After all, you'll need someone to look after you.'

Such appalling contempt for the terrible grief of a man would ill become the Devil himself. But on many occasions, I had betrayed such dismal proof of my humanity that I had lost face to say anything in honest protest. That day I felt how the Inspector's friendship insulted me like a whiplash.

However intense one's bereavement, the wheel of work knows no respite. One has to go about full steam obtaining the food to eat and clothes to wear, down to the firewood and the last petty detail regularly as before. After my work, when I sat alone in my house, that piteous question often rang in my ears: 'Baba, why was the old man crying like that at your feet?' I got Harinath's decrepit hut thatched at my expense, gave away my milch cow, and redeemed his land from the moneylender.

For quite some time, on lonely evenings and sleepless nights, in the unbearable agony of recent loss, I was constantly haunted by the thought that the tender-hearted daughter of mine, even after undergoing life's travails, knows no peace in the other world because of her father's cruel misdeed. She seemed to be hovering around me asking in distress, 'Baba, why did you do that?'

It so happened over a period that I could not ask poor patients for fees. If a little girl fell ill, I thought it was my Shashi suffering the affliction of every sick girl in the village.

It was monsoon in full swing, and the entire village had flooded; one had to go by boat through paddy fields and courtyards of houses. It had begun to rain early in the morning and had not stopped yet; I got a summons from the zamindar's courthouse. Their boatman who had come to fetch me was too impatient to wait a minute and had started being imperious.

Earlier, when I had to go out in such foul weather, there had been someone around to pick up my old umbrella and look out for any holes in it; an anxious voice to warn me repeatedly to guard against blasts of wind and gusts of rain. That day, I had to find out the umbrella for myself from the silent, empty house and as I was coming out, I stood a while remembering that loving face of hers. Looking at her closed bedroom, I reflected: if a man could be so indifferent to the sorrows of others, why would God keep so much affection in store for him in his house? When I arrived at the door of that empty room, wails of anguish rose in my heart. Hearing the rich man's servant bellowing outside, I quickly controlled myself and went out.

While getting into the boat, I noticed a canoe tied to the *ghat* near the police station: a farmer in a loincloth was getting wet in the rain. 'What's happened?' I asked him. He said his daughter had been bitten by a snake the previous night. The poor wretch had brought her body all the way from his distant village to report the death. I noticed that he had taken off his only upper garment to cover the dead body. The impatient boatman from the zamindar's office cast off immediately.

When I came back at around one, I saw the man still sitting there huddled up in the rain; he had not been able to see the Inspector yet. I sent him a portion of my meal; he did not touch it.

After a hasty meal, I set out again to visit the patient at the courthouse. When I got back in the evening, the man was still there, sitting in a daze: he could not answer a question, simply stared. To him at this moment this river, the village, the police station, this damp grimy beclouded earth seemed unreal. Questioning him repeatedly, I gathered that a constable had come out once to ask if he had any money. He had said he was very poor and had nothing. 'Then perish, you wretch. Keep sitting,' the constable had said leaving him there.

I had seen such things often enough in the past, but nothing had ever struck my mind. Today I could not tolerate it. The whole inclement sky resounded with the piteous inarticulate voice of Shashi. The immeasurable grief of that mute farmer having lost his child seemed to well up in me thrusting at my ribs.

The Inspector was lounging in a wicker stool serenely puffing away at his hookah. His uncle still encumbered with his unmarried daughter had recently come from his native home with an eye on me; he was sitting on a mat and they were chatting. I stormed into their midst. 'Are you humans or fiends?' I shouted. Depositing my day's earnings with a bang in front of him, I said, 'Is it money you want? Here it is. Put it away for the next world. Now let that man go; let him do the funeral of his daughter.' The camaraderie between a police inspector and a doctor, which had thrived on the tears of the oppressed, crashed to the ground in this tempestuous encounter.

Before long, I fell at the Inspector's feet, showered encomiums especially for his magnanimity, and denounced my own folly. Nevertheless, in the end I had to leave my homestead.

*Bhadra 1307* (1900)

NOTE

1 A 'native doctor' is one who has received formal attestation of professional competence in basic medicine.

2 See Glossary

# Wish-fulfilment
# (*Ichchhapuran*)

The name of Subalchandra[1]'s son was Sushilchandra[2]. But people rarely match their names. Subalchandra was rather frail, and Sushilchandra was not too docile.

The boy went around tormenting the entire neighbourhood, so his father sometimes ran after him trying to give him a thrashing; but he had arthritic legs, and his son could run like a deer. Naturally, the raps, slaps and whacks he flailed around most often missed their target. But the day Sushilchandra was by chance caught, there was no escape.

Today, Saturday, the school was to break up at two o'clock. But Sushil was in no mood to go to school today. This had some reasons: not only was a geography test looming at school, but in the evening, there was going to be a fireworks display at the Boses' house in the nearby locality. Since morning, a great flurry of activities had been going on; Sushil's wish was to spend the entire day there.

After much pondering, when finally it was time to go to school, he took to bed. His father Subal came and asked, 'What's this? Why are you lying in bed? Aren't you going to school today?'

'I've got a stomach-ache,' said Sushil, 'I can't go to school today.'

Subal saw through his malingering. 'Just wait,' he said to himself, 'you'll get a taste of your own medicine.' So he told him, 'Stomach-ache did you say? Then you had better not go out. Hari alone will go to watch the fireworks at the Boses'. I had bought some toffees for you; better not eat that either. Lie here quietly; I'm going to get you some mixture.'

With this, after bolting the door from outside, he went on to prepare a horribly bitter herbal decoction. Sushil found himself in a great quandary: on the one hand, he dreaded the decoction as much as he loved toffee; on the other, for visiting the Boses' house, he had been restive since the previous night; that was going to be banned as well.

When Subal-babu returned with a big bowl of mixture, Sushil sprang to a sitting posture, saying, 'My stomach pain's completely gone! I'll go to school.'

'No, no, better not,' said Subal, 'Now take the medicine and lie down quietly.' With this, he forced the medicine down his throat and went out, locking the door from outside.

Sushil, lying in bed weeping, kept brooding all day, 'Oh, if tomorrow itself I were to be my father's age, I could do whatever I liked; no one could shut me in.'

His father Subal-babu, sitting alone outside the room, kept thinking, 'Only because my parents indulged me too much did I never make any progress in study. If only I got back my childhood, wasting no time in anything else, I would have done nothing but study.'

*Ichchha-thakruṇ*[3], incidentally at that time was passing by their house. Knowing the wishes of the father and the son, she decided, 'All right, let their wishes be granted for a few days.' So, she said to the father, 'Your wish is fulfilled. From tomorrow you will be your son's age.' To the son she said, 'From tomorrow you will be as old as your father.' Both of them were exhilarated to hear this.

The old Subalchandra could never sleep well at night; during the small hours of the morning, he would have some sleep. But whatever happened to him that day! Suddenly waking very early, he leapt out of the bed and discovered he had become a diminutive figure; all his lost teeth had sprouted; where the beard and moustache on his face had gone there was no trace at all. The shirt he had worn before going to bed at night was so loose in the morning the sleeves almost touched the floor, the neck hung down to his chest, and the fall of the dhoti swept so widely over the floor that it was practically impossible to take a step without tripping.

Sushilchandra used to get up early and go about making mischief; but today, he showed no sign of waking any time soon. When his father Subalchandra's hollering roused him, he found his clothes so tightly fitting to his body, they nearly ripped apart; he had grown big physically; salt-and-pepper beard half covered his face; running his hand over his head, which earlier had a luxuriant shock of hair, he felt a glossy bald patch with no frontal hair.

This morning, Sushilchandra did not at all feel like leaving his bed. He yawned noisily several times with a characteristic clicking of fingers, kept tossing and turning in bed, and at last with his father Subalchandra disturbing him, to his great annoyance, he got up.

Their wishes had been fulfilled no doubt, but they were in for trouble. As I said earlier, Sushilchandra had contemplated that if he became adult and independent like his father Subalchandra, he would wander around, climbing trees, jumping into water, eating green mangoes, and plucking chicks of birds as often as he wished; whenever he wanted he would get back home to eat whatever he liked, with no one to stop him. But surprisingly, today after rising in the morning he felt no urge at all to climb trees. Looking at the pond covered with algae and hyacinth, he felt that a jump into it meant an almost certain fit of shivering with fever. He spread out a cane mat on the veranda and sat down brooding quietly.

For once, he thought: giving up games altogether was not a good idea; let me try it. There was an *amra* tree nearby: to climb it he scrambled in various ways. The same tree that he would have shinned up like a squirrel only yesterday, today with his frail body he could not climb by any means: when in the process he dangled from a low-hanging branch, the tender branch broke under his weight, and an elderly Sushil fell to the ground with a thud. People were going along the road nearby; they burst into a gale of laughter at the spectacle of an old man trying to climb a tree and falling flat. Sushilchandra, his head hanging in shame, returned to his mat on the veranda and called out to his servant, 'Hey, go buy me a rupee's worth of candies!'

Sushilchandra was very fond of candies. At a shop near his school, he often saw candies of various colours stacked in glass jars. The odd coin he got from his father he used to spend buying only those. He had promised himself that once he had money like his father had, he would only stuff his pockets with candies and suck away to his heart's content. Today his servant bought him a heap for a rupee; taking one, slipping it into his toothless mouth, he started rolling it around with his tongue. But an elderly man's tongue by no means relished a child's toffee. He contemplated: let my father have them; a little boy that he is, he will like them. Next moment, he thought: better not; so many lozenges may upset his stomach.

Boys who had until yesterday played *kabaddi*[4] with Sushilchandra, today coming to seek him out, on stumbling upon an elderly Sushil, ran off into the distance. Sushil had imagined that if he were to be independent like his father, he would spend all day playing the game with his friends—intoning *du-du-du-du.* But today the sight of Rakhal, Gopal, Akshay, Nibaran, Harish, and Nanda irritated him: I wanted to be alone sitting quietly, and here are the lads going to kick up a shindy, he panicked.

As I said earlier, his father Subalchandra, sitting on his mat in the veranda every day, cogitated: when I was a boy, I wasted time making mischief. Once I get back those days, I will be a most obedient boy, shutting myself in, sitting with books, and learning lessons all day. I will even stop listening to grandmother's stories in the evening, and instead study in candlelight until late in the night.

But when he got back his childhood, Subalchandra abhorred the thought of ever going to school. Exasperated, Sushil would ask, 'Baba, aren't you going to school?' Scratching his head with eyes cast down Subal would mumble, 'I've got a stomach-ache; I can't go to school today.'

'Can't go, indeed!' said Sushil irritably, 'I too had stomach-ache like that when it came to going to school. I know all about it.'

In fact, Sushil had shirked school on so many pretexts and they were so fresh in his memory that it was beyond his father to outwit him. He started sending his little father forcibly to school. After school, coming back home, Subal would be itching to go out for a good round of running and playing, but just at that time, the elderly Sushilchandra, spectacles on his eyes, would be reading with intonation from *Krittibas's* Ramayana; Subal running about noisily would disturb his reading. So he would force Subal to sit in front of him, hold a slate in his hand and do sums. He set such long sums it took his father a good one hour to work out just one. In the evening, several old fellows gathered in Sushil's room to play chess. To keep Subal restrained at that time, Sushil engaged a tutor who taught him until ten at night.

Sushil was very strict about the diet of his father, because when Subal had been Sushil's present age, he suffered from poor digestion ; if he ate a little too much, he would suffer from acidity. Sushil remembered this well, so he would never allow his father to eat much. Now that Subal was a boy's age, he had such voracious appetite that he could have digested pebbles! But the less Sushil gave him to eat, the more famished he got. Eventually, he grew emaciated until his bones began to show. Sushil decided Subal must be seriously ill, so kept stuffing him with medicine.

The elderly Sushil too was in a fix. Whatever he did following his old habit did not go down well with him. Earlier, once he heard the announcement of an open-air opera anywhere around, no matter whether it was rain or winter, he would arrive there straight away. The old Sushil of today going to do it ended up in bed for three weeks with cough and cold, and pain all over his body and head. He had all along bathed in the pond; trying to do the same thing today as usual, he got swollen joints in his limbs resulting in severe arthritis, which took six months of treatment. Thereafter, he used to bathe in warm water on every third day and never allowed Subal either to bathe in the pond. He went to get down from his bed, as usual with a leap, forgetfully, and all his bones tingled and rattled. Soon after slipping a whole *paan* into his mouth, he discovered there were no teeth: paan-chewing was out of the question. Going to comb or brush his head absently, he found most of the scalp was bald. Sometimes he suddenly forgot that he was as old as his father, and forgetting, as before naughtily, pelted Aunt Andi's water-pot with stones enjoying the clang. Seeing this childish prank of an elderly man, people chased him with aggressive intent, and he scurried for shelter from shame.

Subalchandra too on some days suddenly forgot that he was now a small boy. Thinking he was an old man as before, he would go and sit in the assembly of old men playing cards or dice and try to talk like an elderly man. At this, shouting 'Shoo, you cheeky boy, go play. Such effrontery!' they would send him packing. Forgetfully, he would approach the teacher, saying, 'Well, can you give me your hookah? I'll have a few puffs.' The teacher made him stand up on the bench on one leg. He would go and tell the barber, 'Hey Beja, why didn't you go to shave me for the last few days?' The barber appreciated that the boy was quite adept at cutting jokes. 'After ten years or so, I'll go,' he would quip. On some days, again, he would go and beat up his son Sushil, as he had been used to doing. Enraged, Sushil would say, 'Is this what you are learning at school? Raising hands against an old man, you little rogue!' Soon people would gather, someone beating him, someone slapping and someone else abusing.

Then Subal began to pray desperately, 'Oh, had I been old and free like my son Sushil, I'd have been relieved.' Sushil also prayed with joined hands every day, 'O god, make me as small as my father, so I can play around merrily. My father has become so naughty I cannot control him any more; I'm worried to death because of him.'

Ichchha-thakrun reappeared and said, 'How now? Hope you have no more regrets?'

Both of them prostrating themselves before her said, 'For heaven's sake, O *Thakrun*, yes. Now make us what we were.'

'All right, tomorrow morning you will wake up to what you were before.'

The next morning Subal woke up an old man, and Sushil a boy. To both of them it seemed they had woken from a dream. Subal called out gravely, 'Sushil, won't you memorise your grammar?'

'Baba, I've lost my book,' said Sushil, scratching his head.

*Ashwin 1302* (1895)

NOTE

1 *Subal* is the first name and *Chandra* is the middle name 'Subal' means well-built or strong.
2 'Sushil' means well-behaved or good-natured.
3 Goddess of wishes; not one of the 330-million-strong Hindu pantheon, she is an ad hoc deity made up just for this story.
4 An Indian outdoor team game requiring much stamina.

# The Rift
## (*Byabadhan*)

Going by relationship, Banamali and Himangshumali were cousins; even that relation could be found out by an elaborate detour. Their two families had been living as next-door neighbours for long years; only a garden separated their premises. For this reason, even though the connexion was not too close, there was no lack of intimacy.

Banamali was vastly senior to Himangshu in age. When Himangshu had not yet cut his teeth or learned to talk, Banamali, carrying him in his arms, had strolled in this garden mornings and evenings, played with him, placated his cries, and lulled him to sleep. Moreover, for entertaining babies, whatever frivolities and abnormal efforts incongruous to age, like vigorous head-shaking, loud chattering and so on, which mature adults have to undertake, Banamali had done faultlessly.

Of studies, Banamali had done very little. He had the hobby of gardening, and he had this little cousin as a distant relation. Banamali had been nurturing this infant as a rare and pricey creeper sprinkling him with all the affection of his heart. When he started creeping around his whole entity, inside and outside, Banamali considered himself blessed.

It is not usually noticed, but we do come across an occasional character who for the sake of a small fancy or child or an ungrateful friend very easily sacrifices himself completely. In this vast world, he blithely invests his entire life's capital in a single small trade of affection. Thereafter, perhaps on a small usufructuary right he spends the rest of his life very contentedly or suddenly one morning, after selling off his house and property, stands as a beggar on the street.

When Himangshu grew a little older, in spite of the great disparity in age and the tenuousness of relations, he seemed to have developed a bond of friendship with Banamali. Between them, the differences did not matter.

There was some reason for this, too. Himangshu was a student and naturally very keen to acquire knowledge. Whatever books he found he sat down to read. Thereby he had read many bad books no doubt, but some way or the other, there had been an overall development of his mind. Banamali with somewhat special respect for his cousin used to listen to him, to seek his counsel, to discuss all matters, big or small, and never ignore him for a child. If someone who has been raised on the first milk of affection eventually commands respect by virtue of his talents, wisdom and good moral character, such a cherished creature is not found elsewhere in all the world.

Himangshu was fond of gardening as well. But in this matter, there was a difference between the two friends: Banamali's was motivation of the heart; Himangshu's, of the head. Banamali had a natural inclination to nurture with utmost care those tender trees and plants of the earth, those insensate masses of life that never crave for care, but if cared for, thrive like our own children, yet are even more childish than humans, But Himangshu had a curious eye for plant life: how seeds germinate, leaves sprout, buds spring, flowers blossom—all this deeply engaged his attention.

About the various stages of gardening: sowing, grafting, manuring, trellising, and so on, various ideas would come to Himangshu's head, and Banamali would be very glad to accept them. Whatever addition or alteration to this little garden was possible they would effect by working together.

In front of the door, there was a paved platform in the garden. Every day punctually at four in the afternoon, Banamali, with a light cotton shirt on, and a crimped chuddar flung over his shoulder, would go and sit there in the shadow, his hubble-bubble in hand; he had no friends, no books, not even a newspaper for company. He would puff away and look sideways indifferently, now to his right, now to left. In this way, like the spiralling smoke from his hubble-bubble, time would slowly, very breezily evaporate, collapse and vanish without leaving any trace anywhere.

At last, when Himangshu, after having returned from school, washed and taken some food, made his appearance, Banamali would hurriedly put aside his smoking tube and get up. At that time noticing his avidity one could realise who he had been expecting patiently all this while.

Thereafter their tête-à-tête began as they walked. When darkness began to fall, they would sit on a wooden bench. A southerly wind would begin to blow raising a murmur in the leaves; on some days, there was no breeze; the trees would keep standing still like a picture; stars twinkled all over the sky.

Most of the time Himangshu would do the talking and Banamali would listen quietly. Even what he did not understand, he would enjoy listening all the same. Things that might seem very disgusting if heard from anyone else would be quite interesting to hear from Himangshu. With such an admiring adult listener before whom to practise, Himangshu's faculties of oratory, memory and imagination would find full play. Partly he talked after reading, partly after thinking; other points came to his mind on the spot, and sometimes his lack of knowledge he would make up for with imagination. Much that he said was right, but much else was wrong as well; in any case, Banamali would listen solemnly. At times, he would utter a word or two, but when Himangshu gave his counter-explanation Banamali would accept it, and next day sitting in the shade puffing at his hubble-bubble contemplate those things for a long time with wonder.

In the meantime, trouble ensued. In between Banamali's garden and Himangshu's premises passed a drain. Somewhere down the drain, a lemon tree had grown. When the tree bore fruits, Banamali's servant tried to pluck them, and Himangshu's servant resisted him. Had there been any substance in the swearing and cursing that flowed freely between them, it could well nigh have filled up the drain.

Banamali's father Harachandra and Himangshu's father Gokulchandra got embroiled in a bitter feud over it. Eventually, the two parties landed in court over the ownership of the drain.

Stalwarts among the lawyers were pitted against each other, and engaged in a prolonged war of words. The money that was spent by the two sides would out-measure the water that had ever flowed down the drain during the *Bhadra* floods.

In the end, Harachandra won. It was proved that the drain belonged to him, and nobody else had any right to the lemons. Gokulchandra appealed, but the drain and the lemons remained Harachandra's absolutely.

Until completion of the litigation, friendship between the cousins had suffered no setback. Not only that, lest the dispute should overshadow it, Banamali would try to tie Himangshu to his heart even more intimately; neither would the latter betray the least apathy.

The day Harachandra won the suit, there started a great jubilation in the house, particularly the women's quarters; only in Banamali's eyes there was no sleep. Next day in the afternoon, he went and sat on that platform in the garden so lugubriously as if nothing had happened to anyone else in the world, only he had suffered a terrible defeat.

The usual time went by. It was six, but Himangshu did not turn up. With a long sigh, Banamali looked at Himangshu's house. Through the open window, he could see Himangshu's school uniform hanging from the clothes rack. He looked for and found a couple of familiar signs: Himangshu was home. Casting aside his tobacco tube, with a sad face he kept pacing up and down the garden and looked every now and then at that window, but Himangshu did not come.

When the evening lamp was lit, Banamali sauntered up to Himangshu's house.

Gokulchandra was sitting at the doorstep cooling off in the evening breeze. 'Who's there?' he said.

Banamali was startled, as if he had been caught with intent to steal. '*Mama*, it's me,' he said, his voice trembling.

'Whom do you want? No one is there'.

Banamali came back to his garden and sat down quietly.

As the night advanced, the windows of Himangshu's house closed one after another; the slits of light that had been coming through chinks in the doors also went out in ones and twos. Standing in the dark night, Banamali thought that all of Himangshu's doors had been shut on his very face, only he was left forlorn in the darkness outside.

Next day again, he came and sat in the garden; he thought today perhaps the boy might come. The thought that he who for long years had been coming every day would not come even for a single day he could scarcely accept. He had never thought that it was in any way possible for this bond to break; he was so contented that he could never even know when all his joys and sorrows of life had surrendered themselves to that bond. Today suddenly, he came to know that the bond had broken. Nevertheless, that his ruin had come in one fell swoop was too much for him to believe in his heart.

He used to sit in the garden every day as usual, just in case Himangshu came by chance. But such was his misfortune that what used to happen every day as a matter of course did not happen one day even by chance.

On Sunday, Banamali thought as usual today also Himangshu

would come to breakfast with them. He did not exactly believe it, yet he could not give up hope altogether either. Breakfast time came, but Himangshu didn't come. 'Then he'll come after lunch,' he assured himself. But after lunch he did not come. He then thought: today perhaps he's taking a nap after his meal; when he wakes, he'll come.

When he awoke I do not know, but he did not come.

Again, evening fell, night came on, the doors of Himangshu's house shut one by one, and the lights went out one after another.

In this way, when his miserable fate had snatched away from his hand all seven days of the week from Monday to Sunday, with not a single day left to harbour his hope, his two tearful melancholy eyes sent a complaint of heart-rending resentment at Himangshu's closed-door house. With all the anguish of his life packed in a single spurt of affliction, he sighed, 'O Benevolent One!'

? 1298 (1891)

# Reciprocation
## (*Daan-Pratidaan*)

The invectives hurled by the elder brother's wife were as sharp as they were venomous. The hapless woman at the receiving end taking them to heart suffered terribly.

Her husband Radhamukunda was principally the butt of this tongue-lashing, and he, having finished his night's meal, was sitting nearby helping digestion with a mix of betel juice and tobacco smoke. The tirade entered his system through his ears, apparently with no adverse effect on his digestion. With unperturbed solemnity he finished his puffs and went to bed at the usual time.

However, such extraordinary digestive power cannot be expected of everyone. Today Rashmani, after coming to their bedroom, behaved with her husband in a manner she had never dared before. On other days, going to bed quietly she would devote herself to massaging her husband's feet without a word. Today, all at once shaking her bangles and turning back to him, she lay crouched up on one side, and set up a regular quake in the bed with a paroxysm of sobs.

Without taking any notice of it, Radhamukunda tried to catch sleep clutching a huge bolster. But when he saw that his indifference was only aggravating his wife's impatience, he at last told her mildly in a grave voice that he would have to rise early for some urgent work and must have some sleep now.

Hearing her husband's voice, Rashmani could no longer hold back her wail, and it gushed out.

'What's the matter?' Radhamukunda asked.

'Didn't you hear?'

'I did. But I don't think sister-in-law said anything wrong. Aren't we living off my elder brother? Your clothes, your ornaments, everything—have I bought them with my father's money? Look, someone who gives you your food and clothes might tell you a harsh word or two. You should accept it in good grace, with the food and the rest.'

'Why take such food and shelter?'

'You've to live after all.'

'I'd better die.'

'Until you do, try to have some sleep; you'll feel better.' And he went on to set an example of his precept.

Radhamukunda and Shashibhushan were neither brothers nor any close relation: say, almost relation by domicile. But their bond of love was no less strong than that between siblings. This the elder housewife Brajasundari found somewhat intolerable. Particularly, when it came to making gifts, Shashibhushan never betrayed any preference for his own wife over the younger woman. On the contrary, if anything were by chance not available in pair, he would give it to the younger wife rather than his own. Besides, there is evidence that he often relied more on his brother's counsel than on his wife's importunities.

Shashibhushan was an extremely careless and unmethodical person. So, managing the household as well as the estate entirely lay on Radhamukunda himself. Brajasundari always suspected that Radhamukunda was conspiring secretly to cheat her husband. Since she never got any proof of her suspicion, her malice for him grew apace. She suspected proofs themselves to have been hostile to her;

she then hated proofs altogether and sat in her room fortifying her suspicion. The fire she carefully kept ablaze in her mind often erupted like a volcano in fiery words with accompanying tremors.

Whether Radhamukunda's sleep had been disturbed that night is not known, but in the morning, when he came and stood before Shashibhushan, he looked wan. 'What makes you look like this, Radha?' Shashibhushan asked him solicitously. 'Aren't you well?'

Radhamukunda said slowly, in a mild voice, 'Dada, it seems we can't stay here any longer.' He then reported his sister-in-law's verbal assault of the previous night briefly with his usual calmness.

Shashibhushan said with a smile, 'Is that all? That is not anything new. She's from a different family, you see; she can't resist a dig whenever she gets an opportunity. Do you have to leave us just because of that? Look, she doesn't spare me either; so do you think I can leave her?'

'And do you think I can't stand a few words from a woman?' said Radha. 'Why then am I a man after all? All I fear is we might cause some strife in your family.'

'What peace shall I find if you leave me?'

There were few words after this. Radhamukunda left with a sigh; his heart remained as heavy as ever.

Meanwhile, Brajasundari's rancour was soaring. She lost no opportunity to make stinging insinuations at Radha on a thousand pretexts. She riddled Rashmani's heart every moment with a hail of verbal arrows. As for Radha, though he puffed away at his hookah placidly, and started snoring with his eyes shut the moment he saw his wife on the point of crying, yet from all appearances, he too was beginning to lose his patience.

Nevertheless, his was no fledgling bond with Shashibhushan. It dated back to a distant past when the two brothers went to school together, after their breakfast of soaked rice, with books and slates under their arms. Together they slipped from school escaping their teacher's notice to play with cowherds. Together they lay in their bed in dim lamplight hearing stories from their aunt. Together they sneaked out at night to watch operas at far-away villages, and when found out in the morning, shared the blame and punishment equally. Where was Brajasundari or Rashmani then? Could one snap one's ties of so many days all of a sudden? But the suspicion or the slightest hint that this bond had been promoted by selfishness, that this profound love was but a clever guise of mendicancy was sickening to Radhamukunda. It is therefore anybody's guess how things would have turned out if the present conditions were to persist any longer. However, at this point there was a serious turn of events.

According to the law in force at that time, if government revenues were not paid by sundown on the due date, the estates of the zamindar would be sold off by auction to realise it.

One day, Shashibhushan heard that his sole landed estate had been auctioned off because of outstanding revenues payable to the governor.

Radhamukunda said with his usual mildness and composure, 'The fault is entirely mine, Dada.'

Shashibhushan said, 'How can it be your fault? You remitted the money all right. If it was to be looted during transit, what possibly could you have done?'

It was useless now trying to ascertain whose fault it was; now the household had to get going. Shashibhushan had neither the temperament nor the training to get down to any job all at once. It seemed as if slipping off the paved steps of a *ghat* he had fallen straight into deep waters in a moment.

He moved to mortgage his wife's ornaments as an immediate step. Radhamukunda forestalled it by depositing a whole sack of money before him; he had already collected adequate money by pawning *his* wife's ornaments.

There was at least one great change in the family: someone the mistress had tried assiduously to throw out once in prosperity, she clung to anxiously now in adversity. She was not late in realising which one of the two brothers was the more dependable at this juncture. That she had ever had any ill feeling against Radhamukunda was never betrayed now.

Radhamukunda had already equipped himself to earn an independent income. He began to practise as an attorney in a near-by town. In those days, the avenues of income from attorneyship were wider than they are today, and an astute and circumspect Radhamukunda set up a thriving practice right from the beginning. By and by, he took up briefs for almost all major zamindars of the district.

Rashmani's present status was just opposite of what it had been before. Now Shashibhushan and Brajasundari lived off *her* husband. Whether or not Rashmani had ever boasted it openly, I do not know, but once perhaps she had betrayed that feeling by hints and gestures: perhaps, stamping her feet and swinging her arms proudly, she had had her way against the wishes of the elder mistress in a certain matter. But that was just once; from the following day, she became even more docile than she had ever been. The fact is that word had reached her husband's ears: whatever arguments Radhamukunda may have applied that night, from the next morning there was no word on her lips; she behaved as if she were Brajasundari's handmaiden. One hears that very night he had all but sent her packing to her father's house and had not seen her face for a week. In the end, Brajasundari stepped in to mediate and brought about their reconciliation, saying, 'Look brother, the younger one's come only the other day, and I've been here for so many years. What should she know about the eternal relation of affection between you and me? She is a mere child. Forgive her.'

Radhamukunda placed the entire money for household expenses at Brajasundari's disposal. Rashmani received her necessary expenses from Brajasundari as a rule or on request. In the household, the elder mistress's condition was certainly not worse now, if not better, than before, because, as you might recall, Shashibhushan out of affection and other considerations had treated Rashmani often rather preferentially.

Although Shashibhushan wore his usual winsome smile, he was languishing from some secret malaise. No one else had taken much notice of it, only Radha lost his sleep at the sad face of his elder brother. Waking late on some nights, Rashmani found Radha sighing and tossing restlessly.

Sometimes, Radhamukunda would go and assure Shashibhushan, 'Don't worry, Dada. I must get back your ancestral property. I shall not desist in any case. And the day is not too far off either.'

Indeed, it was not. The person who had bought off Shashibhushan's property on auction was a businessman, quite incompetent as a zamindar. He had acquired it with aspirations for fame, but had to pay his revenue dues from his personal resources, never making a single paisa of profit. Radhamukunda used to realise the rents once or twice a year plundering the tenants with the help of *lathiyals*. The tenants were loyal to him as well. They secretly hated this zamindar, who was from a lower caste; with Radhamukunda's counsel and connivance, they began to betray their hostility to him in every possible way.

Eventually, the poor fellow, after several unsuccessful litigations, became eager to get rid of this troublesome appendage once and for all. At a throwaway price, Radhamukunda bought back their old property.

The span of these developments was not as brief as it might appear. Nearly ten years had passed in the meantime. Shashibhushan was barely at the beginning of his middle age. Now he looked old having aged fast only these last few years, as if riding a steam engine driven at speed by the internal heat of his distressed heart. Even though he got back his ancestral property, no one knows why he was no longer his usual cheerful self. Long into disuse, the lyre of his heart had perhaps become dud; no matter how often the strings were now tightened, they slackened off, never emitting the familiar tune again.

People of the village expressed a great deal of jubilation and went to Shashibhushan insisting on a feast. Shasibhusan turned to Radhamukunda. 'Now, what do you say, *bhai*?'

'Of course,' said Radhamukunda, 'there has to be some rejoicing on an auspicious day.'

There had not been such a feast in the village for long years. Everyone, high or low, ate to their fill. The Brahmins got their honorarium; the poor and the destitute, their clothes and coins. They blessed the host heartily and went away contented.

At the approach of winter, it was a bad spell in the village; moreover, in connection with the feast Shashibhushan had worked hard and had been rather irregular in his habits for some days. His frail body could take it no more; he fell seriously ill. Along with other severe complications, he had high temperature with shivers. 'The case is serious,' said the doctor.

At two or three in the morning, ordering all men out of the patient's room, Radhamukunda said, 'Dada, advise me how I have to allocate your property in your absence.'

'*Bhai*, what do I have that I can give others?'

'Why, everything is yours.'

'Yes, once it was; not any more."

Radhamukunda sat silently for some time, fiddling with the bedspread smoothing out a part with his hands. Shashibhushan's respiration became laboured.

Radhamukunda then sitting at the edge of his bed, clasping his feet, said, 'Dada, let me confess the heinous crime I have committed. It's now or never.'

Shashibhushan gave no reply. Radhamukunda went on—the same composure, the same slow speech, only with a deep sigh at times. 'Dada, I am unable to express myself properly. The Omniscient One knows what is going on in my heart, and if anyone in the world can realise it, it is you. Ever since childhood, there was no difference between you and me at heart; whatever difference we had was external. We differed only on one point: you were rich; I was poor. When I realised that because of this trifling issue the possibility of a separation between us was growing stronger I had wiped it out; I had the revenue looted and your estate auctioned off.'

Shashibhushan, without showing the least surprise, smiled gently, and then said in faltering words in a faint voice, 'Bhai, there was nothing wrong in what you did. But do you think all you did it for has been fulfilled? Can you hold it any longer? Good God !' Two drops of tears rolled down his eyes over his serene smile.

Radhamukunda bowed his head at his feet and said, 'Dada, did you forgive me?'

Shashibhushan drew him near, and holding his hand said, 'Listen then, Bhai. I knew this from the very beginning. Those you had conspired with divulged this to me themselves. I have forgiven you from that moment.'

Radhamukunda began to weep, his blushing face covered with his hands. After a long while, he said, 'Dada, if you have forgiven me, take back your property. Do not refuse in anger.'

Shashibhushan could not reply; by then his voice had choked. Keeping a fixed gaze at Radhamukunda's face, he lifted his right hand once. Whatever that gesture signified, Radhamukunda may possibly have understood.

*Chaitra 1299* (1892)

# Retaliation
# (*Pratihinsa*)

## 1

The granddaughter of the former dewan[1] of Mukunda-babu's estate and wife of the present manager, Indrani, was present at an inauspicious moment at the Babus' house attending the bridal feast of their daughter's son. Why it was inauspicious would be clear from a brief narration of the previous history.

Now, Mukunda-babu was deceased, so was his dewan Gourikanta; following the call of time, neither of them was present in person at his respective position. But when they had lived, there was a rigid bond between them. When Gourikanta, who had lost his parents, had no means of livlihood, Mukundalal, simply being impressed by his appearance, had trusted him with the management of his small estate. It was proved in course of time that he had made no mistake. Like termites building up their mound, like seekers after God accumulating virtue, Gourikanta went on adding to Mukundalal's property bit by little bit day after day with untiring effort. Finally, when he added the Bankagari Pargana to his estate tactfully purchased at a surprisingly low price, Mukunda Babu's family was elevated to the class of respectable zamindars. Naturally, when the master prospered, his servant did too; gradually he acquired a brick-house, some landed property, and a thriving practice of priesthood. Thus, one who had once belonged to the class of *tehsildar*[2] came to be known as the respectable dewan-*ji*.

So much for the previous story. Currently, there was Binodbihari, Mukundalal's adopted son, and Ambikacharan, Gourikanta's well-educated grandson-in-law, who worked as their manager. The dewan did not trust his own son Ramkanta; that is why when he retired because of old age, he had engaged his grandson-in-law in his place superseding his son.

Things were going on smoothly, everything remaining more or less the same as before except for a slight change in one matter: now the master-servant relation was strictly professional, not one of the heart. In those days money was cheap, and people's hearts were rather cheap too. These days, according to a unanimous opinion, the wasteful expenditure of the heart has been virtually abolished; when even the relatives' share has dwindled to a trickle, how can others get any?

In the meanwhile, the dewan's granddaughter Indrani arrived at the babus' house in connection with the wedding feast of their grandson.

The world is, as it were, the chemical laboratory of Providence, where people of various shades of character are assembled to interact constantly with one another creating countless variegated new histories. On this joyous occasion of the wedding feast, two persons of diverse types encountered each other, and in no time there crept up a thread of a new colour in the tireless crocheting among the world's people, which resulted in a different kind of loop in the network.

Indrani arrived at her master's house rather late in the afternoon when everyone had finished eating. When Binod's wife Nayantara enquired about the reason for the delay, Indrani cited preoccupation with housework, ill health and one or two other reasons which saisfied no one. Though she had suppressed the true reason, no one failed to surmise it. The reason was this: the Mukunda-babus were their masters, and no doubt they were rich, but in lineage Gourikanta was far superior to them. Indrani could not afford to forget that superiority. She had been deliberately late to avoid taking food at their house. Having understood her motive, they had repeatedly requested her, but Indrani was not one to acknowledge defeat; she refused to be persuaded to eat.

On one occasion, even when Mukunda and Gourikanta were alive, there had been a greater revolt over sensitivity to lineage. That story can be recounted in this context.

Indrani was extremely beautiful. In our literature, beauty is celebrated as static lightning. The metaphor is often misplaced, but it fitted Indrani. It seemed she had captured a violent speed and intense pain in a trap of imperturbable gravity within herself quite effortlessly with an inborn power. Lightning stood perpetually still in her face, in her eyes, and all over her limbs. Here its fickleness was forbidden.

When Mukunda Babu had seen this beautiful girl, he submitted to Gourikanta a proposal of his adopted son's marriage with her. Gourikanta was inferior to no one in loyalty to his master; he could die for his master's sake. No matter how much his condition improved, and no matter to what extent his master might indulge him like a friend, he had never in his dream, never even inadvertently forgotten the respect due to his master. In front of the latter, and even in reference to him, he was almost bowed down in reverence. Nevertheless, he could not bring himself to agree to this marriage proposal. He would have paid off his debt of loyalty to the last paisa; why should he give up his claim due to ancestry? It was not honourably possible for him to give his granddaughter in marriage to Mukundalal's son.

Mukundalal did not take this pride in ancestry from a servant in good grace. He had hoped that with this proposal he would be showing favour to his loyal servant. When Gourikanta did not take it in the way he had intended, Mukundalal stopped talking to him for some time, to his great distress. This apathetic behaviour of his master struck Gourikanta's heart like a deadly spear. Nevertheless, getting his granddaughter married to a poor orphan *kulin* boy, he went on to educate him at his own expense keeping him in his family.

This then was the man full of ancestral pride whose granddaughter Indrani came to her master's house but refused to dine. This certainly cannot have made her mistress Nayantara's heart overflow with sweet love. She could now imagine seeing with her hate-filled eyes several instances of audacity in Indrani's behaviour.

First, Indrani was wearing too many ornaments and was dressed too flamboyantly. What was the need for her trying to compare with her masters with such ostentatious display of opulence?

Second, Indrani's vanity of beauty. Indrani was no doubt beautiful, and for a social inferior to have such extraordinary beauty might be unnecessary and even unfair, but the imputation of vanity was altogether Nayantara's imagination. You cannot blame one for her beauty, so if blame you must, you have willy-nilly to ascribe conceit to it.

Third, Indrani's hubris or what in common parlance is called arrogance. Indrani had a nartural gravity. Except very close and familiar persons, she could not mix freely with anyone. Moreover, to obtrusively create a fuss or officiously interfere with some work was not her habit.

Over many such baseless or valid reasons, Nayantara gradually became increasingly irritated: finding unnecessary pretexts, referring to Indrani as 'our manager's wife' or 'our dewan's granddaughter', she kept introducing and addressing her repeatedly. She primed her favourite shrewish maidservant who at once went about her brief: fussing over Indrani like a friend she kept fiddling with her ornaments and examining them critically; praising her necklace and bracelet, she asked, 'Well, sister, are these gilded things?'

'No, made of brass,' Indrani said with extreme solemnity.

Calling out to Indrani, Nayantara said, 'You! What are you doing there standing alone? Why don't you carry this food-tray to the palanquin from Hatkhola?' The maidservant stood nearby. Just for a moment opening her profound faraway eyes under the shadow of their long lids, Indrani looked at Nayantara's face, and the next moment picking up the tray of sweets proceeded to the palanquin downstairs.

The guest for whom the gift of sweets was meant felt embarrassed. 'Why are you taking the trouble yourself, sister? Why don't you hand it to the maid over there?'

'Where's the trouble in it?' Indrani demurred.

The other woman said, 'Then please give it to me, sister.'

'No, no, I shall carry it myself.' With this, she bore away and laid the trays in the palanquin just as graciously as goddess *Annapurna* could offer rice to her devotee affectionately with her own hands. And that short interaction made the housewife from the rich Hatkhola family avid for making the soft-spoken, gently-smiling Indrani her dear friend for the rest of her life.

Thus all the barbs of insult, which Nayantara shot with her cruel womanly deftness, Indrani deflected with the impenetrable shield of her blemishless, shining natural spiritedness—each one, instead of piercing her body, broke on impact. Her grave imperturbability aggravated Nayantara's malicious resentment which Indrani could very well perceive, and at a convenient point of time she came back home without taking anyone's leave.

## 2

Those who suffer calmly are hurt deeper than others. The hurt of humiliation, although Indrani had ignored most disdainfully, had nevertheless touched her heart. In the same way that there had been a proposal of Binodbehari's marriage with Indrani, once there had been a proposal of Nayantara's marriage with Indrani's distant and destitute cousin Bamacharan. Indrani could still remember the day in her childhood when Nayantara's father had come to their house along with Nayantara and requested Gourikanta appealingly for his daughter's marriage with Bamacharan. On that occasion, the extraordinary glibness of the little girl Nayantara had surprised and amused everyone in Gourikanta's family, and compared to her precocity, a shy, tongue-tied Indrani had considered herself utterly incompetent and inexperienced. Gourikanta was very much pleased with the girl's looks and loquacity, but because of a slight taint in her family history, did not approve the proposal of her marriage with Bamacharan. Eventually, his own choice and his own efforts had brought about Nayantara's marriage with the non-*kulin* Binod.

Indrani found no consolation in remembering all this; on the contrary, the insult kept assailing her even more incisively. She remembered the story of Sharmishtha and Shukracharya's daughter Debjani[3] in the *Mahabharata*. If Indrani could emulate Debjani who had made her master's daughter Sharmishtha[4] her servant crushing her vanity, only then would she have avenged herself. There was a time when her grandfather Gourikanta was as indispensable to Mukunda-babu's family as the demon-guru Shukracharya to the demons. At that time, if he had wished, he could have brought Mukunda-babu to his knees, but instead he had himself taken his property to its peak and established an orderliness in every sphere. So, no longer today was it necessary for the masters to be grateful in his memory. Then, the Bankagari Pargana: this, Indrani thought, her grandfather could easily have purchased in his own name itself; at that time he had had the wherewithal, instead he had purchased it for his master: did anyone in the master's family remember today that this was virtually a donation? 'Ours was the gift, the money and fame, which gives you the arrogance to insult us today,' she contemplated, as her heart grew rebellious.

Coming back home she found that her husband who had returned after attending the wedding feast at the master's house and his managerial work was sitting on an armchair in his bedroom reading the newspaper.

There is a general perception that husband and wife are very often of a similar nature. The reason for this perception is that if we come across a stray instance where they have common traits, it seems so proper and reasonable that we tend to generalise it. Anyway, in the present case, Indrani and Ambikacharan actually shared one or two traits. Ambikacharan was not much of a sociable type. He went out only to do his work. After completing his own work and getting others to complete theirs, when he returned home, it seemed as if to protect himself from the intrusion of unrelated people he had entered an impregnable fortress. Outside, he and his work, and inside the house, he and Indrani, were all that constituted his entire life.

Well-dressed and sparkling with ornaments, Indrani entered the room when Ambikacharan, going to say something in jest, suddenly stopped short looking worried. 'What's happened to you?' he asked.

'What could have happened?' said Indrani trying to laugh off his worry. 'Presently I've met my gem of a husband.'

Putting aside the newspaper, Ambika said, 'That I can see; what happened before that?'

'Before that, received cordial reception from the mistress,' said Indrani as she took off her ornaments one at a time.

'What was the reception like?'

Drawing near, Indrani sat on the arm of of his chair, then putting her arms round his neck, said, 'Not exactly the kind I get from you.' She then narrated bit by bit all that had happened. She had promised herself that she would not talk about these unpleasant things with her husband, but could not keep the promise in the end; neither could she ever keep similar promises before. To her husband Indrani discarded all the normal inhibitions of her nature to the extent she remained restrained and abstracted to outsiders; to him she could not conceal even a small part of herself.

Hearing the entire story, Ambika became furious. 'I'll resign my job this moment,' he fumed, and at once set out to write a stern letter to Binod-babu. Indrani then got down from the arm of the chair, and sitting near her husband's feet on the carpeted floor, resting her hands on his lap, said, 'No need to hurry. Better not write today. Tomorrow morning decide whatever you like.'

Ambika flared up. 'No, there should not be a moment's delay.'

Indrani had bloomed as a lone water-lily on the stalk of her grandfather's heart. While she had extracted the milk of affection from his heart, she had unconsciously imbibed several of his emotions stored there. Even though Indrani had not fully inherited Gourikanta's loyalty and devotion to Mukundalal's family, a conviction had been firmly rooted in her heart that they should devote their lives to the welfare of their master's family. Her well-educated husband could have taken up a lawyer's profession or any respectable job if he liked, but honouring his wife's feelings he was quite content to manage Binod's estate devotedly. Though Indrani had been seriously offended by the humiliation, she could by no means accept that her husband should relinquish Binodbihari's job.

Indrani, trying to sound reasonable, said in her mild, sweet voice, 'After all Binod-babu is not to blame. He knows nothing of all this. Angry with his wife, why should you rush off to quarrel with him?' Ambika burst out laughing; his own decision seemed utterly ridiculous to him. 'That's true,' he said, 'but masters or whatever they may be, I'm not going to send you to their house ever again.' This slight storm blew away the cloud for that day; the house brightened up, and her husband's tender fondness made Indrani forget all the neglect from outside.

## 3

Binodbihari, entrusting the entire management of his estate to Ambikacharan, never bothered to supervise it personally. Some husbands, because of absolute dependability and trustworthiness have a nonchalant attitude towards their wives; Binod too had a similar indifference to his own estate. Income from the estate was so guaranteed, so fixed that it was hardly noticed as an income at all; like something habitual it held no charm for him.

Binod cherished the wish that finding out some secret channel he would overnight enter *Kuver*'s vault. Therefore, relying on the counsel of various people, he would launch into various kinds of preposterous enterprises. One time it might be decided that holding the entire *babla*-tree population of the district on lease he would manufacture bullock-cart wheels; at another time he might be advised to collect honeycombs from the Sundarbans; yet some other time he might go on to contract the forests of the western region to monopolise the cultivation of myrobalan. Binod knew in his mind that others would laugh at his plans, so he would not divulge them to anybody. He was particularly shy of Ambikacharan; lest Ambika should think he was wasting the money, he was always diffident. He behaved with Ambika in a manner as if Ambika was himself the zamindar and he was just getting a yearly salary for his sinecure.

From the day after the wedding invitation, Nayantara began to poison her husband's mind. 'You never look after things personally,' she moaned, 'Whatever money Ambika thinks fit to hand you, you accept ungrudgingly. Meanwhile, what disaster is going on secretly nobody knows. Your manager's wife wore such jewellery the like of which I have never seen since I came to your house. Where does she get all these ornaments? And how did her arrogance rise to this level?' And so on and so forth. Of the ornaments she gave an exaggerated account, and what Indrani herself had told her maidservant she recounted largely from her imagination.

Binod was a man of weak character: on the one hand, he could not help depending on others; on the other, whatever suspicion anyone whispered into his ears he believed entirely. The conviction that the manager was misappropriating funds became firmly rooted within a minute. Especially because he did not look after the work personally, he began to see all sorts of frightful possibilities in his imagination; yet, how to detect the manager's theft he had no idea either. To confront him with the question was beyond his courage. What a bother!

Because of Ambikacharan's preeminence, all the employees were jealous of him. Particularly, his distant nephew Bamacharan whom Gourikanta had hand-picked for the job harboured the most powerful grudge against Ambika. He had his reasons: in respect of relationship and other factors, he considered himself Ambika's equal, and firmly believed that despite being his relation, only out of jealousy was Ambika not giving him a higher post. Once someone gets a post, requisite competence comes automatically to him, he held. This was particularly true because he regarded the manager's job as extremely trivial. He would say: in these days a manager in office work is just like a flag fluttering on a chariot earlier; the wretched horse dies of toiling, and all Mr Flag does is wave proudly and sway along with the chariot.

Hitherto, Binod had never cared to enquire about the goings-on in his estate. Only when he needed a big sum of money in connection with his business would he send for the treasurer secretly and ask about the extent of cash in hand. When the treasurer named the sum, he would hesitate a little and then finally ask for it, as if it was someone else's money. The treasurer would hand him the money after getting it receipted. For sometime thereafter, Binod was inhibited before Ambika-babu. Only if somehow they did not meet did he feel relieved.

Sometimes this left Ambikacharan in a predicament: after setting apart the zamindar's dues, the rest of the fund was meant for payment of the government revenues and employees' salary. If that money was spent on irregular heads, he had to suffer a great deal of trouble managing the estate. But Binod, after withdrawing the money, went about it so surreptitiously like a thief that Ambika hardly had any scope to talk to him in the matter; it was no use writing letters either, because the man was shy only of committing an act in full view, not of anything else, so he was scared only of encounters.

Gradually, when Binod began to cross all limits, an exasperated Ambika kept the key of the iron safe in his own custody, thereby forestalling any further secret withdrawal by Binod. Yet, he was such a craven fellow that despite being the master, he could not enforce his authority. But Ambika was making futile efforts: with whom the demon of evil fortune collaborated, no key of an iron safe can lock in his money; on the contrary, the reverse was the result. But more of that later.

Discomfited by the stringent arrangement of Ambikacharan, Binod was seething under the surface. At this point, when Nayantata planted the seeds of doubt in his mind, he felt somewhat elated. Privately, he started making enquiries with the employees individually. Bamacharan then became his principal spy.

When Gourikanta was the dewan, he had applied force to appropriate lands of neighbouring zamindars, thus grabbing a good many lands of a number of people. But Ambikacharan never did anything of the sort. On the contrary, if matters came to a head threatening to end up in court, he would try his best to compromise. To this very point Bamacharan drew his master's notice. He explained to him convincingly that Ambikacharan must have been bribed by the other party to compromise at his master's expense. Bamacharan's own perception was no different: that a man in authority can abstain from taking bribes is something he would never believe .

Thus fanned by various sources, Binod's flame of suspicion kept rising steadily, but he could not summon up the courage to have recourse to any direct action whatever: first his shyness; second, his apprehension lest Ambika who knew the ins and outs of his estate should try to harm him. In the end, exasperated by this cowardice of her husband, Nayantara, one day calling Ambikacharan without Binod's knowledge, told him from behind the doorscreen[5], 'Your services are no longer required. Hand over the charge to Bamacharan and leave.'

Ambika had already got scent of the demonstration of opposition to him that was agitating Binod, and so was not too much surprised at Nayantara's words. At once he went to Binodbihari and asked, 'Do you want to relieve me of my duties?'

'No, never,' said Binod, flustered.

'Has there been any reason for you to suspect me?' Ambika asked again.

'Absolutely not,' said Binod, very much embarrassed.

Ambikacharan made no mention of what Nayantara had told him and came back to office. He did not say anything to Indrani either. Things went on like this for some time.

Meanwhile, Ambikacharan came down with influenza. Though it was not serious, he had to absent himself from the office for quite some time on account of debility. Around that time, the government revenue was payable, and there was pressure of other kinds of work. Considering this, one morning while still convalescing, he went to office without notice. Nobody had expected him then, and everyone said, 'You had better go back home. You are too weak now to work.'

Heedless of their reference to his weakness, Ambikacharan sat down at his desk. The officials seemed somewhat agitated and suddenly with inordinate attention engaged in their respective work.

Opening his desk, Ambikacharan saw there was not a single personal paper there. 'What's this?' he asked all of them. Everyone seemed to be shocked; whether the papers had been removed by a thief or by a ghost they could not ascertain.

'My dear sirs,' said Bamacharan, 'don't feign innocence. All of you know that the master himself has called for his papers.' 'Why?' asked Ambika, white with suppressed anger. Bamacharan, busy writing, replied, 'How can we say that?'

Taking the opportunity of Ambikacharan's absence, Binod at the instigation of Bamacharan, making a duplicate key and opening his manager's private desk, had taken away all his papers for examination. The shrewd Bamacharan made no secret of the fact that Ambika resigning from his work from humiliation was not undesirable to him.

After locking his desk, Ambikacharan, his body trembling, went to seek out Binod, who sent word that he had a headache. From there going back home, suddenly feeling weak he lay down on his bed. Indrani came rushing and covered him as if with her whole heart. By and by, Indrani heard everything.

The static lightning no longer remained immobile today: her breast began to heave; her dark eyes aghast, flames of lightning flaring from their corners began to spew intense virulence of anger. So much insult to such a saintly husband! Such reward for so much loyalty!

The sight of Indrani burning silently with such fierce rage calmed down Ambika's anger. As if to save the sinner from the wrath of God, he said to Indrani holding her hand, 'Binod is but a child, weak by nature; he's been confused by listening to different people.'

Indrani, then throwing her arms round her husband's neck, hugging him close to her heart embraced him passionately, and all at once, bedimming the glint of fury in her eyes, tears began to stream down in torrents. Clutching at him with both hands from all the wrongs, all the affronts of the world, she wanted, as it were, to enthrone her life-deity in the shrine of her heart.

It was decided that Ambikacharan would immediately resign; today there was no disagreement on this score. But this small retribution was no consolation for Indrani: when the suspicious master was himself going to dismiss Ambika, how could he have avenged it by resigning? Once Ambika resolved to lay down office, his anger was pacified. But Indrani's anger smouldered in her heart all through her work, all through her leisure and pleasure.

EPILOGUE

Just then, the servant came to announce that the treasurer of the zamindar was come. Ambika decided that Binod, out of decency, not saying it himself, had sent the treasurer to convey his dismissal. So, on his own, writing a letter of resignation, he handed it to the treasurer. Without asking anything about it, the treasurer said, 'Disaster has struck.'

'What has happened?'

Then he heard the details. Ever since Ambika's preventive measures had stopped Binod withdrawing money from the treasury, he had been raising huge loans from various sources. Dabbling in one trade after another, the more he was cheated and suffered losses, the more he became reckless: trying to recoup the losses with newer and newer absurd means, ultimately he was up to his ears in debt. When Ambika was ill, Binod taking the opportunity had withdrawn the entire money from the coffers. Bankagari Pargana had long been mortgaged with the neighbouring zamindar, who, never insisting on the redemption of mortgage so far, had allowed interests to accrue. Now at an opportune moment he was all set to obtain a decree. This was the crisis. Ambika was stunned to hear this and stood still for a while. 'I can't think of anything now,' he said. 'Let's discuss it tomorrow.' When the treasurer rose to leave, he took back his resignation letter.

Coming into the inner rooms, narrating everything to Indrani, Ambika said, 'In this critical time for Binod, I cannot leave the job, can I?' Indrani sat for a long while like a statue. At last with great effort repressing all the conflict and hesitancy of her heart, she said with a sigh, 'No, you cannot.'

Thereafter began a frantic search for funds; sufficient money was by no means forthcoming. Ambika advised Binod to collect the ornaments from his wife. Earlier, in connection with his business, Binod had tried this, never successfully. This time, with much pleading, much weeping and self-abasement, he begged for the ornaments. Nayantara did not relent. She contemplated that everything was going to fall apart from all sides, now these ornaments were her sole and final support, and with extreme desperation held on to them .

When no funds could be managed from any possible source, Indrani's revengeful frown reflected a lustre of ecstatic glee. Pressing her husband's hand warmly she said, 'Haven't you done what you needed to do? Now just withdraw yourself. Let things take their own course.'

Realising that the fire of Sati's[6] fury incensed by her husband's humiliation had not been extinguished yet, Ambika smiled inwardly. Like a helpless child in his days of danger, Binod relied on him so urgently that he felt a surge of pity for him: by no means could he desert him in this state. He was contemplating to raise the money by mortgaging his own property. But Indrani with an oath, said, 'No. You cannot do that.'

Finding himself in a quandary Ambika sat brooding. No matter howsoever he tried to persuade Indrani gradually, she did not let him speak. Ambika sat silently, somewhat sad and sullen.

Then Indrani, opening the iron chest, took out all her ornaments on a big platter, and lifting that heavy platter with great effort with both hands placed it near her husband's feet with a wan smile.

Her grandfather's sole repository of love, Indrani had received many costly ornaments year after year since her birth. Most of the savings of her thrifty husband too had been converted into gold in the casket of this childless woman. Gathering up all that gold before her husband, she said, 'With this jewellery I'll retrieve the gift once made by my grandfather and then give it away again to his masters.'

Having said this, closing her tearful eyes, lowering her head she imagined that her old grandfather—with sparse white hair, innocent and handsome countenance, with a benign smile of affection, bright fair skin, beaming with intellect—was present there at that moment, and putting his soothing hand of love on her bent head blessing her silently.

When Bankagari Pargana was bought back, breaking her vow Indrani, shorn of her jewellery, once again went on invitation to Nayantara's house; no longer in her mind was there any affliction of humiliation.

*Asharh 1302* (1895)

NOTES

1 Chief minster or finance minister of a state ruled by a former Indian prince, a post now abolished.
2 Revenue collector.
3 Daughter of the demon-guru Shukracharya and wife of king Yajati.
4 Daughter of Vrishaparva, king of demons; youngest wife of Yajati.
5 A Hindu married woman, customarily, out of modesty, at the time of the story, does not show her face to males, not even to the elderly male members of her family except her husband. When it becomes urgent, she talks either from behind a screen or with her veil pulled down low enough to hide her face.
6 Sati, consort of Shiva and daughter of king Daksha. When she went to attend her father's sacrificial ceremony, Daksha denounced Shiva in the most derogatory terms for his eccentric and reckless lifestyle in the presence of the invited gods, which enraged Sati. Hence the allusion.

# Resentment Appeased (*Maanbhanjan*)

Gopinath Shil's wife Giribala lived on the top floor of Ramanath Shil's three-storey mansion. In front of the southern door of her bedroom, there stood some flowerpots of jasmine and rose saplings. The roof had a high parapet, built like a grid of bricks with gaps to allow outside view. The bedroom walls were hung with framed engravings of variously dressed foreign women and those in various states of undress; but in the mirror opposite the front door, the image cast by the sixteen-year-old mistress was no way inferior in beauty to anyone on the wall.

Giribala's beauty was like a sudden flash of light, like surprise, like consciousness after sleep: coming in a trice it strikes; a single impact could be overwhelming. If you saw her, you would feel, 'I was not prepared to see her. She is altogether different from what we see around us or have ever seen.'

Giribala was rippling all over with her surging charm. Just as the froth of wine spills over the goblet, so did her blossoming youth and fresh beauty inundate her body. They romped riotously in her dress and jewellery, in her movements, in the flourish of her hand and tilt of her neck, in the wild rhythm of her nimble feet, in the jingle of her bracelets and tinkle of her anklets, in her fluid laugh and fluent speech, and in her sharp glances.

Giribala was fascinated with the intoxicating juice that seemed to flow through her body. She would often be found draped in a colourful sari of soft texture, fidgeting around on the terrace, without cause as if her limbs wished to dance to an unheard, muffled tune in the core of her mind. Twirling, turning her body and pirouetting in various curlicues she seemed to derive a kind of joy she alone knew: as if, by exciting ripples in the different aspects of her beauty, she felt with a mystifying thrill strange impulses and their recoil in the warm blood-stream throughout her body. Suddenly plucking off a leaf, she might let it float the next moment lifting her right arm into the air: simultaneously with it, her bangles tinkled, her sari-end slithered, and the graceful gesture of her arm soared into the realm of clouds, like an invisible bird freed from its cage. Or, suddenly picking up a clod of earth from the flowerpot, she might fling it freakishly. Standing tall on her toes, she might take a quick view of the outside world from the opening in the parapet, and turn back the next moment with a swish of her sari-end, jangling the keys tied to it. Yet again, sitting in front of the mirror, undoing her chignon she might start doing it all over again at an odd hour: gathering the hair at the back with a ribbon, then biting that ribbon between her jasmine-white teeth and lifting both arms overhead, she would weave plaits and coil them up tightly. This done, she had finished all she had to do, when she would sprawl lazily on her soft bed like a streak of moonlight deflected from the cover of leaves.

She had no children; in the wealthy family, she had no work either. Only accumulating her self every day within herself, now she could contain herself no more. She had her husband; but the husband was not accessible to her. Even though from childhood she had fully blossomed into youth, she had somehow escaped her husband's notice.

Rather, in her childhood she had had love from her husband. In those days, her husband, playing truant from school and evading his sleeping elders, used to drop in on solitary afternoons for amorous talks with his child bride; despite living in the same house, they used to exchange love letters on fancy notepads and he took pride in showing those billets-doux to selected friends at school. Fits of pique and sulks were not rare either.

At this point, his father having died Gopinath was catapulted into the position of the head of the family. Unseasoned wood soon gets infested with woodworm: when Gopinath became independent at an unripe age, he got into bad company. Then his movements gradually became rarer in the inner quarters to extend elsewhere.

Leadership has an excitement of its own; addiction of man to his fellow men is too strong to overcome. Napoleon had an overweening ambition for leaving a permanent impression on the minds of the masses and their history down the ages. The head of a small band of lackeys in a small drawing room has an aspiration of similar nature, albeit on a smaller scale. If one can organise around oneself a spoilt circle of cronies glued together by flippant waggery, dominating them and winning their applause can be a source of great excitement. Many people do not flinch from courting debt, scandal and even ruin for the mere thrill of it.

Having graduated to number one among his cronies, Gopinath was beside himself with excitement. He kept pulling off newer feats and achieving greater glory in tomfoolery everyday. His friends said Gopinath was unparalleled in cracking jokes in the company of his brothers-in-law[4]. Blinded by the vanity and excitement of it to all other feelings of happiness and sorrow, duties and obligations, the wretched fellow kept being swept around as in a whirlpool.

On the other hand, Giribala with her imperial beauty continued to shine on the vacant throne of her bedroom in the unpopulated territory of her inner quarters. She knew that the Lord had empowered her with the sceptre: the vast world, which was visible through the eyehole in the parapet, she knew she could conquer simply with an oblique glance, yet not even one man in the entire world she had so far been able to captivate.

Giribala had a very witty maidservant; her name was Sudhamukhi, called Sudho for short. She used to sing, dance and recite rhymes for her. She would expatiate on the beauty of her master's wife lamenting that such beauty went to waste at the hands of a philistine. Giribala could never manage without this Sudho in attendance at any time. She would listen to Sudho's elaborate critical appreciation of her facial charm, figure and the brightness of her complexion; at times, she would protest, and with a rapturous heart rebuke her for a liar and flatterer. Sudho then sat proving with hundreds of oaths the genuineness of her views, which Giribala found not too difficult to believe.

Sudho used to sing for Giribala: *I have signed up as a slave at your feet.* In this song, Giribala could hear the echo of a hymn to her own impeccably beautiful feet painted in lac dye, and with it the image of a lover wallowing at her feet flashed in her imagination. Alas, the two hallowed feet with the tinkling of their anklets danced about on the empty terrace singing their own paeans, yet no self-sold devotee came to sign up the bond of slavery.

The woman to whom Gopinath was enslaved was Labanga by name. She was a theatre artiste: she could wonderfully enact fainting on the stage. When she, in a nasal artificially whining voice, with a gasping half-articulate childish drawl, let out screams, 'O Lord of my heart! O God of my soul', the audience dressed in fine dhotis with waistcoats over them and stockings on their feet, would rhapsodically yell, 'Excellent, excellent!'

About the astounding talent of this artiste Labanga, Giribala had heard on many occasions straight from her husband. Her husband had not yet turned a permanent absconder then. Even being unaware of her husband's infatuation, she then used to feel jealous. That any other woman was endowed with any such captivating art, which she herself did not have, was intolerable to her. With jealous curiosity, she had expressed on many occasions her desire to go to the theatre, but never could persuade her husband.

At last one day, she sent Sudho with money to watch the show. Sudho came back shocked: screwing up her nose and brow, and uttering Lord Rama's name, she prescribed lashes of broomstick on the artistes' foreheads. Men who fell for their hideous figures and spurious gestures also received the same treatment. Giribala felt greatly reassured.

Thereafter, when her husband severed ties with her, doubts arose in her mind. When she expressed disbelief in Sudho's words, Sudho reaffirmed on oath that Labanga did look as shrunken and ugly as a burnt log wrapped in a piece of cloth. Giribala could not ascertain the cause of her attractive power, and with battered pride kept smouldering within.

Finally, one evening taking along Shudho she secretly went to visit a show. A forbidden act is most exciting: by the impulse of the faint throbbing it had set up in her heart, the stage aglitter with lights, abuzz with people, resounding with music, and decked up with sets appeared even more wonderful in her eyes. From her walled-in, desolate, cheerless home, to what magnificent world of festivity she was transported! Everything seemed like a dream.

That day's programme was the musical play 'Maanbhanjan'[1]. The final bell rang, the music band stopped, the restive spectators immediately quietened and sat still, the floodlights became brighter, the curtain rose, a troupe of dancing girls dressed as the milkmaids of *Braja*[2] started dancing with accompanying music, and the theatre resounded frequently with claps and applause from the audience. Then the bloodstream began to course through Giribala's youthful body in agitated excitement. The tempo of music, the brilliance of lights and costumes, and the exuberance of applause together made her forget society and the world altogether for a while: she thought she had come to a place where there was no hindrance to enjoying liberal and aesthetic freedom.

Sudho came to her several times during the show and whispered in a tremulous voice, 'Ma'am, we'd better return now. If Dada-babu finds out, there's no saving us.' Giribala paid no heed; there was not a trace of fear in her mind now.

The play progressed far: Radha was languishing from the unconquerable offence of injured pride; in that sea of resentment Krishna found himself entirely out of his depth; no amount of supplication, coaxing or whining could make her relent. Giribala began to swell with exultant pride; at this discomfiture of Krishna, she delighted in her own infinite prowess vicariously through Radha. No one had ever cajoled her in this way; she was a neglected, humiliated, abandoned wife, yet in some strange infatuation, she concluded that she too was capable of persecuting so mercilessly. How terribly powerful beauty could be she had heard from others and only guessed; today in the brilliance of lamps, amidst tunes of songs, on the colourful stage she saw its vivid demonstration. A feeling of intoxication completely filled her head.

Finally, the curtain fell, the gaslights dimmed, the audience began to leave, Giribala sat spellbound. That leaving the place she would have to return home was not on her mind: she was contemplating that the play would never end; the curtain would rise once again; other than the defeat of Krishna at the hands of Radha, nothing mattered. Sudho said, 'What are you doing, Ma'am? Get up. Lights will go out any moment.'

Giribala returned to her bedroom very late at night. In a corner, a lamp was flickering; there was no man, no sound in the room; on the empty bed at the end, an old mosquito net was waving gently in the breeze. Her familiar everyday world seemed utterly disgusting, dull and mean. Where was that world full of beauty, light and music—the world where she could occupy centre stage resplendent in all her glory, where she was no mere ordinary woman, unknown, neglected and inconsequential?

From then on, Giribala kept visiting the theatre every week. In course of time, the wonder of her first visit dwindled largely; now she could discern the performers' garish make-up, lack of beauty, artificial acting and everything else, but her addiction nevertheless did not wear off. Just as on hearing the war-trumpet, a soldier's heart begins to flutter, she felt a similar turmoil as soon as the curtain lifted over the stage. Behold that magnificent elevated imposing pulpit segregated from the world, lettered in gold, adorned in painted canvas, steeped in poetical and lyrical magic, visible to an enraptured audience, mysterious in background secrecy, revealed in bright illumination—can there be a more magical throne for an earth-conquering empress of beauty?

The day she first saw her husband at the theatre, and when Gopinath indulged in mad outpourings over the performance of an actress, profound hatred for him arose in her mind. With a stricken heart, she decided that if ever a day were to come when her husband fascinated by her beauty would fall at her feet like a moth with singed wings, and she could walk away in umbrage spitting disdain from her toenails, only then would her wasted youth and wasted beauty be fulfilled.

But when was that rosy day to come? At present, Gopinath could be sighted only rarely. At the head of the storm of his own madness, gathering a gaggle of cronies as a banner of dust he had gone away in a whirl nobody knew where.

One full moon night of spring in *Chaitra*, Giribala was sitting on the terrace wearing an orange-yellow sari, her sari-end flowing in the southerly breeze. Even though her husband had stopped coming home, she used to embellish herself with a different set of new ornaments every day. Diamond and gem-studded ornaments transmitted a maddening thrill to her limbs; their sparkling and tinkling raised a wave around her. Today she wore armlets, a necklace with beads of rubies and pearls, and a sapphire ring on her left little finger. Sitting next to her feet, Sudho was at times stroking her perfectly shaped, tender lotus feet, and saying with genuine upsurge of emotion, 'Ah, *Bouthakrun,* if I were a man, I would be happy to die clasping these feet to my breast!' Laughing proudly, Giribala retorted, 'Would have died perhaps without ever getting to do it. Would I then have stretched my feet out in this way? Stop talking nonsense. Sing me that song.'

On the lonely terrace flooded by moonlight, Sudho sang, 'Here I abase myself at your lotus feet. / Let everyone in *Vrindaban* witness it.'

It was about ten at night. All others in the house had finished their meal and gone to bed. Suddenly Gopinath arrived, smelling of attar, with a scarf flowing from his shoulder. Looking abashed and pulling a long veil over her face, Sudho ran off speedily.

Giribala thought her day had come at last. She did not look up and sat unperturbed with as towering a pride as Radha's. Nevertheless, the curtain did not rise; neither did any Krishna in his crown of peacock feathers roll at her feet; no one sang out in a *raga*, 'Why darken the moonlight by hiding your moonface?' In an unmusical prosaic voice, Gopinath said, 'Give me the key please.'

In such enchanting moonlight and such springtime after a long separation, could these be the first words from a lover? Whatever is written in poems, plays and novels: is that entirely false? Only on the stage, the lover comes singing a song to roll at his sweetheart's feet, and the mere sight melts the heart of a spectator. To imagine that the same person comes on a spring night to ask his matchless young wife, 'Give me the key please'! Is there any music in it or is there any love? Absolutely devoid of charm and grace, it is utterly trivial.

Just then, the southerly wind blew moaning like the heartrending sighs of all humiliated poetry of the world. The fragrance of blooming jasmine wafted from the pot; ringlets of Giribala's hair flowed over her eyes and her face, and her scented orange-yellow sari kept fluttering its end. Swallowing her pride, Giribala rose to her feet.

Taking her husband's hand, she said, 'I'll give the key; come into the room.' She had firmly resolved that today she would cry and make him cry, fulfil her secret fantasies, and by applying her infallible missiles[3], come out victorious.

Gopinath said, 'I can't wait long enough. Give me the key.'

'Not just the key,' said Giribala, 'I'll give you everything it locks. But tonight you must not go anywhere.'

'That can't be. I've something urgent to do.'

'Then I won't give the key,' said Giribala.

'Won't give indeed!' said Gopinath, 'Let me see how you don't.' With this, he seized her sari-end, saw there was no key; then entering the room, pulled open the dressing table drawer, saw the key was not there either. He then broke open her hair-dressing casket; mascara, vermilion, ribbon and various other things were there—but no key. Then rummaging through the bedding, overturning the mattress, battering the cupboard he turned the room upside down.

Giribala stood stiffly like a statue, clutching at the door and looking at the roof. A frustrated Gopinath, seething with rage, growled, ' Give me the key I tell you or it won't do you any good.' Giribala did not say a single word. Then Gopi caught hold of her, wrested away the armlets, necklace and ring from her body, and kicking her aside, went away.

No one in the house woke up; nobody in the neighbourhood knew anything; the moonlit night remained as quiet as before, as if an undisturbed peace was prevailing everywhere. But if screams of the heart could be heard outside, that moonlit Chaitra night sleeping happily would have been suddenly torn asunder by a sudden and most intense cry of agony. Such heart-breaking events happen in such a completely silent way!

Still, even that fateful night did end. So stunning were her defeat and humiliation that Giribala could not open up even to Sudho. She contemplated killing herself: by defacing her immense beauty and youth with her own hands, she would avenge the neglect done to her. But the next moment it occurred that it would matter little to anybody: no one would even feel what loss it would mean to the world. Neither was there any happiness in life nor was there any consolation in death.

'I'm going back to my father's house,' declared Giribala. Her father's house was a long way from Calcutta. Everyone tried to dissuade her, but the mistress of the house heeded no advice; neither did she take along anyone with her. Meanwhile, Gopinath too had set out on a boat-trip with his complement of cronies no one knew where or for how long.

## 2

Gopinath visited almost every show at the Gandharba theatre. There Labanga played in and as *Manorama.* Gopinath and company, sitting in the front row, used to cheer her loudly and lob bunches of currency notes onto the stage. Occasionally on some days, creating ruckus he caused great annoyance to the audience. Yet, the theatre authorities never dared to forbid him.

At last one day, Gopinath in a slightly drunken state barged into the green room and kicked up a great row. Feeling humiliated on some trivial imaginary issue, he severely beat a certain actress. Her screams and Gopinath's cursing alerted the whole theatre.

At the end of their patience that day, the authorities threw him out with the help of the police.

Gopinath was determined to settle scores for this insult. Since a month before the *puja* season, the management had been giving wide publicity to the extended shows of *Manorama.* They had wrapped the entire city of Calcutta in posters, as if it was wearing a *namabali* inscribed with the famous playwright's name.

At this point of time, Gopinath decamped with their principal actress Labanga, vanishing by boat to some undeclared place.

The authorities suddenly found themselves in a great predicament. After waiting a few days for Labanga, they finally made a new recruit rehearse for the role of Manorama, which deferred their show. But that did not affect the box office: the play drew full houses, hundreds being turned away from the gates; there were rave reviews in the papers as well. The news reached Gopinath's ears. He could not hold himself any longer; driven by rancour as well as curiosity, he came to see the play.

In Act I, Scene 1, Manorama is in her in-laws' house, living like a servant in shabby dress, going about her chores in a subdued, self-demeaning, diffident manner, never uttering a word, never properly lifting her face.

In the last Act, sending Manorama back to her parents' house, her venal husband proceeds to marry a millionaire's only daughter. After the wedding, when in the bridal chamber the husband takes a good look at the new bride, he discovers that she is also Manorama, except that she no longer has that servant's dress: today she is dressed like a princess, her incomparable beauty enhanced by jewellery and gorgeous attire radiating to every corner. In her childhood, Manorama had been kidnapped from her rich father's house and brought up in poverty. Many years later, her father recently having traced her brought her back home and now has married her off afresh to her own husband with great ceremony.

Then in the bridal chamber begins the scene of smoothing ruffled feathers.

In the meantime, a great uproar had begun in the audience. As long as Manorama was in the shabby servant's dress hiding her face behind her veil, Gopinath had been watching quietly. But in the bridal chamber she stood up discarding her veil, sparkling in jewellery, blazing in red attire and sending out waves of beauty. Tilting her head in indescribable arrogance and pride, she darted a sharp contemptuous lightning glance at the audience, especially at Gopinath; the audience were filled with admiration, and the house resounded with their thunderous applause. Then suddenly, Gopinath jumped up and burst out shouting, 'Giribala, Giribala!' Surging forward he tried to hop onto the stage, but was stopped by the musicians.

Furious at this sudden interruption by the spoilsport, the audience shouted in English and Bengali, 'Drive him out, throw him out!

Gopinath kept screaming wildly in a broken voice, 'I will kill her, I will kill her.'

The police came and dragged him away. Spectators from the entire city of Calcutta continued to feast their eyes on Giribala's acting, only Gopinath did not find a place there.

*Baishakh 1302* (1895)

NOTES

1 Maanbhanjan: Resentment Appeased; this is how the story gets its title; Radha is having the sulks and Krishna is trying hard to coax her out of them; this is the theme of the play.
2 Vrindavan (see Glossary)
3 The text has *Brahmashtra* which means arms consecrated with the divine power of Brahma, hence most potent.
4 The wife's younger brothers and sisters are traditionally on bantering terms with the husband.

# The Wedding Garland (*Malyadaan*)

The morning was slightly chilly. As the day advanced, the air warmed up somewhat, and a breeze started from the south.

Jatin was sitting on the veranda; from there, through the gap between a jackfruit tree on one side and a rain tree on the other in a corner of the garden could be seen the vast open field stretching away endlessly under the *Phalgun* sun. Bordering one side of that field ran a mud path along which an unloaded bullock-cart was wending its way to the village, the cart man singing leisurely, a *gamchha*[1] folded twice over placed on his head.

Just then, a female voice called out with laughter from behind, 'Hallo Jatin, are you contemplating someone from your previous birth?'

'Why, Patal?' protested Jatin, 'Am I so wretched that if I have to contemplate, I have to fall back on my previous birth?'

'Don't brag any more,' countered the girl with the nondescript name of 'Patal' [a vegetable] in her family circle. 'Every detail of your present life is at my finger tips, my dear sir,' she continued, 'Shame, shame! You've advanced so far in age, yet couldn't find yourself such a paltry thing as a wife. Look at that Dhana, our gardener: even he has a wife; quarrelling with her mornings and evenings he alerts the whole neighbourhood that he indeed has one. And you staring at the field pretending you're meditating on some moon-faced creature, do you suppose I cannot see through all these tricks? That's just posturing to impress people. Look Jatin, a known Brahman doesn't need to show his sacred thread[2]. Have you ever seen our Dhana staring like you and pretending to be languishing for his wife? Even in his saddest days of separation, I've seen him sitting with his weeding trowel under the tree; he didn't seem to have that far-away look in his eyes like you. And you, dear sir, never saw the face of a wife, wasted your youth simply by dissecting corpses and cramming books. Why do you sit staring at the midday sky expectantly? I hate such wiles; They get on my nerves.'

'Please stop it. That's enough,' replied Jatin placing his hands together. 'Don't embarrass me any more. Your Dhana is blessed indeed. He is the one whose example I'll try to follow. No more words, please. I'll exchange garlands with the first wood-gathering girl[3] I come across tomorrow morning. Can't bear such contemptuous talk any longer.'

Patal: That's final then?

Jatin: Yes, of course.

Patal: Come along then.

Jatin: Where to?

Patal: You just come.

Jatin: Oh, no, you must be up to some mischief. I'm not going to move now.

Patal: All right. Sit here then.

Saying this, she went away hurriedly.

Let me introduce them at this point. Jatin and Patal differed in age by just one day. Because Patal was senior by only a day, Jatin was unwilling to show her any formal respect as elder. They were cousins and had been playmates. Since Jatin never called her 'Didi', Patal in her childhood had often expressed her grouse to her father and uncle, but by no disciplinary proceedings achieved any result: even to her only younger cousin, she remained Patal.

Patal was quite chubby and plump, bubbling over with cheerfulness. There was no social authority to restrain her fun-loving joviality. Even before her mother-in-law, she could never assume a sober posture. During the early days of her marriage, her in-laws often talked about it, but in the end, everybody had to capitulate: 'Let her be. She is like that.' Eventually, the solemnity of the elders fell flat on the ground from the impact of her irrepressible joviality. Patal could not stand any sulky, morose or worried faces around her: the atmosphere was, as it were, laden with sparks of energy from her endless gossip, laughter and jest.

Patal's husband Harakumar-babu was a deputy magistrate. He had been transferred from Bihar to the Excise Department in Calcutta. For fear of plague in the city, he had taken a garden house on rent at Bally[4], and used to commute to and from Calcutta. As he was required from time to time to leave station on departmental tour, he had been planning to have his mother and one or two other relatives shifted from his native home, when Jatin arrived on a week's visit at his cousin's call; he had recently got his medical degree and not yet set up much practice.

On the first day of his visit, coming straight from the Calcutta lanes, Jatin was lounging on the quiet shady veranda, rapt with the indulgent torpidity of a spring afternoon. It was then that the teasing ordeal by his cousin had begun. When Patal left, he felt relieved for the time being and sat quite comfortably in a fresh posture; in the context of the wood-gathering girl, his mind kept wandering in the lanes and alleys of his childhood fairy-tale world.

The chirping of Patal's playful voice startled him once again. Holding another girl's hand, she forcibly stood her before Jatin. 'O, Kurani!' she cooed.

'Yes, Didi?'

'How do you like this brother of mine?'

The girl stood looking at Jatin without the least shyness.

'What would you say? Isn't he good looking?' asked Patal.

The girl scrutinised him solemnly and nodded. 'Yes, he is.'

Jatin coloured, and leaving his seat said, 'Oh, Patal, what childishness is this?'

'Am I being a child or are you playing an oldie? You pretend you're as old as the hills.'

Jatin fled the scene. Patal ran after him, calling, 'O Jatin, don't be afraid. You won't have to exchange garlands right now. There's no auspicious date in this month or the next. You can take your time to decide.'

The girl whom Patal called Kurani[5] stood surprised. Her age was about sixteen; she was slim: there was nothing remarkable about her looks; only her face had an extraordinariness that brought the impression of a wild deer to one's mind. An expression, which in uncharitable language might perhaps be called unintelligent, but it was not stupidity, just immaturity of the intellectual faculty that instead of taking away from the beauty of her face, rather lent it a distinct quality.

In the evening, after returning from Calcutta and finding Jatin, Harakumar-babu said, 'So you've come, Jatin. Very good, we'll be requiring some medical advice from you. While in Bihar, we had picked up a girl during the famine[6]; we have been raising her since. Patal calls her Kurani. The girl and her parents had been lying under a tree near our bungalow. On being informed, when we went to enquire, her parents had already been dead and the girl was barely alive. Patal saved her life with great effort. Nobody knows what caste she is. If anybody raises a question, Patal says, "She is *Dwija*[7]; she died, and then was reborn into our family, so her original caste no longer matters." In the beginning, she used to address Patal as Ma. Patal told her sternly, "Don't call me Ma, mind you. Call me Didi." If a girl her age were to call her mother, she would feel herself like an old matron, Patal had argued. Perhaps because of starvation during the famine, or maybe any other cause, she has developed a colic in her abdomen which she feels acutely at times. You have to examine her thoroughly and find out what's wrong.' He called out to his servant Tulsi to fetch Kurani.

Kurani who was doing up her hair came hastily into Harakumar-babu's room, her half-done plaits swinging on her back. She stood looking with her doe-like eyes fixed on the two of them.

Finding Jatin hesitating, Harakumar said, 'You are feeling embarrassed for nothing, Jatin. She looks so big, but is like a green coconut: only liquid splashing inside; no kernel has begun to form yet. She doesn't understand a thing. Do not mistake her for a woman. She is a wild deer.'

Jatin got down to his job, Kurani showing not a trace of bashfulness. 'So far as her body functions are concerned, there's nothing wrong apparently,' he declared.

Abruptly entering the room Patal said, 'There's nothing wrong with her heart either. Shall I demonstrate it ?'

Going up to Kurani and touching her chin, she said, 'O Kurani, do you like this brother of mine?'

Nodding her head, Kurani said, 'Yes.'

Patal asked, 'Will you marry him?'

'Yes,' she said, nodding again.

Patal and Harakumar burst out laughing together. Unable to see the point of the joke, Kurani in imitation of them, kept up a beaming face staring vacuously.

Jatin blushed scarlet and quickly said, 'Ah, Patal, you're going too far; that's very wrong of you. Harakumar-babu, you indulge Patal too much, I must say.'

'If I don't, I can't expect indulgence from her,' Harakumar quipped. 'But anyway, Jatin, you are getting so flustered only because you do not know her. Being so shy yourself, I think you'll be teaching her to be shy, too. Don't feed her with the fruit of the wisdom tree. Everybody behaves jocularly with her; if suddenly now, you start showing gravity, she will find it strange.'

Patal: And that is precisely why I could never get along with Jatin. We have been quarrelling ever since childhood. He is too serious.

Harakumar: I see! That's how quarrelling has become a habit with you. Now that your cousin has given you the slip, you –

Patal: Lying again! There's no fun quarrelling with you; I don't even try.

Harakumar: I acknowledge defeat straightaway at the beginning.

Patal: Great indeed! If instead of conceding defeat at the beginning, you did it at the end, how happy I'd have been!

At night, keeping doors and windows in his bedroom open, Jatin sat reflecting: What an ominous shadow must have been cast on the life of a girl who had seen her parents die of starvation! How immensely she must have grown up through that terrible experience! Could one make fun of her? Her Lord had mercifully laid a veil over her intellect. If that screen were to be removed, what terrible marks of destiny's rampages would be revealed! This afternoon when Jatin had been looking through the trees at a slice of the vernal sky, and the faint fragrance of the distant jackfruit buds reached him, he had seen the world with his mind's eye through the mist of a charming sweetness. The unintelligent girl with her doe-like eyes dispelled that golden mist. The famished and parched world hardened by grief standing imposingly behind the cooing, humming, murmuring spring loomed large.

Next evening, Kurani had a recurrence of her chronic colic. Patal at once sent for Jatin. Jatin came and found that Kurani's hands and feet were cramping from pain, her body was stiff. He sent a man to buy medicines and asked for a hot-water bottle. 'A great doctor indeed,' teased Patal, 'Why don't you rub some warm oil on her feet? Can't you see her soles are cold as ice?'

Jatin started massaging hot oil vigorously on her soles. The treatment continued until quite late in the night. After returning from Calcutta, Harakumar began to ask after Kurani every now and then. Jatin could see that just back from work in the evening, not finding Patal in attendance, Harakumar was in an awful state: that was the implication of his frequent inquiries about Kurani.

'Harakumar Babu has become impatient, he said. 'You'd better go, Patal.'

'Come, come, you must find someone for a pretext,' quipped Patal, 'I know who's really become impatient. All you now want is I should leave. And yet, you're blushing at every word! Who would have thought you had such scheming bottled up?'

Jatin: All right, for heaven's sake, stay on here. Only keep your mouth shut and spare me. I was wrong: Harakumar Babu must be relaxing peacefully, he rarely gets such an opportunity.

At last finding relief, when Kurani opened her eyes, Patal said, 'Your man was pressing your feet all this while, begging you to open your eyes. Is that why today you're so late coming round? Shame, shame, pay him your respects.'

Dutifully, Kurani at once picked the dust from Jatin's feet solemnly. Jatin hurriedly went out of the room.

From the next day on, Patal started a full-scale torment on Jatin. He had sat down to eat when Kurani came and without more ado started fanning away the flies. Feeling uneasy, Jatin at once dismissed her, 'No, no, there's no need.' Taken aback at this dismissal, Kurani looked back for once enquiringly at the room behind, and then kept swinging her fan again. Addressing the person behind the scene, Jatin called out, 'Patal, if you keep tormenting me like this, I just won't eat. I'm getting up now.'

As soon as he made to get up, Kurani dropped the fan. Jatin could discern deep lines of pain in Kurani's vacuous face; remorsefully, he sat down again. That Kurani did not understand anything, that she felt no shame, felt no pain was something even Jatin had begun to believe. Today at a rare instant, he realised that there was exception to every rule, and just when that exception would suddenly occur, nobody could tell in advance. Kurani discarded the fan and went back.

Next morning, Jatin was sitting on the veranda, with cuckoos among the trees calling rapturously, the air heavy with the scent of mango buds, when he noticed Kurani waiting hesitantly with a cup of tea at some distance. In her doe-like eyes, there was something of a pitiful fear: she seemed unable to decide whether by taking him the tea she would be causing him annoyance. Feeling a prick of pain, Jatin walked the distance to take the cup from her hand: how could he hurt this young deer of human birth on a flimsy ground? He had just taken the cup when he found Patal suddenly appear at the other end of the veranda flourishing a fist at him laughing soundlessly, as if to say, 'How now! Caught you finally.'

That evening, Jatin was reading a medical journal when startled by the scent of flowers, he saw Kurani enter the room with a garland of *bakul* flowers in her hand. Jatin said to himself, 'Really, things are going too far. Patal ought not to be allowed to go on with this cruel joke any longer.'

To Kurani he said, 'Shame, Kurani! Can't you see that your Didi is having fun at your expense?'

He had hardly finished before Kurani turned back to leave, alarmed and disconcerted. Jatin at once called her back and said, 'All right, Kurani, give me your garland.' He took it from her; a glow of delight flashed on her face. The same moment, a burst of loud laughter could be heard from behind the curtain.

Next morning, going to tease him as usual, Patal saw Jatin's room was empty; on a piece of paper just two words were written: 'Gone. Jatin.'

'O Kurani, do you know your bridegroom has fled? Couldn't hold him?' Giving a gentle pull to her plait, Patal went back to her chores.

It took Kurani some time to get at the meaning. She stood still like a picture, staring vacantly. Then walking slowly into Jatin's room, she saw it for herself: it was empty, her last evening's gift of the garland lying on the table.

It was a fine soothing morning of spring. The sunlight, filtering through the quivering foliage of a *gulmohar* tree and interweaving with shadows, lay across the veranda; squirrels were scampering with their tails turned up, and birds singing their apparently inexhaustible thoughts, each in a different note. In this secluded corner of the earth, in this segment of the world conjured up by the chiaroscuro of thick foliage and patch of sunlight, there was joie de vivre blooming bright. Amidst that, the foolish girl seemed unable to find any reasonable meaning of her life, of her surroundings; everything seemed an impenetrable enigma. What happened and why did that happen so that this morning, this house, everything whatever, turned completely void? Here was a girl who had but a modicum of sensibility: who had cast her into the misty cavern of her heart's unfathomable pain even without a lamp in her hand? Who could lift her back into this realm of spontaneously teeming life of the world, amidst this oblivious din of plants, birds and animals?

Patal, after finishing her housework came to have a word with Kurani and found her in Jatin's room, lying on the floor clutching a leg of his bedstead: as if she was supplicating at the feet of the empty bed, as if the nectar-bowl hidden in her heart she was pouring out at the feet of emptiness in futile assurance. The woman lying in a heap with flowing hair and dishevelled clothes seemed to be saying in the language of silent dedication, 'Take me. Take me to you. O dear, please take me.'

Surprised, Patal said, 'What's going on, Kurani?' Kurani did not get up and lay as before. When, coming near, Patal touched her, she burst into spasms of sobs.

Patal was startled. 'O, poor wretch,' she cried out, 'What have you done! You are lost![8]'

Apprising Harakumar about Kurani's condition, Patal said, 'Big trouble for us! What were you doing? Why did you not forbid me?'

Harakumar said, 'Because I was never used to forbidding you. Even if I did, would there have been any result?'

Patal: What kind of a husband are you? If you find me doing something wrong, won't you force me to stop? Why did you let me play this game?

Rushing to the prostrated girl and putting her arms round her neck, she said, 'My good sister, my darling, tell me frankly all you have to say.'

Alas, what language did Kurani have so she could articulate the untold mystery of her heart with words? She was lying pressing down on an inexpressible agony: what that agony exactly was, whether anyone else in the world ever felt it or how people described it Kurani knew nothing whatever. All she could do was tell it in tears; she had no other means to express her feelings.

Patal said, 'Kurani, your Didi is very naughty indeed, but she never thought you would take her words seriously. Nobody ever trusts her words: why did you make such a mistake? Kurani, dear, look up for once at your Didi's face. Forgive her.'

But Kurani's mind had then turned away from her: she could not bring herself to look Patal in the face; she lay with her face buried harder in her hands. Even without comprehending everything clearly, she was, rather stupidly, angry with Patal. Patal, then slowly unlocking her arms, withdrew from her. Standing at the window like a statue in stone, she kept looking at the row of areca trees, their leaves shimmering in the Phalgun sun, her eyes filled with tears.

Next day, Kurani could be found no more. Patal used to dress her lovingly in the best of clothes and ornaments. Herself disorganised in her ways, she never cared about her own dress or looks, but whatever fancy she had for dress and make-up she realised it all through Kurani. All those clothes and ornaments put away over the years lay on the floor of Kurani's room; everything, even the bangles and the nose-ring, which she constantly wore, she had discarded before leaving. So many years of her Patal-didi's affection she had, as it were, tried to wipe away from her body.

Harakumar Babu set the police in a search for Kurani. In the panic whipped up by the campaign for plague-control that year, so many people were fleeing in so many directions that the police were hard put to track down a particular individual in the exodus.

Harakumar-babu, after knocking on the wrong door on two or three occasions to his great misery and embarrassment, at last gave up on Kurani. Whom they had picked up from the lap of the unknown, into it again she went hiding.

Jatin had managed to get a doctor's post in the plague hospital that year. One afternoon, having finished his meal at home, when he came back to the hospital, he was told that a new patient had been admitted into the female ward. The police had picked her up from the street.

Jatin went to visit her. A rug pulled over her body covered much of her face. Picking up her hand, he felt her pulse the first thing; the pulse indicated no high fever, but extreme weakness. Then to examine her thoroughly, he removed the cover from her face: it was Kurani.

Meanwhile, Jatin had learnt everything about Kurani from Patal. Her two doe eyes darkened by the gloom of unspoken emotions, with their tearless melancholy, had persistently overshadowed Jatin's thoughtful mood in his leisure hours. Today, the long lids of those drooping eyes shut by ailment had lined her emaciated cheeks in black streaks. The moment he looked at her, it seemed someone clutched at his heart. Here was a girl whom God took the best of care to make as pristine as a flower: why did He then cast her from a famine into an epidemic? How could this frail creature languishing in bed today from affliction have borne, and where could she have contained, so many blows of adversity, so much burden of pain in this short span of life? Not only this, how had even Jatin happened in her life interposing like a third crisis? Repressed sighs kept pounding at his heart's door, but their impact set up a resonance of happiness in his heartstrings as well. The love such as rarely found in the world, even without Jatin asking for it, drifting on its own had suddenly dropped at his feet like a full-bloomed *madhabi* twig one phalgun afternoon. What soul on earth deserved that heavenly offering—a love that could survive such odds until finally collapsing at death's door?

Jatin sat beside Kurani feeding her some warm milk in small quantities. After a long time, heaving a deep sigh she opened her eyes. Looking at Jatin's face, she seemed to be trying to recall him from a distant dream. When Jatin gave her a gentle shake with his hand placed on her forehead, and called 'Kurani', the last spell of her unconsciousness suddenly broke. She recognised Jatin, and at once, the soft mist of another trance fogged her eyes; like the *Asharh* sky made sombre by the advent of clouds, an extensive curtain of dewy freshness descended on her two dark eyes.

With solicitous appeal in his voice, Jatin said, 'Kurani, finish off the rest of the milk.'

Kurani sat up reclining, and looking from above the cup fixedly at his face, finished drinking the milk in slow sips.

If a doctor in a hospital keeps sitting by a single patient, not only does it hamper work, but it looks odd as well. When Jatin got up to attend other calls, Kurani's eyes grew anxious in fear and despondency. Holding her hands, Jatin said reassuringly, 'I'll come back soon, Kurani. Don't worry.'

Jatin reported to the authorities that the new patient was not suffering from plague; she had become weak from starvation. Staying here with other patients, she might get infected.

With special permission to shift her elsewhere, Jatin took Kurani to his rented house, and then wrote a letter to Patal giving her all the information.

That evening, there was no one in the room except the patient and her doctor. At the head of her bed, a kerosene lamp with a coloured paper shade was burning dimly giving a soft diffused light, and the pendulum of a clock on a bracket was oscillating with a ticking sound in the silent room.

With a hand on Kurani's forehead, Jatin said, 'How do you feel, Kurani?'

Kurani gave no answer and instead pressed Jatin's hand tight to her forehead.

'Do you feel better?' Jatin asked again.

Kurani took a pause and then said with her eyes closed, 'Yes.'

'What's it you are wearing on your neck, Kurani?' asked Jatin.

Kurani tried to cover it quickly with her sari.

Jatin saw it was a withered bakul garland. He at once remembered which garland it was. With the clock ticking away, Jatin sat reflecting quietly. This was the first time Kurani had attempted to hide anything, her first effort to conceal her emotion. Kurani had been an innocent fawn. When did she metamorphose into a young woman weighed down by a heart with its emotions? What sun's light, what sun's warmth dispelled the mist over her faculties, exposing her shyness, her misgivings, her anguish so suddenly?

It was two o'clock or later in the night; Jatin had fallen asleep sitting in his chair. The door suddenly opening with a creak, he woke up with a start and saw Patal and Harakumar-babu enter the room, the latter carrying a large bag in his hand.

Harakumar said, 'After receiving your letter, deciding to come here tomorrow morning, we had gone to bed; half way through the night Patal pleaded, "Dear, tomorrow morning will be too late to see Kurani; I must go right now." Patal could not be dissuaded: then and there hiring a carriage we set out.'

Patal told Harakumar, 'Come, you'll sleep in Jatin's bed.' Affecting some reluctance, Harakumar retired into Jatin's room and was not too late falling asleep either.

After returning from Jatin's room, calling Jatin to a corner, Patal asked, 'Is there any hope?' Jatin went to Kurani, felt her pulse, and shaking his head indicated that there was no hope.

Keeping herself out of Kurani's sight, Patal took Jatin aside and said, 'Tell me frankly, Jatin, don't you love Kurani?'

Without giving Patal any reply, Jatin came and sat beside Kurani's bed, and then taking her hand in a firm grip and giving a shake, called, 'Kurani, Kurani!'

Kurani opened her eyes and with a trace of a sweet, benign smile on her face, answered, 'Yes, Dada-babu?'

'Kurani, put this garland of yours round my neck.'

Kurani kept looking at Jatin's face, her eyes unblinking and uncomprehending.

'Won't you give me your garland? asked Jatin, sounding urgent.

This indulgence of affection revived a streak of her resentment from old neglect. She said, '"What's the use Dada-babu?' Jatin holding her hand in both of his said, 'I love you, Kurani.'

Kurani remained silent for a moment; then tears kept rolling down her eyes in endless streams. Jatin knelt on the floor beside the bed, keeping his head lowered near Kurani's hand. Kurani took the garland off her neck and put it round Jatin's.

At that point, Patal came near and called, 'Kurani!'

Kurani's shrunken face brightened up. She said, 'Yes, Didi?'

Patal moved closer and holding her hand said, 'You are not still angry with me, sister?'

Kurani replied with a calm, gentle look in her eyes, 'No, Didi.'

Patal asked Jatin to go into the next room for a while.

Patal then opened her bag and took out all Kurani's clothes and ornaments from within it. Without disturbing the patient much physically, she draped her cautiously in a red *Benarasi* sari over her shabby clothes, then slipped one after another a bangle and a bracelet into each arm, and then finally called Jatin.

When Jatin came, Patal sat him on the bed and handed a gold chain of Kurani's. Gently lifting Kurani's head, Jatin placed it round her neck.

When the light of dawn fell on her face, Kurani did not see that light. From the undiminished charm of her face, it seemed she had not died, but, as it were, drowned in a bottomless dream of happiness.

When it was time to carry off the body, Patal fell on Kurani's breast, weeping, 'Sister, dear, you are lucky. You are happier in death than in life.'

Looking at that calm and serene picture of death, Jatin mused: 'To Him she went to whom she belonged. Neither was I deprived.'

*Chaitra 1309* (1902)

## NOTES

1 A coarse piece of cloth used as a bath towel, especially by rural people.
2 The sacred thread is a Brahman's distinctive mark; the Bengali proverb means that a well-known person needs no identification.
3 Literally, a woman who collects dry twigs and branches for fuel or for selling them to buy her food; one who lives by scavenging; an utterly destitute woman. It is a recurring theme of Bengali fairy-tales.
4 Across the Ganga, then a sleepy township secluded from the hubbub of the city of Calcutta.
5 The name of a girl child, born after all her previous siblings had died one after another, given by her mother in apparent neglect, hoping this one would survive; a stray, waif, a foundling; a similar name is *Phelna* (See Return of the Little Master); quite fitting with the girl's state in the context of the story.
6 The great famine of 1176 of the Bengali era (1769 AD), popularly known as *Chhiyattarer manwantar* (the Famine of '76 in which nearly ten million people died in Bengal, Bihar and Orissa which were a single state then).
7 Literally, twice-born, a Brahman is said to undergo a spiritual regeneration, a second birth, when he takes the sacred thread.
8 The Bengali *Moriachhis!* (in formal writing) literally, 'You're dead!' or 'You're doomed!' is a common exclamation at some near and dear one's almost certain peril, usually brought about by one's own folly; especially uttered to a woman, it simply means she is doomed to languish in unrequited love.

# The Intervening Woman (*Madhyabartini*)

## 1

Nibaran's world was out-and-out ordinary; there was not a shade of romance in it. That there was any need for that sentiment in life had never occurred to him. Just as one's feet pass quite carelessly into the old pair of slippers, in the same way in this old familiar world, Nibaran used to occupy his accustomed place without ever contemplating or philosophising on it even by mistake.

After rising in the morning Nibaran used to sit bare-chested at his doorstep beside the lane puffing away serenely at his hookah. People walking along, carriages moving by, a Vaishnava beggar singing, a pedlar hawking discarded bottles: this passing sight kept his mind lightly occupied. On the day when the vendor of green mangoes or *topshi*-fish happened to come, after much haggling, he would buy a few to make a somewhat special meal that day. Thereafter at the usual hour rubbing oil on his body, he took his bath, ate his meal, put on the *chapkan* hanging on the clothesline, and then finishing a *paan* while puffing at the hookah, popped another paan in his mouth and finally set out for his office. After returning home, spending the evening placidly at the house of his neighbour Ramlochan Ghosh, he had his meal and at night in the bedroom met his wife Harasundari.

So far no poet had versified the brief critical analysis that went on there about a present for the wedding of the Mitras' son, the insolence of the newly engaged maidservant and the suitability of a particular spice to a certain curry, and for that, no grievance had ever arisen in Nibaran's heart.

Meanwhile, during the month of *Phalgun,* Harasundari fell critically ill; her fever continued obstinately without remission. The more she received quinine, the higher, like an impeded current of water, her temperature kept rising. In this way, the disease dragged on for twenty days, twenty-two days, and right up to forty days.

Nibaran had stopped going to office; he had not been visiting Ramlochan's evening sessions for long; there was no knowing what to do. Now he went into the bedroom asking after the patient; now he sat in the outside veranda smoking tobacco worriedly. He kept changing doctors and *vaids*[1] mornings and evenings, even as he wanted to try whatever medicine anyone might suggest.

In spite of such haphazard treatment born out of love, Harasundari recovered from her illness in forty days. But she was left so feeble and frail that her body seemed barely able to utter in a faint voice from far away, 'I exist.'

It was spring; the south wind had started blowing, and on balmy nights, moonlight had been given the right of entry with silent footsteps into the open bedrooms of married women.

Right beneath Harasundari's bedroom was her neighbour's backyard garden. Not that it was a particularly charming sight. Once, someone had fancifully planted some croton trees, and thereafter had not taken much notice of it. Pumpkin vines crept onto the trellis of dead twigs; a thicket grew beneath an old jujube tree; a portion of the compound wall near the kitchen had collapsed, and the pile of bricks was gathering cinders and ashes everyday.

Even so, looking from the window at the garden, Harasundari kept imbibing a sip of delight every moment such as she had never done before in her insignificant life. When a small stream grown sluggish in summer is a sliver lying on the sandy bed, its water becomes most transparent so the morning sunbeam keeps quivering up to the bottom, the touch of wind tingles it all over with delight, on its crystal mirror are distinctly reflected the stars of the sky as pleasant memories. In the same way, a joyous Nature seemed to be touching the delicate string of Harasundari's life with each of her fingers, arousing some music in her heart, the mood of which she could not fully comprehend.

At such moments, sitting beside her, when her husband asked, 'How are you?' tears welled up in her eyes. In her emaciated face, her eyes appeared enormous; lifting those large, yearning, grateful eyes at her husband's face, holding his hand with her skinny hand, she kept lying silently; her husband too felt some strange new ray of joy creeping into his heart.

A few days went by in this way. One night, when from behind the trembling branches of the small peepul tree on the dilapidated wall, a big disc of the moon was emerging, and sweeping the sultriness of the evening a night-faring breeze had risen, Harasundari, caressing Nibaran with her fingers wandering into his hair, said, 'Look, dear, we're not ever going to have a child. You marry again[2].'

For some time now, Harasundari had been mulling it over. When there appears an ecstatic joy, a sublime love in one's heart, one feels: 'I can do anything.' Suddenly, an urge for self-sacrifice becomes dominant. Just as the surge of waves violently collapses on the hard ground of a shore, so an emotion of love, an exuberance of delight, a noble sacrifice wants to hurl itself on an enormous sorrow.

In such a state of mind, one day Harasundari joyfully decided: 'For my husband I will do something that is ideally the greatest. But alas, whoever had the ability as much as the desire? Well, what is at my disposal that can be given? No wealth, no talents, no power, only a life is all I have: all right, if even that life is to be laid down for someone, so be it and right now. Nevertheless, what is even that life worth?

'Besides, had I been able to give my husband a darling doll of a child, fair as milk-froth, soft as cream, graceful as an infant-god! But that is never to be, howsoever I may wish.' Then she thought she must get her husband married again. She wondered why wives were so squeamish about it. It was by no means a difficult task. For one who loved her husband, how was it impossible to love her co-wife as well? Her heart swelled with pride.

When he heard the proposal for the first time, Nibaran laughed it off; he paid no heed the second and the third time as well. This disapproval, this reluctance of her husband enhanced Harasundari's trust and happiness as much as they reinforced her determination.

On the other hand, the more he heard the request over and over, the more its impossibility was dispelled from his mind, and as he sat on the doorstep smoking tobacco, the more the happy picture of a house swarming with children kept brightening up in his mind.

One day, he broached the subject on his own and said, 'I can't marry a little girl at this ripe age and then take the bother of bringing her up.'

'You don't need to worry about that,' said Harasundari. 'Bringing her up is my responsibility.' Simultaneously in the mind of this childless woman, there appeared the visage of an adolescent, tender, bashful bride barely separated from her mother's lap, and her heart melted with affection.

Nibaran said, 'I've my office, and other kinds of work, besides you. I won't have the time to listen to the whims of a tiny girl.'

She assured him repeatedly. 'You won't have to waste a moment for her.' In the end, she said jokingly, 'All right, all right. I will see then what becomes of your work, what becomes of me, and what of you.' Nibaran did not think it necessary to give any reply to it and returned the jest by tapping her cheek with his forefinger. So much for the preface.

## 2

With a nose-ring wearing, tear-laden, small girl Nibaran got married eventually; her name was Shailabala.

Nibaran thought: the name sounds very sweet; the face is also suffused with fullness. Her expressions, her features, her movement, everything I wish so much to watch and have a good look at, but it just doesn't happen. On the contrary, I have to pretend, 'All she is, is a slip of a girl, and see what trouble she's been. Somehow evading her, if I could go back to the sphere of work suitable to my age, I would have been relieved.'

Noticing this predicament of Nibaran, Harasundari felt a great deal of amusement. On some days, grabbing hold of his hand she would say, 'Come, come, where are you scooting off? Surely that slip of a girl isn't going to eat you up, is she?' Pretending to be busier than he was, Nibaran would say, 'Away with it! I've some special work,' looking unable to find where to escape. Guarding the door, Harasundari would laugh and say, 'Today you can't evade me.' At last, as if compelled, Nibaran would sit down on the bed, looking sad.

Harasundari would whisper in his ears, 'Fie on you, after bringing home another man's daughter, you ought not to neglect her so unfairly.' She would then make Shailabala sit on Nibaran's left, and forcibly parting her veil and lifting her bent head by the chin, say, 'Oh, see how beautiful like the moon her face is.'

Another day she would excuse herself leaving the two alone in the room, and shut the door behind with a bang. Nibaran knew for certain that two inquisitive eyes were glued to one slit or another; turning over with extreme indifference, he would pretend to sleep; crouching with her veil pulled down and face turned away, Shailabala would disappear into a corner. At last, Harasundari, having completely failed, gave up in desperation, but without much regret.

When Harasundari's efforts ceased, Nibaran himself entered the fray. It was such a curiosity, such mystery: a piece of diamond evokes the wish to watch from different sides, different angles, then what to say of the human mind, the mind of a cute little human being. It has to be appreciated in so many ways: by touching it, by caressing it, by watching it—from behind, from the front, from the side. Sometimes tweaking the earring, sometimes slightly lifting the veil, sometimes suddenly with a start like lightning, sometimes staring long like viewing the stars as newer and newer frontiers of beauty have to be discovered.

The head clerk of the McMoran Company Sri Nibaranchandra had never before had such an experience. When he had first married, he had been a mere boy. By the time he attained his youth, his wife had become long familiar, married life extremely habituated. He did love Harasundari, but never in his mind had gradual and conscious awakening of love occurred.

An insect that has germinated right within a ripe mango, that has never had to explore the juice, never had to taste it little by little— just release such a one in a bower of full-blosommed flowers of spring, and then watch: what avidity in flitting round and round at the half-open mouth of a blooming bud of rose! A little whiff of fragrance it smells, a little drop of nectar it tastes makes it so drunk!

Nibaran started giving Shailabala little presents in secret: sometimes a glass doll in a gown, sometimes a bottle of perfume or some sweetmeat. In this way, a little intimacy developed. At last one day, Harasundari, coming at an opportune moment in between her household chores, peeping through the door slit found that Nibaran and Shailabala were playing '*ten-twenty-five*'[3] with cowries.

A game indeed for a mature man! Hadn't Nibaran, after eating his meal in the morning, set out for the office? So then, instead of going to office, he had sneaked into the inner rooms! What was the need of this deception? Suddenly with a burning poker of thunder, as it were, someone opened her eyes wide, and in that intense heat, the tears in her eyes dried up by evaporating. To herself she said, 'Who had brought her home? Who had united them? If it is me, then why do they behave with me in this way—as if I am a thorn in their happiness?'

For some time now, Harasundari had been training Shailabala in household work. One day, Nibaran brought himself to speak, 'She's a mere child. You're working her too hard; she's not so strong physically, you see.'

A sharp riposte had come to her lips, but without saying anything, she fell silent.

From then on, she would never allow the bride to perform any chore; cooking, scrubbing, washing, everything she would do by herself. Eventually, Shailabala was reduced to a sitting doll, Harasundari waiting upon her like a handmaiden, and Nibaran entertaining her like a court jester. Shailabala never learned the lesson that doing housework and caring for others were primary duties of life. The way Harasundari carried on working as a maidservant had an aura of pride; there was no inferiority or meanness about it. She said to herself, 'Together you two children, you keep playing. Alone I take up the charge of this house.'

## *3*

Alas, where was that strength today which had once empowered her to contemplate that for her husband's sake, she could relinquish without demur half her own claim to love? Suddenly one full-moon night when a tidal wave enters one's life, then overflowing the shores, one thinks, 'I have no boundaries.' One's entire being is put to great strain in trying to keep the lofty promise, made impulsively, during the long ebb tide of life. In times of sudden affluence, the deed of gift one signs with a single stroke of the pen, one has to repay every fraction of a second pie-by-pie[4] in times of perpetual poverty. Then one realises how poor man is, how feeble the heart is, and how meagre one's power.

Lean, anaemic and pale following her prolonged illness, Harasundari resembled the crescent moon of the second lunar day; she led an attenuated existence in the domestic world. She had thought, 'It seems even without having anything whatsoever, I can get along.' By and by, her body regained its strength, her blood circulation improved, and then a faction of co-sharers from somewhere crowded her mind; they raised a clamour: 'It is all very well for you to have signed up to sacrifice yourself, but we won't give up our claims.'

The day Harasundari first realised her condition clearly, vacating her own bedroom for Nibaran and Shailabala, she went to sleep alone in a separate room.

The bed she had first slept in on her wedding night at the age of eight, she relinquished today after twenty-seven years. After blowing out the lamp, when this married woman with an unbearably heavy heart threw herself on her new bed of widowhood, a fashionable young man was then singing a woman flower-vendor's song in raga *behag* at the other end of the lane; another man was accompanying him on the *tabla*, with the audience appreciating the synchronisation of beats with loud applause. That song in that silent moonlit night did not sound discordant in the next room. Girlish bride Shailabala's eyelids were then drooping in drowsiness, with Nibaran cooing sweet nothings into her ears.

By now, Nibaran had read Bankimchandra's *Chandrashekhar*[5] himself and to Shailabala he had read out the works of several modern poets as well. Deep down in Nibaran's life, a fountain of youth that had remained plugged all along, now being unplugged, gushed forth suddenly at a most inopportune moment. No one was prepared for that, and so his sensibility and judgement as well as the entire system of the family were thrown into utter confusion. The poor fellow had never known that such disruptive elements did exist within human beings, such devastatingly wild powers that threw all calculations and assumptions, order and symmetry into complete disarray.

Not only Nibaran, but Harasundari too experienced a new sense of anguish. What was this yearning for? What was giving her this unbearable torment? What her mind now wanted it had never wanted, and never received either. When Nibaran used to go to office regularly like the average person, when for some time before going to sleep they used to discuss the milkman's bill, rising cost of articles, and social obligations, this inner turmoil was not even incipient. She did love him, indeed, but that love of course had no lustre, no warmth. It was merely like unlit fuel.

Today she felt as if someone had all along been depriving her of the fulfilment of life, as if her heart had forever been starving. Her feminine life had been spent virtually as a destitute. All she had done spending twenty-seven invaluable years was slaving with shopping, cooking and paan making. Today, halfway though her life, she saw that right next to her bedroom, by unlocking a secret vault of priceless treasure a little girl was enthroned as the empress straightaway. True, a woman was a servant, but at the same time she was a queen as well. Nevertheless, dividing the dual role one woman had become servant; the other, queen. Thereby the servant's pride was gone, and the queen's happiness was lost.

For, neither did Shailabala ever get a taste of the genuine happiness of a woman's life: she received such unremitting caresses that not a moment was left for love. Heading for the sea, sacrificing itself into it, perhaps a river has a noble mission to fulfil. But if the sea, heaving under the pull of high tide, were to be increasingly anxious for the river, then the river would only keep accumulating itself within. The world with all its care and affection kept waiting solicitously day and night for Shailabala; consequently, Shailabala's narcissistic admiration kept soaring without bounds; to the world in turn, not a trickle of her love could ever flow. She came to know: 'Everything is for me; I am for no one whosoever.' In such conviction, there is hubris, but no contentment at all.

## 4

One day, inky black clouds had gathered; it had become so dark that even indoors it was impossible to do any work. Outside, it was raining in sheets. The jungle of weeds and creepers under the jujube tree was almost submerged, and muddy water was burbling down the drain along the broken wall. In the solitary darkness of her new bedroom, Harasundari was sitting silently beside the window.

At that time, gingerly like a thief, Nibaran drew up to the door, unable to decide whether to return or to approach. Harasundari noticed this, but did not say a word. Then Nibaran, suddenly going straight like an arrow to her, blurted out in one breath, 'A few ornaments have become necessary. As you know, I have run into several debts. Creditors are harassing badly. Something needs to be pawned. I think I can redeem it soon enough.' Harasundari gave no reply; Nibaran kept standing like a culprit. At last, he asked once again, 'So you're not going to give any today?'

Harasundari said, 'No.'

Exiting from the room was as difficult as entering into it had been. Nibaran, looking this way and that, and hesitating a little, muttered, 'Then, let me try elsewhere,' and left.

Where the debts had been incurred and where ornaments were to be pawned Harasundari knew it all. She deduced that the previous night the newly-wed wife had hectored this bemused and biddable man of hers, saying, '*Didi* has a safe full of jewellery. And you think I can't wear even one piece?'

When Nibaran was gone, taking her time Harasundari got up, unlocked the iron safe and took out all the ornaments one by one. Calling Shailabala in, first she gave her own wedding *Benarasi* sari to wear, and then decked her from head to foot with the entire set of ornaments one after another. Doing up her hair tastefully, and then lighting a lamp she found time to have a good look at her: the girl's face was very nice indeed; like a recently ripened, sweet-smelling fruit, well-formed and luscious. When Shailabala walked away, the sound of her ornaments kept jangling in Harasundari's veins, in her blood for a long while afterwards. She thought, 'Today what is there with which I can compare with you, dear? But one day, I too was that age, wasn't I? I too filled out to the last curve of youth, did I not? Then why did someone not give me the message? When that day had come, when that day went by I was not even informed either. But look at the pride, the swagger, with which Shailabala is walking away, the waves she makes.'

When homemaking was all Harasundari knew, how precious these ornaments had been to her! Then, like a fool, could she have let this go out of hand in this way in a moment? Now besides homemaking, she had sensed another thing, something great; now the price of ornaments, provision for the future, everything had become insignificant.

On the other hand, Shailabala walked away sparkling with gold to her bedroom, not even for a moment realising the extent of what Harasundari had given her. She knew that coming from all sides, all the attention, all the wealth, all the good fortune would as a matter of course end ultimately in her; for, she was Shailabala; she was her husband's sweetheart.

## 5

In his somnambulism, someone can walk fearlessly along a perilous path without a moment's thought. There are people, who even in their waking state have similar spells of trance when all judgement vanishes, and they dash forward through the narrow path of danger blithely, until finally waking up to a catastrophe.

Our head clerk of the McMoran Company was just such a person. In the centre of his life, Shailabala kept whirling like a powerful vortex, and sucked in from afar various costly things kept disappearing into it. Not only Nibaran's humanity and salary, Harasundari's happiness and ornaments, but it surreptitiously tugged at McMoran Company's cash fund as well: bundles of currency notes kept vanishing in ones and twos. Nibaran resolved each time that he would replenish the fund from his salary over the next few months. But the moment the next month's salary came to his hand, it was pulled by that vortex, down to the last two-anna coin, coruscating for a trice, before it vanished at lightning speed .

Finally, he was caught. His was a hereditary job. The sahib liked him very much; he allowed him two days' time to replenish the cash. How he had defalcated a staggering two and a half thousand rupees over a period was even beyond Nibaran's own comprehension. Almost driven mad, he turned to Harasundari. 'I'm ruined.'

Harasundari went pale on hearing everything.

Nibaran said, 'Immediately take out the ornaments.'

'Where do I get them? I've given them all away to *chhotobau.*'

Utterly impatient like a child, Nibaran cried out, 'Why did you give it to chhotobau? Why did you? Who told you to give?'

Instead of giving the true reply, Harasundari said, 'What was the harm there? Has it gone to waste?'

A timid Nibaran ruefully said, 'Then possibly you can find some pretext to get them back. But for heaven's sake, don't tell her I want it or for that matter, why I want it.'

Now Harasundari burst out in utter disgust and scorn: 'Pretext? Is this the time for pretexts or pussyfooting? Come with me.' Along with him, she entered chhotobau's room.

Shailabala refused to see reason. To everything they said, she replied, 'How does it concern me?'

Had there been any understanding with her that she would ever have to worry about any family concern? Everyone was supposed to think of oneself, and all the others together were to think about Shailabala's comfort: suddenly now this is sought to be violated. What gross injustice!

Nibaran then fell weeping at Shailabala's feet. Shailabala only kept saying, 'I don't care. Why should I give away my personal possessions?'

Nibaran discovered that the delicate, tender-looking, puny weakling was even harder than the iron safe. Seeing this cowardice of her husband at a critical time, Harasundari was mortified with shame; she tried to wrest the key from Shailabala. Shailabala pre-empted it by flinging the bunch across the wall into the pond.

Harasundari exhorted her confused husband, 'Why don't you break the lock?'

'In that case, I'll hang myself,' said Shailabala with a placid face.

'I'm going to try another source,' said Nibaran and rushed out, in a dishevelled state.

In just two hours, Nibaran sold off his ancestral house for two and a half thousand rupees.

After great effort, he escaped jail, but lost his job. As for movable and immovable property, all he was left with was two wives only; of them, the sorrow-laden girl wife, meanwhile being pregnant, became virtually immovable. In a small damp house in the lane, this small family then took shelter.

## 6

Chhotobau had no end of grievance and discontent. By no means was she going to recognise that her husband was incapable. All right, if he was incapable, why had he got married?

There were only two rooms upstairs. One room was Nibaran and Shailabala's bedroom; in the other, lived Harasundari. Shailabala used to grumble, 'I can't spend day and night in a bedroom.' Nibaran, giving false assurance would assure, 'Looking for a better house. We'll soon shift.'

Shailabala said, 'Why, isn't there another room next to this?'

Shailabala had never cared to have a good look at her former neighbours. Disturbed by Nibaran's recent plight, they came on a visit one day. Shailabala shut herself in, after bolting the door, adamantly refusing to open it. When they left, she threw a tantrum, fuming, weeping, fasting, and having hysteric fits, almost driving the neighbours mad. Such disturbances happened frequently.

In the end, at a critical stage of her pregnancy, Shailabala fell seriously ill; she even ran the risk of miscarriage. Nibaran begged Harasundari, holding her hands, 'You must save her.'

Harasundari kept nursing Shailabala day and night without rest. If there was the slightest lapse, Shaila would rebuke her with harsh words; she would not give a single reply. Shaila hated to take sago-water: she would throw it away with the cup, and while running a temperature, insist on rice with green mango chutney. If denied, she would raise hell. With blandishments like, 'My Lakshmi[6]', 'My good sister', 'My darling *Didi*', Harasundari would try to comfort her like a child.

But Shailabala did not survive. Having received all the care and affection of the family, an utterly unhappy and disgruntled girl's brief futile life ended prematurely.

## 7

Nibaran at first received a great shock, but next moment realised that some mighty shackles had snapped. Even in bereavement, suddenly he felt a joy of liberation; it struck him that the load of a nightmare had been weighing him down. As soon as he recovered his senses, his life became insubstantially light. Was this his darling Shailabala, tender like a myrtle creeper, his life-snare just detached? Suddenly taking a deep breath, he felt no, it was his halter.

Then, what was his lifelong companion, Harasundari? He discovered that occupying his entire world all by herself, she alone was sitting in the shrine of memories of all his joys and sorrows; nevertheless, there was a chasm in between. It was just as if a small, shining, handsome, cruel knife had cut a painful incision along the median line of his heart.

At dead of night one day, when the entire town was asleep, Nibaran quietly entered Harasundari's secluded bedroom, silently lay down on their old bed occupying the right side following the old system. But this time, into his perpetual domain he entered like a thief.

Neither Harasundari nor Nibaran spoke a word. Just as they used to lie side by side previously, now too they lay side by side; but right in the middle the apparition of a girl kept lying; neither could disregard her.

*Jyaishtha 1300* (1894)

NOTES

1 Physician practising ayurvedic medicine.
2 See 'polygamy' in Glossary.
3 A simple game played by small girls in rural Bengal.
4 A very small former Indian coin worth one-third of a pice, the latter worth one-sixteenth of a rupee.
5 A historical novel based on the conflict between Mirkassim and the East India Company. The extramarital romance between Pratap and Shaibalini, her husband Chandrashekhar's idealism, and the pair's redemption through mortification and death are the principal motifs.
6 See 'Lakshmi' in Glossary.

# The Haldar Family
# (*Haldargoshthi*)

This was one family with no reasonable ground for conflict. It was well-to-do, and its members were none too bad. Yet, a conflict arose.

It had to: if everything in life were to happen only on reasonable grounds, the world would resemble an exercise book of arithmetic: if you approached a bit carefully, no mistake would occur in your calculation; even if it did, all you needed to do was to erase and correct.

But providence has a wry sense of humour. Whether he is or is not proficient in mathematics is anybody's guess, but certainly, he has no interest in it: he does not bother to work out the net result of transactions in human life. Therefore, he has interlaced his system with an element called incongruity. With abrupt intervention, it plays havoc with what is seemingly possible. This is what thickens the plot of drama, overflowing the shores of the domestic sea with waves of laughter and tears.

This is exactly what happened in this case: where there was a lotus pool, there descended a rogue elephant. Mire and the mire-grown ended up in an incompatible association. Were it not so, this story would not have been written.

The worthiest member of this family was Banwarilal; there is no doubt about it. He knew it all too well himself, which is what had been agitating him. Competence, like the steam of an engine, drove him from within; if he found a road ahead, well and good; if not, he rammed into whatever he encountered on the way.

His father Manoharlal had the traditionally maintained airs of the affluent. His cherished desire was that ascending the top rung of the society he dominated, he would remain its crown. So he had no connection with its hands and feet. Ordinary mortals are used to doing work; they move about. What Manoharlal used to do was to stay firmly at the centre of the elaborate arrangement of not doing any work and not making any movement.

Such people are often found to attract at least one or two tough and genuine persons to themselves quite effortlessly as if magnetically. This is simply because a tribe of people are born with the instinct to serve. Just to fulfil that instinct, they look for such worthless fellows as can entrust their well-being entirely to their care. These natural servants find no pleasure in serving their own interests; but making someone else carefree, keeping him in the best of comforts, shielding him from all adversity, enhancing his prestige in society—this is what gives them utmost pleasure. They are, as it were, a sort of male mother, and that too, not of their own sons, but another's.

Manoharlal's servant was Ramcharan: his sole object of keeping fit and toiling hard was to keep his master's body protected. If his own breathing could spare his master the necessity of breathing, he would willingly have panted day and night like a blacksmith's bellows. Outsiders often thought that perhaps Manoharlal was unfairly torturing his servant by making him work unnecessarily. Not without reason, though: the tube of his hubble-bubble might drop from his hand on the floor; picking it up was no difficult job; yet, for this purpose if he were to holler out to Ramcharan making him run from another room, it did look most unseemly. Nevertheless, in countless such dispensable matters making himself indispensable was what gave Ramcharan utmost satisfaction.

As was his Ramcharan, so was another attendant Nilkantha. The charge of managing the estate lay on this Nilkantha. Nourished by his master's favours, Ramlochan was quite plump and glossy, but Nilkantha's body was virtually all skin and bone. At the door of his master's treasury, he stood guard like the embodiment of famine. The property was Manoharlal's, but the attachment for it was entirely Nilkantha's.

Discord between Banwarilal and Nilkantha had been continuing for long . Suppose, by pleading with his father, Banwarilal managed to obtain the approval for ordering a new ornament for his wife. Now, he would expect the money to be released in advance so he could place the order according to his own choice. But that was not to be. Every expense-related work must be handled exclusively by Nilkantha. The result would be two-fold: the ornament delivered would be to no one's liking and Banwari would be convinced that Nilkantha received a cut from the jeweller. Men of strict principles do not lack enemies. From a good number of people, Banwari had been hearing the same thing: the more Nilkantha deprived others, the more he lined his own pocket.

Yet, the conflicts that had been brewing on either side involved quite petty sums. Nilkantha, being a man of shrewd judgement, did recognise that unless he was on good terms with Banwari, he might in future get into trouble. Nevertheless, Nilkantha was parsimonious vis-à-vis his master's wealth. What he considered unjustified, he could by no means spend, notwithstanding his master's orders.

On the other hand, Banwari had been frequently feeling the need for unjustified expenditure. The factor lying at the root of many improper affairs of males was present here too in no small measure. There might be various opinions about the beauty of Banwari's wife Kiranlekha; we need not go into that; Banwari's own opinion is alone material to the present context. In fact, the other women of the family considered his passion for his wife nothing but an excess. In other words, it was just as much attention as they would have wished from their husbands, yet were deprived of.

Whatever Kiranlekha's age might be, from her figure it seemed she was a mere child. Hers was nothing of the matronly appearance and demeanour befitting the eldest daughter-in-law of a family. Overall, she seemed like a speck of a thing.

Banwari endearingly called her Anu[1]. When he found this too big to convey his love, he called her Paramanu[2]. Those who know chemistry are aware of the enormous power of these particles in the phenomena of the universe.

Kiran had never asked anything of her husband. She bore such an indifferent attitude as though she had no necessity of anything in particular. In the family, many were her sisters-in-law; she was fully preoccupied day and night with their concerns alone: she scarcely felt any need for the quiet contemplation demanded by the newly awakened love of early youth. For this reason, she evinced little enthusiasm in her interaction with Banwari. Whatever he gave her she accepted without demur, never advancing to solicit anything. Naturally, Banwari had to think out for himself just how to please his wife. When the wife puts up her demands candidly, it can be cut down at least to some extent through negotiation, but how can one negotiate with oneself? In such a case, an unsolicited gift proves costlier than a solicited one.

If that was not enough, there was no knowing how pleased she was on receiving her husband's gifts of love. If asked about this, she would say, 'Fine! Good!' But Banwari's doubts just lingered: it kept recurring in his mind that perhaps she did not like it. Mildly reproving her husband, Kiran would say, 'That is but your nature. Why keep repining? Why, it's quite fine.'

Banwari had read in his textbooks that contentment is a great virtue. Nevertheless, its presence in his wife's nature pained him. His wife had not merely satisfied him, she had enchanted him; he too wished to enchant her in turn. His wife did not have to make any special effort: the gracefulness of youth overflowed quite naturally and the skill in her manner of caring for him was openly manifest. But a man has no such privilege; to demonstrate his masculinity, he has to build up something tangible with his talents. Unless he can prove that he has some special power, a male's love remains pallid. Even if he has nothing other than wealth, which at any rate is an expression of power, if like a peacock's tail he can display that wealth in all its splendour, it gives his mind some consolation after all. Nilkantha had time and again stood in the way of Banwari executing this plan to exhibit his love. Banwari was the eldest son of the family, yet had no authority over anything; Nilkantha, emboldened by the master's indulgence, despite being a servant lorded it over him. The constraint and humiliation of it was not so much due to anything as much as his inability adequately to load the quiver of Cupid.

Eventually, the right to all this wealth would devolve exclusively on him, wouldn't it? But would his youth last forever? The colourful cup of spring would not fill spontaneously with nectar as it did now. His wealth would by then solidify into a coagulated mass, like ice on mountain peaks, allowing no waves of carefree abandon and wasteful expenditure to play in it. If money was any use, now was the time, when the vigour to squander it merrily had not been lost yet.

Banwari had three habits in the main: wrestling, hunting and cultivating Sanskrit. His notebook was heavily laden with Sanskrit absurd verses[3]: on rainy days, in the south wind or on moonlit nights, they proved very useful. The advantage was that Nilkantha had no authority to cut back on the rhetorical ornaments of these verses. Howsoever extravagant the hyperboles might be, there was no compulsion to explain it at the office of the treasurer. There might have been stinginess about the gold content in Kiran's earrings, but in the metre of the *mandakranta*[4] verse hummed into her ears, not even one measure was missed, and in its passion, there was practically no limit in the extent.

Tall and robust Banwari had a wrestler's figure. When he became angry, people were struck with fear. But the mind of this robust man was very tender at the core. When his younger brother Bangshilal was small, Banwari had nurtured him with motherly affection. It seemed as if in his heart there was a hunger for rearing.

The fact that he loved his wife so much was associated with this aspect as well, this yearning to nurture. Kiranlekha was as slight as a stray sliver of light in the shadow of trees, and just because she was small, she had kept a special compassion ever awake in her husband's heart. This little wife of his he was very eager to adorn variously in clothes and ornaments and then behold admiringly. This was not the joy of lust, but the joy of creation, of making many out of one, of watching Kiranlekha in different hues and different attires from different perspectives.

But merely reciting Sanskrit verses could scarcely satisfy Banwari's urge. Neither could he display the masculine power in him; nor could he fulfil his desire to embellish the object of love with opulent gifts.

Thus did the son of a rich man, for all his honour and fame, a beautiful wife, his vibrant youth, everything that people generally desire, eventually grow into a sort of nuisance in the family.

Sukhada was Madhu Kaibarta's[5] wife, a tenant of Manoharlal's. She came into the inner quarters one day and fell crying at Kiranlekha's feet. The fact of the matter is this: a few years ago, to buy dragnets, fishermen had taken a loan of a thousand rupees giving a joint undertaking as in previous years. If there was a good haul, there was no problem paying up the loan together with interest, so they did not hesitate to borrow the money even at an exorbitant rate of interest. That year, the catch had not been up to expectation, and incidentally, for consecutive three years, there was such a low influx of fish at the river bend that the turnover hardly covered their costs; moreover, they were entangled in a web of debt. Those members of the syndicate who had come from different areas simply disappeared, but Madhu Kaibarta being a resident tenant had no scope to evade payment, and so the entire responsibility for the loan had fallen on him. Sukhada had come to seek Kiran's aid with the appeal to save them from ruin. As was known to everybody, it was no use approaching Kiran's mother-in-law, because that lady could not even imagine that anyone could so much as interfere with Nilkantha's administration. At the same time, Madhu knew that Banwari harboured a grudge against Nilkantha, so he had sent his wife to plead with Kiran.

Despite his anger and blustering, Kiran knew definitely that Banwari had no authority to interfere with Nilkantha's decisions. She repeatedly tried to explain the matter to Sukhada. 'What can we do after all? As you know, we have no say in this matter. The master is there; tell Madhu to approach him directly.'

That attempt had already been made. Whenever any complaint was made to Manoharlal, it was invariably referred back to Nilkantha for disposal, which only aggravated the predicament of the complainant. If anyone wanted to appeal for a second time, the master would be furious: if he were to undertake the bother of management of property, where was his happiness in enjoying property?

While Sukhada was whining away before Kiran, Banwari was in the next room, oiling the barrel of his gun. He had heard every word of their conversation. Kiran's oft-repeated miserable pleas that they were unable to help in any way pierced his heart as a shaft.

That day was the full moon day of *Magh* on the eve of *Phalgun*. The sultriness of the day suddenly in the evening broke into a wild wind. The cuckoo kept cooing incessantly, by repeatedly sounding a single note trying to overturn some listlessness somewhere. And the sky was overflowing with the fragrance of flowers, as if there was the hustle and bustle of a fair. From the inner garden right beside the window, the scent of *champak* flowers lent a heavy intoxication to the vernal sky. That day, Kiran was wearing a *latkan*-dyed[6] sari and a garland of jasmine on her bun. As was customary with this couple, for Banwari also a latkan-dyed chuddar and a thick garland of jasmine suitable for celebrating the Phalgun festival had been laid out. The early hours of night went by, yet there was no sign of Banwari. The brimming cup of youth did not appeal to his taste then. How could he enter Lord Krishna's abode of love with such overwhelming diffidence in his heart? He had no power to relieve Madhu Kaivarta's distress; Nilkantha had that power! Whoever had woven the wreath to garland such a coward?

First, he called Nilkantha into his outer room and forbade him to forfeit Madhu Kaibarta's property for unpaid debt. Nilkantha argued that if Madhu was given a reprieve, everyone else would make similar demands and a huge sum on the verge of forfeiture would have to be written off. When he failed to best him in argument, Banwari started reviling Nilkantha right and left. He called him low-born[7]. Nilkantha retorted, 'If I were not low-born, why should I have to depend on the high-born[8]?" He called him a thief. Nilkantha said, 'Of course! One whom God has not given anything to own has necessarily to survive on other's wealth.' All Banwari's invectives he bore gracefully. Finally, he said, 'The lawyer is waiting. I must go. If you find it necessary, I'll come later.'

Banwari decided that enlisting his younger brother Bangshi to his side, he would confront his father forthwith. He knew that going alone would be counterproductive: just a few days ago, he had had some altercation with his father over the same Nilkantha; his father was already annoyed with him. Yet, there was a time when everyone used to believe that Manoharlal loved his eldest son most of all. But now, from all appearances, his preference was for Bangshi. That is why Banwari wanted to include Bangshi as a party to his deputation.

Bangshi was a perfectly good boy. In the family, he alone had passed a couple of examinations. He was now preparing for the law examination, staying up all day and night preparing his lessons. God knows whether he was accruing anything inwardly, but physically, he looked run-down.

Even on this evening in early spring, the windows in his room were closed. He dreaded the transitional period of seasons; he had not the least compatibility with the open air. A kerosene lamp was burning on the table; some books were lying in a pile on the floor beside his bed, some others were on the table; in the recess in a wall were some bottles of medicine.

Bangshi was totally opposed to Banwari's proposal. Banwari flared up, 'So you're scared of Nilkantha!' Bangshi made no response to that and kept silent. In fact, he did always try to keep Nilkantha favourably disposed towards him. He used to spend most of the year in lodges in Calcutta, where as a matter of course, he required more than his fixed allowance. In this context, he was used to keeping Nilkantha in good humour.

Banwari called Bangshi a craven, a coward, a toady of Nilkantha and went off to settle with his father all by himself. Manoharlal was sitting on the *ghat* of their garden pool baring his plump body to the evening breeze. Clustered around him were his henchmen recounting a flattering tale of how the neighbouring zamindar Akhil Majumdar had recently been harassed in the district court by their barrister from Calcutta. On that spring evening, this story enhanced with the fragrant air had become a most delightful treat to him.

Banwari's sudden intrusion spoilt the mood. He was not in a position to broach his point with much ceremony. Pitching his voice right away to the top, he came out straight: Nilkantha was damaging their interests; he was a thief, misappropriating his master's funds and filling his own coffers. The allegation had no proof and it was not true either: Nilkantha had brought them prosperity; neither was he a thief. Banwari had thought that it was because of the master's unshakeable trust in Nilkantha's honesty that he relied on him with total unconcern in every matter. This was a wrong perception. Manoharlal had the firm idea that Nilkantha did steal whenever he had the opportunity. Nevertheless, on that score, he had no hatred for him, because from time immemorial, such had been the way of the world: it is on the leftovers of filching retinues that the affluent had forever subsisted. Whence would one, who was not smart enough to steal, have the shrewdness to preserve the property of one's master? After all, it was not for a *Dharmaputra* Yudhishthira[9] to manage an estate. 'All right, all right,' he cut in petulantly, 'you need not worry about what Nilkantha does or does not do.' He further said, 'Look at Bangshi. Does he ever bother about anything? How well he is carrying on with his studies! That lad is rather something of a man.'

After this, the tale of Akhil Majumdar's harassment no longer seemed entertaining enough. Naturally, as far as Manoharlal was concerned, thereafter the spring breeze blew in vain and the shimmering of moonlight on the dark waters of the lake proved useless. Only for Bangshi and Nilkantha did the evening not turn out to be futile. After closing his windows, Bangshi studied until late into the night and Nilkantha spent almost half the night in discussions with the lawyer.

Kiran was sitting by the window after putting out the lamp. Today, she had finished her work rather early. The night meal was not taken, but Banwari had not returned yet, so she was waiting. Kiran had altogether forgotten about Madhu Kaivarta. She had no grievance at all that Banwari had no power to alleviate Madhu's sorrow. She had never expected her husband to display any special talent. The family glory lent itself to her husband. He was her father-in-law's eldest son: that he must outgrow this identity had never even occurred to her. They were after all the renowned Haldar family of Gossainganj.

After pacing about in the veranda until late in the night, Banwari came into the room. He had forgotten that he had not eaten. The fact that Kiran had been waiting for him without having eaten particularly struck him that day. This self-inflicted austerity of Kiran seemed to be at odds with his own worthlessness. Every morsel of food almost choked him. Very excitedly, he told his wife, 'I shall save Madhu, whatever it takes.' Kiran was surprised at this unwarranted vehemence. 'Just listen to him!' she said, 'How can you—of all men—save him?'

Banwari would pay off Madhu's debt himself; this was his resolve, but he had hardly any savings to speak of. He decided to sell off one of his three vintage guns and a costly diamond ring. But such quality goods would not fetch suitable price in a village, and even trying to sell them would set off rumours. Therefore, finding some pretext, Banwari went away to Calcutta. Before he left, he called Madhu and assured him that he need have no fear.

Meanwhile, understanding that Madhu had sought Banwari's intervention, Nilkantha became furious with Madhu. The persecution by his bailiffs banished all semblance of dignity from the Kaibarta settlement.

The very day Banwari returned from Calcutta, Madhu's son Swarup came running and panting, and clutching his feet started a howling wail. 'What's up, eh? What's the matter?' Nilkantha had kept his father locked up in the estate office since the previous night, said Swarup. Banwari trembled in rage. 'Go report to the police immediately,' he said.

Heavens! Report to the police! Against Nilkantha! His feet refused to budge. In the end, urged by Banwari, he did go and report. The police swooped down on the estate office, freed Madhu, and taking Nilkantha and a few bailiffs into custody despatched them as the accused to the magistrate.

Manohar found himself in a predicament. His counsels, on the pretext of paying bribes swindled him, splitting the money with the police. A barrister arrived from Calcutta; he was a novice who had just started taking his briefs. The advantage with him was that what was accounted for as his fees did not go entirely to his pocket. Fielded for Madhu, on the other hand, was a veteran lawyer from the district court. Who exactly was affording his fees was not clear. Nilkantha was sentenced to six months' imprisonment. He appealed to the high court, but the sentence was upheld.

Not in vain had the diamond ring and the gun sold at good prices: for the time being, Madhu escaped and Nilkantha went to jail. But how after this incident could he possibly survive in his homestead? Banwari told him reassuringly, 'Stay put. You don't have to fear.' Just what had emboldened him to give the assurance he alone knew: maybe it was the sheer arrogance of his masculinity.

Banwari had made no special effort to hide the fact that he was at the root of this untoward event. It was out; it even reached the master's ears. The master sent word through his servant: 'Banwari must never come in front of me.' Banwari did not disobey his father's orders.

Kiran was staggered at her husband's behaviour. What was this! Eldest son of the family: not on speaking terms with his father! Moreover, by sending their own official to jail he had lowered the prestige of the family before the entire world! And that too, for an underling like Madhu Kaibarta!

Strange indeed! In this family, so many eldest sons had been born over so many years, and never were Nilkanthas scarce, either. Nilkanthas had themselves taken the entire responsibility of the estate and the eldest sons in complete idleness had minded the family name. Such preposterous happenings had never taken place.

Today the lowering of the eldest son's position in the family undermined the eldest daughter-in-law's prestige. Today after all these years, Kiran found reason enough to disrespect her husband. After all these years, her springtime latkan-coloured sari and the jasmine garland on her hair went pale in shame.

Kiran had come of age, yet had not borne a child. This Nilkantha, one day persuading the old master, after inspecting a bride had almost settled another marriage for Banwari. Banwari was the eldest scion of the Haldar family; this had to be kept in mind foremost of all. That he should remain without a son was out of the question. Kiran had felt a tremor in her heart in this matter. Nevertheless, she could not hold herself from admitting that the point was reasonable enough. Even then, she had not been angry with Nilkantha, rather blamed her own fate. If her husband had not confronted Nilkantha aggressively, and quarrelling with his parents forced them to cancel the negotiation, Kiran would still not have thought it unjust. In fact, Kiran had felt an insidious disrespect for his manliness for not giving a thought to the family's interests. Was the demand of a noble family a trifling matter? It certainly had the right to be cruel. Compared to that, what was the value of the joys and sorrows of some young wife or some indigent Kaibarta?

If what happens as a matter of course does not happen occasionally, nobody can forgive it; Banwari could not realise this. He ought to have proved himself the perfect eldest son of this family; that it was wrong for him to disturb the continuity of the system by deliberating on other just or unjust things was very clear to everyone except him.

On this score, Kiran had often expressed her discontent to her younger brother-in-law. Bangshi was intelligent; he was dyspeptic and on slight exposure to the elements had a terrible bout of sneezing and coughing, but he was calm, composed and astute. Putting down his law book, with the chapter he had been reading turned over on the table, he said, 'This is sheer madness.' Kiran nodded anxiously and said, 'You know your brother, *Thakurpo*. When he is in good humour, there's no problem, but once he loses his cool, he becomes unmanageable. Tell me what am I to do?'

When Kiran's opinion fully concurred with that of every sensible person of the family, it upset Banwari most of all. This wisp of a woman, delicate as a half-bloomed magnolia: to make her share his own anguish all his male strength proved inadequate! Now, if Kiran could perfectly identify with him, the laceration in his heart would not have assumed such proportions.

That Madhu must be protected was simply a matter of duty, which, due to external provocation, really became an obsession with Banwari; compared to this, everything else seemed trivial to him. Meanwhile, Nilkantha returned from jail, looking so healthy as though he had gone visiting his father-in-law's house on the special invitation of *Jamai-shashthi*[10]. He resumed his work with total nonchalance.

Unless Madhu was evicted, Nilkantha could not uphold his prestige before the tenants. He was not much concerned about prestige, however, but if the tenants did not respect him, his work would be impeded, which was why he had to be cautious. Nilkantha started sharpening his weeding trowel to uproot Madhu like a tuft of grass.

This time Banwari no more stayed behind the scene. He unambiguously told Nilkantha that he would do everything in his power to prevent Madhu being evicted. First, he repaid Madhu's debt in full out of his own resources; thereafter, finding no other alternative, he personally went and informed the magistrate that Nilkantha was conspiring to implicate Madhu wrongly.

Banwari's well-wishers convinced him that the way things were turning out, Manoharlal in all probability would disown him any day. Had there been none of the troubles involved in disowning, he would by now have thrown him out. But there was Banwari's mother, and as for the relatives, different people had different opinions: Manohar was still holding his peace just because he was strongly opposed to raising a hue and cry over the matter.

Things were going on in this way, when suddenly one morning, Madhu's house was found padlocked. He had gone away overnight nobody knew where. Since the matter was taking an ugly turn, Nilkantha, with funds from the zamindari exchequer, had despatched Madhu along with his family to Varanasi. The police had knowledge of this, so there was no trouble. Yet, Nilkantha tactfully spread the rumour that on the new moon night Madhu along with his wife and children had been sacrificed to goddess Kali, and their bodies stuffed in sacks had been drowned in mid-Ganga. People shivered in horror, and their respect for Nilkantha increased manifold.

Banwari's compulsive preoccupation was thus set at rest, albeit for the time. But his family life no longer remained the same.

Once, Banwari had been extremely affectionate to Bangshi. Today, he discovered that Bangshi meant nothing to him; rather, he was of the Haldar family. And his very own Kiran—whose meditative image, ever since the days of his youth by and by entwining the trellis of his heart had been shrouding it—did not completely belong to him, either; she too belonged to the Haldar family. There was a time when Banwari would moan and groan because ornaments made to Nilkantha's order did not quite match Kiran who throbbed in his heart. Now he saw that all the sensual poetry of Kalidasa through Amaru and Chaura[11] with which he had adorned his beloved, ill befitted this eldest wife of the Haldar family.

Yet, the spring breeze blew, the raindrops resonated in the *Shravan* nights, and the pangs of unrequited love roamed the alleys of the empty heart, forlorn and forsaken.

Not everyone feels the need for intense love; the little *kunke*[12] measure of rations of everyday life serves most people quite well. That meagre dispensation causes no problem for the greater world, but for one or two individuals that is just not adequate. They cannot, like unborn chicks, survive just on the yolk of the egg; they have hatched out of the shell and must have pasture vast enough for procuring their own food from. Banwari was born with just that hunger: he was eager to fulfil his own love with his own manliness; but whichever direction he wanted to escape, he was confronted by the juggernaut of the Haldar family edifice and ended up banging his head against its walls.

Days passed by as before again. Banwari now pursued his avocation of hunting with even greater interest; except for this, no remarkable change in his life was noticeable from outside. He used to visit the inner quarters for his meals, and thereafter have some limited talk with his wife as well. Madhu Kaibarta was one man Kiran had still not forgiven: Madhu was the root cause that her husband had lost his standing in the family. For this reason, every now and then, somehow her malice against Madhu burst forth in strong words: Madhu was a scoundrel to the backbone, an arch-fiend; to show him any kindness was simply to be deceived. Even though she castigated him repeatedly with these words, she was not content. Banwari, for one or two days at the outset trying to protest, had managed to excite her vehemently; from then on, he made no protest at all. In this way, he was preserving the domestic norms. In this, Kiran felt no absence or insufficiency of anything, but as far as Banwari was concerned, his life, inwardly, was pallid, insipid and forever starved.

About this time, word went round that the younger daughter-in-law of the family, Bangshi's wife, was expecting. The whole family was exhilarated with hope. Kiran's omission of duty to this noble family was likely to be rectified at last; now by the grace of *Shashthi*[13], if a son rather than a daughter were to be born, that would be the most welcome saviour.

It was indeed a son. The younger master had passed his college examinations; now he qualified in the family examination too. He had been receiving increasingly greater attention for some time; now it knew no bounds.

Everyone in the house started making a great fuss over the baby. For Kiran, there was simply no putting him down from her lap for a moment. She was so ecstatic about it that even the memory of Madhu Kaibarta's lowly nature was almost erased from her mind.

Banwari was extremely fond of children. Whatever was small, helpless and tender evoked his love and pity. In the nature of every human being, there is an inherent contrary trait; were it not so, you could not explain how Banwari could ever bring himself to shoot birds.

That Kiran would be blessed with a child was one wish that had remained unfulfilled for Banwari. So when a son was born to Bangshi, Banwari had at first felt a twinge of jealousy, but it did not take him long to expunge that feeling. Banwari could indeed have loved this child very much, were it not for the constraint that with time Kiran became overly preoccupied with the child. Banwari's meetings with his wife became fewer and fewer. He realised that now at last Kiran had found something which could truly fill her heart. So far, Banwari had been like a tenant in Kiran's heart. As long as its rightful owner had been away, he had had free access to the entire house; now that the owner had arrived, the tenant was shoved into a corner of the house. How intimately absorbed Kiran could be in her affection, how passionate she could be in her dedication of self were revelations to which his mind nodded its head and said, 'This heart I never could arouse, though I had done all I possibly could do.'

This was not all. In the context of this boy, for Kiran it was Bangshi's room that seemed to have grown closer to her heart. All her discussions and deliberations were livelier when conducted with Bangshi. Banwari had been growing more and more disdainful of that pusillanimous fellow of keen intellect and fragile, anaemic body. The entire world thought Bangshi in all respects worthier than him. Banwari had accepted this ungrudgingly; but when in various instances he found that his wife appreciated Bangshi as a man more than she did him, Banwari was left disgruntled with his fate and the world at large.

About this time, one day on the eve of Bangshi's exams, news came from Calcutta that he was severely ill; doctors feared the worst. Banwari went to Calcutta and nursed him day and night, but to no avail.

Death removed the thorns from Banwari's memory. The fond remembrance that Bangshi had been his dear little brother and that in his infancy his Dada's lap had been his affectionate shelter, now washed clean with tears, shone brightly in his mind.

He returned from Calcutta with the resolve to bring up the child with all the care of his heart. But regarding this child, Kiran had lost her faith in her husband. She had noticed from the very beginning that her husband was ill-disposed towards the baby. It was her conviction that whatever was normally expected of other people would be just the opposite for her husband: this child was the family's sole surviving scion; everyone realised how precious he was, and certainly for that reason her husband did not realise it. Kiran had a persistent fear that Banwari's malicious eye would bring harm to the boy. Her brother-in-law was no more; there was no hope of her ever bearing a child herself; naturally, this child had to be kept from harm's way. Thus, caring for Bangshi's son did not come quite naturally to Banwari.

The boy was growing up with the indulgent care of everyone in the family. He was named Haridas. With so much pampering, he grew into a somewhat wispy and fragile form. He wore tourniquets and talismans all over his body; his well-wishers kept him constantly encircled.

Amidst all this, he sometimes came across Banwari. He was very fond of brandishing his uncle's riding whip. He would lisp *chabu*[14] whenever he met anybody. Taking out the whip from his room, Banwari would keep swishing it around, to the great delight of the child. On some days, Banwari would set him down upon his own horse, bringing the entire family rushing in with a desperate wail of disaster. Again sometimes, he would fiddle with his gun in front of the amused child; if Kiran happened to see this, she would whisk away the boy to safety. Nevertheless, these forbidden games were the amusements that interested Haridas most. Therefore, in spite of all hurdles, he became most friendly with his uncle.

After a long respite, suddenly death started visiting the family. Manohar's wife was the first to die. Thereafter, when Nilkantha was looking for a bride for the old master, Manohar died. Haridas was then eight years old. On his deathbed, Manoharlal entrusted this little heir especially to the care of Kiran and Nilkantha; to Banwari, he said nothing whatever.

When the will was fetched from his chest, it was found that Manohar had bequeathed his entire property to Haridas. Banwari was entitled to a monthly allowance of two hundred rupees for life. Nilkantha was the executor of the will, and he would manage all the affairs including the estate of the Haldar family as long as he lived.

Banwari realised that no one in the family could trust him, whether with the child or with the property. He could do nothing, spoilt everything he undertook: there were no two opinions about this in this family. It was therefore ordained for him that after eating his rationed food, he would sleep in the corner room.

He told Kiran, 'I'm not going to live on Nilkantha's pension. Let us go to Calcutta leaving this house.'

'Goodness, what are you saying? It's your father's property and Haridas is like your own son. Why are you angry that the property has been given away in his name?'

Alas, how hard her husband's heart was! He could bring himself to envy even this small child! The will her father-in-law had written Kiran fully approved in her mind. She strongly believed that if the property had been placed in Banwari's hand, all the lowbred riffraff of the land, all the Jadus and Madhus, all the Kaibartas and Aguris[15] would have cheated him out of the last paisa; the Haldar family's prospects would have been cast adrift in a boundless sea. To light up the family line, the all-important lamp had arrived at last; all that was now necessary was to see that the oil reserve was not wasted, for which the appropriate guard was none except Nilkantha.

Then one day Banwari saw Nilkantha enter the inner quarters, and going to each room in turn was making an inventory of the articles and securing every chest and trunk with new locks. Finally, he came into Kiran's bedroom and started listing Banwari's articles of daily use. Nilkantha was used to frequenting the inner quarters, so Kiran did not feel shy in his presence. In a voice choking with tears at the loss of her father-in-law, she kept explaining things in the intervals of wiping her tears.

'Get out from my room this moment,' Banwari burst out roaring like a lion.

'*Baro-babu*,' said Nilkantha politely, 'I've no fault after all. As per the master's will, I have to take stock of everything. All this furniture is Haridas's.'

'Just look at that,' said Kiran to herself. 'Is Haridas an outsider? Where is there any shame in enjoying the property of one's own son? Besides, are goods and chattels to go with us when we go? Today or tomorrow, it's our children who'll enjoy them any way.'

The floors of this house felt like thorns under Banwari's feet; the walls seemed to burn his eyes. There was not a soul in this vast family to whom he could confide what tormented him.

Banwari grew anxious to walk away that very moment casting aside everything from household to homestead. But his smouldering anger just would not abate. He could not bear to think that he would leave and Nilkantha would lord it over without hindrance. Unless he could inflict some severe damage right now, he could not pacify his mind. 'I'll see how Nilkantha can protect the property,' he said to himself.

Going into his father's room, he found there was no one. They had all gone to the inner rooms taking stock of the ornaments and utensils. Lapses do occur even in the precaution taken by a most cautious man. Nilkantha had forgotten that after taking out the will, he had not locked the chest. In that chest, there were bundles of documents substantiating the titles to the family estates.

Banwari knew nothing about the contents of these documents, but he knew that they were of utmost importance, and that without them there would be setback at every step in any litigation. He wrapped the papers in a handkerchief, went into the garden and sitting on the platform under the champak tree, kept brooding for a long time.

Next day, Nilkantha came to Banwari to discuss the arrangements for the *shradh*[16] ceremony. Nilkantha's body language was all humility, but in his expression, there was something, or wasn't, observing or imagining which Banwari seethed with anger. He thought that with his politeness Nilkantha was mocking him.

Nilkantha said, 'About the master's shradh – '

Banwari spoke without letting him finish, 'What do I know about that?'

'How can that be? You alone have the right of performing the shradh.'

'What a right! Right of shradh! In the family, that's all I'm any use for; I'm worth nothing else,' Banwari muttered to himself. He thundered, 'Go away! Don't disturb me.'

Nilkantha went, but from behind him, Banwari thought he went away laughing. It occurred to him that all the menials and lesser staff of the house were laughing and jeering among themselves at this discredited, discarded fellow. Who was ever mocked at by fate like the man who was of a family yet did not count as one of the family? Not even a beggar on the street.

Banwari went out with that bundle of documents. The neighbouring and rival zamindar of the Haldar family were the Banerjees of Pratappur. 'I'll surrender all these deeds to them,' Banwari decided, 'Let the estate go to ruin.'

As he was going out, Haridas called out from upstairs in his boyish dulcet, '*Jyatha-mashai*, you're going out? I'll come with you, too.'

'The evil star of the boy had these words uttered by him,' Banwari thought to himself. 'I've already taken to the street; him too I will bring out with me. Go out you will, don't worry; everything will go to destruction.'

Going as far as the outer garden, he could hear a great noise. Not far away, near the market place, a widow's hut had caught fire. As was his wont in such cases, Banwari could not stay at rest. Leaving his bundle of papers under the champak tree, he ran to the site.

When he came back, he saw the bundle had vanished. Instantly piercing his heart like a shaft, the thought occurred, 'Once again I am defeated by Nilkantha. What harm would there have been if the widow's hut had been burnt to ashes?' He concluded that it was the clever Nilkantha who had retrieved it.

Like a storm, he rushed straight away into the estate office. Nilkantha, after hurriedly closing the box, standing up respectfully, made a *pronam* to Banwari. It seemed to him that Nilkantha had hidden the papers in that very box. Without saying anything, right away opening it, he began to rummage through the papers. All he found was a ledger book and supporting papers. Inverting and shaking the box yielded nothing further.

In an almost choked voice, Banwari asked, 'Did you go to *champatala*[17]?'

'Yes, sir, I did, of course. I saw you were running hurriedly, so I went out to see what had happened.'

'So it's you who have picked up my papers wrapped in a handkerchief.'

'No, sir,' said Nilkantha, looking most innocent.

'You're lying. Give them back at once, or you'll face trouble, mind you.'

Banwari blustered for nothing; neither could he tell what he had lost, and aware that he had no right to the stolen goods, kept cursing himself for a careless fool.

Having behaved madly in this way at the office, he came back to champatala and started scouring the area all over again. Swearing by his deceased mother, he resolved, 'I will not give up till I have found out those papers.' Unable to think how he would proceed, all he did was to stamp his feet like an enraged boy, saying, 'Find out I must, I must, I must.'

He sat down under the tree, quite exhausted. There was no one beside him; he had no one his own and he had absolutely nothing his own. From now on, alone and without any resources, he would have to battle against his destiny, against the world at large. For him, there was no honour, no respectability, no love, no affection, nothing whatever, except only the tenacity to kill and be killed.

Thus, he kept agitating within himself until he fell asleep in utter fatigue on the *chatal*[18] under the tree. When he woke up, he could not at once ascertain where he was. After finding his bearing, he sat up and found Haridas sitting near his head. Haridas burst forth, 'What have you lost, uncle? Tell me.'

Banwari was stunned; he could not answer this simple question from Haridas.

'If I can give it back,' asked Haridas, 'what will you give me?'

Banwari thought that perhaps he was referring to something else. He said, 'All I have is yours.' This he said half in jest; he knew he had nothing to give.

Haridas, undoing a fold of his dhoti, took out the handkerchief-bound bundle. The coloured handkerchief had the picture of a tiger printed on it, which his uncle had often shown him. Haridas had a special fascination for it. In the commotion of fire, when the servants had been away, he had come out into the garden and happened to notice the familiar handkerchief.

Banwari plucked the boy up close to his chest and sat there silently. After a while, tears began to gush out of his eyes. He remembered how a long time back, to tame a newly bought dog he had been compelled to whip it repeatedly. One day he had forgotten his whip somewhere, and after searching everywhere, had given up when the dog itself brought it in its mouth to its master, contentedly wagging its tail. Never again could he bring himself to whip the dog.

Banwari quickly wiped his tears and said, 'Haridas, tell me what you want.'

'I want that handkerchief, Jyatha-mashai.'

'Come, Haridas, I will carry you on my shoulders.'

Lifting him up, Banwari went into the inner quarters. On entering the bedroom, he saw Kiran collecting a daylong-sunned blanket from the veranda and spreading it on the floor. Seeing Haridas perched on Banwari's shoulder, she cried out anxiously, 'Put him down, put him down; you'll drop him.'

Fixing Kiran with a steady gaze, Banwari said, 'Don't be afraid any more; I won't drop him.'

With this, he put the child down and advanced him towards Kiran's lap. Then he took out the bundle and handing it to Kiran, said, 'These are documents of Haridas's property. Put them away carefully.'

Taken aback, Kiran asked, 'Where did you get them from?'

'I stole them.'

Then hugging Haridas close, he said, 'Here it is, son; your Jyatha-mashai's valuable property that took your fancy. Take it.' And he pressed the handkerchief into his hand.

Then he took another good look at Kiran. The slim girl she had been was no longer slim; she had put on weight he had not noticed when. So long after, she had grown into the elderly stature befitting the Haldar household. Why dither? Now Banwari had better sacrifice Amarushatak's[19] poems as well along with all his other property.

That very night Banwari was seen no more. Only, he had left a one-line note saying he was going to look for a job.

He could not even wait until his father's shradh! Everyone far and near denounced him for that.

*Baishakh 1321* (1914)

NOTES

1 Literally, molecule; very small, diminutive.
2 Literally, atom, the smallest conceivable particle.
3 The text has *udhbhat-kabita* meaning absurd, anonymous verses.
4 A seventeen-syllable metre of Sanskrit poetry in which the 1st, 4th, 10th, 11th, 13th, 15th, 16th, and 17th letters are of long measure and the rest short; it occurs in Kalidasa's romantic poem Meghadutam.
5 A caste name for fishermen and peasants.
6 Reddish green fruit of a foreign tree so named; its seeds dissolved in water give a red solution used chiefly by sannyasis for dyeing their clothes.
7 The text has *chhotolok*, a derogatory term, never used in its literal sense of a 'diminutive' or 'poor' man.
8 The text has *barolok*, always used to mean a rich man;
9 The allusion is to Yudhishthira in the Mahabharata who as the son of *Yama*, the custodian god of virtue (see Glossary), is traditionally held as the model of truth, virtue and honesty.

10 A ritual reception to the son-in-law on the sixth lunar day of the bright fortnight in the month of *Jyaishtha*.

11 Kalidasa: The most celebrated Sanskrit poet and dramatist of all time, associated with King Vikramadiyta, three plays of whom have survived, 'Malavika and Agnimitra', 'Urvasi Won by Valour' and 'The recognition of Shakuntala'; Amaru: a seventh-century Sanskrit poet known for his love lyrics, often voluptuous, rarely humorously tender, and always showing a sound understanding of feminine psychology; Chaura: Chaurapanchashika [Fifty Stanzas of the Thief], a work of the Kashmiri poet Bilhan of the eleventh and twelfth centuries, which purports to describe the secret love of a bold housebreaker and a princess.

12 Alternatively *Kunika* from Sanskrit *kunchika* is a now-obsolete measure of rice or pulses; a wicker basket of that measure; approx. one-sixteenth of a ser.

13 In Bengali *Shashthi,* another name for Brahma's daughter Devasena, the greatest of the sixteen mother figures, and held to bless one with babies and protect them; a local deity of Bengal.

14 *Chabu* for 'chabuk' the Bengali word for whip.

15 'Every Jadu and Madhu' (or, Ram, Shyam, Jadu) is the Bengali equivalent of 'Every Tom, Dick and Harry'. Aguris are Muslim weavers by profession.

16 A Hindu ritual of offering libation to the departed soul; solemnised on a prescribed day (usually, $11^{th}$ or $13^{th}$) after death, rightfully by the eldest son or wife by default.

17 *Tala* as a suffix to the name of a particular object is a raised paved area around or at its base. Hence, champa (magnolia)-tala, tulsi (basil)-tala, kuyo (well)-tala.

18 Paved courtyard.

19 A book of Sanskrit love poems by Amaru.

# Rasmani's Son
# (*Rasmanir Chhele*)

Rasmani was Kalipada's mother. Nevertheless, she had been obliged to double as his father; for, if besides the mother, the father too is dotingly affectionate, it is no good for the son. Her husband Bhabanicharan could never take his son to task.

If asked why he pampered his son so much, the reason he used to offer has a history of its own.

The fact of the matter is this:

Bhabanicharan was born in the renowned, traditionally rich family of Shaniyari. Bhabanicharan's father Abhayacharan's son by first marriage was Shyamacharan. After his wife's death, when Abhayacharan got married for the second time, his father-in-law had the Alandi *Taluk* assigned particularly in his daughter's name. Considering his son-in-law's age, he had calculated that in the event of his daughter being widowed, she would not have to depend for her subsistence on her co-wife's son.

The first part of his calculation proved true in no time: soon after his grandson Bhabanicharan's birth, his son-in-law died. Having witnessed his daughter taking possession of her own property, on the eve of his departure for the other world, he too went reassured to a great degree about the present world of his daughter.

Shyamacharan had then come of age. Moreover, his eldest son was senior to Bhabanicharan by one year. Shyamacharan brought him up with his own sons without differentiating between them. From the income of his stepmother's property, he had never taken a single paisa for himself, and year after year submitting the clear statement of her income and expenditure under acknowledgement had charmed everyone with his honesty.

In fact, almost everyone had felt that so much honesty was unnecessary, even tantamount to foolishness. That a part of the integral ancestral property should be ceded to the second wife was generally not taken with good grace. If deceitfully by any stratagem Shyamacharan nullified this deed, his neighbours would of course have praised his manliness; neither would he lack experienced people to advise him how to accomplish it flawlessly. But Shyamacharan, even at the cost of impairing their traditional family title, kept his stepmother's property entirely segregated.

Because of this, as well as her affectionate nature, his stepmother Brajasundari loved and trusted Shyamacharan no less than she did her own son. Since Shyamacharan used to treat her property as completely isolated, on many occasions she had reprimanded him, saying, 'Dear son, all this is but yours. Certainly, I will not carry this property along with me to the other world. They will all remain yours. Why do I need to go into so much accounting?'

Shyamacharan had paid no heed to her words.

Shyamacharan kept his sons under strict control, but on Bhabanicharan, there was no control at all. At this, everyone said in one voice that he was more affectionate towards Bhabanicharan than to his sons. In this way, Bhabani ended up with little education, and forever remaining a child in practical wisdom, kept advancing in years while completely depending on his elder brother. He never had to worry about property, except occasionally put one or two signatures. Why he was signing, he never tried to understand, because if he did, he would not have succeeded.

Meanwhile, Shyamacharan's eldest son Tarapada, who had been

assisting his father in every task became an expert in all kinds of work. After Shyamacharan's death, Tarapada told Bhabanicharan, 'Uncle, I think we can no longer stay together. There's no knowing when a small issue may lead to discord; then the whole family will be ruined.'

Bhabani had not imagined even in his dreams that one day living separately he would have to look after his own property. The family where he had been brought up since childhood he knew only as an integrated whole: that somewhere in it, there was a joint and at that joint, it could be split in two was a revelation the suddenness of which filled him with anxiety .

When Bhabani saw that loss of family honour and anguish of the relatives were of least concern for Tarapada, he had to engage in the impossible thought of how to effect the division of property. Utterly surprised to notice his worry, Tarapada said, 'Uncle, what's the problem? Why are you so worried? The division of the property has already been done . Why, my grandfather himself had completed the partition.'

Bewildered, Bhabani said, 'Is it true? But I know absolutely nothing about that.'

Tarapada said, 'Indeed! Does it matter if you don't know? The entire village knows that in the likelihood of having a dispute with you, my grandfather, after allocating the Alandi taluk to your share, had separated you from the beginning: that is how things have been going on so far.'

Bhabanicharan thought that everything was possible. 'And what about this house?' he asked.

'If you like, you can keep the house for yourselves,' said Tarapada. 'If we get the bungalow at the sub-divisional town, we will somehow manage.'

Tarapada agreed so easily to forgo the ancestral home that Bhabanicharan was astonished at his magnanimity. He had never seen their bungalow at the sub-divisional town, and he had no attachment to it at all.

When Bhabani told everything to his mother Brajasundari, she exclaimed, expressing deep disappointment, 'My goodness! What a thing to say! Alandi Taluk I had received as my female share of the property and the basis for my maintenance, and the income from it is not much either. Why won't you get your rightful share in the paternal property?'

Bhabani said, 'Tarapada says my father had not given us anything other than that Taluk.'

Brajasundari said, 'He may say that; why shall I accept it? Your father had written out the will in his own hand in duplicate, one of which he kept with me; it is in my safe.'

The safe was opened. The gift deed for Alandi Taluk was there, all right, but no will. It had been stolen.

Counsel was called in. This fellow was their family priest's son Bagalacharan. Everyone said he was a man of shrewd judgement. Father was the giver of secret chant and son of secret counsel to the village. Between themselves, father and son had shared the worldly and other-worldly concerns of the village. Whatever its effect may have been on others, to them it had caused no inconvenience.

Bagalacharan said, 'So what if the will is not found? Will or no will, brothers must have an equal share in the father's property.'

At this point, the other side produced a will. It allocated nothing to Bhabanicharan's share; the entire property had been bequeathed to the grandsons. Abhayacharan's son had not been born yet.

With Bagala as the helmsman, Bhabani set out to navigate the ocean of litigation. On reaching the port, when he opened the iron safe for stocktaking, he found that the nest of *Lakshmi's* owl[1] was empty: just one or two gold feathers it had moulted lay strewn around. The paternal property went into the hands of the other party. As for the Alandi Taluk, the tip that projected from beneath the bottom of ruin could at most afford a shelter for bare survival, let alone maintain the dignity of the family. Having acquired the old house, Bhabanicharan thought he had made a good bargain.

Tarapada and his men repaired to the headquarters. There remained no further contact between the two sides.

## 2

Shyamacharan's treachery struck Brajasundari like a spear. Committing the crime of stealing her husband's will, he had deprived his brother and at the same time betrayed his father's trust: this she could not forget all her life. As long as she lived, everyday heaving a deep sigh she had lamented, 'Such grave wrong will not go unpunished.' Almost everyday, she had reassured Bhabanicharan, saying, 'I understand no law or litigation; I tell you, the will of my husband will not remain hidden forever. Surely you will get it back.'

All along, having heard this from his mother, Bhabanicharan had begun to rely on it a great deal. As he was himself incompetent, such words of assurance were a source of great consolation to him. Words from the mouth of a pious woman must come true, and what was legitimately his would on its own come back to him: deciding this for certain, he ceased to make any further effort. After his mother's death, this conviction grew even stronger, because filtering through the estrangement of death, his mother's holy aura manifested itself even more gloriously to him. The scourge of poverty did not seem to affect him at all; as if this privation for bare subsistence, this departure from the previous lifestyle was just a day or two of play-acting; nothing was real. For this reason, when, after having worn out the traditional dhoti from Dacca, he had to buy and wear a cheap coarse dhoti, he suppressed a smile. During the *Durga-Puja* the traditional pomp and splendour was dispensed with altogether; the puja was a perfunctory affair; the guests, on observing this poor arrangement, heaving long sighs brought up reminiscences of the past. Bhabanicharan laughed inwardly ; he thought, 'They do not know that all this is only for some time; thereafter one day the puja will be performed with such ostentatious ceremony that they will be amazed.' The certain grandeur of that future he could visualise so distinctly that the present destitution seemed to escape his notice.

To discuss about this, his main partner was Noto the servant. On several occasions, sitting in the midst of an impoverished puja festival, the master-servant duo engaged in debating the details of the arrangements to be made in times of prosperity. Who were to be invited and who were not, whether it was or was not necessary to book an opera party from Calcutta, too, were topics on which there were serious disagreements and arguments between them. Because of his ungenerous nature, Notobihari, to give him his full name, having shown stinginess in preparing that future list had received severe rebukes from Bhabanicharan. Such things happened almost regularly.

Overall, as far as the estate was concerned, there was no worry at all in Bhabanicharan's mind. He had only one cause for anxiety: who would inherit his property. So far, he had had no son. When well-wishers with unmarried daughters requested him to get married once again, sometimes his mind would be agitated. It was not because he had any particular fascination for a newly married wife; rather, like servant and rice[2], for wife also his preference was for the old rather than the new. However, for someone who had any prospect of finding wealth not to have the probability of an offspring was in his opinion an embarrassing predicament.

At this time, when a son was born to him, everyone said: now the destiny of this family will turn for the better; the beginning has been made; the late master Abhayacharan in person has been reborn in this family: the same large eyes. The boy's horoscope too revealed that stars and planets had formed such a favourable conjunction that retrieval of the embezzled property was a certainty.

Ever since his son was born, some changes could be observed in Bhabanicharan's conduct. So far, he had borne his poverty quite effortlessly with fun as mere play, but for his son, he could not maintain that feeling. For the sake of stoking up the guttering ancestral lamp in the famous Chaudhuri family of Shaniyari, the child who had descended on earth thanks to the immensely favourable juxtaposition of stars and planets certainly enjoined some obligation upon him. Until today, continuously down the ages in this family, the kind of pampering which any male child had received since birth was for the first time denied to Bhabanicharan's son; this was something he could not forget. 'As a conventional right in this family what I had been accorded I could not afford for my own son.' As he contemplated this, it kept recurring in his mind, 'It is I who deceived him.' Therefore, for his son, Kalipada, the money he could not spend he tried to make good with copious affection.

Bhabani's wife Rasmani was a woman of a different type. About the ancient pride of the Chaudhuri family of Shaniyari she had never felt any concern. Bhabani was aware of it, and contemplating this, he was amused. He thought, coming as she did from an abjectly poor *Baishnava* family, she indeed deserved to be forgiven this fault: to form a proper notion about the honour and dignity of the Chaudhuris was just not possible for her.

Rasmani herself admitted as much. She used to say, 'I am a poor man's daughter; I care little for honour and dignity. May Kalipada, my darling, survive, he is my greatest treasure.' That the deed would be recovered, and thanks to Kalipada's luck, the dry river bed of this family's lost wealth would once again be flooded by a high tide, were idle talk to which she paid no heed at all. There was not a person around with whom her husband would not discuss the lost will. Only, this most cherished thought of his he could hardly ever share with his wife. Once or twice, he had tried to discuss it, but found no interest. His wife would not pay any attention at all to either past or future glory; the present necessity alone had kept her mind entirely preoccupied.

That necessity was not small either. She had to take great pains to keep the household running. This was because, even after *Lakshmi* departs, she leaves behind some of her encumbrances, when, although there may be no wherewithal, hazards do persist. In this family, the shelter had almost crumbled, but those sheltered even now would not give them respite. Neither was Bhabanicharan the kind who, for fear of penury, would have sent anyone packing.

To keep this burdened and broken-down family running was Rasmani's responsibility. Yet, from no one in the family did she ever get much help. For good reason too. In the halcyon days of this family, all the spongers had lived in exclusive comfort and indolence. Under the vast banyan tree of the Chaudhuri family, upon their bed of comfort, a bracing shade had come and spread on its own and all their needs were met spontaneously: for that, none of them had had to make the least effort. Today, if asked to do any work, they felt extremely insulted; going into the kitchen, they invariably got headache by inhaling smoke, and the slightest attempt to make any movement was thwarted by such terrible arthritis as knew no amelioration even from the most costly ayurvedic oil. That apart, Bhabanicharan used to say that in lieu of shelter, if the sheltered were made to work, that would be tantamount to extraction of labour, frustrating the very virtue of giving shelter: this was by no means the practice in the Chaudhuri family.

Hence, the entire onerous duty lay on Rasmani alone. Day and night, by various tactics and toil, she had discreetly to meet all the wants of this family. In this way having to keep fighting ceaselessly against privation, having to scrimp and save, having to haggle and wrangle harden one inexorably; one's tenderness disappears. The very persons for whom she works to death eventually grow intolerant of her. Not that Rasmani used merely to cook food in the kitchen; also, the responsibility to procure that food was in most part hers. Yet, after partaking of that food at noon those who went blissfully to nap not only spoke ill of that food but also refrained from praising the provider of that food.

Apart from the domestic chores, Rasmani had to examine the accounts and look after the collection of rents all by herself in respect of whatever taluks and *brahmatras* had survived the onslaught of poverty. As regards revenue collection, previously such strictness had never been enforced: Bhabanicharan's money was just the reverse of Abhimanyu[3]; it knew only how to exit; the art of entry was not known to it. Ever to pursue anyone for unpaid dues was completely alien to his nature. Rasmani, when it came to realising her own dues, never gave a single paisa worth of remission to anybody. For this, the tenants used to criticise her; even the *gomastas*, exasperated by her stringency did not hesitate to revile her for the mean-mindedness befitting her lineage. Even her husband, deploring her niggardliness and rudeness as disgraceful to their world-famous family, would sometimes object in a feeble voice. Completely ignoring all this disparagement and admonition, she used to carry on in her own way; the entire fault she took upon her own shoulders. She was from a poor family; she knew nothing of the ostentation of the rich : acknowledging this repeatedly, and both within and outside the house becoming unpleasant to everyone, girding the sari-end tightly round her waist she kept working at the speed of a hurricane; nobody dared to come in her way.

Far from calling upon her husband for any work, she was always afraid in case Bhabanicharan, suddenly in an authoritative vein, happened to take it upon himself to do anything himself. With dampeners like, 'You don't need to worry about anything; you need not be involved in all this,' to keep her husband uninterested in every matter was her main concern. The husband having been used to it all his life, the wife had not had to suffer much on that score. Rasmani had not borne a child until at a late age. By handling the good-for-nothing, simple-minded, dependent husband of hers, both her wifely love and motherly affection had been fulfilled. Bhabani, to her, was virtually a grown-up boy. Therefore, after her mother-in-law's death, the work of both the posts—the master as well as the mistress of the house—she had had to take on upon herself. To shield her husband from the priest's son and other perils, she used to carry herself with such a stern attitude that it acted as a deterrent to her husband's companions. She never had the opportunity to display her feminine side of keeping her severity concealed, smoothing out the edges of her words, and maintaining adequate bashfulness with the males.

So far, Bhabanicharan had been behaving quite obediently with her. But when it came to Kalipada, it became difficult for him to obey Rasmani.

This is because Rasmani did not look upon Bhabanicharan's son in the same way as Bhabani did. About her husband, she used to think, 'Poor fellow, what will he do? What is his fault? He comes of a rich family: he is really helpless.' Naturally, she did not at all expect that her husband would ever undertake any labour. Therefore, in spite of countless wants, she with her utmost ability used to meet her husband's habitual needs as far as possible. In her household, she would skimp on the food and other necessities of other people, but in respect of Bhabanicharan, as far as possible, she allowed no deviation from the conventional rules. In times of particular hardship, if any lapse ever occurred in any matter, she would by no means let her husband know that it had occurred because of scarcity. Maybe, she would say,' Oh! The wretched dog mouthed and spoiled the food.' And she would curse her imagined carelessness. Or maybe, blaming the poor Noto for losing the recently purchased dhoti, she would express profuse disregard for his common sense. Bhabanicharan, then taking sides with his favourite servant would be anxious to rescue him from his wife's ire. Even sometimes it so happened that the dhoti his wife had not even purchased and Bhabanicharan had never seen with his eyes, and which Notabihari was accused of having lost, Bhabanicharan serenely admitted that Noto had pleated, he had used and thereafter—well, thereafter what had happened, his imaginative faculty failed him. Then Rasmani, herself lending a plausible ending, said, 'Certainly, after changing, you had left it the sitting room. There all sorts of men come and go; someone must have stolen it.'

Such was the strategy for Bhabanicharan. But her own son she did not consider in any respect her husband's equal. Her son came from her womb: how did any question of a luxurious lifestyle arise for him? He had to be a hardy and industrious man: he would easily endure suffering and work for a living. 'Without this I can't do. Without that I feel ashamed': such tantrums would not at all befit him. For Kalipada, Rasmani stipulated a veritably spartan regime in food and clothing: she arranged for mere puffed rice and treacle for his breakfast, and a cotton mantle to cover his head and ears for keeping out the cold. Personally summoning the teacher, she instructed him to see that her son should by no means show any laxity in his studies; he should be kept under especially strict discipline and taught his lessons.

Here big problem arose. The docile Bhabanicharan started showing signs of revolt occasionally, but Rasmani overlooked it. Bhabani had forever yielded to his powerful opponents; this time too, he had willy-nilly to surrender, but he resented it. A son of this family swathed head and shoulders in a cotton mantle, eating puffed ice with molasses: how could one suffer such an incongruous sight day after day?

During the Durga-puja, he remembered his father's time when they had all felt so enthusiastic wearing new clothes. This time, on the puja day, the cheap dhoti and shirt Rasmani arranged for Kalipada would have been taken exception to in those days even by their servants. Rasmani had taken great pains to explain to her husband, 'Look, Kalipada is content with whatever he is given; he knows nothing about the old practice. Then why do you sulk unnecessarily?' But Bhabanicharan could not at all forget that only because poor Kalipada was unaware of his own family's glory he was being short-changed. In fact, on receiving a small gift, when dancing for joy and pride he came running to show it to him, that very sight seemed to hurt Bhabanicharan even more acutely than anything else. He was emotionally too weak to bear it; turning his face, he had to retreat.

Since taking up Bhabanicharan's case, there had been a handsome accrual of income in their priest's family. Not content merely with that, the priest's son, every year shortly before the pujas, purchasing various showy, cheap fancy goods from Calcutta, carried on trade for a few months. Vanishing ink, a triad of fishing rod–stick–umbrella, picture letter pads, auction-purchased rotten wool and satin sheets of various colours, saris with rhyme-printed border, and so on, were the merchandise with which he excited the minds of the people of the village. Knowing that in the fashionable circles of Calcutta, it was not possible to keep up with the neighbours nowadays without articles like these, no one in the village aspiring to cleanse himself of his rusticity refrained from spending even more than he could afford.

Once, Bagalacharan had brought an amazing wax replica of a memsahib[4]. One had to wind the device at a particular point and the lady, at once standing up from her stool, would start fanning herself vigorously.

For this summer-afflicted fanning lady-in-wax, Kalipada developed an overwhelming fancy. Kalipada knew his mother all too well, so instead of approaching her, he presented his appeal piteously to Bhabanicharan. Bhabanicharan at once assured him, but when he heard the price, his face went pale.

Collection of rents was Rasmani's preserve; custody of funds was hers as well; expenditure too was done only by her. Bhabanicharan, arrived like a beggar at the door of his *Annapurna*. Through a devious route of irrelevant talk, at last at an opportune moment he abruptly voiced his fond desire.

'You've become mad!' was her short reply.

Bhabanicharan kept thinking for some rime. Then suddenly he spoke out, 'With my rice, everyday you give me ghee and *payes.* Surely that is not necessary!'

'Who says it is not?'

'The *Kabiraj* says it increases bile secretion.'

'As if your kabiraj knows everything!'

'I think if at night discontinuing *luchi*, rice was arranged, it'd be better; luchi causes a heavy feeling.'

'That has never done you any harm. Since birth you have been living on luchi, haven't you?'

Bhabanicharan was ready to sacrifice everything else, but when it came to luchi and payes, he had been uncompromising. Ghee was becoming dearer, yet the number of luchis was the same. At the midday meal, when payes was mandatorily present, the *doi* or yoghurt was quite redundant, but even so, the masters in this family traditionally had been taking both yoghurt *and* payes. If on some day, the omnipresent yoghurt was missing, Rasmani could not bear the sight at all. Hence, there had apparently been no probability for the image of that fanning memsahib to worm its way through any interstices in the doi-payes-ghee-luchi combine.

Bhabanicharan one day went to the house of his priest's son as if casually, and after prolonged desultory talks enquired about that wax doll. He knew there was no reason his present financial hardship should have remained secret to Bagalacharan. Nevertheless, just because today he had no money, he could not buy his son a most trivial thing like a toy: to indicate it even by implication, his head hung in shame. Even so, subordinating that mortal embarrassment, he brought out from within his chuddar a costly old *jamiyar* covered in a piece of cloth. In an almost choked voice, he said, 'Passing through a rather bad time; er, running short of hard cash—so I've decided that by mortgaging this jamiyar I'll take that doll for Kalipada.'

Had it been a cheaper article rather than the jamiyar, Bagalacharan would have had no qualms, but he knew that it was too large a bait to swallow: because not only would people condemn him, on top of that what would come out of Rasmani's mouth would be anything but palatable. Hiding the jamiyar once again within his chuddar, Bhabanicharan had to go back, disappointed.

Kalipada asked his father every day, 'Baba, what's happened to the mem I wanted?'

Every day with a smiling face, Bhabanicharan said, 'Wait – how can it be right now? Let the *saptami* puja day[5] come first.'

To frame a smile on the face every day proved increasingly harder.

Today was *chaturthi*, three days ahead of the puja. On some pretext, Bhabanicharan made an untimely visit to the inner quarters. As if suddenly in course of conversation, he spoke out, 'Look, for a couple of days I've observed that Kalipada's health is deteriorating fast.'

Rasmani said, ' God forbid! Why should it deteriorate? At least I don't see any illness.'

'Why,' said Bhabanicharan, 'haven't you noticed? He keeps sitting silently. He seems to be brooding.'

Rasmani said, 'If he actually kept still for a moment, I'd be relieved. And to think he's brooding! Where and what mischief has to be done is what he must be brooding over.'

No weakness could be detected on this side of the fortress too: not even a dent was left on the stone by the cannon ball. Exhaling a sigh, stroking his head Bhabanicharan came out of the room. He sat all by himself on the veranda, smoking his hookah vigorously.

On the *panchami* day, yoghurt and rice pudding on his platter remained untouched. In the evening, he finished his refreshment merely with a *sandesh*; luchi he could not touch. 'No appetite at all,' was his explanation.

Now a big hole appeared in the wall of the fortress. Next day, Rasmani, after calling Kalipada into a secluded corner, addressing him by his affectionate nickname, said, 'Bhentu, you're not a child any more, yet there's no end to your unreasonable demands! Shame! What you can't get by any means, if you covet, you've half-stolen it, d'you know that?'

On the verge of tears, Kalipada said, 'What do I know? But Baba said he would give it.'

Rasmani then sat explaining what 'Baba said' meant. In these words of his father, what affection, what anguish there was, and if he were to give this toy, what deprivation, what misery it would entail for their poor family, she explained to him thoroughly. Rasmani had never elucidated anything so tenderly to Kalipada. Whatever she did, she did bluntly and forcefully: she felt no necessity at all to sugar-coat an order. So today when he saw she was talking so pleadingly and so earnestly, he was astonished, and even though he was a mere boy, somehow he realised in his own way how much affection there was in some corner of his mother's heart. But how difficult it was instantly to divert the mind away from the mem will not be difficult for an adult reader to comprehend. So, Kalipada, putting on a very grave face, picking up a stick began scratching on the floor.

Then Rasmani once again became stern. In a grim voice she said, 'No matter whether you sulk or cry, what you can't get you won't get by any means.' With this, without wasting any more time she quickly went away for housework.

Kalipada went outside. Bhabanicharan was then smoking, sitting all alone. As soon as he noticed Kalipada from a distance, rising quickly, he began to walk as though he had some urgent work. Kalipada came running and said, 'Baba, that mem I wanted – '

Today no smile played on Bhabanicharan's lips; hugging Kalipada he said, 'Wait, my son, I've work to do. Let me come back; then we'll talk over it.' And he went out of the house. To Kalipada it seemed he quickly wiped tears from his eyes.

At that time, at a house in the neighbourhood, flautists for the festival were being booked on demonstration of their skills. In that concert, in the melancholy morning tune, the first sunbeam of autumn was, as it were, being sprinkled by invisible tears. Standing by the door of their house, Kalipada kept looking at the street silently. That his father was going nowhere for any work was apparent from the very nature of his movement: that at every step he was dragging along a burden of despair and that nowhere he could dump it was all too evident even by observing him from behind.

Coming back into the inner rooms, Kalipada said, 'Ma, I do not want that fanning mem.'

His mother with a nutcracker was then cracking areca nuts with a swift hand. Her face brightened. Between the mother and the son what understanding was reached nobody could possibly know. Putting aside the nutcracker, leaving the basketful of cracked and whole nuts, Rasmani immediately went off to Bagalacharan's house.

Today, Bhabanicharan was late returning home. After having his bath, when he sat down to eat, from his face it seemed that today also doi-payes was not going to be disposed of properly; moreover, the fish-head was destined to go entirely to the cat's lot.

Then, fetching a paper box bound in ropes, Rasmani presented it before her husband. After the meal, when Bhabanicharan would go to retire, only then she would reveal this mystery: Rasmani had wished so, but finding the neglect of doi-payes and fish-head, this had to be taken out right now. Emerging from the box, the mem-doll without delay very enthusiastically started cooling off from the summer heat. The cat had to go back, disappointed. Bhabanicharan said to his wife, 'Today the preparation has been excellent. I haven't eaten such fish curry in a long time. As for the yoghurt, it has set so fine I am at a loss for words!'

On the *saptami* day, Kalipada received his long-cherished treasure. All through that day, he kept watching the fan-swinging white lady and by exhibiting it to the friends of his age excited their envy. In any other circumstance, watching this daylong monotonous fan-waving, he surely would have been completely bored in a single day, but as he knew that on the second day itself his idol was to go, his interest remained intact. Rasmani, by giving her priest's son two rupees in cash, had brought the doll on hire just for a day. Next day, letting out a long sigh Kalipada himself went and returned the doll along with the box to Bagalacharan. This happy memory of a day's reunion remained fresh in his mind for a long time to come: in the realm of his imagination, the swinging of the fan knew no rest.

From now on, Kalipada became an associate in his mother's consultation and from now on, too, every year Bhabanicharan could so easily give him such costly puja gifts that he himself would be amazed.

The deeper Kalipada realised, by being close to his mother, that nothing in the world can be achieved without a price and that that price is to be paid in sorrow, the sooner he seemed to be growing up from within. At every turn he now became his mother's right hand. That the burden of the family had to be borne, not increased, was a realisation which even without counselling became ingrained in his marrow.

For the sake of assuming the responsibilities of life, he would have to prepare himself: bearing this in mind Kalipada began to study perseveringly. When he passed the junior scholarship examination, becoming entitled to a monthly scholarship, Bhabanicharan contemplated that further studies were not necessary: now Kalipada had rather look after the estate.

Kalipada came and told his mother, 'Unless I go to study in Calcutta, I won't be able to grow up properly.'

His mother said, 'That's true, son. Of course, you have to go to Calcutta.'

'For me, you don't have to make any expenses,' Kalipada assured his mother. 'I'll manage with this scholarship and find some odd job as well.'

Bhabanicharan required a great deal of persuading. That there was not much property worth looking after was an argument, which, because it would greatly hurt Bhabanicharan, Rasmani had to withhold. 'Kalipada has to be enabled to stand on his own feet, you know,' was all she said. But again, had not the Chaudhuris, through generations, never leaving Shaniyari, become big men? Outside places were as frightful to them as *Yama's* city. To send a boy of Kalipada's age to Calcutta—how the mere proposal of it could come to one's mind he was at a loss to contemplate. In the end, even Bagalacharan, the most intelligent person of the village, approved of Rasmani's opinion. He said, 'Kalipada, becoming a lawyer, will ultimately avenge the deceit of the forged will. Certainly, this is his destiny, and so there is no preventing him from going to Calcutta.'

Bhabanicharan derived a degree of comfort to hear this. Taking out the old documents wrapped in a *gamchha*, he started discussing the fraud repeatedly with Kalipada. Recently, his mother's ministerial job Kalipada had been performing quite efficiently, but in his father's council, he lacked that force of argument: because about this old injustice done to their family there was not sufficient excitement in Kalipada's mind. Nevertheless, he went on nodding at his father's words. Just as the mythical hero Rama had made a voyage to Lanka[6] to rescue Sita, so Bhabanicharan regarded Kalipada's passage to Calcutta as an equally momentous event: it was not simply a matter of passing examinations, but an endeavour to bring the family deity of fortune back home again.

On the eve of his departure for Calcutta, Rasmani hung a protective talisman round Kalipada's neck, and then giving him a fifty-rupee note, said, 'Keep it; it will help in times of need.' Saved by economising with difficulty on the household expenses, this currency note Kalipada accepted as a truly sacred talisman: this note he resolved he would keep away forever as his mother's blessing and never spend.

## 3

From Bhabanicharan the will-theft was no longer heard as often now as it used to be. Now his sole topic of discussion was Kalipada. His was the news he now roamed the entire neighbourhood to tell people about. Whenever he got his letter, in connection with reading it out from house to house, his spectacles hardly ever descended from his nose. Just because never and in no generation had anyone in his family gone to Calcutta, a sense of pride in Calcutta greatly excited his imagination. Our Kalipada studies in Calcutta and no news whatever concerning Calcutta is outside his knowledge: a second bridge is coming up on the Ganga near Hooghly; even such big news is just household talk to him. 'Have you heard, brother? They're building a second bridge on the Ganga—just now, I've received Kalipada's letter; there he's written everything.' And, taking out his spectacles, carefully wiping the glasses, he read out the letter to his neighbour very slowly from beginning to end. 'Just imagine, brother! Who knows in course of time what other things will happen? Ultimately, even the dogs and foxes with their dirty feet will cross the Ganga—in *Kaliyug*, even such nasty things happen, brother!' Such desecration of the Ganges was no doubt a most heinous thing. But the fact that the great message of Kaliyug's triumph Kalipada had recorded and sent him and that it was thanks to him that the utterly ignorant fellows of the village had come to know of this caused enough exultation for him even to forget his worries about the endless misery of creatures in the present age. To whomever he came across, he said nodding sagely, 'Take it from me, the Ganga's days are numbered.' In his mind, he persisted in hoping that as soon as the Ganges prepared to depart, that news would be known first of all from Kalipada's letter.

Meanwhile in Calcutta, Kalipada carried on with his studies staying in someone's house, managing with great difficulty by giving tuition and at night copying accounts books. Even so, he just about managed to pass the Entrance examination, securing a scholarship. To celebrate this amazing event, Bhabanicharan grew impatient to throw a grand feast for the villagers. He thought, 'The boat has all but reached the shore; so from now on I can spend rather freely.' As no encouragement from Rasmani was forthcoming, the feast was cancelled.

This time Kalipada found his lodging in a mess near his college. The manager of the mess had given him permission to stay in a rather unsatisfactory room on the ground floor. Kalipada, in lieu of teaching his son at his house, got two meals a day, and that damp, dark room of the mess was his shelter. One great advantage of that room was that Kalipada did not have to share it with anybody. Therefore, even though the ventilation was bad, there was no hindrance to his studies. In any case, Kalipada was in no position to judge its merits.

Those who were paid boarders of this mess, particularly the higher altitude ones of the first floor, had no connection with Kalipada. But even with no connection, there was no escape from confrontation. How tyrannical for the low the thundering of the high could be Kalipada was soon to realise.

In the heaven that was this mess, the person who occupied *Indra*'s throne needs some introduction. His name was Shailendra. He was a rich man's son; while reading in college, it was unnecessary for him to stay in a mess, yet that was where he loved to stay.

His parents had proposed that from their large family a few female and male relatives be brought over to Calcutta, then renting a house he stay with them; despite persuasion he had not agreed.

He had reasoned that staying in the company of family members would utterly hamper his studies. However, the true reason was different. Shailendra loved company very much, but the problem with relatives is that there is no getting away just with company; their numerous obligations have to be acknowledged—for someone, doing this is forbidden; for someone else, not doing that is blameworthy, and so on. That is why a mess was the most convenient place for Shailendra. There, companions were many, yet they burdened him with no responsibility. They came and went, laughed and talked; they were like the river, which only keeps flowing, yet nowhere leaves the slightest gap.

Shailendra's own notion about himself was that as a man, he was a model of goodness, whom people call genial. Everybody will know that one great advantage of this notion is that to maintain it to oneself, one need not necessarily be a good man. Vanity is not something like the elephant or the horse: practically at no cost and with no fodder one can keep it nourished.

But Shailendra had the wherewithal as well as the propensity to spend. For this reason, he would not let his own vanity to graze without costing him anything; instead getting costly feed, it had thrived handsomely.

In fact, there was no dearth of kindness in Shailendra's mind. He really loved to remove the sorrows of people. But he loved it so passionately that if anybody refused to seek his help, he would not flinch from inflicting the sorrow the man deserved. When his kindness turned unkind, it assumed a very fierce form.

Entertaining the boarders with theatre shows, hosting mutton feasts, after lending money not giving reminders—such things happened quite often. At the time of going back home on puja vacation, when a newly married youth, in a daze, after fully paying up the boarding charges would be left with little funds, he did not need to worry too much for buying his wife some fancy soap and captivating perfume and along with it, one or two currently imported cheap foreign jackets. Relying entirely on Shailen's taste, he would say, 'But you'll have to make the choice, friend.' Taking him along to the shop, he would pick up very cheap and low-quality stuff when Shailen would rebuke him, saying, 'For shame! What sort of a choice is that?' And he would pick out the most fashionable one. The manager would come up and say, 'Yes, this gentleman is discerning, indeed.' When the customer, on hearing the price looked glum, Shailen took upon himself the simple task of footing the bill, without heeding the repeated objection of the other party.

In this way, wherever Shailen stayed, to everyone around him he had become as good as a shelter in every sense. If anyone refused to accept his shelter, he could not at all tolerate the arrogance of that person. So keen was his benevolence.

Poor Kalipada, sitting on a wicker mat in his dank ground-floor room, with a tattered *genjee*[7] on and his eyes focused on the book, used to prepare his lessons all the while swaying to the cadence of his reading. He must win the scholarship, no matter how.

On the eve of his departure from home, his mother, uttering a self-imprecatory oath, had warned him that he must not indulge in merry-making and idle pastimes mixing with rich men's sons. Not only because of his mother's dictate, but if he were to preserve the destitution he had had to accept, it was impossible for him to fraternise with boys from affluent homes. He had never tried to make Shailen's acquaintance. Though he knew that if he won over Shailen's heart, most of his difficult problems could be simplified in a moment, yet even in the most critical situation, Kalipada had not craved for his favour. He lived with his wants hidden in the lonely gloom of his poverty.

Though he was poor, he would stay aloof: this was too much of a pride for Shailen to tolerate. That apart, in his food and dress, Kalipada's poverty was so conspicuous that it was a veritable eyesore. His abjectly poor clothes, his bed, and his mosquito net, whenever noticed by the boarders on their way upstairs, struck them as an offence. If that was not enough, he had an amulet dangling from his neck and he used to sit in prayer piously mornings and evenings. All this strange rusticity appeared as extremely ridiculous to the upper-floor occupants. One or two flunkeys of Shailen, to discover the mystery of this innocent recluse, frequented his room on a couple of days, but failed to get much out of this tongue-tied fellow. To keep sitting in his room was not pleasant, and by no means hygienic, so they had to quit.

If this indigent person were to be invited to their mutton feast, he would certainly be obliged: contemplating this, one day they rendered him the favour of an invitation. Kalipada told them that to digest the fare of a feast was beyond his capacity; his habits were different. At this rejection, Shailen, together with his retinue, was very much enraged.

For several days, in the room directly above his, thumping, stamping and music went on with such obtrusive loudness that it became well nigh impossible for Kalipada to concentrate on his studies. He used to do his studies by day, as far as possible repairing to Goldighi[8], sitting under a tree, and rising in the small hours, lighting a lamp.

While in Calcutta, because of unhealthy food and shelter, and hard labour in particular, Kalipada developed the symptoms of migraine. Sometimes, it became so severe that he had to keep to his bed for three or four days at a stretch. He knew it for sure that if his father got the news, he would no longer permit him to stay in Calcutta and in his anxiety, maybe, come all the way to Calcutta. Bhabanicharan knew that in Calcutta Kalipada was living in such comfort that it was impossible for the village folk even to imagine. In his perception, just as in the country, trees and plants, bushes and brambles grow spontaneously, so in the atmosphere of Calcutta, all kinds of creature comforts materialised, as if on their own, and everybody could enjoy their fruits. Kalipada had never tried to correct his father's misconception. Even in times of great suffering for his illness, never for a day had he refrained from writing a letter to him. But in those days of distress when Shailen and party raised a fearful din, Kalipada's misery knew no bounds. He would only toss and turn in his bed and lying in the empty room call for his mother and recall his father. The more he suffered the disgrace and distress of privation in this way, the more the resolve to liberate his parents from its bonds kept strengthening in his mind.

Kalipada, as far as possible by shrinking within himself, tried to avert the notice of others, but there was no respite from the torment. One day, he might find one of his old pair of cheap local shoes swapped with a superfine duplicate of foreign make. Going to college wearing such a dissimilar pair was out of the question. Without making any complaint about this, he kept the other one outside his room and from the shoe-mending cobbler purchasing a second-hand pair at a low price managed temporarily. Another day, a boarder from upstairs suddenly coming into Kalipada's room said, 'Have you by mistake brought back my cigarette case from my room? I can't find it anywhere.' Annoyed, Kalipada replied, 'I did not go to your room.' 'Oh, here it is.' Saying this, the man picked up a fancy cigarette case from one corner of the room, and without saying another word went away upstairs.

Kalipada promised to himself, 'If I can qualify for a handsome scholarship at the FA examination, I shall shift elsewhere leaving this mess.'

Every year, the boarders organised the *Swaraswati-puja* in an impressive way. The major part of its expenses Shailen used to bear, but everybody else also contributed. The previous year, in sheer disdain, no one had even approached Kalipada for subscription. This year, with the sole purpose of disturbing him, they produced the bill-book before him. Here was a fraternity from which Kalipada had never sought any aid, whose almost daily-celebrated revelry he had refused the good fortune of joining: when the same people approached Kalipada for subscription, I do not know from what consideration, he signed up all of five rupees. Five rupees Shailen had never received from anyone of his associates.

Because of Kalipada's niggardliness out of poverty, so far, they had despised him, but today this five-rupee donation was simply intolerable. 'What his actual condition is, is not at all unknown to us. Then why this arrogant pride? It appears he wants to score a point over everyone.'

Swaraswati-puja was celebrated with due pomp: the five rupees Kalipada had given made little difference. But this cannot be said as far as Kalipada was concerned. He had to eat in another's house; not everyday was food available in time either; besides, it was the servants of the kitchen who decided his lot; naturally, good or bad, adequate or scanty, without going into any unpleasant nit-picking, he had necessarily to keep away something in reserve for breakfast and tiffin. That little provision together with heaps of stale marigolds sank with the immersed idol.

Kalipada's chronic headache got worse. This time, he did not fail the examination but missed the scholarship. Necessarily, therefore, curtailing his study time, he had to seek out another tuition assignment, and in spite of much provocation, he could not forgo the rent-free accommodation.

The upper-floor residents had expected that this time surely Kalipada would not come back from his vacation to this mess. But at the right time, the door of the ground-floor room swung open. Over his dhoti, wearing that age-old square-painted china coat Kalipada entered his pigeonhole, and putting down a tin trunk along with a huge bundle wrapped in a dirty rag, the porter from Sealdah station squatting in front of his room, after much haggling, agreed to his charge. Inside that bundle, in earthen pots of various sizes and shapes, Kalipada's mother had neatly arranged various tasty preparations from green mango, jujube and other fruits prepared with her own hands. Kalipada was aware that in his absence, the curious upper-floor troupe used to make forays into his room. He had no other cause for worry, except that he was keenly anxious lest any memento of his parents' affection should fall in the hands of these taunting fellows. The goodies his mother had given him were heavenly food for him, but again, all this was a treasure of love from his poor rustic home. Even the containers in which they had been preserved—those earthen-lidded pots sealed with home-made adhesive—showed no signs of urban affluence: they were not glassware, or chinaware, but the thought that any town boy should look down upon them was unbearable to him. Last time, all these special things of his he used to keep hidden from view covered by old newspapers beneath his bed. This time, he took recourse to lock and key. Whenever he went out, even for five minutes, he used to lock the room .

This struck everyone as unseemly. Said Shailen, 'Wealth and jewels are aplenty! Pooh! Even a burglar, after entering the room, feels like weeping. And that room is being frequently locked—it's another 'Bank of Bengal', I see! None of us he can trust—in case, we couldn't resist the temptation of that Pabna[9] calico china coat.

Hey Radhu, I think we can no longer defer buying him a decent coat; what do you say? I'm thoroughly disgusted, seeing that single coat of his all along.'

Shailen had never entered Kalipada's damp, dark room with walls of peeling plaster. On his way up the stairs, just taking a glance from outside, he would feel a revulsion. Especially in the evening, when he saw that under a flickering lamp in that close stuffy room Kalipada sat bare-chested leaning over the book doing his lessons, he would feel suffocated. To his lackeys he said, 'Go and find out what treasure from the seven kings Kalipada has brought back this time.'

Everyone expressed enthusiasm anticipating the fun.

The lock on Kalipada's room door was a very cheap one; it was not forbidding enough; almost any key could open it. One evening, when Kalipada had gone to give tuition, taking that opportunity, two or three very fun-loving boys laughingly opened the lock to enter the room. From beneath the bed, they discovered the jars of pickles, chutney, *aamsattwa*[10], etc. However, it did not seem to them that these were very valuable things to be secreted away.

Further search yielded from under the pillow a key in a metal ring. With that key, when the tin trunk was opened, out came a couple of dirty dhotis, books, exercise books, scissors, penknife, pen and sundry other articles. After closing the trunk, they were about to go away when beneath all the clothes, handkerchief-bound, something was noticed. On beginning to unravel the handkerchief, peeped out a bundle wrapped in rags. When it was unwrapped, one after another peeling off about three or four layers of papers, out came a fifty-rupee note.

Seeing this note, no one could suppress his laughter; they burst into a boisterous laugh. Everyone was convinced that it was for this very note that Kalipada was now and again locking his room; he could not trust a soul in the world. At the stinginess and suspicious nature of the fellow, the toadying companions of Shailen were astonished.

Just then, someone's cough, maybe Kalipada's, was heard from the road outside. At once closing the lid of the trunk, even as the note was in someone's hand, they rushed upstairs. One of them hastily replaced the lock on the door.

Shailen had a hearty laugh to see the note. Fifty rupees was nothing at all to Shailen, yet nobody could have surmised from Kalipada's conduct that there could be even so much money in his box. Then again, for this small note such precaution! 'Well, let us see,' they decided, 'how oddly the bizarre fellow reacts on missing this money.'

Returning after nine at night, tired out from labouring with students, Kalipada had not noticed anything unusual about the room. Besides, his head was almost splitting. He could realise that this pain would keep racking his head for some days more.

Next day, for taking out his clothes, pulling up his trunk from under the bed he found it open. Even though Kalipada was not careless by nature, he thought that maybe he had forgotten to lock it. If any thief had come, the door would not have remained locked.

On opening the trunk, he saw that it was in a complete mess. His heart missed a beat. Hurriedly taking everything out, he found that the packets in paper and cloth were there but the note from his mother was missing. Repeatedly, Kalipada vigorously shook all his clothes; the note did not appear. Meanwhile, the upper inhabitants in ones and twos, as if on their own work coming downstairs, casting furtive glances at that room, went up and down frequently. Upstairs, a torrent of guffaws rent the air.

When there was no hope left of the note being retrieved and with his headache, moving things was no longer possible for him, he lay on his bed supine like a corpse. This note was his mother's token of many sorrows: it was the product of much pain suffered day after day, little by little.

There was a time when he knew nothing of the history of these sorrows; then, he had only heaped load upon his mother's load, until, in the end, the day his mother made him a sharer in her ever-returning daily sorrows, he felt proud as he had never felt before. The greatest message, the noblest blessing in his life that Kalipada had ever obtained had permeated this note. He regarded as a most fiendish curse the theft of that small invaluable gift of sorrow churned out of his mother's bottomless ocean of affection. The sound of footsteps down the adjoining stairs could be heard repeatedly today; needless comings and goings went on continually. It was as if in a fire in the village, everything is burning down to ashes, and right alongside it with an amused murmur, the river is flowing along ceaselessly.

Hearing the tumultuous laughter upstairs, suddenly it occurred to Kalipada that this was no thief's work. Instantaneously, he realised that Shailendra and company out of fun had taken away this note. Even if an outsider had stolen it, it would not have hurt him so much. It kept striking him that blinded with the arrogance of wealth, the young men had laid hands on his mother. For quite some time Kalipada had been staying in this mess, yet not even once had he gone upstairs. Today—that torn vest on his body, his feet bare, his face flushed from passion, and in the fever of his aching head—he rushed up.

It was Sunday: no compulsion of going to college; in the wooden-ceilinged veranda, some sitting on the bed, some on wicker stools, the friends were chatting. Kalipada stormed into their presence and in a voice choking with rage, burst out, 'Give back my note.'

If he had said this entreatingly, it would have been effective, no doubt. But seeing his madly furious attitude, Shailen became infuriated. Had the guard of his house been present, he would certainly have got this uncivil bumpkin summarily expelled. Rising to their feet, all of them shouted together, 'What are you saying, sir? What note?'

Kalipada said, 'From my trunk, you have taken away my fifty-rupee note.'

'You dare to say this? You mean we are thieves?'

If Kalipada had some weapon in his hand, that very moment he would have ended up in a murderous bid. Seeing his menacing attitude, four or five of them grabbed hold of his arms. He kept growling like a trapped tiger.

He had no power, no evidence to take steps against this wrong: whoever would hear him would dismiss his suspicion as crazy. Those who had assailed him with a deadly arrow kept blustering, finding his insolence intolerable.

How that night passed for Kalipada nobody knows. Taking out a hundred-rupee note, Shailen said, 'Go give it to the yokel.'

His companions said, 'Have you gone mad? Wait until his hauteur dies down; let him first submit a written apology addressed to us. Thereafter we will consider.'

They all went to bed as usual and took no time to fall asleep either. In the morning, almost everyone had virtually forgotten about Kalipada. Some of them, while descending the stairs could hear words coming from his room. They thought that perhaps he was taking counsel from a lawyer. The door was bolted from within. Putting ears against the door, what they heard had no connection with law; it was all incoherent muttering.

Going back, they reported the matter to Shailen. Shailen came down and stood near the door. What Kalipada was mumbling was not comprehensible properly; only, every few minutes he was crying out, 'Baba', 'Baba'.

Shailen was alarmed that maybe, mourning for the money, he had gone mad. Twice or thrice, he called, 'Kalipada-babu'. No one replied; only, that mumbling went on. Shailen, once again in a louder voice, called, 'Kalipada-babu, please open the door. That note of yours has been found.' The door did not open; only, a low recriminatory moan could be heard. Shailen had not even imagined that the matter could take such a serious turn. To his colleagues he did not express regret, but in his mind, it kept pricking him all the same. 'Let us break open the door,' he proposed.

Some of them advised, 'Call the police: in case, going berserk, he suddenly does something untoward; yesterday what aggressive attitude we saw makes one fear.'

Sailen said, 'No. Immediately, one of you go and call in doctor Anadi.'

Doctor Anadi lived nearby. After arriving, on putting his ears against the door he said, 'Most probably, it is delirium.'

After breaking open the door, going inside, they saw: the bed was rumpled, part of the bedclothes having slipped off lying on the floor, and Kalipada sprawled on the ground; he was unconscious. He was tossing about, at times throwing his hands and legs about and muttering deliriously. His blood-shot eyes were staring and his face was flushed blood-red.

The doctor, sitting beside him after examining him long, asked Shailen, 'Does he have a relative?'

Shailen's face went pale. Alarmed, he said, 'Why do you ask?'

'It is better to inform; the symptoms are not good.'

'We are not well acquainted with him; we know nothing about his relatives. We will make enquiries, but in the meantime, what ought to be done?'

The doctor said, 'The patient should be immediately shifted from here to a better room upstairs. Moreover, nursing is also necessary day and night.'

Shailen took the patient to his own room. Forbidding his friends to crowd round, he bade them all leave. Putting an ice bag on Kalipada's head, he kept fanning with his own hands.

As you will recall, lest the upper-storey men of this house should in any way express disdain or ridicule, Kalipada had kept the identities of his parents a secret. The letters he used to write them he would carefully drop at the post office, and at the post office address itself, letters in his name used to come which he would go and collect personally.

To get any clue about Kalipada's home, once again his trunk had to be opened. There were two bunches of letters, both very neatly tied with a tape. One bunch was his mother's letters, the other his father's. Mother's letters were rather few; father's were far more numerous.

Taking back the letters with him, Shailen closed the door and sitting beside the patient's bed started reading. The moment he read the sender's address, he was startled. Shaniyari, Chaudhuri House, Six-anna Tehshil! Subscribed: Bhabanicharan Devasharma[11]. Bhabanicharan Chaudhuri!

Putting aside the letters, sitting in a daze he kept looking at Kalipada's face. Some time back, once someone among his colleagues had said that his face very closely resembled Kalipada's. It did not sound pleasant to his ears, and the others had outright dismissed it. Today, he realised that the observation was not baseless. His grandfather Shyamacharan had a brother, Bhabanicharan; this much he knew. Subsequent history had never been discussed in their house. The fact that Bhabanicharan had a son and that his name was Kalipada was entirely unknown to him. So this was Kalipada! His uncle!

Then it kept coming to Shailen's mind: Shailen's grandmother, Shyamacharan's wife, as long as she was living, used to speak of Bhabanicharan until the end. Mere mention of Bhabanicharan's name would bring tears in her eyes. Bhabanicharan was her brother-in-law, indeed, but in age, he was even junior to her son; she had raised him virtually as her own son. In the property feud, when their family had been divided, she longed dearly just to hear a bit of news about Bhabanicharan. She had repeatedly told her sons, 'Because Bhabanicharan is an innocent simple lad, you have surely cheated him. My father-in-law loved him so much. I cannot believe that he should have deprived him of property.' Her sons would chafe at such words, and Shailen could remember he too would be very angry with his grandmother. So much so, that since his grandmother used to support Bhabanicharan's cause, he would be very angry even with him. He did not know at all that Bhabanicharan was so poverty-stricken: only from Kalipada's condition, he could comprehend everything, and he felt great pride contemplating that so long despite a thousand temptations Kalipada had not enlisted in his circle of sycophants. In case accidentally Kalipada had abased himself before him, there would have been no end to his shame now.

## 4

So far, almost every day the boys in Shailen's circle had tormented and insulted Kalipada. Shailen could not persuade himself to keep his uncle in their midst. Consulting the doctor, he shifted him to a decent place with great care.

On getting Shailen's letter, Bhabanicharan relying on a companion immediately rushed to Calcutta. Rasmani, solicitously handing most of her savings built up at great strain to her husband, said, 'See that there's no neglect in his treatment. If you feel it necessary, I'll go whenever you ask me to.' For a wife of the Chaudhuri family, the proposal of abruptly stepping out of home for as faraway a place as Calcutta was so improper that at the first call, her visit just did not happen. She vowed an offering to her deity[12] and sent word to the family astrologer to perform the propitiatory[13] rites.

Bhabanicharan was dumbfounded to see Kalipada's condition. Kalipada had not fully regained his senses : he called him master-*mashai*; this rent his heart. Frequently, in his delirium he called out, 'Baba', 'Baba'. And his father, holding his hand, bending over his face, spoke loudly, 'Here I am, son, I have come.' But Kalipada showed no sign that he had recognised him.

The doctor came and said, 'The temperature has dropped somewhat; now probably he will turn for the better.' That Kalipada would not turn for the better was for him an inconceivable eventuality. Especially, ever since his childhood, people had been saying that when he grew up, he would accomplish some impossible feat, which Bhabanicharan had not taken merely for hearsay; the conviction had been ingrained into his constitution. Kalipada must survive; he was destined to. For this reason, whatever little hope the doctor expressed, he ended up hearing far more than that, and in the letters he wrote to Rasmani there was absolutely no word that might be cause for any concern.

Bhabanicharan was completely amazed at Shailendra's conduct. Who would say he was not his dearest relation? Especially, despite being a well-educated, well-mannered boy of Calcutta, the way he respected him was quite unusual. He concluded that the boys of Calcutta were perhaps like this. He mused, 'That is only proper. As for our village boys, where do they get to receive education, and where will they learn their manners?'

The fever started remitting and Kalipada gradually regained his consciousness. He was startled to see his father at his bedside: he feared that now his condition in Calcutta was going to be revealed to his father. More worrying than this was the thought that his rustic father would become an object of ridicule to the townspeople. Looking around, he could not ascertain which room it was. 'Am I dreaming?' He wondered.

He had not the power then to think deeply. He thought that his father, after coming over to Calcutta, had shifted him to a better room. How he had moved him, where he was managing the expenses from, and if he kept spending like this, what crisis he would have to face afterwards—he was not in a frame of mind to ponder. His only thought now was that he must recover, for which seemingly he had a claim on the entire world.

Once Kalipada noticed that with his father somewhere else, Shailen came to him carrying some fruits in a tray. Surprised, Kalipada looked on at his face, wondering if this was not a mockery. His immediate concern was anyhow to save his father from this man's hands.

Shailen put down the tray, touched Kalipada's feet and said, 'I have done you grievous wrong. Please forgive me.'

Kalipada was in a nervous hurry. A mere look at his face convinced him that he had no hypocrisy in his mind. The first time Kalipada had come to the mess, this handsome face shining with a youthful glow had often attracted him, but inhibited by his own poverty he had never even approached him. If he were his equal, if the right to approach him like a friend were normal for him, how delighted he would have been! But, in spite of being very near to each other, there was no way to cross the insurmountable gulf in between. Whenever Shailen ascended or descended the staircase, the scent of his costly chuddar wafted into his dark room; then he could not refrain from putting aside his lessons taking a glance at this cheerful face unmarked by any lines of worry. At that time, only for an instant, in that damp corner room did the opulent resplendence of a faraway land of beauty come on a visit. We know how disastrous the same Shailen's ruthless youth had thereafter turned for him. Today, when Shailen held the tray of fruits in front of him on his bed, with a deep sigh Kalipada took another good look at that attractive face. As to forgiveness, he did not utter anything expressly: picking up the fruits, he began to eat, thereby conveying what he had to say.

Every day, Kalipada found to his surprise that Shailen had a growing intimacy with his upcountry father. Shailen called him *Thakur-da* and they freely exchanged jokes and banter. The butt of all their fun was the absent grandmother[14]. So long after, inspired by the waves of this south wind of jest, the reminiscences of youth seemed to be instilling rapturous delight in Bhabanicharan's mind. *Thakrun-didi*'s homemade pickles and mango goodies Shailen, taking opportunity of the patient's unwariness, had made short work of completely, which he acknowledged today without shame. This revelation of theft brought great delight to Kalipada's mind. He would have wished to invite the whole world to taste the delicacies made with his mother's own hands, if only they appreciated their value. For Kalipada, his sickbed turned into a get-together of rejoicing: rarely had he enjoyed such bliss in his life. Only, it kept occurring to him, 'Alas, had my mother been present!' Had his mother been present, he wondered, how dearly she would have loved this handsome fun-loving youth.

In their sickroom meeting, there was only one topic of discussion which would sometimes impede the flow of joy. Kalipada seemed to nurture a feeling of injured vanity for his poverty: he felt very ashamed to boast that once upon a time, they had plenty of wealth. 'We are poor.' This stark reality he was not at all willing to qualify with the addition of a 'but'. Neither would Bhabanicharan boast about their affluent days. But those were his happy times, after all; they were his days of youth. The horrible image of the treacherous world had not been revealed yet. Particularly, when Shyamacharan's wife, his very affectionate *Baudidi* Ramasundari was the mistress of their family, standing at the door of that *Lakshmi's* storeroom, what bounties of affection there were for the taking! The afterglow of the memory of those bygone days of glory was what had kept the evening of Bhabanicharan's life tinged with gold. But in course of the rumination of all this happy memory, relentlessly that incident of the theft of the will kept coming back. This one context left Bahabanicharan very agitated: even now, there was hope of getting back that will; about this, there was not a shade of doubt in his mind; his virtuous mother's words were never to prove fruitless. Whenever this context cropped up, Kalipada grew restive inwardly. He knew that this was but an obsession with his father. Mother and son amicably had even indulged this idée fixe; yet he could by no means accept that this weakness of his father should be betrayed before Shailen. How many times he had told his father, 'No, father, that is a false notion of yours.' But such contradictions would prove counterproductive: To substantiate his suspicion of fraud, he would keep recounting the entire story in minute detail. Then there was no stopping him despite Kalipada's various efforts until he had finished.

Especially, Kalipada had clearly observed that Shailen did not like discussion on this topic. He too, seemingly a bit excitedly, would try to refute Bhabanicharan's argument. In every other matter,

Bhabanicharan was willing to accept others' opinions, but in this matter, he could not concede defeat. His mother was literate: she had personally kept his father's will as well as the other deed in a box and put them away in the iron safe. Yet, when in his very presence, his mother opened the box, the deed was there all right, but the will was not: if this was not theft, what was? To appease him, Kalipada would say, 'All right, Baba, I accept your point, but those who have been enjoying the property are only like your sons, aren't they? They are your nephews. After all, the property continues to be in your father's family itself: this is happiness enough.' Shailen could not bear these discussions for too long; he would excuse himself and leave the room. Inwardly hurt, Kalipada was afraid that perhaps Shailen was thinking his father a grasping, mercenary man. If he were somehow to convince Shailen that on the contrary, there was not a shade of materialism in his father's nature Kalipada would have been greatly relieved.

By now, Shailen would surely have revealed his identity to Kalipada as well as Bhabanicharan, were it not for these references to the will. He could by no means believe that his father and grandfather had stolen the will. Yet, neither could he deny that there was a cruel injustice in Bhabanicharan having been deprived of his legitimate share. From now on, he altogether stopped arguing in this matter: he would keep silent, and at the least opportunity withdraw from the discussion.

Still now, in the afternoon Kalipada had spells of headache with slight temperature, but this he ignored as of no consequence. He became avid for studies. He had missed the scholarship once, and certainly could not afford to repeat the failure. Averting Shailen's notice, he resumed his studies; even knowing the doctor's advice to the contrary, he ignored it.

To Bhabanicharan, Kalipada said, 'Baba, you'd rather go back: there mother is all alone. As for me, I'm quite well, as you see.'

Shailen added, 'Now if you go, there's no harm. At least I don't think there's any cause for worry; the little that lingers will get well in a couple of days. And we are here, after all.'

Bhabanicharan said, 'That I know quite well; with all of you here, there's nothing to worry about Kalipada. After all, there was no need of my coming over to Calcutta in the first place; yet, son, how could I convince myself ? Especially, for your *Thakrun-didi*: whenever and whatever she insists, there's no getting away from it.'

Shailen smiled and said, '*Thakur-da,* isn't it you who spoilt Thakrun-didi with all the doting?'

'All right, son, all right,' said Bhabanicharan with a laugh. 'Let me wait till my granddaughter-in-law arrives, then I'll see how strict your administration can be.'

Bhabanicharan was essentially a creature of Rasmani's tending. Even the various comforts of Calcutta could not make up for the want of Rasmani's care. Naturally, he did not require much persuading to go back home.

In the morning, he was ready with his goods packed, when going into Kalipada's room to take leave, he found that his face and eyes were extremely flushed, his body burning hot. Almost half the night he had been studying and memorising logic; the rest of the night, he had not had a wink of sleep.

Kalipada had not quite recovered from his weakness; on top of that, there was this virulent relapse of the ailment: the doctor was particularly worried. Taking Shailen aside, he said, 'This time I don't find the indications good.'

Shailen told Bhabanicharan, 'Look, Thakur-da, you're suffering hardship; neither is the patient getting proper nursing. So I suggest that without further delay Thakrun-didi be brought over.'

Howsoever Shailen might try to play it down, a horrible fear overcame Bhabanicharan; his hands and legs trembled violently. He said, 'Do what you think proper.'

A letter went to Rasmani. Immediately along with Bagalacharan, she came over to Calcutta. After arriving in the evening, just for a couple of hours she could see Kalipada alive. In his delirium, every few moments he had called for his mother: those sounds remained stuck in her heart.

Apprehensive about how Bhabanicharan would survive this blow, Rasmani found no scope to express her own bereavement properly. The thought of her son now merged in her husband: the burden of both of them she now took upon herself. Her heart said, 'I can bear it no more.' Nevertheless, she had to bear.

## 5

It was quite late in the night. In the exhaustion of profound grief, only for a while Rasmani had fallen asleep, senseless. But Bhabanicharan had no sleep. He tossed about in his bed for some time, and then with a long sigh saying 'O Gracious Hari', he got up. With a lamp held in his trembling hand, Bhabanicharan entered the corner room where Kalipada used to sit reading when he was in the village school before he had not gone over to Calcutta. The torn *kantha*[15] embroidered in Rasmani's hand was still spread on the bed, patches of ink at various places of it even now showing. On the dirty wall, charcoal-painted geometrical lines could be seen; at one corner of the bed, along with some hand-bound soiled exercise books a tattered copy of Royal Reader, Part III, was lying even today. And—alas!—a single slipper of his small foot of childhood, which had been lying in a corner, and so far no one had cared to notice, today dwarfing everything else became prominent to his eyes: in the world, there was no precious thing that could overshadow that tiny shoe.

After putting the lamp in the recess, Bhabanicharan sat on the bed. No tears came to his dry eyes, but within his breast, something kept tormenting him: his ribs seemingly wanted to burst open to inhale sufficient amount of air. Opening the eastern door of the room, holding the bar of the window, he stood looking out.

The night was dark; it was drizzling. In front of him, there was dense jungle surrounded by the compound wall. Within it, right in front of his reading room, in a small tract of land Kalipada had fashioned a garden of his own. The bellflower creeper he had planted with his own hands, spreading abundant foliage on the bamboo fence, was still vibrant with life, laden with flowers.

Today, as he kept looking at the carefully tended garden of that boy, a lump seemed to form in his throat. There was nothing more to hope for; during the summer, during the puja, the college would close as usual for vacation, but the one for whom his decrepit home lay empty would never again on any holiday return home. 'O my darling son!' Uttering this, Bhabanicharan flopped down right there upon the ground. Solely with the aim of removing his father's poverty had Kalipada gone to Calcutta, but when he departed, how utterly destitute in the whole wide world he left behind this old man! Outside, the rain came down in torrents.

Suddenly then, in the darkness, footsteps could be heard on the grass and leaves. Bhabanicharan felt a pounding in his heart. What was not to be expected even in the wildest dream, he ended up to expect. It seemed to him that Kalipada had come to visit his garden. But it was raining heavily, so he would be drenched; this unreasonable anxiety made him restive, when outside the window bars in front of his room, someone came and stood for a moment. His head was shrouded all over with a chuddar—his face could not be recognised. But he looked as tall as Kalipada. 'So you have come, my son?' Saying this, Bhabanicharan hurriedly went to open the door. Coming into the garden, he arrived in front of that room. Nobody was there. Braving the rain, he wandered across the garden, but found none. At that dead of night, standing in the dark, he screamed out once in a cracked voice, 'Kalipada!'; no one responded. Alerted by that call, the servant Notu came out of the cowshed, and after much persuasion brought back the old man into his room.

Next morning, Notu, on going to sweep the room, found near the window something tied up in a bundle. He took it to Bhabanicharan. On opening it, the latter found something like an old deed. Putting on his spectacles, just taking a glance he hurriedly came to Rasmani and opened it up in front of her.

'What's that?' asked Rasmani.

'The will.'

'Who gave it?'

'Last night he came; he left it.'

'What will you do with it?'

'I don't need it any more.'

And he tore that document into shreds.

When this news spread in the village, Bagalacharan, nodding his head, said proudly, 'Did I not say that ultimately it is by Kalipada that the will would be recovered?'

Ramcharan, the grocer, said, 'But, Dada-*thakur*, last night when the ten-o'-clock train arrived at the station, a good-looking *Babu* came to my shop and asked me about the direction of the Chaudhuri house; I showed him the way. I seem to have seen something in his hand.'

'Stuff and nonsense!' Bagalacharan dismissed it altogether.

*Ashwin 1318* (1911)

## NOTES

1 In the Hindu iconography, goddess of fortune, Lakshmi (see Glossary) rides a white owl; 'gold feathers' is the author's imagination, perhaps in keeping with its association with wealth.

2 There is a saying in Bengali, which in rough translation stands thus: seasoned grains are the most plentifully productive of rice.

3 Son of Arjuna in the Mahabharata. A valiant fighter at a very tender age; he had not yet learnt the tactics of exiting the chakravyuh (circular battle formation) though he had mastered the art of entering it. Eventually, he was slain by seven charioteers fighting together in a most ignominious violation of the Kshatriya code of conduct.

4 A term of respect used for a European, esp. British, married woman; 'mem' in short.

5 Seventh lunar day of the bright fortnight of *Ashwin*; *Durga-puja*

begins on the seventh and ends on the tenth when the idol is immersed (see Glossary).

6 The island state of Ceylon (now Sri Lanka).

7 A knitted, cotton inner wear for the upper body of males, a vest (originally, from Guernsey in the Channel Islands).

8 A public park in central Calcutta.

9 A district in Bangladesh.

10 Sunned and dried ripe-mango pulp.

11 A general surname for Brahmans.

12 The text has *Rakshakali*, an aspect of goddess Kali (see Glossary) in which form she is worshipped seeking protection (*raksha*) from danger.

13 The text has swastyayan: the term is shanti-swastyayan; the first part means appeasement, the second part, bringing prosperity.

14 The text has *Thakrun-didi*, feminine forms of the corresponding parts in *Thakur-da*; traditionally, grandparents in rural Bengal were and still are on crude jocular terms with their grandchildren up to a certain state of maturity; as, for example, 'How do you like me for a bridegroom?' or, 'bride', as the case may be.

15 Several sheets of discarded cloth stitched together, sometimes embroidered with needle-work, used as substitute for quilt in winter, and even as bedspread in villages and slums.

# Fertility Sacrifice
# (*Putrayajna*)

Baidyanath was reputed in his village to be a prudent man. Naturally, what he did in the present he did with an eye to the future. When he married, he could envision the future newborn's face more distinctly than he saw the newly-wed's face. Such foresight at the time of the traditional *shubhadrishti*[1] is rarely seen. He was a shrewd man, and therefore understood rituals[2] better than conjugal love. One marries only to beget a son: this was his motto[3] when he married Binodini.

But here, in this world, even a wise person can be deceived. When Binodini did not perform her principal duty in spite of being well into her youth, Baidyanath was deeply concerned over condemnation to *punnamnarak*[4] being a certainty. Then again, a concern about who would enjoy his vast wealth after his death made him rather averse to enjoying that wealth in his lifetime. The future, rather than the present, was the only truth to him, as I said.

But such profound sagacity cannot be expected from a young Binodini all at once. The poor girl's precious present and blossoming youth were passing away without love, without fruit: that was the most pitiable thought for her. The fiery longing in her heart made her forget any hunger she might have had for the posthumous rice.

Manu's holy injunction[5] and Baidyanath's spiritual exposition did not help assuage her famished heart in the least.

After all, at her age giving love and receiving love is what a woman naturally considers superior to all other pleasures, all other duties of life.

Instead of being sprinkled with the raindrops of sprouting love, Binoda [a variant of Binodini] had to endure the hailstorm of hectoring and roars from the lofty sky of her husband, aunt-in-law and other weighty and weightier persons; everyone reproached her as a barren woman. Her wasted youth found itself in a situation similar to that of a flowering plant kept in an enclosure cut off from air and light.

Unable to bear the continuous nettling and scolding, when she went to Kusum's house, the hour she spent playing cards gave her a great deal of joy. With the terrible shadow of *Puth-hell* not haunting her there, laughter and banter flowed freely.

On any day when Kusum had no partner for the game, she would rope in her young brother-in-law Nagendra, laughing off any objection from him or Binoda. Here in this world, one thing leads to another; what is now mere sport can eventually turn into a crisis: such serious matters do not immediately seem plausible at a young age.

About this, any firmness of objection from Nagendra was not noticeable either; no longer now could he wait for much persuasion. Thus, Nagendra and Binoda came to meet often enough.

When Nagendra sat down to play, his eyes and his mind remaining glued to something more animate than cards, he often lost the game. The real reason for his defeat was not beyond Kusum or Binoda to recognise. As I have said, the gravity of the consequences of action is not for the immature to comprehend. Kusum used to think that what was going on was good fun; she was rather keen that the fun would eventually grow into its fullest form. Secretly watering the germinating seed of love is a highly amusing pastime for young women.

No less interesting was it to Binoda either. For a woman to wish to hone her skill of winning hearts on a man may be wrong, but is not quite unnatural.

The game thus continuing in cycles of win and loss, and the cards turning up kings and queens repeatedly, the two minds became one, which, apart from the Omniscient, was noticed by another observer who felt amused.

One afternoon, Binoda, Kusum and Nagendra were playing cards. After a while, Kusum went off to attend to her sick baby who had started crying. Nagendra kept chatting with Binoda. But what he was talking about, he himself was unable to make out; streams of blood surged from his heart along the veins throughout his body. Suddenly at a point, his wild youthful passion got the better of his sense of modesty; seizing hold of her arms and forcibly drawing her close, he kissed her. Terribly angered, grieved and ashamed at this insult, Binoda was struggling to wrest her hands free when suddenly they noticed that a third person had entered the room. Nagendra, his face lowered, began to look for the way out of the room.

'*Bauthakrun,*' said the maidservant in a grim voice, '*Pishima*'s calling you.' With her eyes brimming with tears, darting fiery glances at Nagendra, Binoda went away with the maidservant.

Making a molehill of what she had seen and a mountain out of what she had not seen, the maidservant managed to raise a storm in Baidyanath's household. The misery Binoda was reduced to is easier imagined than described. That she was absolutely without fault she did not try to explain to anyone, and bore it all, in abject humility.

Baidyanath, after calculating that his chances of begetting an heir to perform his funeral rites was extremely remote, castigated Binoda, 'Unchaste woman! Get out of my house.'

Binoda lay down on her bed after shutting the door of the bedroom, her tearless eyes blazing like the desert at noon. When the evening grew darker, and the crows in the garden fell silent, looking up to the serene star-studded sky, she remembered her parents, and then tears kept rolling down her cheeks.

That night, Binoda went away leaving her husband's home forever. Nobody even cared to trace her. At that time, she did not know about *Prajanartham mahabhaga*[6]: she had acquired a woman's greatest blessing; her husband's salvation in the next world had germinated in her womb.

Ten years passed by after this episode. Meanwhile, Baidyanath's financial condition had improved considerably. Now, leaving the village, he had purchased a big house in Calcutta for his residence. But the more his wealth mounted, the more anxiously his heart agitated for an inheritor of the wealth.

He married twice more in succession; they yielded only quarrels but no son. Swarms of soothsayers, faith healers and sannyasis filled his house; roots, amulets, consecrated waters and patent medicines kept pouring down like rain. If the bones of goats sacrificed at Kalighat[7] were gathered, the pile would have dwarfed Tamerlane's victory-tower made of skeletons. Yet, not even a tiny baby—just a few bones packed in a small lump of flesh—came to occupy a corner in Baidyanath's palatial house. Worrying about which unknown man's son would eventually feed off his estate, he lost all appetite for food himself.

Baidyanath married yet again: for in the world, hope springs eternal, and there is no lack of marriageable daughters either. Astrologers, on examining the bride's horoscope pronounced that the girl's conjunctions for sons were so favourably aligned that it was not long before Baidyanath's house would be swarming with offspring. Six long years passed thereafter; still the conjunctions never became active.

Baidyanath sank into despair. At last, on the advice of pundits versed in the scriptures, he performed an enormously expensive fertility sacrifice[8] that fed scores of Brahmans for scores of days.

Meanwhile, in the nationwide famine, people of Bengal, Bihar and Orissa had been reduced to only skin and bones. While sitting amidst his inexhaustible stock of rice, Baidyanath wondered, 'Who will eat my rice', the starving nation was staring vacantly at her empty platter despairing, 'What shall I eat?'

Over a period of four months then, Baidyanath's fourth wife had been drinking the water in which a hundred Brahmans had dipped their feet, while one hundred Brahmans eating extravagant lunches and lavish dinners had been filling the municipality's rubbish vats with their discarded pots and plates, and banana-leaves smeared with curd and ghee. Drawn by the smell of food, crowds of starving people kept buzzing at the gates; additional doorkeepers had to be employed to keep them away day and night.

One morning, in Baidyanath's marble mansion, a pot-bellied sannyasi was treating himself to a meal of two seers of *mohanbhog*[9] and one-and-a-half seers of milk; Baidyanath wearing a chuddar on his body sitting obsequiously on the ground with joined palms, was piously watching this holy gastronomic sight. Then, somehow evading the doorkeepers, an extremely thin woman with an emaciated boy entered and said, 'Babu, give us something to eat.'

An irritated Baidyanath yelled out, 'Gurudayal! Gurudayal!' Fearing worse, the woman wailed piteously, 'Babu, give the child something to eat; I don't want anything.'

Gurudayal came and chased the boy and his mother away.

That hungry unfed boy was Baidyanath's only son.

One hundred plump Brahmans and three stout sannyasis alluring Baidyanath with the false prospect of a son went on gorging themselves on his food.

*Jyaishtha 1305* (1898)

NOTES

1 A ritual of Hindu weddings among Bengalis, when the bride is unveiled for the first time in front of the groom.

2 According to Hindu custom, *pinda* is a morsel of rice offered by a son to his departed father and ancestors in propitiation of the soul as part of the funerary rites.

3 The Sanskrit saying ascribed to Manu: *Putrarthe kriyate bharya.*

4 The hell named *Puth* where sonless people are condemned after death.

5 See *Note* 3.

6 *Prajanartham mahabhaga*: fertility is a woman's greatest blessing.

7 A religious spot in Calcutta, famous for its Kali Temple, visited by lakhs of devotees all the year round to offer their prayers including animal sacrifice as part of the ritual.

8 This is the *yajna* that gives the story its title.

9 A sweetened dessert made of coarse flour of wheat usually cooked in milk and ghee sprinkled with raisin and cardamom.

# Nature's Child
(*Balai*)

The biography of human beings is said to appear as an epilogue to the history of all other forms of life on earth. In humans, we find latent shades of the various species of animal life. In fact, what we call human is the trait that tames and harmonises the animal in us—that puts the cow and the tiger in us in the same enclosure, the snake and the mongoose in the same cave. A raga is nothing but the notes in it—only synthesised into music when none of them can go out of tune, except that a certain note dominates the scale—'ma' in one, soft 'ga' in another, 'pa' in a third.

My elder brother's son Balai: in his nature, somehow, the principal traits of plant life were the dominant ones. Since his childhood, looking on quietly was his habit, not moving around. In the eastern sky, black clouds piled up menacingly; his entire mind was filled with the smell of a rain-sodden forest that seemed to be wafted in by damp monsoon winds. Rain fell in torrents; his entire body seemed to take in that sound of rain. On the terrace, the afternoon sun reclined; he would move about with his upper body bare: from all the sky, he would imbibe some indefinable thing. At the end of *Magh*, mango trees blossomed; his veins throbbed with an intimate joy from some ineffable memory. Like the blooming *shal* trees in

*Phalgun*, his inner nature branched out on all sides, filled up to the brim and took on a deeper hue. At these times, sitting alone he liked to talk to himself, patching up whatever stories he had ever heard, like the story of the old pair of tattler birds[1] nesting in the hoary old banyan tree, and so on.

With his big round eyes always staring at things, the boy could not talk much, and so in his mind he had to do a lot of thinking. Once I took him to the hills. In front of our cottage, there was a lush green carpet of grass that rolled down a slope as far as the foot of the hills. He looked on, and his heart filled with great joy. He did not think the layer of grass was stationary; he imagined it to be a game on the roll, continuously moving. Quite often, he would himself roll down that slope; with all his body, he would become a reel of grass: as he turned, its blades would tickle his neck, and he would giggle.

After rain at night, in the early morning, from above the top of the hill ahead sunlight the colour of pure gold spread over the deodar forest: without alerting anyone, going quietly to that deodar forest he would stand fascinated all alone under its shade. He had an eerie sensation: he seemed to visualise the men embodied within these huge trees; they did not speak, but seemed to know everything. They were like ancient grandfathers, of the once-upon-a-time-there-was-a-king antiquity.

It was by no means that his dreamy eyes were set only upwards. I often found him walking in the garden, scanning the ground for something. Saplings with their curled up heads sprouting in sunlight he had no end of interest in watching. Every day bending over them, he seemed to ask, 'What next? Then? And then?' They were his ever-incomplete story. With the newly sprouted tender leaves he had a sort of camaraderie; how could he express exactly what it was like? They too were eager to ask him a certain question. Perhaps they would ask, 'What is your name?' Or, 'Where is your mother?' Balai would answer in his mind, 'My mother is no more, don't you know?'

That anyone should pluck flowers from trees hurt him most. At the same time, he also realised that this sentiment meant nothing to others, and so he wanted to conceal his agony. Boys of his age by repeatedly stoning the tree brought down *amla* fruits; he could not protest, and turning his face went away from there. Simply to tease him, his friends, while walking through the garden lashed away at the trees on either side with sticks, or suddenly snapped a *bakul* twig: he felt ashamed to cry, lest they should consider it crazy. He had his worst distress when the grass-cutter came to clip the shrubs. In them, he had watched marvels everyday—small creepers, nameless flowers—violet and yellow, very tiny; here and there nightshade creepers, their blue flowers with a golden blob at the centre; alongside the fence, medicinal herbs—a *kalmegh* here, an *anantamool* there; bird-eaten *neem* seeds had sprouted into saplings: how pretty their bluish green leaves! Each one was trimmed with the weeding trowel most cruelly. They were no prized collections; there was no one to heed their protests.

On some days, he would come to his aunt, and sitting on her lap embracing her, say, 'Please tell the grass cutter to spare those favourite plants of mine.'

'Balai, don't be silly,' his aunt would say, 'Those are weeds. Can they be left to grow?'

Balai had long begun to realise that there were certain agonies which were exclusively his own: in no one around him did they leave any sensation.

This boy had originated aeons ago, when the future flora of the earth had let out its birth cry in the marshlands sprung up from the womb of the ocean when there were no beasts, no birds, no din and bustle of life, when there were only rocks and mud and water. That day, the plant, as the forerunner of all life in the march of time, had reared its head to the sun, and prayed with joined hands, 'I have come to stay; I will live. I am an eternal traveller. I will survive cycles of death and cycles of time, on my journey to the holy grail of endless life'. That spirited vow of the progenitor of plants reverberates to this day through the woods, the hills, and the meadows. Through their leaves and branches echoes the earth with all her heart, 'I must live; I must live'. The plant as the foster-mother of life on earth has been drawing from the heavens since time immemorial the sap, the vigour, and the flavour of life for the nectar-bowl of earth, and flooding the skies with the message of beleaguered life, 'I want to live'. That message of universal life Balai could hear in some inexplicable way in his veins. We had a good laugh at his expense.

One morning, I was intently reading the newspaper, when Balai came and took me hurriedly into the garden. Pointing at a particular plant, he asked me, 'Uncle, what kind is this?'

I saw it was a silk-cotton plant that had sprouted in the middle of the pebbled walk.

Poor boy! He had made a mistake of calling me out. Balai had noticed the plant when it had just germinated, like the first babbles of an infant. Since then, he had watered it everyday, eagerly watched it grow mornings and evenings. Silk-cotton trees grow fast, though not fast enough to keep pace with Balai's eagerness. When it had grown about three feet high, looking at its luxuriant foliage he thought, 'It is a marvellous tree,' just as any mother, when she notices the first signs of intelligence in her child, wonders, 'An amazing child!" Balai thought he would astonish his uncle as well by showing the plant.

I said, 'I'll tell the gardener to uproot it and throw it away.'

Balai was appalled. What a horrible thought! He said, 'No Uncle, I beg you, please don't.'

'That's a silly thing to say,' I chided him. 'Don't you see it has grown right in the middle of the path? When it comes to blossom, it will scatter cotton all around and be a big nuisance.'

When he could not bring me round, the motherless child went to his aunt. Sitting on her lap, hugging her and whimpering, he said, 'Dear Aunt, tell Uncle not to cut down the tree.'

He had hit upon the right plan anyway. His aunt told me, 'Can't you spare it for the poor child, please?' I did spare it in the end.

If Balai had not shown it, perhaps I would not have noticed the plant in the first place. Now it attracted my notice every day. Within a year, the tree grew shamelessly tall. It also became his favourite.

Every day the tree made its presence felt like a most stupid thing. Rooted to an unusual spot, it stayed put, regardless of anyone, and grew straight into the sky. Whoever looked at it wondered, 'What on earth is it doing here?' I had proposed its extermination another couple of times, and even tried to coax Balai by promising some choice rose saplings to forget the cotton plant.

In the end, I said, 'All right, if you must have a cotton tree, I'll get another sapling planted near the fence; it will look good there'. But every time I proposed to cut down the plant he was aghast, and his aunt would say, 'Whatever you might say, it doesn't look so bad, after all'.

My elder brother's wife had died when Balai was a few months old. Perhaps because of this shock, my elder brother had taken a fancy to studying engineering, and gone to England. The boy was left to grow up in my home in the care of his childless aunt. My brother came back after about ten years. He decided to provide British-style schooling for Balai, and took him to Shimla[2] with the idea of later moving him to England.

Balai wept much for having to leave his aunt. Our home became childless again.

Two years passed thereafter. All these days, Balai's aunt had shed secret tears for him, and going into Balai's empty bedroom fiddled with a torn shoe, a ripped rubber ball and illustrated books of animal fables, even as she thought that by now Balai must have outgrown his fancy for these things.

At one point, I thought that the wretched cotton tree had grown too big—too much of an eyesore—to be ignored any more. One day, I felled it.

About this time, Balai wrote to his aunt from Shimla, saying, 'Aunt, please send me a photograph of my silk-cotton tree.'

He had thought of visiting us before finally leaving for England. Somehow, it did not come about. Therefore, he wanted to carry a picture of his friend with him.

His aunt told me, 'Please call in a photographer.'

I asked why.

She showed me the letter Balai had written her in his novice hand.

I told her I had already cut down the tree.

Balai's aunt refused to take any food for two days, and did not talk to me for a long time. When Balai's father had taken him away from her lap, it was as if by cutting her umbilical cord. Now, when his uncle removed his dear tree, it similarly dealt a severe blow to her world of motherly affection, and left a wound in her heart.

After all to her, that tree was Balai's prototype, his alter ego.

*Agrahayan 1335* (1928)

NOTES

1 Banghama, banghami < bangama, bangami < bihangam, bihamgami, Sanskrit words for bird couple; a kind of telltale or tattler birds mentioned in many Bengali fairy-tales, as for instance, those by Abanindranath Tagore.

2 One of the hill resorts where such residential schools followed a wholly British system of schooling.

# Woman Bereft of Jewels (*Manihara*)

I had moored my boat beside that dilapidated paved *ghat.* The sun had set then.

The oarsman was reading his *namaaz*[1] on the roof of the boat. In the blazing canvas of the western sky, the gestures of his silent worship were being silhouetted intermittently. Mirrored on the motionless placid water, the myriad streaks of colour were fast shading from lighter into deeper, from golden into steel, from one tint into another.

In front of a big ramshackle mansion with broken windows and a half-collapsed balcony, on the ghat ruptured by the roots of a peepul tree, I was sitting alone in the evening abuzz with the call of crickets. My eyes had just begun to moisten, when my hair stood on end as I heard the words, 'Where is the gentleman coming from?'

The man looked emaciated from malnutrition, very much like the long-withered uncared-for appearance of an average Bengali working elsewhere not favoured by fortune. He wore a dhoti and a dirty oil-stained unbuttoned *chapkan* of some coarse silk from Assam; he looked as if he had returned from his work a short while ago, and when he should have taken some refreshment, had come for some evening air instead.

The stranger sat beside me on the steps. 'I am from Ranchi,' I introduced myself.

'What do you do?'

'Business.'

'What trade?'

'Myrobalan, silk-worm, and timber.'

'Your name?'

After a pause, I gave a name, which was not my real name.

He was still curious. 'What brings you here?'

'Change of climate.'

The man was somewhat puzzled. 'Look, sir,' he said, 'For nearly six years I've been taking in this air together with an average dose of fifteen grains of quinine each day. But no result so far.'

'You must admit that the climate here is very much different from Ranchi's.'

'That's true, sir, very much different. Where are you putting up?'

'In this house,' I pointed to the rickety building overlooking the ghat.

Perhaps, the man suspected that I had discovered some hidden treasure in this deserted house, but he raised no further question in that context, only recounted the event that had happened fifteen years back in this ill-fated house.

He was a local schoolmaster. His famished and sickly face beneath his bald head had a pair of large deep-set eyes that shone with extraordinary brightness. He reminded me of the Ancient Mariner created by the English poet Coleridge.

The oarsman, after finishing his prayer, went about his cooking. As evening descended, the dark abandoned building stood like a giant apparition of its former self.

The schoolmaster began his story:

About ten years before I came to live in this village, Phanibhushan Saha had been living in this house. He had inherited the huge estate and business of his uncle Durgamohan Saha who had died without a son.

But Phanibhushan was a product of the modern times. He had received education. He would not hesitate to walk straight into the sahib's office with his boots on, and speak in chaste English. Moreover, he wore his beard. Naturally, he had no chance of ever getting any sahib merchants' patronage. One look at him gave the impression of a 'Young Bengal' association.

Moreover, he had a permanent trouble in his home as well. His wife was beautiful. What with his college education and his wife's beauty, a traditional lifestyle was given the go-by. Even when they fell ill, they used to call in the Assistant Surgeon. Their taste in food, clothing and ornaments soared coorrespondingly.

You must be a married man, so you will know that women are generally fond of green mangoes, hot chillies and stern husbands. The unfortunate man who is deprived of his wife's love is not necessarily bad looking or impecunious; he is extremely docile. If you ask me why, I have my own explanation.

No one is happy without cultivating individual instincts and faculties. To rub his horns, a deer looks for the trunk of a hard tree; a banana trunk is no good for him. Ever since men and women appeared as distinct species, women have been practising the art of taming imperious men with various deceptive tricks. The husband who willingly capitulates denies his wife her job. Weapons like the *varunashtra, nagpash* and *agnivan*[3], which have been honed through the ages and handed down by her grandmothers, all go to waste. What a woman wants is to enthral her husband and then exact his love in her own capacity. If the husband is too submissive to give his wife that opportunity, it is most unfortunate for him and even more so for his wife.

Indoctrination into the modern culture has divested males of their inborn god-gifted noble barbarity reducing conjugal relations to a rather tame affair. The wretched Phanibhushan had emerged a perfect gentleman from the machine of modern civilisation. He could neither prosper in his business nor make much headway in his marital relations.

Phanibhushan's wife Manimalika used to get love without effort, Dacca-saris[2] without tears and bracelets without sulks. In the process, her feminine instinct, and with it her passion, had become inert. She was used to receiving only; she never gave anything. Her innocent and stupid husband believed that perhaps gifts alone begot gifts from others. Who could have been farther from the truth? Eventually, she came to regard her husband as a machine to turn out her Dacca-saris and bracelets, and befittingly enough, the machine was so perfect that never once did it require even to be lubricated with a drop of oil.

Phanibhushan's birthplace was Phulbere and he conducted his business here. He had to stay here most of the year under business compulsions. At Phulbere, though he did not have his mother, there were his parents' sisters and several other relatives. However, it was by no means to serve their interest that Phanibhushan had brought an especially beautiful bride home. Therefore, he segregated his wife from the others, keeping her to himself alone in this house. But the wife differs from other possessions in that keeping to oneself does not always mean ownership to a greater degree.

The wife was not much disposed to talking; neither did she mix with her neighbours too much. Feeding Brahmans on a religious vow or offering coins to religious mendicants was not her wont. Nothing in her care was ever wasted; except for her husband's hugs and kisses, whatever else she had received, she had stored away carefully. Astonishingly, even from her exquisite beauty of youth, she had not, as it were, allowed the least bit to dissipate. Rumour had it that even at twenty-four, she looked as callow as if she were fourteen. People whose hearts are chunks of ice, whose hearts have no room for the aches and stings of love can perhaps keep fresh for a long time; like a miser, they can keep themselves hoarded externally as well as internally.

God left Manimalika barren like a vibrant creeper with thick foliage; He denied her a child. This means He did not give her some such thing, which she could appreciate far more than the jewels stored away in her iron chest; something, which, like the rising sun of spring, could melt the chunk of ice in her heart with its own tender warmth, releasing a fountain of affection over the household.

Nevertheless, Manimalika was very adept at housekeeping. She had not employed a single servant too many. She could not stand the idea of someone doing for a price what was within her ability to do. She never spared a thought for anyone, never loved anyone; she only worked and saved whatever she received. That is why she had no illness, no grief and no agony; with her overflowing exuberance, undisturbed peace and burgeoning wealth she lived ever so imposingly. For most husbands, this much is sufficient—not just sufficient, indeed rare. That our waist is part of our body we hardly care unless we have a sciatic pain. That there is a wife as the linchpin of the household, recognising this at every step, and that for twenty-four hours driven by love, is what is called the sciatica of domesticity. Obsequious devotion to the husband may be a matter of pride for a wife, but is not satisfying to the husband. Or so I feel.

Sir, to sit down daily to measure the wife's love on an accurate balance—precisely how much has been received and how much is the deficit—is that at all a man's business? Wife will discharge her own duties and I will do mine: this is the broad understanding in homemaking, isn't it? How much is manifest in the inarticulate, what is lacking in friendship, how much is implied in the overt, or what is the immensity in the minuscule—God did not endow males with so delicately keen a perception about measuring the nuances of love; it was not found necessary. Of course, women indulge in analysing the faintest sign of male affection and apathy: the real intent in what is spoken and the quintessence in the manner it is spoken they keep extracting by splitting and scanning. For, men's love is the source of women's power, their capital for the business of life. Only if they can follow the direction of this love's wind and orient their sails correctly at the right time do their boats sail over to the other side. That is why the equipment called love-meter finds a place in women's hearts, not in men's.

But men have since acquired what they have been denied by providence. Going one up on the Maker, poets have indiscriminately handed over to the masses this rare instrument, this compass needle of ascertaining affliction. I have no complaint against the Almighty; He made man and woman distinct enough, but civilisation has wiped out the distinction; now both species are acquiring the dominant traits of each other, giving rise to domestic chaos. The wedding couple have no means to ascertain each other's identity in advance, so have to wait with anxious apprehension.

You are getting annoyed! I stay here alone, banished from the wife. A detached view offers many deeper insights into the domestic world. These are not topics for students; I have told you this in the course of our conversation; you may like to think it over.

What I essentially mean is that though Phanibhushan never had to complain about inadequate salt in his food or excess lime in his *paan*, his heart was unbearably tormented by some indefinable something. The wife had no fault, nothing exceptionable about her, yet the husband had no happiness. He only kept sending diamonds and pearls targeting his partner's empty heart, but they ended up in her iron chest, leaving her heart as empty as ever. His uncle Durgamohan did not understand love so delicately, did not want so solicitously or offer so lavishly and yet from the aunt, obtained it copiously. If you want to be a businessman, you can't afford to be a parvenu, and if you want to be a husband you have to be a man. Let there be no doubt about that.

Just then, jackals started yelling from the nearby jungle. There was a couple of minutes' interruption in the teacher's flow of story telling. It seemed as if in that dark conference ground, whether hearing the conjugal code expounded by the schoolmaster or amused at the conduct of Phanibhushan enervated by the creed of the new culture, the fun-loving jackal tribe burst into intermittent guffaws. Their surge of emotion having subsided, when the surrounding became twice as quiet as before, the teacher resumed his story, rolling his large bright eyes in the darkness of the evening.

Phanibhushan's complex and extensive business was suddenly faced with a crisis. For a non-professional like me it is difficult to realise and explain its nature. Overall, his creditworthiness in the market had somehow dipped alarmingly. If only he could raise one and a half lac rupees or so from somewhere just for five days to produce once before the market, his business would immediately tide over the crisis and move ahead rapidly.

The money was not forthcoming. Any rumour that he was trying to borrow from local money-lenders would doubly hamper his business prospects, so he had been sounding out outside sources; there, adequate security was a prerequisite.

Pawning jewellery obviates the hassles of documentation, and hence, is a simple and speedy way out. Phanibhushan approached his wife. Phanibhushan was incapable of going to his wife as freely as other husbands can approach theirs. It was his misfortune that he loved his wife: it was such love as the hero of lyric poetry has for the heroine; such love as requires cautious advances and hinders easy articulation of feelings; the love whose strong attraction, like that between the sun and the earth, leaves an insurmountable gulf in between.

Nevertheless, if he falls in a desperate situation, even a lyric hero has to broach to his sweetheart matters like mortgage, IOUs and promissory notes, but his voice trips, words falter, and even such plain business talk is inhibited by confusion of thought and tremors of mortification. Poor Phanibhushan could not boldly utter, 'Look, dear, I am in dire need. Give me your ornaments.'

He did speak, however, but spoke very feebly. When Manimalika's face hardened and she said neither yes nor no, he received a cruel blow, but did not return it, for he totally lacked any masculine roughness. Where he ought to have forcibly snatched what he wanted from her, he smothered even his deep resentment. He seemed to believe that even if he were to suffer disaster, he would not allow force to intrude into the domain which is exclusively for love. If you admonished him over this, he would probably raise a delicate point: if I forfeit my credit in the market, even if for the wrong reasons, I have no right to loot the market just because of the unfairness. If my wife does not give me her ornaments willingly on trust, I cannot plunder them. As credit counts in the market, so does love at home; brute force is needed only in the battlefield. Was it for cutting such superfine threads of logic at every step that man was made so liberal, so formidable, of such large size? Does he have the time to sit contemplating the most delicate sentiments with utmost subtlety, or does it befit him? Anyway, too proud of his exalted faculties of heart to touch his wife's jewellery, Phanibhushan went off to Calcutta to collect money by other means.

Generally, a wife knows the husband far better than a husband knows the wife. But a husband with a nature of great subtlety does not come wholly within the focus of his wife's microscope. Phanibhushan's wife did not quite understand Phanibhushan: the antiquated beliefs down the ages that build up woman's untutored skills cannot accommodate ultramodern males. These men are a class apart and are growing as mysterious as women. They do not quite fit into any of the broad categories of the ordinary male, such as brute, idiotic or blind.

Manimalika had therefore to call her counsel for consultation. A brother of Manimalika's by old acquaintance or distant relation worked under the steward in Phanibhushan's office. He was not the type who would improve his prospects by means of performance: on any pretext, on the strength of the relationship, he used to collect his salary and even some perquisites into the bargain.

Manimalika called him in and told everything. 'Now what is your advice?' she asked. He nodded sagely. This meant the indications were not good: astute men never find them good, anyway. 'The master can never raise the money,' he said. 'Eventually, he is sure to fall back on your ornaments.'

Going by her own perception of human beings, Manimalika concluded that this eventuality was the most probable and only this was reasonable. She grew extremely worried. She had no children; she did have her husband, but his existence she never felt in her heart. Therefore, that which was her only cherished treasure, which like her son was growing gradually by the year, which was no mere metaphor but real gold, real gems–of her breast, of her neck, of her head—which she had prized over the years was now to be cast into the bottomless pit of business: the thought froze her. 'What can be done?' she asked.

'Taking the ornaments, let's start for your father's house right away,' said Madhusudan even as he planned how to appropriate some of the ornaments, maybe most of them.

Manimalika at once agreed to this proposal.

One evening towards the end of *Asharh,* a boat came and moored at this ghat. In the intense darkness of the densely clouded morning, amidst the croaks of sleepless frogs, Manimalik boarded the boat, covered all over in a thick shawl. Madhusudan, waking up from within the boat said, 'Better pass the casket to me.' Mani said, 'That I'll see later. Now cast off.'

The boat set sail and was driven along by the swift current. Throughout the night, Manimalika had put on all her ornaments one after another covering her body; there was not an inch left from head to toe for another. She had calculated that carrying the ornaments in a box was not safe because the box might somehow get out of her possession; but if she had them on her body, no one could take them before killing her.

Not finding any box with her, Madhusudan could not sense anything: that under the thick shawl, along with Manimalika's body and soul were shrouded her even dearer ornaments was beyond his imagination. If it was true that Manimalika did not understand Phanibhushan, it was even truer that she saw through Madhusudan all right.

Madhushan had left a note with the steward that he was taking his mistress to her father's house. The steward had been with them since Phanibhushan's father's time. Extremely irritated, he wrote out a letter to his master with execrable spellings; he did not write good Bengali, but managed to convey that it did not behove a man to give improper indulgence to his wife.

Phanibhushan rightly guessed what was on Manimalika's mind. It hurt him most that despite confronting severe losses, renouncing his wife's ornaments he had been trying his utmost to collect the money, yet she suspected him; she had not recognised him even today. The grievous wrong done to him that ought to have made him angry merely left him aggrieved. Man is God's sceptre packed with thunder: if he cannot light up in a flash to encounter the wrong done to himself or to others, shame on him. Man ought to flare up like a forest fire on the slightest pretext, and woman to shed torrents of tears like monsoon clouds without pretext: this was the divine dispensation, but it no longer holds.

Phanibhushan, addressing his guilty wife said to himself: if this is your judgement, so be it; I will go on doing my duty. Phanibhushan, the man who should have been born five or six centuries hence when only spiritual power would move the world, having descended in the nineteenth century happened to marry a woman of the ancient times, the archetypal woman whose wisdom the scriptures denounced as catastrophic. He did not write a word to his wife and resolved never to mention anything about it to her. What a harsh penal code!

After about ten days, Phanibhushan, having somehow collected the money and overcome his crisis, finally returned home. He was sure Manimalika would have come back by then after keeping her ornaments with her father. He imagined how she would be embarrassed and a bit repentant too, to see her successful husband, mission accomplished, who had once stood as a supplicant and had been subjected to needless labours. Contemplating this, he had arrived at their bedroom door.

He found the door locked. Breaking it open, he found it empty. The iron safe in the corner stood open, with no trace of ornaments in it. Phanibhushan received a stunning blow deep inside. The world seemed purposeless, and everything from love to livelihood, futile. He thought to himself: we husbands are struggling to erect each single spoke of this cage of domesticity, but there is no bird in it; it just refuses to stay. What then are we embellishing with the rubies of our heart's blood and the pearl garland of our tears? He kicked away from his mind that empty cage he had built up with all his life's treasure.

Phanibhushan was reluctant to take any initiative about his wife's whereabouts, deciding to leave it entirely to her discretion to return or not. The old Brahman steward said, 'What's the point of remaining silent? After all, she is the mistress of the house and we must make enquiries.' He then sent a messenger to her father's house, who brought back the news that neither Mani nor Madhu had so far reached there. It was then that thorough enquiries were made. Men were sent asking people along the riverbank. A missing diary on Madhu was filed with the police. Which boat, which boatman took them, which route they took or where they finally reached: there was no clue whatever.

After he had given up all hopes about her, one evening Phanibhushan entered his abandoned bedroom. It was Lord Krishna's birthday; it had been raining incessantly since morning. To mark the festival day, a fair used to be organised in the open space in the village; there under a thatched shed a public *jatra* was being performed; the songs made fainter by the sound of torrential rain reached his ears. He was sitting in the dark by the window you see there with shutters hanging loose from the hinges. Gusts of damp wind drove in, and with it splashes of rain and snatches of song: he sat completely oblivious to it all. Two art-studio paintings of goddesses Lakshmi and Saraswati were hung up on the wall. A coarse bath towel, one Turkish towel, one thin-bordered sari, another striped one, as if ready to wear, hung from the clothes hanger. On a tripod in a corner, in a brass tray a couple of paans made by Manimalika with her own hands lay dried up. In the glass cupboard were neatly put away her childhood relics of China clay dolls, bottles of perfume, decanters of coloured glass, costly cards, large marine cowries, down to the empty soap boxes. The fancy kerosene lamp with a tiny glass bulb, which she cleaned and lit every day herself and then placed in the recess in the wall, now extinguished, stood there as before; that tiny lamp was the only silent witness to Manimalika's parting moments in the bedroom. To think that one who could tear herself away from everything should still leave so many signs, so many relics, and so many stamps of affection on all the lifeless matter! Come, Manimalika, come and light your lamp, illumine your home, and standing in front of the mirror put on your carefully pleated sari; all your items are waiting for you. Nobody wants anything from you, except that you reappear, and with your ever-lasting youth and ever-fresh beauty enliven this huge scattered mass of matter with a unifying thread of life; the inarticulate sobs of these mute, inanimate objects have made a cemetery of the house.

It was dead of night when the rain as well as the opera songs stopped. Phanibhushan was still sitting at the window as before. Outside the window, there was such an all-pervasive solid darkness that he seemed to be facing the royal portal of *Yama*'s abode, as though if he cried aloud from here, what he had lost forever just might reappear once, ever so briefly; on this inky black canvas of death, on this rock-solid touchstone, that lost gold might as well leave a streak.

Suddenly, a tapping sound accompanied with the tinkling of ornaments was heard. Unmistakably, it seemed to be approaching from the ghat. The river's water and the night's darkness had then merged with each other. An elated Phanibhushan kept trying to see with his avid eyes pushing back and penetrating the darkness farther and farther: his swollen heart and eager eyes began to ache, but nothing was visible. The more intensely he tried to descry something, the denser the darkness and the more shadowy the world seemed to be growing: seeing an unexpected visitor at dead of night at the window of her own house of death, Nature promptly let down one more curtain.

The sound began to advance towards the house from the topmost step of the ghat and finally stopped in front of it. The security guard had gone to visit the jatra after closing the main gate. Now those taps and clangs kept pelting the closed door as if simultaneously with the ornaments, something hard was striking the door. Phanibhushan could hold himself no more. Crossing the dark rooms and going down the dark stairs he stopped at the closed main door, which was locked from outside. As he shook it violently with his hands, the impact and the sound startled him awake. He realised that he had come down all the way from upstairs in his sleep. He was perspiring all over, his hands and feet cold as ice, his heart beating like a guttering lamp. Emerging from his dream, he noticed that there was no sound outside except the continuous patter of the *Shravan* rain, and along with it the sound of the jatra players singing a tune of the dawn.

Although the matter was entirely a dream, it was nevertheless so palpably near and true to life that Phanibhushan felt he had been a whisker away from the miraculous fulfilment of his impossible desire. The distant *Bhairavi* tune mixing with that sound of raindrops kept telling him that this waking itself was a dream; the world itself was a fiction.

The following day also had a jatra programme, and the guard had been granted leave as well. Phanibhushan ordered the main gate to remain open all night. The guard pointed out, 'On the occasion of the fair, various kinds of people from different places have gathered. I do not want to take a risk by keeping the gate open.' Phanibhushan rejected his argument. The guard said, 'In that case I'll stand guard all night.' 'No, you must not,' said his master. 'You have to go to watch the jatra.' The guard was bewildered.

In the evening, Phanibhushan sat at the same window of his bedroom after putting out the lamp: in the sky, there was the glare of rainless clouds, and all around, the stillness of expectation of the approach of something indefinite. The incessant din of frogs and the loud jatra songs could not break that stillness, and was only infusing an incongruously strange mood into it. Long afterwards, the frogs, the crickets and the jatra boys fell silent, wrapping the dark night with an extra blanket of darkness. It was evident, the time had come at last.

The same clattering and jangling rose from the ghat. But Phanibhushan did not turn his eyes in that direction, lest his impatient expectation and restive attempts should frustrate all his hopes, all his efforts. Lest the impulse of his eagerness should overwhelm his senses, he summoned up all his energy to control his mind and sat stiff and rigid like a wooden statue.

The clanking sound now came progressively from the ghat through the open gate; he could hear the sound winding up the spiralling staircase of the inner quarters. Phanibhushan could barely restrain himself. His heart kept thrashing like a canoe on the tempestuous sea, nearly choking his breath. After traversing the spiral, the sound continued along the veranda gradually approaching the bedroom. Finally, at the bedroom door, the clattering and tinkling stopped just short of crossing the threshold.

Phanibhushan could not control himself any longer. His pent-up emotion surged up violently in a moment; leaping out of bed like a flash of lightning, he cried out weeping, 'Mani!' The same moment, waking up with a start, he noticed that from the impact of his own eager cry even the window panes of the room were vibrating; outside, there was the same noise of frogs and songs of the jatra boys in tired-out voices.

He struck his own forehead mightily in frustration.

The following day, the fair had wound up. Stall-owners and the jatra party had left. Phanibhushan ordered that there should be no one else present in the house after evening. The servants concluded that their master must have been performing some tantric[4] rites. Phanibhushan observed a fast all day.

In the deserted house in the evening, Phanibhushan came and settled beside the window. Today, there were no patches of cloud in the sky, and the stars shone brightly through the rain-washed clear air. The waning moon of the tenth lunar day was still a long time away in rising. With the fair closed down, there was not a single boat in the brimming river, and the entire village, tired out by two nights of watching the festival, was in deep slumber.

Sitting on a chair leaning his head on its back, Phanibhushan was watching the stars. He was reflecting: one day at nineteen, while studying in a Calcutta college, when in the evening, lying supine on the bed of grass resting his head on his palm in a park, he would keep gazing at those timeless stars, Mani's bright immature face would come to his mind; she was fourteen, barely past puberty, and staying in his father-in-law's house across the river. How sweet the alienation then was! How marvellously like raga *Basant*[5] with *Yati tala*[6] the stars had twinkled rhythmically with the beating of youth in his heart! Today the same stars had inscribed the sloka from *Mohamudgar*[7] in letters of fire on the sky, declaring: 'Strange indeed is this world!'

Soon all the stars vanished. A sheet of darkness descending from the sky and another rising from the earth met like the upper and the lower lids of the eye. Today Phanibhushan's heart was calm and peaceful. He was certain that today his desire would be fulfilled: death would reveal its mystery to the seeker after truth.

As on the previous night, the same sound rose from the river on to the steps. Phanibhushan composed himself and sat resolutely with his eyes closed in a meditative posture. The sound entered through the unguarded gate into the house, spiralled up the winding stairs, traversed the long veranda and then paused for a moment outside the bedroom door. Phanibhushan's heart grew anxious, and goosebumps sprouted all over his body, but today, he did not open his eyes. Crossing the threshold the sound came into the room. The clothes rack where the pleated saris hung, the niche where the kerosene lamp stood, the tripod where the paan had dried, and the cupboard with the curios—at each place halting for once, the sound finally stopped very near Phanibhushan.

It was then that Phanibhushan opened his eyes, and saw that moonlight of the tenth crescent had entered the room and a skeleton was standing right in front of his chair. The skeleton had a ring each on its eight fingers, discs on its palms, bangles on its wrists, armlets and necklaces in place, complete with a tiara on the parting of her hair: an ornament on each bone from head to foot coruscating with gold and diamond. The ornaments were loose-fitting, and flapping from side to side, yet not slipping off the limbs. Most terrible, on its skeletal face, within the bony eye socket, the two eyes were alive—the same dark pupils, the thick long eyelashes, the dewy lustre and the same unwaveringly firm and placid gaze. The same beautiful dark large expressive eyes he had seen for the first time—on the wedding night eighteen years back amidst tunes of *Sahana* in an illuminated assembly—he now saw in the wan moonbeam on a *Shravan* night, and as he saw, blood froze in all the veins of his body. He tried his utmost to close his eyes, but no way could; they stared fixedly like those of a dead person.

Then the skeleton, its gaze fixed on a stupefied Phanibhushan, raising its right arm motioned to him with its fingers. All four diamond rings sparkled on the bones. Phanibhushan rose to his feet as if spellbound. The figure turned towards the door. Bones rattled and ornaments jangled as they brushed against each other. Phanibhushan followed it like an ensnared puppet. They traversed the veranda, and then winding along the dark spiral staircase, rattling, clattering, jingling all the way, climbed downstairs, crossed the portico, went through the unmanned unlit gate and finally came out on the pebbled walk through the garden. The pebbles crunched with each step. There the pale moonlight was enmeshed in the thick foliage of trees, finding no way to escape. Moving through swarms of fireflies along the damp-smelling, dark shadow-path, they arrived at the ghat.

Down the same steps of the ghat from which the sound had begun, the bejewelled skeleton clattered down in an erect steady motion one step at a time. A long streak of moonlight shimmered on the onrushing water of the vigorous monsoon river. The skeleton stepped into the river; Phanibhushan who was following it also stepped into the water. The moment he touched water, his somnambulant spell broke off: there was no longer his guide in front of him; only across the river, the trees were standing still, and above his head, a crescent moon was watching, calm and astonished. Repeatedly shivering all over, his feet staggering, Phanibhushan tripped in the forceful current. He could swim, but his nerves failed him. After coming out of a dream only for a moment on the threshold of consciousness, he sank the next into unfathomably deep slumber.

His story over, the schoolmaster paused for a while. As he stopped all of a sudden, it became clear that except him everything else in the world had fallen silent and still by now. For quite a long while, I did not say a word; nor in the dark could he notice the expression on my face.

'Don't you believe this story?' he asked me.

'Do you believe it?' I retorted.

'No,' he said. 'And I have my reasons too. First, Nature is no fiction-writer; her hands are full. Second –'

'Second,' I said, 'It's me; my name is Phanibhushan Saha.'

Not at all embarrassed, the schoolmaster said, 'I guessed it right then. And what was your wife's name?'

'Nrityakali.'

*Agrahayan 1305* (1898)

## NOTES

1 The Muslim ritual of worshipping the Almighty prescribed by the holy Koran, which consists in silently uttering prayers with some gestures of hands in a specified posture of sitting.

2 Saris made by the especially skilled artisans of Dacca; their fineness and floral designs have made them a class apart widely acclaimed and still now coveted by women with eclectic tastes, particularly Bengali women.

3 *Varunashtra*: the sanctified arrow invoking the Hindu water god *Varuna* (water) potentised to bring in clouds followed by showers; *nagpash:* an arrow potentised with hymns to invoke serpents as a device to bind the enemy and incapacitate him; *agnivan:* an incendiary arrow in the name of the fire god *Agni.*

4 A follower of Tantrism: a movement within Hinduism combining magical with mystical elements, and with sacred books in the form of dialogues between Shiva and his wife Shakti.

5 A raga appropriate to spring and set to rouse a mood (*bhava*) of joy and sentiment (*rasa*) of love, besides a general euphoria.

6 An eight-beat rhythmic pattern played on the tabla accompanying light classical Hindustani music chiefly *thumri.*

7 An anthology of religious sermons by the great Shankaracharya dispelling one's delusions.

# The Ending
# (Samapti)

## 1

Having recently passed his BA examination, Apurbakrishna was returning to his native village from Calcutta.

The river was small; it almost dried up after the monsoon every year. Now at the end of *Shravan,* it was in full spate skirting the village and lapping the bottom of bamboo clumps. After many days of heavy rain, today the sun was up in the cloudless sky. If we had a glimpse of the heart of Apurba, who was sitting in a boat, we would have found there also a youthful stream full to its brim sparkling in the sun and splashing in the wind.

The boat arrived at the *ghat.* From the riverbank, the concrete roof of their house was visible through gaps between trees. Apurba had come unannounced, so nobody had come to receive him. When the boatman extended a helping hand for the luggage, Apurba waved him away, swung it up and leapt on to the ground breezily. The riverbank was slippery; he fell on the mud with his luggage. Instantly a wave of high-pitched tinkling laughter burst forth in a dulcet tone startling the birds in a nearby peepul tree.

Apurba, being extremely embarrassed, quickly recovering his poise looked around. He saw that on the riverbank kiln-fresh bricks, unloaded from a merchant's boat, had been kept in stacks; sitting there, a girl was nearly doubling up with laughter.

Apurba recognised her: she was Mrinmayi, daughter of their new neighbour. Their original home had been near the big river far away, which they had to abandon because of erosion of banks; for two or three years now, they had been living in this village.

The girl had acquired quite a bit of notoriety. Though males of the village affectionately called her Paagli,[1] women were always scared, wary and apprehensive about her wayward nature. Boys were her exclusive playmates; for the girls of her age she had profound indignation. In the realm of children, the girl was something of a marauding thug[2].

Her mother always complained to her friends that it was only because Mrinmayi was a pampered child of her father that she had such a formidable sway. Yet, when she contemplated that he loved her, and tears in Mrinmayi's eyes hurt him no end, in deference to her husband who stayed away from home she could never bring Mrinmayi to tears.

Mrinmayi was light-brown in complexion. Her short, curly hair fell over her back. Her facial features were strikingly like a boy's. In the two wide black eyes, there was neither any shyness nor any fear nor the least hint of coyness. She was tall, with a developed physique, healthy and strong, but whether her age was tender or advanced did not occur to anybody; if it did, they would have criticised her parents for her still remaining unmarried. Occasionally, when the boat of some unknown zamindar arrived at the ghat, awe-struck village people would be in a nervous flurry, the women would suddenly drop their veils down to the tips of their noses like curtains descending on the stage. But Mrinmayi popped up at the ghat running, clutching a a naked infant picked up from somewhere, her curly locks swinging on her back. She would stand gazing at the stranger with dauntless curiosity, like a fawn in a land where there are no hunters or dangers. She then went back to her boy companions and regaled them with an exaggerated account of the ways and manners of the newly arrived creature.

Our Apurba, earlier, coming home on holidays, had seen this unfettered girl a couple of times, and both when he had leisure and even when he had none had thought about her. In this world, so many faces invite our eyes, but one or two, quite surprisingly, go straight into our hearts. That is not entirely due to beauty; some other attribute is there; I think it is transparency. In most faces, human nature cannot manifest itself; the one that exhibits the mysterious soul dwelling in the cave of the heart stands out in a multitude and is instantly imprinted in our hearts. In this girl, across her face, across her eyes, there always appeared and always romped a wild turbulent femininity like a free, swift forest deer. That is why her vibrant face, once seen, was never easy to forget.

The reader hardly needs to be told that Mrinmayi's amused outburst for all its melodious quality was a bit painful to the hapless Apurba. Quickly passing his bag to the boatman, he walked briskly towards home, red in the face.

It was a perfect backdrop—the riverbank, the shade of the trees, birdsongs , sunlight at dawn, and twenty years of age. Of course, the brick-pile was not remarkable, but the person sitting there had lent a pleasing charm to that hard lifeless mass as well. What, alas, could be crueller of fate than to have reduced the poetry of such a scene to farce as soon as the protagonist took his first step?

## 2

Peals of laughter from that brick-stack ringing in his ears, Apurba, with his mud-stained chuddar and bag, walked on in the shade of the trees and arrived at his home. His unexpected arrival delighted his widowed mother. Forthwith she sent across men for various milk delicacies and fish; even among the friends and neighbours there began a stir of sorts.

After meal, his mother brought up the proposal of his marriage.

Apurba had anticipated it: the proposal had been made much earlier; but taking his cue from the current trends, he had declared, 'No marriage before passing BA.' So long because of this, his mother had been holding her peace, but now that pretext wouldn't do. 'Let's first see the bride,' he said. 'Then we'll decide.' 'Bride has been seen,' said his mother. 'You don't have to worry about that.' Apurba took it upon himself to worry about that and said, 'Unless I've seen the bride, I can't marry.' The mother thought, whoever has heard such a preposterous thing! Nevertheless, she consented.

That night, when putting out the lamp Apurba had gone to bed, and lay lonely and sleepless, coming from beyond all the sounds and all the stillness of the monsoon midnight, the surging laughter of a sweet trilling voice kept ringing in his ears. His mind kept tormenting itself that the morning faux pas ought somehow to be mended. He thought, 'I, Apurbakrishna, have acquired considerable learning and spent long spells in Calcutta. Even though I, having accidentally stepped on a slippery patch, fell on the mud, I am not a nobody like a yokel to be treated with disdain and indifference.' Only the girl did not know this!

The following day, Apurba was to go to see the bride. The bride's family lived fairly close to their house in the same locality. Apurba dressed with special care. Putting aside his usual dhoti and chuddar, wearing a silk *chapkan* and a vest, putting on a round-shaped puggree on his head and a pair of varnished shoes on his feet complete with a silk umbrella in his hand he set out early in the morning.

As soon as he arrived at his prospective father-in-law's house, there was a flurry of activity and much fuss over his reception. Finally, in due time the girl—dusted, cleaned, made-up, tinsel-chignonned and wrapped in a thin garish sari—was presented before the bridegroom, her heart palpitating. She sat silently in a corner, her chin almost touching her chest, with an elderly maidservant sitting behind her as moral support. A little brother of the bride was minutely inspecting the puggree, the watch-chain and the sprouting beard of this potential intruder into their family. After tweaking his moustache for a while, Apurba finally asked the girl gravely, 'What do you read?' No reply emerged from the mound of shyness sunk under clothes and ornaments. After two or three repeats of the question, and several encouraging prods on her back from the elderly maid, the girl in her faint voice poured out very fast in one breath, '*Charupaath* Book Two, Essential Grammar Book I, Simplified Geography, Arithmetic, Indian History.'

At this point, there rose the thudding and stamping of a restless motion outside. In a moment, Mrinmayi rushed into the room panting, her unbound hair swinging on her back. Without so much as casting a glance at Apurbakrishna, she straight away began to pull the bride's brother Rakhal's hand. Rakhal was then raptly cultivating his own potential for observation; he was in no mood to give it up. The maidservant, careful to maintain mildness of voice within tolerable limits of pitch, started berating Mrinmayi as angrily as possible. Gathering up all the gravity and glory he was capable of, and with his turbaned head held straight up, Apurbakrishna stayed put, fingering the watch chain near his abdomen. In the end Mrinmayi, when she could not distract Rakhal in any way, gave him a good smack on his back, whipped the veil off the bride's head and stormed out of the room leaving the maidservant growling in futile rage; Rakhal began to giggle at the sudden discomfiture of his sister. He did not consider the smarting smack on his back entirely unmerited, for they were always exchanging such things. It so happened once, when Mrinmayi's hair fell about halfway down her back, Rakhal had sneaked up behind her and run his scissors into her locks. Mrinmayi had then snatched the scissors away from him in a fit of pique and snipped off the rest ruthlessly. Locks of curly hair fell like bunches of black grapes from a vine. Such were the methods of disciplining each other.

Thereafter, this silent examination session did not last much longer. The girl sitting in a heap managed to stand full length and went into the inner quarters, escorted by the maidservant. Apurba solemnly stroking his sparse moustache got up to leave. Going near the door, he discovered that his new, varnished shoes were not there, and where they were could not be ascertained either.

Everyone in the family felt geatly embarrassed; torrents of abuses and reproaches were hurled at the unknown culprit. After an extensive search, there was no other way than to put on the master's old, tattered, oversize pair of slippers, and a well-dressed Apurba, in pantaloons and other apparel, began to walk very cautiously along the muddy village path.

At a deserted stretch near a pond, there suddenly arose the same babble of laughter in a sonorous tinkle. It seemed as if the fun-loving forest goddess, behind the screen of foliage, amused to see his incongruous pair of slippers, was suddenly unable to check her laughter. Startled and confused, Apurba stood looking around when a shameless female delinquent emerging from the woods put down the new pair of shoes in front of him and instantly turned to escape. Apurba swiftly grabbed her hands taking her prisoner.

Mrinmayi tried in vain to wriggle out of his grip. Sunbeams filtering through twigs fell on her round smiling impish face framed by her curly locks. Just as a curious traveller, stooping beside a limpid flowing sunlit river keeps scanning its bed, so did Apurba look with his deep solemn eyes at Mrinmayi's upturned face and into her two restless eyes. Then very slowly loosening his grip, as if leaving his duty unfinished, he released the prisoner. Had Apurba beaten her angrily, she would have been least surprised, but this strange silent punishment on a lonely path was something quite incomprehensible to her.

Her vibrant laughter ringing like the anklets of a dancing Nature, resonated throughout the sky, and a pensive Apurbakrishna trudged back home.

## 3

Apurba, on one pretext or another all through the day, did not go to the inner rooms to avoid meeting his mother. He had an invitation somewhere, where he lunched. Why Apurba's sort of a learned, reserved and reflective type should be so mortally anxious to reclaim his lost glory and exhibit his inner worth to a simple illiterate girl is difficult to comprehend. What did it matter if a flighty village girl considered him a mere nobody? Having for a moment made him a laughing stock, and then oblivious to his presence, been eager to play with an illiterate foolish boy called Rakhal—after all, what harm did it do? What was the need to prove that he reviewed books for a monthly magazine titled *Bishwadeep*[2]*?* That his trunk contained perfumes, shoes, Rubin's camphor, coloured letter pad, and the book *How to Play the Harmonium*, to say nothing of a full notebook waiting to be published as dawn in the womb of night? But our mind cannot be pacified easily, and by no means to this volatile village girl would Apurbakrishna Roy, Esq., BA, acknowledge defeat to this excitable village girl.

That evening when he went into the inner room, his mother asked him, 'Well, Apu, how was the bride? Did you like her?'

'I've seen, Ma,' said Apurba, a bit embarrassed. 'I liked one of them.'

'How many girls did you see?' His mother was surprised.

Apu hemmed and hawed, but finally spoke: their neighbour Sharat's daughter Mrinmayi was the one he liked. To imagine that such was his choice after so much learning!

At first, Apurba was held back by shyness; at last, when his mother persistently opposed him, he overcame it. 'I'll marry no one but Mrinmayi,' he blurted on impulse. The oftener he thought of that inert doll of a girl, the worse was his aversion to marriage.

After two or three days of mutual resentment, fasting and sleeplessness, Apurba won. Never mind, his mother comforted herself, Mrinmayi is a mere child; moreover, her mother is not competent to train her properly. When it falls to me after marriage, she will definitely change. By and by, she came to believe that Mrinmayi was pretty. But the next moment, to her utter dejection, her short locks appeared in her mind's eye. Even so, she hoped that tight plaiting and liberal pats of oil would mend this shortcoming as well in time.

People of the neighbourhood gave the name of *Apurba-choice*[3] to this preference of Apurba's. It was all very well that many loved *Paagli* Mrinmayi, but the thought of taking her as their son's wife never crossed anyone's mind.

Mrinmayi's father Ishan Majumder was duly informed. He had been working as a goods-cum-booking clerk of a steamer company in a tin-roofed shanty at a distant riverside station. His beloved Mrinmayi's marriage proposal brought tears to his eyes. How much they were tears of joy and how much of sorrow there is no way to ascertain.

Ishan petitioned the head office for leave because of his daughter's marriage. The sahib considered the occasion too trivial and turned down the petition. Ishan then wrote home asking them to postpone the wedding until the *pujas* when a week's holiday was likely. Apurba's mother wrote back, 'There's an auspicious day this month; I can't postpone any more.' With both his prayers turned down, Ishan made no more objections and went back with a heavy heart to weighing goods and selling tickets.

Thereafter, Mrinmayi's mother together with all the elderly women of the village started to advise Mrinmayi day in and day out about her future dos and don'ts. With injunctions on love of play, brisk strides, loud laugh, boys' company, and eating whenever hungry, they completely succeeded in projecting marriage as a horrifying proposition. With a heart full of anxiety and apprehension, Mrinmayi thought she had been sentenced to life imprisonment to be followed by hanging. Stiffening her neck and retracing a step like a recalcitrant pony, she declared, 'I shan't marry'.

## 4

Nevertheless, she did marry.

Thereupon her training began. Overnight, her entire world was hemmed in by the inner quarters of Apurba's mother.

Her mother-in-law got down to the task of reformation. With a stern face she said, 'Look, dear, you're no small child any more. In our house, none of that brazenness is allowed.' The way she said this, Mrinmayi did not take it that way. She thought: if it is not allowed in this house, then perhaps she had to go elsewhere. In the afternoon, she could not be found. 'Where's she? Where's she?' rose the clamour. In the end, a perfidious Rakhal gave her away from her secret niche: she had been sitting in the abandoned chariot of Lord Radhakanta under the old banyan tree. How her mother-in-law humiliated her in tandem with her well-wishers in the neighbourhood is something the readers can well imagine.

At night, dense clouds gathered, and it began to rain. Lying in their bed, Apurba by slow degrees edged closer to Mrinmayi and said in a low voice into her ears, 'Don't you love me, Mrinmayi?'

'No,' she said brusquely. 'And I never will.' All her rage, all her retribution she hurled on Apurba's head with the fury of thunderbolts.

Apurba was hurt. 'But why? What harm have I done you?'

'Why did you marry me?'

A satisfactory explanation for this fault is difficult. But Apurba said to himself: no matter what it takes, I must rein in this mutinous heart.

The next day, her mother-in-law, on discovering all signs of her rebellious nature, locked her in. Like a caged bird fresh from the woods, she flapped around the room for quite some time. At last, finding no way to escape, she shredded the bed-sheet with her teeth in futile anger, and then lying prostrate on the floor wept, mentally calling out to her father.

After some time, she felt someone come silently and sit beside her. Affectionately he tried to lift the dust-laden strands of her hair from her cheek. Mrinmayi moved his hand away shaking her head vigorously. Apurba, then lowering his face to her ears said in a mild voice, 'I've opened the door secretly. Come, let's run away into the backyard garden.' 'No!' said Mrinmayi with force through sobs, shaking her head angrily. Trying to lift her face by the chin Apurba said, 'Just see who's come.' Looking at Mrinmayi lying on the floor, Rakhal stood at the door confusedly. Mrinmayi, her face down, pushed off Apurba's hands. Apurba said, 'Rakhal has come to play with you. Will you go?' 'No,' she said with asperity. Rakhal also realised that the atmosphere was not congenial; he quit the place quickly to his great relief. Apurba sat for some time silently. When Mrinmayi fell asleep tired of weeping, he tiptoed out and latched the door behind him.

The next day, Mrinmayi got a letter from her father. He lamented his failure to attend the wedding of his dearest daughter and blessed the couple heartily. Mrinmayi went to her mother-in-law and said, 'I want to go to my father.' Her mother-in-law reacted reproachfully at this absurd demand all of a sudden. 'No one knows where her father lives, and she wants to go to him. A ridiculous demand, really!' Mrinmayi went away without saying a word, bolted herself in her room, and like a despairing person beseeching God, muttered: 'Baba, come and take me back. I have no one my own here. I shall die if I have to stay here.'

At dead of night, when her husband was fast asleep, Mrinmayi stole out of the room. Though clouds gathered off and on, the paths were visible enough in the moonlight. She had no idea which way to go to reach her father. All she knew was that the road followed by the mail runners led to any address in the world. Mrinmayi took that road. She walked on and on until she felt exhausted; the night was nearly over as well. When one or two birds in the woods were fidgeting about waiting to break out in hesitant notes, but unable to ascertain the time, were still dithering, Mrinmayi arrived at the end of the road near the river at a place that looked like a big market. She was trying to guess which direction to take from there when she heard the familiar jingling. Mailbag on his shoulder and out of his breath, the runner appeared. Mrinmayi rushed to him and said piteously in her tired voice, 'I want to go to my father at Kushiganj. Could you take me with you?' He said, 'I don't know Kushiganj.' With this, he ran to the *ghat,* woke up the boatman of the mail-boat and cast off. He had no time to show pity or answer questions.

Soon the market became abuzz with activity. Mrinmayi went down to the ghat and hailed a boatman. '*Majhi*, will you take me to Kushiganj?' Before he could reply, someone from another boat called out, 'Who's it? Minu Ma, how did you come here?' Brimming over with eagerness, Mrinmayi said, 'Banamali, I want to go to my father at Kushiganj. Take me in your boat.' Banamali lived in the same village and knew this wayward girl only too well. 'Going to your father?' he said. 'That's fine. Come on, I'll take you.' Mrinmayi got into the boat. The boat set sail. Clouds gathered, and soon it began to rain torrentially. The river, which was in full spate in *Bhadra,* began to heave, tossing the boat and overpowering Mrinmayi with drowsiness. She spread her sari-end inside the boat and lay down. Lulled by the rocking river, this turbulent girl slept away like a peaceful child pampered by Nature.

When she woke, she found herself lying on her bed in her father-in-law's house. Finding her awake, the maidservant began to scold her. Her voice brought in the mother-in-law who took her turn with very harsh words. Mrinmayi, her eyes wide open, looked on quietly at her face. Finally, when she made a dig at her father's faulty training, Mrinmayi got up, went into the next room and bolted the door.

Apurba overcame his diffidence, and going to his mother said, 'Ma, what's the harm in sending my wife to her father for a few days?' His mother rebuked him in a manner no one had ever done or ever will. She reproached him severely for picking an execrable tomboy when there were so many girls to choose from across the country.

## 5

All through that day, it was inclement outside and equally so inside the house.

Next day, late at night Apurba woke her up and said, 'Mrinmayi, do you want to go to your father?' Mrinmayi was startled. 'Yes,' she gushed, clutching his hand ardently.

Apurba said in a whisper, 'Come, we'll run away quietly. I've arranged a boat.'

Mrinmayi looked at her husband with profound gratitude. Then scrambling out of bed, she changed her clothes and was ready to go. Apurba left a reassuring note for his mother and together they stepped out. That night, on the dark lonely silent village path, Mrinmayi held her husband's hand with utmost trust for the first time out of her own free will. Her ecstasy and anxiety transmitting through that tender touch throbbed in her husband's veins.

The boat set sail that night itself. In spite of her ebullient thrill, Mrinmayi soon fell asleep. She woke up in the morning to untold freedom and joy—so many villages and markets, cornfields and woods on either bank, so many boats passing by on either side. Mrinmayi enquired of her husband for an uncountable number of times about each trivial detail. 'What's in that boat? Where has that come from? What's the name of this place?' And so on: questions whose answers Apurba neither had found in his college books nor could manage with his Calcutta experience. His friends would have been ashamed to know that Apurba had answered each single question with aplomb and that most answers disagreed with the facts. For instance, he had not hesitated a bit to declare a cargo boat of sesame as one of linseed, the munsiff's court as zamindar's court, and Panchberia as Rainagar. And these outrageous answers took nothing away from the unsuspecting interrogator's satisfaction.

In the evening next day, the boat arrived at Kushiganj. In a tin shed lit with a sooty glass-panelled oil lantern, a bare-chested

Ishanchandra was sitting on a stool, poring over a huge leather-bound journal opened on a small desk. The newly married couple walked in. Mrinmayi called, 'Baba!' Such a voice so sweetly sounded had never been heard in that room.

Tears rolled down Ishan's eyes. He did not know what to say or what to do. His daughter and his son-in-law were, as it were, a prince and princess of an empire. He was utterly confused how best to make their thrones amidst these jute bales.

And what to give them for food? A poor clerk, he cooked his own food—lentils and rice with a a boiled vegetable or two. What would he do, what feast could he arrange to celebrate the day? Mrinmayi said, 'Baba, today we'll cook together.' Apurba could not agree more to the proposal. There was little space, little food and few people in the house; but just as a fountain spurts out in a forceful spray from a nozzle, so did joy in a thousand streams issue forth from the spout of poverty.

Three days passed by in this way. Everyday the steamer arrived twice on schedule; such large numbers of people and their hurly-burly all around. By the evening, the riverbank became deserted, and then there was absolute freedom. The three of them sharing the chores of arranging and cooking, often bungling, aiming for something and ending up differently; later, Mrinmayi serving with her tender hands to the tinkling of bangles the father and his son-in-law eating together; teasing her on numerous slips in her housewifery, her playful remonstrance and resentment. Then one day, Apurba said they ought not to stay any longer. Mrinmayi piteously appealed for a few more days, but Ishan said, 'Better not.'

On the day of departure, Ishan, drawing his daughter close and blessing her on the head, said in a voice almost choked with tears, 'Dear child, be a good wife shining bright in your father-in-law's home. Let no one find fault with my dear Minu.' A sobbing Mrinmayi departed for home with her husband. Ishan went back to his doubly dismal, dingy hut and continued to routinely weigh goods day after day, month after month.

## 6

When this guilty couple returned home, their mother kept up a very grave posture, saying nothing whatever. She found no fault with any one's conduct such as they might try to refute. This silent reproof and unspoken resentment bore down crushingly on the household. At last, at the end of his patience, Apurba came to his mother and said, 'Ma, my college has opened, and I have to go back to study law.'

His mother said indifferently, 'What have you decided about your wife?'

'She'll stay back here.'

"No, son, that won't do,' she protested, 'You take her along with you.' She forsook the familiar form of addressing her son for the formal[4].

'All right,' said Apurba feeling offended.

Preparations were on for the journey to Kolkata. The night before his departure, when Apurba came to bed, he found Mrinmayi weeping. Apurba suddenly felt distressed. 'Mrinmayi, don't you like to go with me to Calcutta?' he asked.

'No.'

'Don't you love me?' There was no answer. Very often, an answer to this question is easy enough, but at times, it has such psychological ramifications that it is too much to expect an answer from a mere girl.

'You'll miss Rakhal, is that the reason?' Apurba asked.

'Yes,' pat came her reply. Like a needle, exceedingly fine yet exceedingly sharp, jealousy against a mere boy Rakhal assailed this well-read BA-passed youth. He said, 'I won't be able to come back for a long time.' Mrinmayi had nothing to say about this information.

'Probably it'll be two years, maybe even more,' he added.

'When you return,' she demanded, 'remember to bring a Rogers three-blade knife for Rakhal.'

Rising from a reclining posture, Apurba said, 'So you'll stay back here?'

'Yes, I will go and stay with my mother.'

'Well, then,' Apurba sighed, 'I won't come back until you write me a letter. Is that fine?'

Deciding that a reply to that question was unnecessary, Mrinmayi went off to sleep, but Apurba had no sleep; he sat propped up with a pillow. Late at night, the moon was up and moonlight filtered on to their bed; Apurba looked at Mrinmayi. As he watched her, she seemed like a princess put to slumber by the touch of a silver wand; only if he found the gold wand, could he awaken the sleeping soul and exchange their wedding garlands. The silver wand meant laughter, the gold wand tears.

At dawn, Apurba woke her up and said, 'Mrinmayi, it's about time I left . Let me drop you at your mother's house.' Mrinmayi left her bed. Apurba took her hands and said, 'Now I have a request. I have often helped you in many ways. Before I leave, would you give me a parting reward?'

'What reward?' asked Mrinmayi, surprised.

'Give me a kiss—freely and lovingly.'

Seeing the bizarreness of the request as well as the seriousness on his face, Mrinmayi gave a laugh. Then restraining herself , she craned forward to kiss, advanced close enough, but could not; she gave up in giggles. After two such attempts, she desisted, and then pressing her sari-end to her mouth, began to laugh. Apurba tweaked her ears by way of punishment.

Apurba's was a very rigid pledge. Grabbing things by snatching and looting like a hoodlum was self-demeaning to him. Like a god in all his glory, he wanted gifts voluntarily offered to him; he would pick up nothing whatever with his own hands.

Mrinmayi stopped laughing. Taking her to her mother's house by a lonely path in the light of dawn, Apurba came back home and told his mother, 'I considered the matter: if I took her along to Calcutta, it would hamper my studies; there she would find no company either. You do not want to keep her in this house, so I left her at her mother's house.'

Amidst a deep sense of wounded feelings, mother and son parted company.

## 7

In her mother's home, Mrinmayi discovered that she could not put her mind to anything. Everything of that house seemed to have undergone a change. Time hung heavy; she did not know what to do, where to go or whom to meet. Suddenly she felt as if there was no one in the house, no one in the entire village, as if there had been a solar eclipse at noon. She could not comprehend that if today she was dying to go away to Calcutta, then only last night where this urge had been. Last night she did not know that the part of her life, which she had left behind and which she was pining for, had already undergone a complete change of flavour. Today willingly without effort she cast away that past life like a withered leaf detached from its stalk.

Story is told of a master maker of weapons who could forge so exceedingly fine swords that a man could not sense its slashing him in two until finally a push separated the halves. Equally fine is the sword of the Almighty: when it had struck Mrinmayi at the seam of her childhood and youth, she had not perceived it. Today, by some sort of a shake, the part that was her childhood fell detached from her youth, and Mrinmayi stood astonished and in agony.

In her mother's house, her old bedroom seemed no longer her own; the one who used to live there had suddenly ceased to exist. All the memories of her heart now hummed around that other house, other room, and other bed.

Nobody saw Mrinmayi out of doors any more. Nobody heard her laughter. Rakhal was scared of seeing her; the thought of games never crossed his mind. To her mother she said, 'Send me back to my father-in-law's house.'

Meanwhile, remembering the depressed look of her son at parting, Apurba's mother was pining away. The thought that he had left his wife with her mother only in anger kept pricking her heart acutely.

Then one day, Mrinmayi with a wan face, her head covered in the traditional way, bowed down at the feet of her mother-in-law, who at once embraced her, her eyes filled with tears. That very moment, the two were united. The mother-in-law was astonished to look at her daughter-in-law's face: she was no longer the Mrinmayi she had known. Not everyone is capable of such transformation. Enormous changes require enormous forces.

Mrinmayi's mother-in-law had planned to correct her faults one by one, but another, an invisible reformer, adopting a mysterious short cut, had metamorphosed Mrinmayi into an altogether new individual. Mrinmayi now understood her mother-in-law; her mother-in-law too discovered her; the entire household became an integrated whole like a tree with its branches.

This solemn, serene, immense feminine nature that suffused Mrinmayi throughout her body and her heart to every line, every curve seemed to cause her anguish. Like the nimbus clouds at the advent of monsoon, an extensive melancholy resentment rose in her mind, which cast a darker shade on her long shadowy eyelashes. She kept saying to herself, 'I may not have recognised myself, but why did you not understand me? Why did you not punish me? Why did you not force me to follow your wish? Wretched that I am, when I refused to go with you, why did you not take me forcibly along? Why did you listen to me and allow my wish? Why did you put up with my disobedience?'

Then she had the recollection of the morning when on the lonely path alongside the pond Apurba, had caught hold of her because she had been naughty, and without saying a word had only looked at her face for once. That pond, that path, that spot under the tree, that morning sun and that deep pensive look in his eyes reappeared in her mind, and all at once, she could comprehend its complete meaning. Then, the parting day kiss, which after advancing to Apurba's face had retracted unaccomplished, now like a thirsty bird heading for a mirage in the desert, kept rushing towards that past spring, but by no means could she quench her thirst. Now frequently, it kept recurring in her mind, 'Alas, if at that moment I had done this, given this reply to that question! Had it been like this then!'

Apurba had a grievance: 'Mrinmayi does not know me fully.' Today, Mrinmayi also sat brooding: 'What did he think of me? What impression did he carry about me?' The thought that Apurba knew her for a wild, flippant, insensible, stupid girl, that he did not know her as a woman capable of slaking his thirst for love with the nectar of her heart, mortified her with remorse, shame and self-reproach. The kisses and caresses she owed him, she now kept repaying vicariously on his pillow. In this way, so many days went by.

Apurba had said, 'Unless you write me a letter, I won't return home.' Remembering this, Mrinmayi one day in her room closing the doors sat down to write a letter. Taking out the golden-bordered coloured letter pad Apurba had given her, she began to think. Grabbing the pen very carefully, straying from the line, forming uneven letters, smudging her fingers, without making any salutation, she wrote these abrupt words: 'Why do you not write me letters? How are you and you come home.' What else there was worth saying she could not think out. All she intended to say had been said no doubt, but when communicating with humankind it is necessary to express one's mind a bit more elaborately. Mrinmayi realised it too, and so after racking her brains for quite some time, added a few words. 'Now you will write me a letter and write how are you and come home, mother is well, Bishu and Punti are well, yesterday our black cow had a calf.' With this, she ended the letter. After putting it into an envelope pouring a drop of love on every single letter she superscripted it: Shrijukta Babu Apurbakrishna Ray. In spite of all the love, line was not straight, letters not well formed, and spelling not faultless. That an envelope requires something more than the name was not known to her. Abashed, in case it came to the notice of her mother-in-law or anyone else, she sent the letter to post through a trusted maidservant.

Needless to tell, the letter did not achieve its purpose; Apurba did not come home.

## 8

The vacation came, and yet Apurba did not come home; his mother thought he was still angry with her.

Mrinmayi also concluded that Apurba was displeased with her; then thinking of the letter, she felt mortally ashamed. As she contemplated how insignificant that letter was, in it practically nothing had been written, none of her feelings had been expressed, that Apurba was thinking her even more childish, and holding her to greater scorn, she kept tossing inwardly as if pierced by an arrow. She repeatedly asked the maidservant, 'Did you post that letter?' The maidservant reassured her as often, 'Yes, of course. I dropped it in the box with my own hand. It must have been so many days now since the master got it.'

At last one day, Apurba's mother called Mrinmayi and said, 'Bou-Ma, it's been a long time Apurba hasn't come home, so I'm thinking of going to Calcutta myself to see him. Would you like to come with me?' Mrinmayi nodded assent, then coming into her room, closing the door, throwing herself on her bed, hugging the pillow to her breast, tittering and slithering gave vent to her pent-up emotion, and then gradually turning sober, melancholic and apprehensive finally sat weeping.

Without giving any intimation to Apurba, these two contrite women proceeded to Calcutta to ingratiate themselves with him. There Apurba's mother went and put up at her son-in-law's house.

That day, despairing of Mrinmayi's letter, in the evening Apurba, in violation of his own promise sat down to write one himself. No word seemed just right: he was groping for a precise address that asserts love, yet at the same time expresses wounded pride as well. Not finding one, he was growing increasingly disrespectful of his mother tongue. Just then, he received a message from his brother-in-law: 'Mother is here. Come immediately. At night you will eat your meal here. All is well.' In spite of the assurance at the end, Apurba grew despondent with an uneasy sense of foreboding. Forthwith, he arrived at his sister's house.

The first thing he asked his mother was 'Ma, is everything all right?'

'Yes, everything is fine,' she said. 'You didn't go home in the vacation, so I've come to take you back.'

Apurba said, 'Did you need to come all the way just for that? You know I've to prepare for the law exam – ' And so on and so forth.

During the meal, his sister said, 'Dada, why didn't you bring your wife along?'

Dada began to explain seriously, 'My law studies... – '

His sister's husband laughed and said, 'That's a bogus excuse. You do not bring her because you are afraid of us.'

His sister said, 'A man indeed to be afraid of. Sudden sight of him might startle a young girl.'

Such quips and banter went on, but Apurba remained sullen. None of this talk seemed to amuse him. He was arguing to himself: when eventually mother had come to Calcutta, Mrinmayi, if she had wished, could easily have come with her; perhaps his mother too had tried to bring her along, but she had not agreed. Inhibited by the awkwardness of expressing it, he could not specifically question his mother: human life as well as the grand design of the world seemed entirely fraught with illusions.

Soon after the meal, a squally wind rose, and it began to pour.

His sister proposed, 'Dada, rather stay back here tonight.'

Dada said, 'No, I've to go back. There's work to do.'

'What's the big thing to do at night?' said his brother-in-law. 'If you stay back one night, you don't have to explain yourself to anybody. Why worry?'

After much insistence, Apurba agreed, albeit very reluctantly.

His sister said, 'Dada, you look tired. Don't sit up. Come, let me show you your room.'

Apurba himself wished as much. Lying on the bed all alone in the dark was what he wanted to his great relief; he did not like any more exchange of words.

Approaching the bedroom, he saw it was dark. His sister said, 'The wind has blown out the lamp, I see. Well, shall I bring you a lamp, Dada?'

'No, that's not necessary. I don't keep a light a night.'

When his sister left, Apurba in the dark room stepped forward cautiously to the bed.

He was on the point of climbing the bed when suddenly a pair of tender arms with bangles tinkling captured him in a tight embrace, and a pair of lips soft as a flowering bud striking like a brigand smothered him with a tearful barrage of passionate kisses giving him no chance to express surprise. At first Apurba was startled, and thereafter realised that an old unfinished venture once thwarted by bouts of laughter was now accomplished amidst a flood of tears.

*Ashwin 1300* (1893)

NOTES:

1 The crazy girl, an address of endearment.

2 The text has *bargi*, a collective name for the *Maratha* cavalry notorious for their freebooting inroads.

2a Light of the Universe.

3 *Apurba,* which is his name, means 'unique' or 'strange'. Hence *Apurba-choice* can mean either 'Apurba's choice' or 'unique choice', take your pick.

4 In most Bengali homes, superiors use certain forms of address for juniors or inferiors; only when the relation is somewhat strained, as in this instance, or when giving any warning, do they use the formal second person singular.

# Glossary

Note: Words and phrases in the text retained as such in translation and not appearing here have been annotated in the ***Notes*** appended to each translated story.

***Bengali calendar months***

***Baishakh/Jyaishtha/Asharh /Shravan/Bhadra/Ashwin/Kartik/Agrahayan/Paus/ Magh/Phalgun/Chaitra***

*Note:* The Bengali New Year commences with Baishakh, correspondingly with the Gregorian calendar, on the 14th or 15th of April. The successive months in the above order begin around the middle of the corresponding Gregorian calendar month.

Subtract the number 593 (or 594 for a leap year) from the year in AD to arrive at the corresponding Bengali Year (*Bangabda*). Bengali Year 1416 commenced on 15 April 2009, for example.

***Bengali seasons***

***Grishma***: summer/***Varsha***: rains/***Sharat***: autumn/***Hemanta***: late autumn/***Sheeth***: winter/***Basanta***: spring

*Note:* Each season is supposed to last for two months. Often overlapping occurs with extended summer and rains.

Briefly appearing before winter, late autumn (hemanta) is generally not experienced as a separate season, often being overlapped by autumn and winter, although it finds an occasional mention in the stories.

***kalbaishakhi***: during the fortnight in late Chaitra and early Baishakh, a strong wind arises in the afternoon from the north-west, often playing havoc with trees and causing widespread destruction of mud houses.

***Rivers***

***Ganges***: the most sacred river to the Hindus with many places of pilgrimage along its banks, especially, Varanasi; length 2507 km; also known as Ganga.

***Yamuna*** (Kalindi): a tributary of the Ganges, the confluence being at *Prayag* (in Allahabad)

*Padma* (now in Bangladesh) is particularly known for its destructive form.
*Hooghly*: a branch of the Ganges, flowing through the West Bengal districts of Howrah and Hooghly.
*Narmada*: the second most sacred Indian river; in central India.
*Godavari*: in central India, sacred to the Hindus.

***Places***

***Lucknow***: the capital of Uttar Pradesh, famous for its own style of thumri and ghazal singing.
***Benares***: a city on the Ganges, in UP, major place of pilgrimage for the Hindus, seat of the Hindu University, famous for its wedding saris named after it.
***Ranchi***: an industrial city in Bihar, also a health resort.
***Puri***: a district town in Orissa, on the Bay of Bengal, a tourist resort and holy place to the Hindus.
***Kalighat***: a place of Hindu pilgrimage in south Calcutta.

***Trees, Plants and Flowers (and a bird)***

***peepul*** (ashvattha): a large tree, resembling the banyan; another name is *bodhitaru* or bo tree, tree of wisdom, from Sanskrit *bodhi*.
***shal***: a tropical tree that grows tall and straight, giving valuable timber for pillars and roof structure of huts.
***jhau***: an evergreen shrub with feathery clusters of blades of leaves.
***kadamba***: spherical-shaped mildly fragrant flower with bright yellow-orange hairy growth, a favourite with children; a flower of the rainy season.
***bakul:*** a large ever-green tree of small, white, sweet-smelling spring flowers
***bel:*** wood-apple tree; it bears sweet-smelling white flowers in summer; the leaves of the tree are an indispensable item of Hindu rituals; the sweet astringent pulp within the fruit's hard shell is a laxative and also makes cool sherbet.
***champa***: golden-yellow summer flower
***kamini***: sweet-smelling white flowers blooming by night and shedding at dawn, during the rains, unlike *shefali* or *shiuli, which* is a winter flower.
***madhabi***: a creeper with pink flowers, grown over a trellis, as part of a grove to give a decorative facade to premises.
***gaab:*** a resinous tree bearing inedible fruits
***neem***: *margosa*, a large tree with crops of small serrated leaves and white flowers; its sweetish fruits are favourite bird feed; leaves have medicinal value; its huge leafy branches offer cool, healthy shade.
***kaash***: milk-white flowers sprouting on long, slender, wavy reed-like stalks that spread a white radiance across vast verdant fields at the advent of autumn, have an appeal to Bengalis as the harbinger of their great annual festival, the Durga Puja; finds frequent mention in the stories.
***amlaki***: generic name, *emblic myrobalan,* medicinal plant bearing small sour fruits, which taste sweet when chewed with water.
***amra***: hog-plum tree. Its sweetish-sour olive-green fruits make good chutney and pickles.
***kalmegh***: another medicinal plant of extremely bitter leaves.

***kochu:*** plant cultivated in the tropics for its large, edible rootstock and tuber.
***koel*:** a generic name for any of the several parasitic cuckoos; it is characterised by a shrill cry ending with a gentle cooing, the name 'koel' is preferred by poets.
*Note:* Words either naturalised into the English language or having their English equivalents have been mostly excluded.

***Gods and goddesses of the Hindu pantheon***

***Hindu pantheon***: believed to be 330 million in number
***Durga***: variously called *Parvati, Basanti, Mahamaya, Annapurna, Sati, Uma*, consort of Lord Shiva, conceived as the prime mover of the universe and the driving force behind human activity; worshipped as the principal goddess by the Hindus, especially the Bengalis, for five days during the bright lunar fortnight of the month of Ashwin (autumn) with fervour and festivity, which goes by the name of *Durga Puja* or the great autumn festival, often mentioned in the stories. It celebrates the slaying of the demon *Mahishasura* (erupting out of the womb of a buffalo), the symbol of all evil.
***Kali*** ( the *a* being pronounced as in *art*): a fierce-looking, with lolling tongue, unsightly manifestation of the consort of Lord Shiva, believed to annihilate evil, and worshipped for empowerment in any enterprise.
***Lakshmi***: goddess of wealth and prosperity; her idol carries a pitcher symbolising never-ending wealth; traditional Hindus associate this perception to their family coffers; thanks to her perceived benign nature, her name has come to be often referred to a docile boy or girl, or otherwise used as an affectionate term of persuasion; she is often alluded to by the epithet *chanchala* meaning fleeting or inconstant, for wealth does not last too long.
***Saraswati***: wife of Brahma; goddess of learning, speech and music; draped in white, which is perceived to symbolise the pure, transparent and serene; she is imagined to dwell in a lotus pool, carried around by a swan and playing on the *veena* (lyre).
***Dashamahavidya***: the ten manifestations of the primordial power, the goddess Durga. *Bharavi* is one.
***Ganesh***: eldest son of Shiva and Parvati, god of fulfilment, worshipped all over India by devout Hindus before launching an auspicious enterprise or proceeding to worship any other deity. Mythologically, Ganesh is elephant-headed; hence, he is also called Gajanan, *gaja* meaning elephant, and *anan*, face.
***Kartik*** (kartikeya): commander-in-chief of the gods, handsome, youngest son of Shiva and Parvati, conceived for slaying the demon Taraka (dramatised by Kalidasa in Kumarsambhava); seldom worshipped as a god except for his good looks by a particular section of the Bengalis. To describe an extremely handsome male, he is traditionally likened to Kartik.
***Madan***: also known as Kamadeva, god of love, lust, desire (cf. Cupid, Eros);
***Indra***: held by the Vedas as the king of the gods, he lives in the palace *Vyjayanta* in the city of *Amaravati,* lounges in the garden *Nandan,* and rides a chariot drawn by two horses *Uchchaihshrava* and also rides the elephant *Airavata.* Yet, he is not commonly worshipped.

*Varuna*: god of the sea.
*Yama*: god of death; also called *Dharmaraj*, dispenser of justice after death for mortal acts according to divine decree of vice and virtue. *Yamapuri*, Yama's city, compares with Hades in Greek mythology.
*Dharma*: a word having wide connotation. From the simplest meaning 'essential property of matter, nature, or being', it extends to cover social, moral, and religious principles, codes, customs, and laws, and the conduct conforming to justice, piety and righteousness. Yama is held to be the custodian of the good, and hence sometimes referred to as Dharma.
*Yaksha*: a demigod supposed to protect treasure buried underground; a man, especially a child, left to die shut up in an underground cellar of treasure is believed to become its custodian; the term is sometimes referred to a niggardly hoarder of money.
*Kubera*: one of the four Lokpalas, guardian deity of the northern quarter of the universe, lord of wealth. He dwells in the jewelled city of Alaka, near Mt. Kailasa. He commands a host of gnomes (yakshas) who guard his treasure (cf. Pluto, Mammon); used to describe someone with immense wealth.
*Krishna*: an incarnation (avatar) of Vishnu, the most celebrated and beloved Hindu icon, whose life story is told in the *Bhagavata-Purana*. Associated with his pranks and feats in childhood in *Vraj* (Gokul in Mathura), his roaming exploits on the banks of the Yamuna, playing the flute and sporting with the *gopis* (milkmaids), his love for his consort Radha and her pique and placation, which is the staple of *Vaishnava* devotion. Celebrated as a perfect human being, and for the ideal he enunciated in the Bhagavad-Gita.
*Shiva*: a self-absorbed ascetic, the destroyer form of the three chief divinities of Hindu pantheon, the other two being Brahma the progenitor and Vishnu the protector, of the universe; used as an epithet of someone notoriously self-forgetful (*Bholanath*) or something fiercely destructive (*Rudra*), and to symbolise the good, austere and auspicious. *Bhutnath* is another name for Lord Shiva who, after drinking, roams the burning *ghat*s with his retinue in a state of narcotised abstraction; *bhut* means 'ghouls and charnel house spirits', and *nath* means 'lord'. Nandi and Bhringi are his chief retainers and accomplices in this. *Bhairav* is one of the eight destructive images of Shiva.
*Brahma:* the creator who, with Vishnu and Shiva, constitutes the triad known as the Trimurti (See above); also called *Prajapati* (butterfly) Brahma who is believed to predetermine the fate of every individual on earth since birth through marriage until death as a fait accompli called *Prajapatir Nirbandha* or *Bidhir Bidhan* (the decree of fate). The phrase occurs in many stories, particularly, in 'The Elder Sister'. Also, the ultimate and divine reality, from which all being originates and to which it returns.
*Kali* (the *a* being pronounced as the o in 'so'): the presiding deity of the fourth and last age of creation called *Kali Yug,* which will end in total annihilation according to the Hindu scripture; used to mean an approaching doomsday or times vitiated by evil instincts and strife, marked by degenerate tastes. The other three *Yuga*s are *Satya, Treta, Dwapar,* the four making up a *kalpa* equal to one day of Brahma.

***Historical, religious and scriptural sites, events and personages***

*Manwantar* (the Great Famine): the term has a mythological allusion: the tenure of each of the fourteen imaginary sons, *Manu,* of Brahma is called a *manwantar* or transfer of power from one *Manu* to another; this is believed to be associated with great upheaval and apocalyptic devastation. Hence, a famine causing large-scale death and destruction has been given this name. The two great famines that ravaged Bengal are that of the Bengali eras 1176 (1769 AD) and 1350 (1943 AD) brought about by governmental negligence, hoarding, black-marketing, and profiteering.

*Sepoy Mutiny*: the great Indian mutiny of 1857 was triggered by the army being required to bite off the cartridges smeared with animal fat, allegedly of the cow, taboo for the Hindus, or of the pig, taboo for the Muslims.

*Aryavarta*: northern part of India where the Aryans settled, as compared to the Deccan separated by the Vindhyas (see *Agastya).*

*Partition of Bengal*: Lord Curzon in 1905, ostensibly to meet administrative requirements, announced partition of Bengal into East Bengal, a Muslim-majority province, and West Bengal, a Hindu-majority province. It sparked off a great agitation, which spun into a national movement; as a result, the partition was revoked in 1911.

*Chanakya* (Vishnu Gupta): a scholar of keen intellect and cunning in the court of Chandragupta Maurya, whose ascension to the throne was facilitated by his machinations against the Nanda dynasty. He is credited with *Arthashashtra* (treatise on economics), and what is popularly called *Chanakya-sloka*, Sanskrit couplets on time-tested lessons of practical wisdom and social morality.

*Subhadra*: sister of Krishna and Balaram.

*Tantia Topi*: a leader of the Sepoy Mutiny, joined the troops of Nana Saheb and later Rani Lakshmi Bai of Jhansi and carried on a desperate fight in Central India. He was hounded from place to place, was given up to the British, early in April 1859, by Man Singh, a feudatory of Sindhia, and was hanged on charges of rebellion and murder.

*Kach and Debjani*: Kach was the son of Brihashpati, pre-eminent in the knowledge of the Vedas and the teacher of the gods. Debjani was the daughter of Shukracharya, teacher of the demons. Though Debjani loved Kach passionately, he refused to marry her, raising intricate points of morality evolving out of the circumstances of her rescue and his resurrection by her father.

***Religious texts, rites, and places***

*Shashtra*: deriving from the Sanskrit root *shas,* which means 'to rule', it signifies the law, code, decree or writ meant to regulate man's behaviour on earth, enunciated by the ancient sages as perceived by or revealed to them through meditation. In a broader sense, any treatise on religious teachings is a shashtra.

*Puranas*: oldest Sanskrit texts recounting the births and deeds of the Hindu gods, the creation, destruction and recreation of the universe; they number eighteen .

*Vedas*: the most ancient scripture of Hinduism, four in number, written in Sanskrit around four thousand years ago. The Rig (nature of God), Yajur (rituals for use by priests), Sama (hymns to gods), and Atharva (spells and incantations) are the source of all mantras and sacrificial rites of the Hindus.

***Vedanta***: one of the six main philosophical schools of Hinduism; the last part of the Vedas, written by Vyasdev, expounding the monism regarded as implicit in the Vedas according to the doctrines of the Upanishads. It teaches that Brahman is the only reality, the whole phenomenal world being the outcome of illusion (maya).
***Vedanta-Bhasya***: eighth-century AD Hindu theologian and philosopher Shankara was the leading exponent of the Vedantic (Advaita) school of philosophy; his commentaries on the Vedanta and the Bhagavad-Gita are esteemed.
***Patanjal-darshan***: the philosophy of sage Patanjali who lived in the third century; it consists of four parts: yoga, meditation, divine glory, and the uniqueness of the soul. He wrote a commentary on Panini's Grammar.
***Yoga***: a Hindu system of philosophy which aims at the mystical union of the self with the Supreme Being in a state of complete awareness and tranquillity through certain physical and mental exercises. Patanjali expounded the essentials. A yogi is a mystic, a master of yoga; a female mystic is a *yogini* (different from the sixty-four companion goddesses of *Durga).*
***Agastya***: a sage of Vedic and Puranic antiquity, said to have subdued the Vindhya Mountains (which divide India centrally into Aryavarta and the Deccan) when they threatened to cut off the sun's rays reaching the Deccan plateau; a phenomenon held to symbolise colonisation of southern India by the Aryans. He is believed to have crossed the mountains (on the first day of *Bhadra),* never to return, thus stunting its growth in height forever. Traditionally, someone setting out on a mission and never returning is said to have gone on an *Agastya jatra* or 'Agastya's journey'.
***Manu***: any one of the fourteen sons of Brahma. *Vaivasvat* (son of the sun) Manu is held as the primordial progenitor of mankind and lawgiver; the Hindu code of jurisprudence is attributed to him.
***Devanagari***: Goddess Saraswati is credited with the invention of the Sanskrit language and its Devanagari script, the script of the devas.
***Mahabharata***: one of the two ancient epics of India, the other being the Ramayana. Written in Sanskrit by Vyasdev, it deals chiefly with the struggle between two families of the same clan and contains many episodes the most notable of which is the Bhagavad-Gita.
***Ramayana***: written in Sanskrit by Valmiki, this epic recounts the feats of Ramachandra (one of the three human manifestations of Vishnu), held as the model of goodness and valour. His wife Sita is the model of Hindu womanhood.
***Bhagavad-Gita***: the most revered and sung Hindu scripture; written in Sanskrit verses, it epitomises the teachings of the Upanishad and is incorporated into the Mahabharata as yoga counsels of Lord Krishna to Arjuna before the battle of Kurukshetra. Krishna, as Arjuna's charioteer, advises him on his duty in times of war, the nature of being and of God. Young Bengali revolutionaries held it as a sacred text.
***Bhagabat***: Puranas narrating the life and exploits of Krishna.
***Puja***: prayer or worship, whether austere (as with just an offer of flowers to one's deity) or ceremonial (as with elaborate ritual and offering on a particular day to a particular god or goddess); in Bengal, it is almost exclusively the goddesses who

are worshipped except for the family deity *Narayana*. Unless specifically mentioned, *puja* in Bengal refers to Durgapuja with wide connotation beyond worship; for instance, puja spirit, puja holidays, puja market.

***pujari***: worshipper or priest, more often a Brahman who officiates for a devotee.

***ishtadevata***: a guardian deity of a Hindu family who is worshipped as part of a routine often in a separate quarter or shrine allotted to it in the household.

***sannyasi*** (sannyasin): originally, a Brahman who having attained the fourth and last stage of life as a beggar will not be reborn; a Hindu male bound by vows of celibacy, poverty, chastity and obedience, living on alms and the barest of clothes. Credulous people often fall victim to the deceptive garb of a fake sannyasi. The corresponding Muslim term is *fakir.*

***sadhu***: a Hindu wandering holy man.

***chariot festival***: the festival of Jagannatha going on a chariot for his sea-bath annually; Jagannatha is an idol of Krishna worshipped throughout Orissa and Bengal; at an annual festival in the month of *Asharh* the idol is wheeled through Puri town in Orissa on a gigantic chariot; centring this event fairs are held with great enthusiasm and merriment.

***mantras***: Vedic metrical psalms; religious incantation during worship; political counsel; instigation.

***namabali***: a chuddar or scarf, usually saffron-coloured, printed with the names of gods, especially, Hari (Krishna) and Rama: *Hare Krishna, Hare Rama,* over and over again, worn by the Vaishnavas and other pious Hindus.

***ekadashi***: Hindu widows observe the eleventh day of each lunar fortnight by keeping fasts.

***Vrindavan***: the grove beside the Yamuna, a rendezvous of flirtation for Krishna with his principal consort Radha and other herdswomen (*gopi*s), regarded as a holy place by the Vaishnavas.

***Vaishnava or Baishnav***: a member of a sect devoted to the cult of Vishnu, strongly anti-Brahmanic and anti-priestly in religious persuasion, and stressing devotion through ecstatic songs and simple rituals. Lyrical poems on Vaishnavism (the cult of *bhakti* or devotion) called *padabali* form an important component of Bengali literature.

***sakhi***: applied to females, a friend or an alter ego, to whom private matters are confided, itself a form of address also. A male friend would be a *sakha.*

***ashram***: a religious retreat or community where a Hindu holy man lives; a cloistered educational community for the hermitage life of learners in ancient India.

***Kalighat***: a spot of pilgrimage in Calcutta, famous for its shrine of the goddess Kali, which devotees visit to: (i) redeem a pledge after supposedly receiving the boon they prayed for, and (ii) perform ritual worship to ward off the evil effects of conjunction of stars. The place has a notorious association with animal sacrifice.

***chandimandap***: a permanent site, public or private, generally with a thatched structure where the goddess Chandi (one of the manifestations of goddess Durga) is worshipped, and hymns in her praise (from the Markandeya Purana) are sung. When not in use as such, it is a favourite spot for village elders to gather and gossip.

***ghat***: stairs or a passage way, usually paved, leading down to a river or any water-body (also means: a mountain pass; mud path; a fault); a jetty or landing place where boats moor, and people gather for taking bath, drawing water or performing pujas and funerals; a meeting ground of women especially in villages to discuss local politics and scandals.

***Writers, literary works and forms***

***Kalidasa***: the greatest poet and dramatist in Sanskrit literature, associated with the court of King Vikramaditya (fifth century?). His works include *Meghaduta, Kumarsambhava,* and *Shakuntala.*

***Jaydev***: fifteenth-century Bengali poet, court pundit of King Lakshman Sen, wrote *Gitagovinda,* a dramatic poem about Krishna and Radha.

***Kasidas*** (Kasiram Das): c. seventh-century poet celebrated for his Bengali translation of the Mahabharata by Vedavyas.

***Krittibas Ojha***: c. fifteenth-century poet celebrated for his Bengali translation of the Ramayana by Valmiki.

***Ishwarchandra Vidyasagar***: a nineteenth-century Sanskrit scholar, so celebrated a name that the honorific title of erudition, *Vidyasagar,* has virtually replaced his surname Banerjee. He was a pioneering force of social and educational reform in Bengal. There is hardly a Bengali who has never read his *Barnaparichay* and *Kathamala* as primers. He was a great philanthropist as well. Kathamala, his book of animal fables, is the Bengali equivalent of Aesop's Fables.

***Madanmohan Tarkalankar***: a Bengali poet with a Sanskrit title for erudition in logic and rhetoric, contemporary of Vidyasagar, with some widely-read primers to his credit.

***Bankim Chandra Chatterjee***: Bengal's first and arguably greatest novelist anticipating Tagore by about a quarter of a century, he wrote fourteen novels, mostly with a historical background. His *Vande Mataram* slogan, from the eponymous song composed in praise of the motherland and appearing in his first novel *Anandamath,* was accepted as the national song and became the rallying cry for nationalist revolutionaries. Besides, he was a redoubtable writer of essays and commentaries, especially satires, on social degeneration of Bengali youths, Hindu rites and even the British Raj, creating a fictitious opium-addict and unsparing character Kamalakanta as his medium for the latter purpose.

***jatra***: an extended dramatic work performed in the open air by itinerant troupes enacting historical, mythological or epic themes.

***panchali***: a type of traditional ballad celebrating the glory of a deity, often set to music with a recurrent refrain. The writer most acclaimed for his *panchali*s is Dashu Ray.

***kabigan***: a type of song-contest where poets sing extempore verses usually on mythological themes.

***kirtan***: a type of traditional religious song, devoted to the love of Krishna and Radha.

***kathakata***: the vocation of a reciter and expositor of Puranas and mythological stories.

***agamani***: a class of folk songs celebrating the homecoming of Parvati from Kailas to her mother Menaka, sung in Bengal heralding her at the advent of Durga Puja.

***baul***: < *batul* (Sanskrit) or madcap. A sect of mendicant singers without religious creed who seek communion with God by making the mind levitate in the omnipresent air in intoxicated abstraction (the euphoric effect nearly always achieved with *ganjika* or *ganja,* that is, marijuana).

***Mangalkavya***: a genre of narrative poems glorifying besides goddess *Chandi* (see above), other lesser deities such as *Manasa* (snake-goddess), *Dharma* (a non-Aryan tribal god conceived from *Yama* and the Sun god of the *Purana*) and *Shitala* (goddess of the scourge of pox). These, Bengal's very own, local deities being finicky have to be kept in good humour with propitiatory offering (by women, each on a particular day in a particular month of the year). *Chandimangal* written by Mukundaram Chakraborti is the most celebrated of the *mangalkavyas*. 'Kabikankan' is an appellation for his distinguished poetic achievement. *Manasamangal* was written by Vijaygupta, and *Dharmamangal* by Ghanaram Chakraborti.

***Vidyasundara***: a narrative poem by Bengali poet Bharatchandra Ray *Gunakara*, a title meaning 'a literary virtuoso'. Vidya is the heroine.

***Meghnadbadh-kavya***: an epic by Michael Madhusudan Datta on the slaying of Meghnad (or Indrajit, Ravana's son); based on the Valmiki Ramayana, composed in blank verse, inspired with the humanism of the nineteenth-century Bengali renaissance, it seeks to alter the original by relegating its divine status to the background, in an ornate, rather convoluted, language, which found little favour with the Bengalis traditionally inspired by the Krittibas version. His genius was dissipated trying vainly to make a name in English literature.

***Nabagopal Babu***: Nabagopal Mitra was the editor of a newspaper started by Tagore's father. Tagore mentions him in *My Reminiscences* while recalling the day his elder brother asked him to his great embarrassment to read a poem to Mitra.

***Kabikankanchandi***: a ballad in praise of the goddess Chandi by the sixteenth-century poet Mukundaram Chakraborti. See 'Mangalkavya' above.

### *Social customs, rites, and festivals*

***Brahmin*** (or Brahman): a member of the highest or priestly caste in the Hindu caste system. By virtue of their supposed superiority, they were the most privileged class of the society; offering them land, food, and money was held to count as a virtuous act in the next world. Bengali *dwija* means 'twice-born'; it refers to a Brahmin who is believed to be regenerated or reformed by wearing the sacred thread; it can also mean 'a bird' because it hatches from an egg.

***kulin***: the highest sub-caste of the Brahmans; a pernicious and degrading system of polygamy was introduced by King Ballal Sen of Bengal, which permitted a kulin Brahman to marry as many girls as he liked—sometimes even girls his granddaughter's age—to extort dowry and satisfy lust. The system died a natural death under the changing social conditions.

***polygamy***: beyond the kulin system, polygamy was socially permissible for the purpose of preserving the continuity of one's family line, as for example, if the first wife proved barren.

***Kayastha***: a member of the traditional writer and other white-collar professional class, such as, lawyers and teachers; second in rank to a Brahman in social hierarchy.

***Shudra***: lowest of the four hereditary classes into which Hindu society is divided; traditionally, the working class. The other two castes are the Kshatriya (warrior class) and Vaishya (trader class), in that order.

***outcastes*** ('untouchables'): those pursuing the so-called 'unclean' trades, such as, oilmen, cobblers, scavengers, relegated to a separate cluster. The lowliest of them is the *dom*, whose duty is to remove corpses and carcasses and burn corpses at the crematorium.

***Santhal***: an aboriginal tribe of India, chiefly inhabiting parts of Bihar and West Bengal.

***kabiraj***: physician practising in the traditional Indian system of medicine, *Ayurveda,* a treatise on the art of healing and prolonging life, sometimes regarded as the fifth Veda.

***pundit*** (pandit): an expert; a learned person; formerly a Brahman learned in Sanskrit language and literature, especially in Hindu religion, philosophy and law (as Pandit Ishwarchandra Vidyasagar), later extended to any scholar as an honorific title, acquired or assumed; sometimes a sarcastic appellation for false pedantry. In British India, teachers at schools, besides those at *tols*, were known as pandits, irrespective of the subjects they taught.

***tol***: a Sanskrit grammar school, but its adjectival form *tulo* was used only to demean someone who had not graduated beyond the primary levels. Often, wrongly, confused with *Chatushpathi*, where the four Vedas would be taught, besides grammar.

***Raja***: king; formerly, also a ruler or landlord, locally within his territory; sometimes used as a form of address or title preceding a name (as Raja Rammohan Ray).

***Ray Bahadur***: an honorific title conferred by the government on aristocratic Hindus as a recompense for their abject loyalty to the British Raj. *Khan Bahadur* is the Muslim equivalent.

***Young Bengal***: a collective term for the young men of nineteenth-century Calcutta, who were progressive-minded, thanks to the advent of English education and culture mostly followers of the progressive Anglo-Indian, Derozio.

***orthodox marriage***: conventional marriage decreed by scriptures, according to which girls had to be given away in marriage, within the same caste, within a certain age, normally twelve years (but sometimes it was even before puberty). Failure meant possible social ostracism.

***sacred thread***: male members of the Brahman caste wear it as an insignia of superiority, in a cluster of several rounds of cotton string, transversely across the left shoulder down to the right knee; also means the ceremony celebrating the auspicious assumption.

***Ramnaam*** (Rama's name): held most sacred by the Hindus to: (i) scare off ghosts by uttering 'Ram' or 'Rama' in a rapid burst, (ii) express their mortification at seeing or hearing something ugly or shameful, by uttering it twice in exclamation, the first being somewhat long-drawn, (iii) express relief from some crisis, (iv) chant in funeral processions, (v) swathe themselves with Rama's name printed in a repeated design on scarves, (vi) as a form of greeting, and (vii) as prayer ('Hey Ram!').

***pranam*** (or ***pronam***): an expression of respect for elders or superiors, either uttered with a gesture of joined palms and bent head, or performed by touching the feet, or more piously, wiping the dust from the feet and placing it on one's own head.

***namaskar***: said with joined palms as a usual form of greeting between two persons less familiar with each other; Muslim equivalent of *salaam.*

***salaam***: a Muslim form of greeting consisting of a deep bow with the right palm on the forehead.

***shradh***: a Hindu ritual of offering libation to the departed soul; solemnised on a prescribed day (usually, eleventh or thirteenth) after death, rightfully by the eldest son, or wife by default.

***shanti-swastyayan***: the first part means appeasement, the second part, bringing prosperity; the ritual for this purpose.

***zamindar*** (jamidar): originally, contract agent holding land, collecting revenue, paying 9/10$^{th}$ to the Viceroy and retaining the rest; he inherited his zamindari and was responsible for policing his jurisdiction. Under the Permanent Settlement Act of Lord Cornwallis in 1793, zamindars were elevated to landowners with (i) the government's land-revenue demand permanently fixed, (ii) recovery provision through sale of proportionate land, and (iii) withdrawal of the magisterial power. The system was abolished after 1947. The Tagores were zamindars in East Bengal (now Bangladesh).

***dewan***: formerly, a chief minister or finance minister of a state ruled by an Indian prince. Extended to similar positions under a zamindar.

***taluk***: part of a zamindar's landed estate, usually named after the place.

***Brahmatra***: rent-free land given to a Brahman.

***tehshil***: firstly, the revenue receipts; secondly, the office where the revenue is paid.

***tehshildar***: the revenue collector of the government.

***gomasta***: the rent collector or steward of a zamindar; the bill collector of a businessman or a mercantile firm.

***korfa***: a cultivator who has no right in the land, but holds it as a tenant-at-will, and is not recognised by the zamindar; a *ryot* under a *ryot.* In *Shashti* (Punishment), Ramlochan is the original tenant; Dukhiram and Chhidam are korfa tenants.

***kachhari***: a court or office where any public business is transacted; thus, there was a government *kachhari* as well as a *zamindari kachhari.*

***nayeb***: the highest official in a kachhari; secretary, steward to a zamindar.

***piyada*** (or peyada): a footman, messenger or agent of a landowner collecting revenue, often using third degree methods; bailiff of a law court.

***paik***: same as piyada except that he often joins a barkandaz as a lathiyal (see below).

***barkandaz***: a sepoy carrying firearms, an armed bodyguard of a zamindar; a member of his private army.

***moktar*** (mukhtar): a legal representative appointed by a defendant or plaintiff with the power of attorney.

***munsiff***: a judge of the lowest civil court.

***chaprasi***: a liveried servant; an orderly or bearer or peon in an office.
***lathi***: a five to six-feet long wooden stick, seasoned by oiling and sunning, used as a weapon.
***lathiyal*** (or lethel): expert in wielding lathis; professional fighter or guard on the payroll of a zamindar.
***lagi***: a ten- to twelve-feet-long bamboo pole used for punting a country boat.
***gadabanduk***: a flintlock gun, in which the charge is ignited by a spark produced by a flint in the hammer.
***kuthi***: office, business house, mansion, or bungalow.
***nilkuthi***: factory producing indigo dye from plantations, and the associated office.
***aatchala***: a house with a roof of thatch in the shape of an octagon, walled up with coarse mats made of palm-leaves or date leaves or bamboo slips and plastered with mud; sometimes left without walls, when meant for public use, for example, for pujas as a chandimandap.
***durbar***: formerly the court of a native ruler or a governor; a formal meeting at such places.
***zenana***: from Hindi *zanana,* a woman; a Muslim's wives and concubines collectively. Part of a house reserved for the women and girls of a household; a seraglio or *harem* in a Muslim palace. In Bengal, a rough equivalent is *antahpur* or *andarmahal,* where strangers, especially males, are forbidden.
***mohar***: or sovereign is an ancient gold coin of India and Persia; seal or stamp.
***mudra***: coin, legal tender; in the context of the stories, gold and silver coins; also means signs made with fingers during prayer; pose or gesture of dancing; mannerism.
***paisa***: in the context of the stories, one sixty-fourth of a rupee or one sixteenth of an anna; since 1956, one hundredth of a rupee; then made of copper, now of nickel.
***rathjatra*** (chariot festival): Lord Jagannath going by chariot; on the second bright lunar day of Asharh, the idol is taken out in a procession.
***brothers' day***: in Bengali, *bhai-phonta* or *bhratri-dwitiya,* a festival where sisters put sandalwood paste marks (tilak) on their brothers' foreheads, wishing them a long and prosperous life, with exchange of gifts and sweetmeats. It is held on the second day of the bright lunar fortnight following Kali-puja.
***kabaddi, or kapati*** (ha-du-du): a simple originally rural game of India, still played, needing strength and stamina. Two teams stand across a line; anyone then starts the game by crossing the line, while holding his breath, uttering 'du-du-du...' or 'chuuu...', at the same time trying to touch any rival player and returning, before running out of breath. If he can do it, the player touched is 'dead'; if he is caught while trying to make good his return, he is 'dead'.

***Wedding:***
***dowry***: the Hindu custom of a bridegroom's father extorting money and goods from the bride's father in consideration for and commensurate with his son's worth.
***engagement and blessing ceremony***: in Bengali *pakadekha,* formal approval of the pair by both sides; legally validated according to the Hindu code of marriage by

signing up a detailed document and solemnised with gifts of gold rings or some such valuable items attended with a feast.

***turmeric ceremony***: in Bengali, *gayehalud,* a ritual in which turmeric paste is touched on the brow of the bridegroom in the small hours of the wedding day, and this turmeric is carried ceremonially along with fish and betel leaves to the bride to dab on her brow before she takes her ritual bath.

***bridal party***: customarily, the bridegroom sets out in a procession of friends and relations for the bride's house where the wedding takes place.

***auspicious sighting***: in Bengali, *shubhodrishti,* a ritual where the bride and the groom formally see each other, and especially in the period of the stories, for the first time. This is an occasion for merriment and exchange of repartees among the couple's friends and cousins.

***seven-turn ritual***: in Bengali, *saatpaak ghora,* the bride sitting on a wooden plank is taken seven times round the groom who keeps standing still. This is held to bind them forever invisibly in sacred ties.

***ritual gifts***: in Bengali, *tattva,* information, message, enquiry, etc., is extended to mean various goods and sweets traditionally exchanged as part of the ritual between the bride's and the bridegroom's families during the wedding ceremony, and thereafter, in its original meaning (exchanging information) on seasonal occasions as a form of courtesy.

***vermilion***: bright red cinnabar powder used in the parting of their hair by Hindu married women not widowed. This also marks the solemnisation of marriage when it is first worn.

***shwashur-bari***: father-in-law's house; for a bride, her husband's father's house where she goes to live; for a groom, his wife's father's house where he goes occasionally on a visit; used in village parlance occasionally as an imprecation to mean prison.

***Dress***

***Benarasi sari***: a rich silk fabric woven with raised design, often in gold or silver threads, once specialised in at Varanasi (Benares), the traditional dress for Bengali brides.

***tusser***: fabric of coarse silk yarn; when ochre-coloured, used during prayer or worship.

***garad***: fabric of the finer quality silk yarn; worn as sari; makes the Bengali bridegroom's wedding attire.

***chapkan***: long, loose upper garment for males, normally worn with *pyjamas,* chiefly as part of official dress.

***choga***: waist coat; a toga-like open-breasted vest worn over chapkan ('choga-chapkan') by the affluent gentry.

***jobba***: a knee-length, open-breasted vest, denoting office, authority or rank.

***chadar*** (chuddar): a length of cloth, decorative or plain, wrapped around the upper part in winter. At other times, neatly folded and put on the shoulder, completes the respectable attire of the average Bengali gentleman going out on social occasions.

***jamiyar***: a richly embroidered shawl, indicating high social position.

*gamchha*: a kind of serviette; a rectangular two-yard length of coarse coloured cloth, used as a towel, sometimes worn as a *lungi* or loincloth, or slung over the shoulder by labourers or domestic servants.
*dhoti*: six-and-a-half yards length of white cloth for men worn in various styles to cover the body from the waist down.
*pyjamas*: full, flared, ankle-length trousers of fine fabrics, used by either sex, especially, for leisure wear.
*kurta*: a long, flowing shirt with full sleeves and without collar, worn with dhoti or pyjamas.
*khaddar*: or *khadi,* is hand-woven coarse cotton cloth made of hand-spun threads, introduced and popularised by Gandhi. Dhotis and caps made of khaddar were once a proud apparel for the *Swadeshi*s.
*puggree*: a man's headdress, worn ethnically by the Sikhs, and occasionally in the past by respectable Hindus, made by swathing a length of linen or silk.
*shamla*: a chiffon-embroidered turban worn by clerks and lawyers.
*ghagra*: an ankle-length skirt worn mainly by north Indian women
*attar*: an oil from flowers, especially the damask rose or jasmine petals, used pure or as a base for perfume; applied to the face or hair, or sometimes dabbed on the earlobes.

***Food***
*rice* (bhaat): the staple food grain of India, especially of the Bengalis, who eat it twice, or even oftener a day, thereby earning the dubious distinction of *bheto* (given to eating rice) due to the lethargy induced by it.
*roti*: or 'ruti' in Bengali, called *chapatti* by North Indians, a type of hand-made unleavened bread made by kneading a mix of coarse flour of wheat and water, rolling out into a disc and baking first on a frying pan and then direct on the flame when it balloons up; forms a staple food of most Indians.
*luchi*: Please see the Notes to The Royal Mark. Paratha and puri are variations on luchi.
*paan*: betel leaf wrapped with a mixture of areca chips, catechu powder, lime paste, and optionally, some addictive and aromatic preparations; the juice aids digestion.
*sandesh*: a Bengali speciality sweet, made of curdled milk (milk coagulated by acid) and sugar or jaggery in various shapes, consistencies, and garnishes; traditionally offered in pujas, and as a treat to guests.
*mohanbhog*: a sweetened dessert made of *suji* (coarse-ground flour of wheat) usually cooked in milk and ghee sprinkled with raisin and cardamom.
*payes*: a milk preparation of sunned rice, sugar or jaggery and raisin, cashew nut, etc.
*doi*: a thick custard-like food, resembling yoghurt, prepared from milk that has been curdled by bacteria, often sweetened.

***Music:***
*shehnai*: a classical wooden wind instrument, consisting of a conical tube fitted with a mouthpiece having a double reed. It has a penetrating nasal but sweet tone,

played during pujas, and especially, at weddings. A recurring instrument in Tagore's stories. The other wind instrument most played is the bansuri or flute, which is Krishna's instrument in his dalliance with Radha and other herdswomen.

***veena***: a seven-string instrument in various shapes and sizes is of the oldest origin, and held as the symbol of music in *Saraswati*'s hand. Other frequently played string instruments are *sitar, sarod* (both played with a plectrum), and *sarangi* with a bow. The main strings in the sitar and sarod overlie others, the tuning depending on the raga being played, rendering the music continuous (*meend*) and melodious.

***taanpura***: a stringed musical instrument, usually of four strings, sometimes of six, played by stroking with the fingers, helps the vocalist maintain a perfect tune.

***tabla***: a percussion instrument for any kind of classical or light music, consisting of a pair of drums played by the fingers and palms of both hands.

***khol*** (or shrikhol): a single-piece variation on the tabla, both ends of which are played simultaneously, to accompany *kirtan* and *baul* songs.

***alap***: similar to talking about a theme, as we do through language, when developing an idea, logically and meaningfully. Thus, it means exposition of the idea of a raga, in a slow tempo without rhythmic accompaniment (*tala*), in vocal or instrumental music.

***raga***: a melodic framework, a basic note-pattern formed by selecting notes from the thirteen tonal intervals conventionally established in the octave space, usually associated with a particular mood, *rasa* (sentiment), time, season, and even region, on which a vocalist or instrumentalist can improvise creating new tonal patterns. The musicological tradition recognises six *ragas* and thirty *raginis*, mirroring, at the metaphysical level, *Shiva-Shakti* or *Purusha-Prakriti* pairs, and represents the masculine-feminine principles in music.

***bhairavi***: a morning ragini exciting a sober, meditative mood with a tinge of sadness.

***desh***: a light, meditative evening raga.

***malhar***: a monsoon group of *ragas,* it forms rich combinations with other *ragas*: *Deshmalhar, Meghmalhar, Mianmalhar,* all late-night ragas.

***basant***: a springtime evening raga evoking a romantic mood.

***sahana***: a late evening exhilarating raga most often used in the stories in wedding references.

***thumri***: with *Ghazal, Bhajan, Tappa,* etc. forms a category known as classical vocal light music. Thumri (from *thumakna*, which means 'to walk with dancing steps so as to make the ankle-bells tinkle') is a form connected with dance, dramatic gestures, mild eroticism, evocative love-poetry, and folk songs of Uttar Pradesh, with regional variations. While the dignified Benaras *gharana* exhibits an approach similar to khayal, the Lucknow *gharana* shows an affinity with ghazal. Originally sung by courtesans and court musicians, it thrived in Lucknow, once the leading centre of Hindustani classical music.

***ghazal***: originally meant 'love-song in Persian'. Later, Urdu literary tradition extended the thematic range. From the beginning, the love of God was interwoven as a strand of the thematic fabric by *sufi* saints.

***bhajan***: a genre of light classical music; derived from the root Sanskrit word *bhaj* which means 'to serve', the name is applied to a class of songs which had been composed as well as sung by saint-poets in the wake of the devotional movement that swept the country from the eighth century onwards. The common ragas used were desh, sarang, bhairav, kalingda, mand, and malhar with rhythms of eight or sixteen beats. Notably, this is different from the kind known as *Kirtan,* which has nothing to do with the ragas or the complexities of classical music.

***Terms of address***

***baba***: father; also, a respectful term for any father figure; reciprocally used as a term of endearment for son and occasionally extended socially to other boys or men.

***ma***: mother; reciprocally used as a term of endearment for daughter and extended socially to other girls or women; applied by a servant to the wife of the master. *Chhoto ma* and *baro ma* are the terms for the youngest and the eldest wife in an extended family; also, uttered in a sigh of desperation *(Ma!),* as Baidyanath in 'The Golden Deer' did when he drew a blank in his search for hidden treasure.

***ma-thakrun***: an address for the mistress of a house used by her servants or others. *Note:* The Bengalis traditionally regard a woman, especially a married one, as a mother figure. Hence, using *ma* as a suffix, they call their father's sister *pishima,* mother's sister *mashima,* uncle's wife *kakima* or *jethima*, and maternal uncle's wife *mamima*, also with their corresponding shorter forms without the suffix.

***kaka*** (kaku) ***or*** khuro: younger brother of one's father, also extended socially.

***jyatha***: father's elder brother.

***dada***: elder brother with respect to younger brothers and sisters, whether siblings or cousins; extended by social courtesy to people of similar age; also, a form of address for grandfather, especially, maternal grandfather, *Thakurda* being the address for paternal grandfather. *Dada* or *dada-babu* is also applied by servants to the son of the master.

***didi***: elder sister with respect to younger brothers and sisters, whether siblings or cousins; extended by social courtesy to people of similar age; also, a form of address for grandmother, and for the wife of one's husband's elder brother.

*Note:* The last two forms of address above are reciprocal between grandparents and grandchildren.

***bhai***: literally, brother, an affectionate term of address for the grandson and extended by social custom to other boys and men. Also, a friendly form of address in general, or when making a request, among men as well as women

***bou-didi***: elder brother's or elder cousin's wife; also used socially for women of similar rank; an alternative form is *bou-thakrun.*

***thakurpo***: husband's younger brother or cousin.

***babu*** (babuji): used by people of lower class, as for instance, by a servant speaking or referring to the master; likewise, Ma (Maji), *ji* being a respectful suffix, for the master's wife. Also used at the end of first names, sometimes surnames as well, but never with both, as a formal address between social acquaintances, e.g., Kailash-babu ; *other meanings:* a term of respectful address like *Mr* or *Sir,* nearly equivalent to *Esquire;* scribe, clerk; the word once meant an indigenous equivalent of a British title like Ray Bahadur and referred to wealthy, fashionable, ostentatious gentry (see the story Grandfather); now used ironically for one given to prodigality, foppishness and triviality.

***thakur***: used to address a Brahman, priest, deity or a saintly person; used after dada (dadathakur) to refer respectfully to a Brahman.

***mashai*** (or mashay): added to babu to mean the master, added to dada to mean grandfather, and to thakur or jyatha to mean the priest and one's father's elder brother suggesting some degree of intimacy mixed with respect; also, used between any two persons of either sex who are on joking terms with each other; used after the surname as an address between two respectable male acquaintances, such as, Chakraborti Mashai and Kundu Mashai; used after *master* as a respectful address for a teacher.

***khoka***: address of endearment for one's son, often the youngest, or any other small boy (see *baba)*; similarly, *khuki* or *khuku* for a girl.

***bouma***: address for the wife of one's son or one's younger brother, and by extension, wife of others of similar age (see *ma*).

***bou***: sometimes the address for a daughter-in-law in an extended family or by social superiors. *Chhotobou* and *barobou* respectively refer to the younger and the elder ones in a joint family.

***sahib*** (or saheb): a white man, a form of address or title placed after a man's name or designation, used as a mark of respect. It is also usually the Muslim equivalent of 'babu'. *Bibisaheb* is the corresponding address for a Muslim married woman. *Memsaheb* is the term for the wives of sahebs.

***shala***: one's wife's brother. See below.

***shyalika*** (shyali): wife's sisters or her female cousins; the younger ones are traditionally permitted to be on bantering terms with the husband, but flirting is taboo. Similarly, her husband's younger brother or his male cousin, *debar,* stands in the same relation to her. Contrarily, her husband's sister, *nanad* is not traditionally on amicable terms with her while the wife's younger brothers bear an affectionate relation, *shala,* to her husband. Strangely, *shala* is a term of abuse also, used as such or muttered under one's breath.

*Note*: The pronoun 'you' in English is universally used in direct conversation, irrespective of age, social status or relative position of the speaker and the person spoken to. Not so in Bengali (or in Hindi, for that matter), where three distinct forms corresponding to 'you' are admitted: *tui, tumi, aapni. Tui* is the affectionate address for children in the same family, and friends, and the pejorative address for so-called low-caste people. *Tumi* is the reciprocal address of endearment among the members of a family irrespective of age, between lovers, and by elderly people to their unrelated juniors. *Aapni* is reserved for teachers and other social or chronological seniors or superiors.